PENGUIN BO...

LOST EMPIRE

Clive Cussler is the author or co-author of a great number of international bestsellers, including the famous Dirk Pitt® adventures, such as *Crescent Dawn*; the NUMA® Files adventures, most recently *Medusa*; the *Oregon* Files, such as *The Jungle*; the Isaac Bell adventures, which began with *The Chase*; and the recent Fargo adventures. His non-fiction works include *The Sea Hunters* and *The Sea Hunters II*: these describe the true adventures of the real NUMA, which, led by Cussler, searches for lost ships of historic significance. With his crew of volunteers, Cussler has discovered more than sixty ships, including the long-lost Confederate submarine *Hunley*. He lives in Arizona.

Grant Blackwood, a US Navy veteran, spent three years aboard a guided-missile frigate as an operations specialist and pilot rescue swimmer. The author of the Briggs Tanner series, and co-author of *Spartan Gold*, he lives in Colorado.

Find out more about the world of Clive Cussler by visiting:
www.clivecussler.co.uk

Lost Empire

CLIVE CUSSLER *with*
GRANT BLACKWOOD

PENGUIN BOOKS

PENGUIN BOOKS

Published by the Penguin Group
Penguin Books Ltd, 80 Strand, London WC2R ORL, England
Penguin Group (USA) Inc., 375 Hudson Street, New York, New York 10014, USA
Penguin Group (Canada), 90 Eglinton Avenue East, Suite 700, Toronto, Ontario, Canada M4P 2Y3
(a division of Pearson Penguin Canada Inc.)
Penguin Ireland, 25 St Stephen's Green, Dublin 2, Ireland
(a division of Penguin Books Ltd)
Penguin Group (Australia), 250 Camberwell Road, Camberwell, Victoria 3124, Australia
(a division of Pearson Australia Group Pty Ltd)
Penguin Books India Pvt Ltd, 11 Community Centre, Panchsheel Park, New Delhi – 110 017, India
Penguin Group (NZ), 67 Apollo Drive, Rosedale, Auckland 0632, New Zealand
(a division of Pearson New Zealand Ltd)
Penguin Books (South Africa) (Pty) Ltd, 24 Sturdee Avenue, Rosebank,
Johannesburg 2196, South Africa

Penguin Books Ltd, Registered Offices: 80 Strand, London WC2R ORL, England

www.penguin.com

First published in the USA by G. P. Putnam's Sons 2010
First published in Great Britain by Michael Joseph 2010
Published in Penguin Books 2011
001

ISBN: 978-1-405-93272-1

www.greenpenguin.co.uk

Acknowledgements

Thanks to the following people, without whom this book wouldn't be what it is:

Sam Craghead of the Museum of the Confederacy, whose insight was truly invaluable; John Koivula and Tim Thomas for their gemological and geological insights; Rich Hartney for helping us crash-land; Doug Lyle and C. J. Lyons for entertaining our medical questions; Geoff Irwin and Peter Bellwood for their willingness to entertain speculative anthropological questions; Tim Roufs and Sandra Noble for their Mesoamerican expertise; Jurgen Theiss for his Zanzibar and Tanzania help; Tom Chaffin, author of *Sea of Gray*, for brainstorming what might have happened; Victoria Lisi for her keen pen; Neil, Peter, Tom, Sara, and Pam for their patience, steadfastness, and candid input; the Kid and his wife for their friendship and support; and finally, Steve Berry: You truly are a big deal, my friend.

LOST EMPIRE

Prologue

London, England, 1864

The man known as Jotun strode purposefully through the predawn fog, the collar of his peacoat up and a scarf wrapped loosely around his throat and mouth. His breath misted in the air before him.

He stopped walking suddenly and listened. Had he heard footfalls? He turned his head to the left, then the right. Somewhere ahead he heard a muffled click. A boot on cobblestone. Moving lightly for such a big man, Jotun stepped back into the shadows between the pillars of an arched gate. In the pocket of his coat, he tightened his fist around the shaft of his lead-and-leather cosh. The side streets and back alleys of Tilbury were never a friendly place, and even less so between sunset and sunrise.

'Damn this city,' Jotun grumbled. 'Dark, dank, cold. God help me.'

He missed his wife, he missed his country. But this was where he was needed, or so the powers that be said. He trusted their judgment, of course, but there were times when he would gladly trade his current duty for a proper battlefield. At least there he would know his enemy and know what to do with him: Kill or be killed. Very simple. Then again, despite the distance, his wife much preferred his current posting to his earlier ones. 'Better to be distant and alive than close and dead,' she'd told him when he'd gotten his orders.

Jotun waited another few minutes but heard no further movement. He checked his watch: three-thirty. The streets would begin to stir in another hour. If his quarry was going to make a run for it, it would have to be before then.

He stepped back onto the street and continued north until he found Malta Road, then turned south for the docks. In the distance he could hear the lonely clanging of a buoy, and he could smell the stench of the Thames River. Ahead, through the fog, he glimpsed a lone figure standing on the southeast corner of Dock Road, smoking a cigarette. On cat's feet, Jotun crossed the street and strode ahead until he could see more of the corner. The man was indeed alone. Jotun stepped back into the alley entrance, then whistled softly, once. The man turned. Jotun lit a match with his thumbnail, let it flare briefly, then crushed it out between his thumb and index finger. The man walked over to Jotun.

'Mornin', sir.'

'That's debatable, Fancy.'

'Indeed it is, sir.' Fancy looked down the block, then up.

'Nervous?' asked Jotun.

'What, me? What would I have to be nervous about? Tiny fella like me walking these alleys in the dark of night. What could be wrong with that?'

'So let's hear it.'

'She's there, sir. Berthed as she's been the last four days. Lines are singled up, though. I chatted up a mate of mine that does odd jobs down on the docks. Rumor has it she's moving upriver.'

'To where?'

'Millwall Docks.'

'Millwall Docks aren't finished yet, Fancy. Why are you lying to me?'

'No, sir, that's what I heard. Millwall. Later this morning.'

'I've got a man at Millwall already, Fancy. He says they're closed down for another week at least.'

'Sorry, sir.'

Jotun heard the distinctive scuff of leather on brick behind him in the alley and immediately realized Fancy was sorry for a different reason entirely. Jotun took some solace in the knowledge that this little weasel of a man probably hadn't betrayed him out of spite but rather out of greed.

'Run along now, Fancy . . . Far away. Out of London. If I see you again, I'll open your belly and feed you your own guts.'

'You won't be seeing me again, sir.'

'For your sake, make sure of it.'

'Sorry again. I always liked – '

'Another word, and it will be your last. Go.'

Fancy hurried off and disappeared into the fog.

Jotun quickly considered his options. The fact that Fancy had lied about the Millwall meant he was lying about the ship, which in turn meant she was going downriver, not up. He couldn't let that happen. Now the question became: Was it wiser to run from the men who were coming up behind him or to fight them? If he ran, they'd chase him, and the last thing he needed was a ruckus this close to the dock. The ship's crew was probably already on edge, and he needed to catch them calm and unawares.

Jotun turned around to face the alley.

There were three of them, one a little shorter than him, two much shorter, but they all had heavy, round shoulders and bucket-shaped heads. Street thugs. Throat cutters. Had there been enough light for Jotun to see their faces, he was certain there would be very few teeth, plenty of scars, and small, mean eyes.

'Good morning, gentlemen. How can I help you?'

'Don't be makin' this harder than it needs to be,' the bigger of the three said.

'Knives or hands or both?' Jotun asked.

'What?'

'No matter. It's your choice. Come on, then, let's get on with it.'

Jotun took his hands from his pockets.

The big one rushed in. Jotun saw the knife coming up from the man's waist, a well-timed slash designed to open up a femoral artery in the leg or tear open the lower belly. Jotun not only had two inches of height on the man but at least four inches of arm's reach, and he used it, lashing out with his own uppercut blow. At the last second he let the palmed cosh swing forward. The leather-wrapped lead bulb caught the big man squarely under the chin. His head flipped up, and he stumbled backward into his partners, then dropped hard on his butt. The knife clattered across the cobblestones. Jotun took one long stride forward, cocked his knee up to waist height, and slammed the heel of his boot down onto the big man's ankle, shattering the bone. The man started screaming.

4

The other two hesitated then but only for a moment. Often in these circumstances a wolf pack like this disperses once the big dog is put down, but these were men accustomed to easy fights.

The one on the right sidestepped his fallen partner, dropped his shoulder, and charged forward like a bull. The charge was a ruse, of course. There was a blade hidden in one of those hands; the moment Jotun grabbed ahold of the man, the knife would come up. Jotun took a quick step back on his left leg, coiled it, then sprung forward, simultaneously swinging his right foot forward. The kick caught the charging man fully in the face. Jotun heard the wet crunch of bone. The man dropped to his knees, teetered for a moment, then collapsed face-first onto the street.

The last man was against hesitating, and now Jotun saw what he was looking for: that watershed moment when a man realizes he's going to die if he doesn't make the right decision.

'They're alive,' Jotun said. 'If you don't turn around and run, I'm going to kill you.'

The man stood rooted, knife before him.

'Come on, son, did they really pay you enough for this?'

The man lowered his knife. He swallowed hard, shook his head once, then turned and ran.

So did Jotun. Ran for all he was worth, down the street, right onto Dock Road, then through a line of hedges and across St. Andrews. A short alley took him to a pair of warehouses. He sprinted between them, vaulted over a fence, landed hard, then rolled to his feet and kept going until he heard the pounding of wood beneath his boots. The docks. He looked left, then right, but saw only fog.

Which way?

He turned around, read the building number above his head, then turned on his heel and sprinted south for fifty yards. To his right he heard the sound of water lapping. He veered that way. A dark shape loomed before him. He skidded to a stop, bumped into the stack of crates, stumbled sideways, then found his feet. He hopped up onto the smallest crate, then boosted himself up one more level. Twenty feet below, he could just make out the surface of the water. He looked upriver, saw nothing, then turned to look downriver.

Twenty yards away he saw the faint glow of yellow light behind a mullioned window; above this, past the deck rail, a ship's wheelhouse.

'Damn it!' Jotun barked. 'Damn it to hell!'

The ship faded into the fog and disappeared.

Chapter 1

Chumbe Island, Zanzibar, Tanzania

The sharks darted at the edges of their vision, sleek gray shapes that offered Sam and Remi Fargo only glimpses of knife-edged fins and flicking tails before disappearing into the curtain of swirling sand. As usual, Remi had refused to pass up the photo opportunity, and as usual she'd asked Sam to serve as scale as she focused her high-speed underwater camera past him and at the feeding frenzy. For his part, Sam was less worried about the sharks than he was the precipice at his back – a hundred-fifty-foot drop off the sandbank into the dark deep of the Zanzibar Channel.

Remi pulled her face up from the camera, smiled with her eyes behind the mask, and gave him an OK sign. Sam thankfully finned forward to join her. Together they knelt in the sand and watched the show. It was July off the coast of Tanzania, which meant monsoon season, which in turn meant the warm East African Coastal Current (EACC) was surging from the southeast until it met the southern tip of Zanzibar, where it split into inshore and offshore currents. For sharks this created a 'food funnel' in the eighteen-mile gap between Zanzibar and the mainland as prey fish were driven northward. An irresistible moving buffet, Remi called it.

Sam and Remi took care to stay within what they'd dubbed the Safe Zone, that fifty-yard, crystal-clear water strip off Chumbe Island. Past that was the drop into the channel. The demarcation was hard to miss: The current, moving at six knots or more, threw up a roiling curtain of sand as it scraped along the island's sandbar. This Sam and Remi had dubbed the Good-bye Zone; step into this rip current without a safety line and you were in for a one-way trip up the coast.

Despite the danger – or perhaps because of it – this yearly trip to Zanzibar was one of their favorites. Along with sharks, prey fish, rip currents, and underwater sandstorms that lasted for months, the EACC offered up treasure – albeit usually bits and pieces worth nothing more than their curiosity factor, but this was enough for Sam and Remi. Over the centuries, ships had been plying Africa's east coast from Mombasa to Dar es Salaam, many of them laden with gold and gems and ivory bound for colonial empire cities. Countless ships had sunk in and around the Zanzibar Channel, the contents of their holds spilled along the bottom, just waiting for the right current to uncover or move them within reach of curious divers such as the Fargos. Over the years they'd recovered gold and silver coins from the Roman Empire to Spain, Chinese ceramics, Sri Lankan jade, silverware . . . From the fascinating to the mundane, they'd uncovered it. So far on this trip, they'd found only one item of note: a diamond-shaped gold coin so barnacle-encrusted they could make out no details.

Sam and Remi watched the sharks feed for a few more minutes and then, by mutual nod, turned and began finning south along the bottom, each stopping occasionally to use a Ping-Pong paddle to waft at the sand, hoping the lump that had caught the eye might be a hidden bit of history.

Chumbe Island, roughly six miles long and two miles wide, is shaped like a woman's boot, with the shin, ankle, and forefoot facing the channel, and the back of the calf, the stiletto heel, and sole facing Zanzibar proper. Just above the ankle there was a break in the sandbar, an inlet that led to the lagoon created by the stiletto heel.

After fifteen minutes of trolling along the sand, Sam and Remi reached this stiletto break, then turned west until they were ten yards off the beach, then swung north again to resume their search. Now they became more watchful. It was along this stretch of the sandbar that the main channel pushed dangerously close to the beach, a bubble-shaped salient that narrowed their Safe Zone to a mere forty feet. Remi swam inshore and ahead of Sam by a few feet, each of them frequently checking to make sure the other hadn't drifted toward the precipice.

In the corner of Sam's right eye he saw a glint, a fleeting flash of gold. He stopped swimming, settled knees first into the sand, then tapped his dive knife on his tank to get Remi's attention. She stopped swimming, turned, and finned back to him. He pointed toward the spot. She nodded. With Sam in the lead, they swam toward shore until the sandbanks came into view. A wall of sand nearly twelve feet tall, these banks marked a precipice of sorts where the water depth dropped from chest height to twenty feet. They stopped before the bank and looked around.

Remi shrugged *Where?*

Sam shrugged his shoulders and kept scanning up and down the bank. There. Twenty feet to his right he saw it again, a flash of gold. They swam to it and stopped again. Here the Good-bye Zone precipice was closer still, not eight feet behind their backs. Even at this distance they could feel the surge of the current, like a vortex trying to sweep them into the deep.

Jutting from the bank at waist height was what appeared to be six or seven inches of a barrel's hoop. Though tarnished and fuzzy with barnacles, in a few places the hoop had been sandblasted by the current, exposing shiny metal.

Sam reached out and fanned the area around the hoop. The exposed portion widened to eight inches, then ten inches, before curving back and disappearing into the bank. Sam moved his paddle upward, hoping to uncover some of the barrel's staves if the wood hadn't succumbed to rot.

Sam stopped fanning. He looked to Remi and saw her eyes were wide behind her mask. Above the hoop was not rotted wood but a curved metal facade, mottled green with patina. Sam dropped to his knees and wiggled forward until his chest was nearly touching the bank, then craned his neck and waved his paddle beneath the hoop. After thirty seconds of work a cavity appeared. Gently, slowly, Sam slipped his hand into the hollow and probed the interior with splayed fingers.

He withdrew his arm and backed away from the object until he was again beside Remi. She looked at him with expectant eyes. He nodded back. There was no doubt: Their barrel wasn't a barrel but rather a ship's bell.

'Well, that was unexpected,' Remi said a few minutes later after surfacing.

'I'll say,' Sam replied after removing his mouthpiece. Until now, the biggest artifact they'd ever found was a sterling silver trencher from a torpedoed World War II Liberty Ship.

She shed her fins and tossed them over the gunwale onto the afterdeck of their rental – a commuter-style twenty-five-foot Andreyale Joubert-Nivelt express cruiser complete with lacquered teak woodwork and retro sub-way windows – then climbed the ladder, followed by Sam. Once they'd shed the remainder of their gear and tucked it away in the Andreyale's cabin, Remi fished a pair of water bottles from the ice chest and tossed one to Sam. They sat down on the deck chairs.

'How long do you think it's been down there?' Remi asked.

'Hard to say. Doesn't take long for patina to set in. We'd have to see the thickness of the growth on the rest of it. The interior felt fairly unblemished.'

'And the clapper?' Remi asked.

'Couldn't feel it.'

'Looks like we've got a decision to make.'

'That we do.'

Not only did the Tanzanian government have some unorthodox laws when it came to maritime salvage, Chumbe Island was officially known as Chumbe Island Coral Park, a good portion of which had been partitioned as a Reef Sanctuary and a Closed Forest Reserve. Before Sam and Remi could do anything, they first had to determine whether the bell officially lay within either of these protected areas. If they passed this hurdle, then they could in good conscience proceed to the next step: determining the bell's provenance and/or pedigree, a requirement should they want to stake a legal claim before alerting local officials to the bell's presence. It was a tenuous tight-rope on which they treaded. If they reached the far side, they may have a significant historical find on their hands, but on either side of the tightrope were laws that could lead to, at best, having the find snatched away, or, at worst, criminal charges. By law they could take any found man-made objects that required 'no extraordinary excavation methods.' Trinkets such as Remi's diamond-shaped coin were fine; a ship's bell was a wholly different matter.

None of this was new to the Fargos. Together and alone, privately and professionally, Sam and Remi had been hunting for treasure, artifacts, and hidden history for most of their adult lives.

Following in her father's footsteps, Remi had attended Boston College, emerging with a master's in anthropology and history, with a focus on ancient trade routes.

Sam's father, who'd died a few years earlier, had been one of the lead engineers on NASA's space programs while Sam's mother, a vivacious lady, ran a charter dive boat.

Sam received an engineering degree from Caltech, along with a handful of trophies for lacrosse and soccer.

While in his final months at Caltech, Sam was approached by a man he would later discover was from DARPA – the Defense Advanced Research Projects Agency – the government's research and development arm. The lure of pure creative engineering combined with serving his country made Sam's choice an easy one.

After seven years at DARPA Sam returned to California, where Sam and Remi met at the Lighthouse, a jazz club on Hermosa Beach. Sam had wandered into the club for a cold beer, and Remi was there celebrating a successful research trip looking into rumors of a sunken Spanish ship off Abalone Cove.

Though neither of them had ever called their first meeting a case of love at first sight, they'd both agreed it had certainly been a case of 'pretty damned sure at first hour.' Six months later they were married where they'd first met, in a small ceremony at the Lighthouse.

At Remi's encouragement Sam dove headfirst into his own business, and they struck pay dirt within a year with an argon laser scanner that could detect and identify at a distance mixed metals and alloys, from gold and silver to platinum and palladium. Treasure hunters, universities, corporations, and mining outfits scrambled to license Sam's invention, and within two years Fargo Group was seeing an annual net profit of three million dollars. Within four years the deep-pocketed corporations came calling. Sam and Remi took the highest bid, sold the company for enough money to see themselves comfortably through the rest of their lives, and then turned to their true passion: treasure hunting.

For Sam and Remi, the engine that drove their lives was not money but rather the adventure and the satisfaction of seeing the Fargo Foundation flourish. The foundation, which split its gifting among underprivileged and abused children, animal protection, and nature conservancy, had grown by leaps and bounds over the last decade, the previous year donating almost twenty million dollars to a variety of organizations. A hefty part of that money had come from Sam and Remi personally, and the rest of it from private donations. For better or worse their exploits attracted a fair amount of media attention, which in turn attracted wealthy, high-profile donors.

The question they now faced was whether this ship's bell was something they could turn into philanthropic funds or simply a fascinating historical diversion. Not that it mattered, of course. The pursuit of hidden history held its own joys for them. Either way, they knew where they had to start.

'Time to call Selma,' Remi said.

'Time to call Selma,' Sam agreed.

An hour later they were back at their rented plantation-style bungalow at Kendwa Beach, on Zanzibar's northern tip. While Remi prepared a fresh fruit salad, slices of prosciutto and mozzarella, and iced tea, Sam dialed Selma. Above their heads, a sixty-inch ceiling fan churned the air while through the French doors a cool offshore breeze billowed the gauze curtains.

Despite it being four A.M. in San Diego, Selma Wondrash picked up on the first ring. Sam and Remi were not surprised, having come to believe Selma slept only four hours a night, save Sundays, when she slept five.

'The only time you call me when you're on vacation is when you're in trouble or about to get into trouble,' Selma said over the speakerphone without preamble.

'Not true,' Sam replied. 'Last year from the Seychelles we called – '

'Because a troop of baboons had broken into your beach house, destroyed the furniture, and made off with

14

all your worldly goods, and the police thought you were burglars.'

She's right, Remi mouthed from across the kitchen island. Using the tip of her knife, she tossed Sam a chunk of fresh pineapple. He caught it in his mouth, and she applauded silently.

'Okay, that's true,' Sam told Selma.

A former Hungarian citizen who'd never quite lost her accent, Selma Wondrash was the stern but secretly soft-hearted head of Sam and Remi's three-person research team behind the Fargo Foundation. Selma was widowed, having lost her husband, an air force test pilot, in a crash ten years earlier.

After finishing her degree at Georgetown, Selma had managed the Library of Congress's Special Collections Division until Sam and Remi lured her away. More than a research chief, Selma had proven herself a superb travel agent and logistics guru, getting them to and from destinations with militaristic efficiency. Selma ate, drank, and lived research: the mystery that stubbornly refused solution, the legend that showed the barest spark of truth.

'So what is it this time?' Selma asked.

'A ship's bell,' Remi called.

They could hear the fluttering of paper as Selma retrieved a fresh legal pad. 'Tell me,' she said.

'West coast of Chumbe Island,' Sam said, then recited the coordinates he'd locked into his GPS unit before heading for the boat. 'You'll have to check – '

'Boundaries of the reserves and sanctuaries, yes,' Selma said, her pencil rasping on paper. 'I'll have Wendy look into Tanzanian maritime law. Anything else?'

'A coin. Diamond-shaped, about the size of a U.S. half-dollar. We found it about a hundred twenty yards north of the bell . . .' Sam looked to Remi for confirmation of this and got a nod in return. 'We're going to see if we can clean it up a bit, but the face is obscured right now.'

'Got it. Next?'

'There's no next. That's it. As soon as possible, Selma. The sooner we can put a hook on that bell, the better. That sandbank didn't look all that stable.'

'I'll get back to you,' Selma replied and hung up.

Chapter 2

Mexico City, Mexico

Quauhtli Garza, the president of the United Mexican States and the leader of the Mexica (pronounced in the traditional way, Meh-SHEE-kah) Tenochca Party, gazed out the floor-to-ceiling windows and down into the Plaza de la Constitución, where the Great Temple had once stood. Now it was nothing more than beautified ruins, a tourist attraction for those who wanted to gawk at the sad remains of the magnificent Aztec city of Tenochtitlán and the great twelve-foot-diameter, twenty-ton Calendar Stone.

'A mockery,' Quauhtli Garza mumbled, watching the milling crowds.

A mockery he'd so far been able to correct with only marginal success. True, the Mexican people had since his election gained a better understanding of their lineage – had come to understand the true history of their country that had been all but obliterated by Spanish imperialism. Even the name, the Aztec Party, which so many news reporters used to describe Mexica Tenochca, was an insult, a nod to falsity. Hernán Cortés and his bloodthirsty Spanish conquistadors had named the Mexica peoples Aztecs, bastardized from the name of the legendary home of the Mexica – Aztlán. It was a necessary artifice, however. For now, Aztec was a term the Mexican people both understood and could take to their collective hearts. In time, Garza would educate them.

It was, in fact, a ground surge of pre-conquest nationalism that had swept Garza and the Mexica Tenochca into power, but Garza's hopes for Mexico's widespread and immediate embracement of its history were starting to fade. He'd come to realize they'd won the election partly because of the previous administration's incompetence and corruption and partly because of Mexica Tenochca's 'Aztecan showmanship,' as one political pundit had termed it.

Showmanship indeed! It was absurd.

Hadn't Garza years ago renounced his Spanish Christian name, Fernando, for a Nahuatl one? Hadn't his entire cabinet done the same? Hadn't Garza renamed his own children in the Nahuatl tongue? And more: Literature and images of Spain's conquest of Mexico were slowly being weeded from school curricula; street and plaza names had been changed in favor of Nahuatl words; schools now taught courses in Nahuatl and the true history of the Mexica people; religious holidays and traditional Mexica festivals were celebrated several times a year. But still, all the polling showed that the Mexican people saw all of it as novelties – excuses to miss work or drink or misbehave in the streets. Even so, that same polling suggested real change could be instituted if they had enough time. Garza and the Mexica Tenochca needed another term, and to get that Garza needed to have the Senate, the Chamber of Deputies, and the Supreme Court of Justice of the Nation more firmly under his thumb. As it stood, the presidency was restricted

18

to a single term of six years. Not long enough to accomplish what Garza had planned, not long enough to accomplish what Mexico needed: a fully realized history of its own, free of the lies of conquest and slaughter.

Garza stepped away from the window, strode to his desk, and pressed a button on the remote. Shades descended from the ceiling, muting the noonday sun; in the ceiling, recessed lighting glowed to life, illuminating the burgundy carpet and heavy wooden furniture. Like the rest of Garza's life, his office reflected his Mexica heritage. Tapestries and paintings depicting Aztec history lined the walls. Here, a twelve-foot-long, hand-painted codex detailing the founding of Tenochtitlán on a marshy island in Lake Texcoco; over there, a painting of the Aztec goddess of the moon, Coyolxauhqui; across the room above the fireplace, a floor-to-ceiling tapestry showing Huitzilopochtli, the 'Hummingbird Wizard,' and Tezcatlipoca, the 'Smoking Mirror,' in union, watching over their people. On the wall above his desk was an oil painting of Chicomoztoc – 'the Place of Seven Caves' – the legendary source of all Nahuatl-speaking peoples.

None of these, however, kept him awake at night. That honor belonged to the artifact standing in the corner of the room. Perched atop a crystal pedestal in a cube of half-inch-thick glass was Quetzalcoatl, the feathered serpent god of the Aztecs. Of course, depictions of Quetzalcoatl were commonplace – on pottery and tapestries and in a multitude of codices – but this representation was unique. A statuette. The only one of its kind. At four inches tall and seven inches long, it was a masterwork carved by unknown hands a millennium ago from a chunk of nearly translucent jade.

Garza walked around his desk and sat in the chair before the pedestal. Quetzalcoatl's surface, lit from above by an inset halogen bulb, seemed to swirl, forming mesmerizing shapes and pools of color that were at once there and not there. Garza's eyes drifted back along Quetzalcoatl's plumes and scales until coming to rest on the tail – or where the tail should have been, he corrected himself. Instead of tapering to a traditional serpent's tail, the statuette widened for a few inches before ending abruptly in a jagged vertical line, as though it had been cleaved from a larger artifact. This was, in fact, the theory Garza's scientists had put forth. And a theory he had worked hard to suppress.

This Quetzalcoatl statuette, this symbol of the Mexica Tenochca, was incomplete. Garza knew what was missing – or, more accurately, he knew the missing piece would not resemble anything in the Aztec pantheon. It was this thought that kept him awake at night. As the symbol of the Mexica Tenochca movement since the day Garza had founded it, this statuette had become a rallying cry for the wave of nationalism that had swept him into office. Should its credibility be called into doubt . . . It was a question Garza didn't dare entertain. The thought that a lost nineteenth-century warship could destroy everything that he'd built was unacceptable. All of it gone because of a trinket or artifact found by a random snorkeler, who in turn shows it to someone with a passing interest in history, who then asks an expert. A falling domino that destroys a nation's restored pride.

The buzz of the intercom on Garza's desk shook him from his reverie. He turned off the case's halogen light and returned to his desk.

'Yes?' he said.

'He is here, Mr. President.'

'Send him in,' Garza said, then turned and sat down behind his desk.

The double doors opened a moment later and in strode Itzli Rivera. At six feet tall and one hundred fifty pounds, Itzli Rivera appeared unsubstantial from a distance – gaunt in the extreme, his narrow face of angles and planes dominated by a hawk nose – but as he came closer Garza reminded himself how deceptive Rivera's appearance was. It showed in the hard set of his eyes and mouth, in his steady, purposeful gait, and in the taut muscles and the tendons of his bare forearms. Even without knowing the man, an astute observer could easily see Itzli Rivera was no stranger to hardship. Of course, Garza knew this to be true. His chief operative had indeed visited hardship upon many poor souls, so far most of them political opponents who didn't share Garza's vision for Mexico. Luckily, it was easier to find a virgin in a brothel than it was to find an incorrupt member of the Senate or the Chamber of Deputies, and Rivera had a knack for finding a man's weakness, then shoving the dagger home. Rivera was himself a true believer, having rejected his Spanish name, Hector, in favor of Itzli, which in Nahuatl meant 'obsidian.' A fitting name, Garza thought.

A former major in the Grupo Aeromóvil de Fuerzas Especiales, or Special Forces Airmobile Group, GAFE, and former Secretariat of National Defense's S-2 Intelligence Second Section, Rivera had left the army to become Garza's personal bodyguard, but Garza had quickly seen Rivera's wider potential and had put him to work as his own private intelligence and operations director.

'Good morning, Mr. President,' Rivera said stiffly.

'And to you. Sit down, sit down. Can I get you something?' Rivera shook his head, and Garza asked, 'To what do I owe this visit?'

'We've come across something you may want to see – a video. I asked your secretary to cue it up.'

Rivera picked up the remote from his desk, aimed it at the fifty-inch LCD television on the wall, and hit Power. Garza sat down. After a few seconds of silence, a man and woman in their mid-thirties appeared, sitting together before an ocean backdrop. Off camera, a reporter was asking questions. Though Garza's English was fluent, Rivera's technical people had added Spanish subtitles.

The interview was short, no longer than three minutes. When it was done, Garza looked to Rivera. 'And the significance is?'

'Those are the Fargos – Sam and Remi Fargo.'

'Is that supposed to mean something to me?'

'Do you remember last year, the story about Napoleon's Lost Cellar . . . the lost Spartans?'

Garza was nodding his head. 'Yes, yes . . .'

'The Fargos were behind that. They're very good at what they do.'

This got Garza's attention. He leaned forward in his chair. 'Where was this interview taped?'

'Zanzibar. By a BBC correspondent. Of course, the timing could be a coincidence.'

Garza waved his hand dismissively. 'I don't believe in coincidences. And neither do you, my friend, or else you wouldn't have brought this to me.'

For the first time since entering the office, Rivera

showed a trace of emotion – a thin shark's smile that never reached his eyes. 'True.'

'How did you come across this?'

'After the . . . revelation . . . I had my technical team create a special program. It monitors the Internet for certain key words. In this case, "Zanzibar," "Tanzania," "Chumbe," "Shipwrecks," and "Treasure." The last two, of course, are the Fargos' specialties. In the interview they were adamant that the trip was simply a diving vacation, but . . .'

'This close to the last incident . . . the British woman . . .'

'Sylvie Radford.'

Radford, Garza thought. Luckily, the idiot woman had had no inkling of the significance of what she'd found, treating it as nothing more than a trinket, showing it off around Zanzibar and Bagamoyo, asking locals what it might be. The necessity of her death had been unfortunate, but Rivera had handled it with his usual care – a street robbery turned murder, the police had concluded.

What Ms. Radford actually found had been the thinnest of threads, one that would've required careful and expert teasing lest it snap. But the Fargos . . . They knew all about following random threads, he suspected. The Fargos knew how to uncover something from nothing.

'Could she have told someone what she found?' Garza asked. 'The Fargos have their own intelligence network of sorts, I would imagine. Could they have gotten a whiff of something?' Garza narrowed his eyes and stared hard at Rivera. 'Tell me, Itzli, did you miss something?'

The gaze that had withered many a cabinet secretary

and political opponent left Rivera unfazed; the man merely shrugged.

'I doubt it, but it is possible,' he said calmly.

Garza nodded. Though the possibility of Ms. Radford having shared her find with someone was disconcerting, Garza was pleased Rivera had no trouble admitting he may have made a mistake. As president, Garza was surrounded daily by sycophants and yes-men. He trusted Rivera to give him the unvarnished truth and to fix the unfixable, and he'd never failed in either respect.

'Find out,' Garza ordered. 'Go to Zanzibar and find out what the Fargos are up to.'

'And if this isn't a coincidence? They wouldn't be as easy to handle as the British woman.'

'I'm sure you'll work it out,' Garza said. 'If history has shown us anything, it's that Zanzibar can be a dangerous place.'

Chapter 3

Zanzibar

After talking with Selma, Sam and Remi took a catnap, then showered, changed clothes, and took their scooters down the coast road to Stone Town, to their favorite Tanzanian cuisine restaurant, the Ekundu Kifaru – Swahili for 'Red Rhino.' Overlooking the waterfront, the Red Rhino was nestled between the Old Customs House and the Big Tree, a giant old fig that served as a daily hangout for small boat builders and charter captains offering day sails to Prison Island or Bawe Island.

For Sam and Remi, Zanzibar (or Unguja in Swahili) personified Old World Africa. The island had over the centuries been ruled by warlords and sultans, slave traders and pirates; it had been the headquarters for trading companies and the staging area for thousands of European missionaries, explorers, and big game hunters. Sir Richard Burton and John Hanning Speke had used Zanzibar as the base for their search for the source of the Nile; Henry Morton Stanley had begun his famous hunt for the wayward David Livingstone in the labyrinthine alleys of Stone Town; Captain William Kidd had reputedly sailed the waters around Zanzibar as both pirate and pirate hunter.

Here, Sam and Remi found every street and courtyard had a story and every structure a secret history. They never left Zanzibar without dozens of fond memories.

By the time they pulled into the parking lot the sun was dropping quickly toward the horizon, casting the sea in shades of gold and red. The scent of oysters on the grill drifted in the air.

'Welcome back, Mr. and Mrs. Fargo,' the valet called, then signaled for a pair of white-coated attendants, who trotted over and pushed the scooters away.

'Evening, Abasi,' Sam replied, shaking the valet's hand. Remi received a warm hug. They'd met Abasi Sibale on their first visit to Zanzibar six years earlier and had become fast friends, usually having dinner with him and his family at least once during their yearly visits. Abasi was never without a smile.

'How're Faraja and the kids?' Sam asked.

'Happy and healthy, thank you. You will come to supper while you are here?'

Remi smiled. 'Wouldn't miss it.'

'I believe they are ready for you inside,' Abasi said.

Just inside the door the maître d', Elimu, was waiting. He, too, had known the Fargos for years. 'Good to see you, good to see you. Your favorite table overlooking the harbor is ready.'

'Thank you,' Sam said.

Elimu led them to a corner table lit by a red hurricane lantern and surrounded on two sides by open windows overlooking the waterfront. Below, Stone Town's streetlights were flickering to life.

'Wine, yes?' Elimu asked. 'You would like the list?'

'Do you still have that Pinot Noir – the Chamonix?'

'Yes, we have a '98 or a 2000.'

Sam looked to Remi, who said, 'I still remember the '98.'

'As the lady wishes, Elimu.'

'Very good, sir.'

Elimu disappeared.

'It's beautiful,' Remi murmured, staring out over the ocean.

'I couldn't agree more.'

She turned her head away from the window, gave him a smile, and squeezed his hand. 'You got a little sun,' she remarked. For some inexplicable reason, Sam Fargo burned oddly – today, only the bridge of his nose and the tips of his ears were pink. Tomorrow they would be bronze. 'You're going to be itchy later.'

'I'm itchy now.'

'So, any guesses?' Remi asked, holding up the diamond coin.

It had spent the afternoon first sitting in a bowl of ten percent nitric acid, followed by Sam's secret formula of white vinegar, salt, and distilled water, followed by a scrubbing with a soft-bristle toothbrush. While many spots remained obscured, they could make out a woman's face in profile and two words: 'Marie' and 'Reunion.' These details they'd relayed to Selma before leaving the bungalow.

'Not a one,' Sam said. 'An odd shape for a coin, though.'

'Private minting, perhaps?'

'Could be. If so, it's well done. Nice clean edges, good tooling, solid weight . . .'

Elimu returned with the wine, decanted, poured for both of them, waited for their nods of approval, then filled their glasses. This particular Pinot Noir was South

African, a rich red with hints of cloves, cinnamon, nutmeg, and something Sam couldn't quite place.

Remi took a second sip and said, 'Chicory.'

Sam's phone rang. He looked at the screen, mouthed, *Selma*, then answered. 'Evening, Selma.' Remi leaned forward to listen in.

'Morning for me. Pete and Wendy just got here. They're starting on the Tanzanian law angle.'

'Perfect.'

'Let me guess: You're sitting at the the Ekundu Kifaru, staring at the sunset.'

'Creatures of habit,' Remi said.

'You have news?' Sam asked.

'About your coin. You have yourself another mystery.'

Sam saw the waiter approaching and said, 'Hold a minute.' They ordered a Samakai wa kusonga and wali – fish croquet and native rice with chapati bread – and for dessert, N'dizi no kastad – Zanzibar-style banana custard. The waiter left, and Sam un-muted Selma.

'Go ahead, Selma. We're all ears,' Sam said.

'The coin was minted sometime in the early 1690s. Only fifty were made, and they never saw official circulation. In fact, they were a token of affection, for lack of a better term. The "Marie" on the coin's face is part of "Sainte Marie," the name of a French commune situated on the north coast of Reunion Island.'

'Never heard of it,' Remi said.

'Not surprising. It's a little lump of an island about four hundred miles east of Madagascar.'

'Who's the woman?' Sam asked.

'Adelise Molyneux. The wife of Demont Molyneux,

28

the administrator of Sainte Marie from 1685 to 1701. According to the stories, for their tenth anniversary Demont had his private stock of gold melted down and minted into these Adelise coins.'

'Quite a gesture,' Remi said.

'The coins were supposed to represent the number of years Demont hoped they would spend together before dying. They came close. They both died within a year of each other, just shy of their fortieth anniversary.'

'So how did this one get all the way to Zanzibar?' Sam asked.

'Here's where truth gets mixed up with legend,' Selma replied. 'You've heard of George Booth, I assume?'

'English pirate,' Sam said.

'Right. Spent most of his time in the Indian Ocean and Red Sea. Started as a gunner aboard the *Pelican* around 1696, then aboard the *Dolphin*. Around 1699 the *Dolphin* was cornered by a British fleet near Reunion Island. Some of the crew surrendered; some, including Booth, escaped to Madagascar, where Booth and another pirate captain, John Bowen, combined forces and hijacked the *Speaker*, a four-hundred-fifty-ton, fifty-gun slave ship. Booth was elected captain, and then around 1700 he took the *Speaker* to Zanzibar. When they went ashore for supplies, the landing party was attacked by Arab troops. Booth was killed and Bowen survived. From there, Bowen took the *Speaker* back to the waters around Madagascar, before dying a few years later on Mauritius.'

'You said the *Dolphin* was cornered near Reunion Island,' Sam repeated. 'How close to the Sainte Marie commune?'

'A few miles offshore,' Selma replied. 'Legend says Booth and his crew had just finished raiding the commune.'

'Having made off with the Adelise coins,' Remi finished.

'So says the legend. And so said Demont Molyneux in an official letter of complaint to Louis XIV, the king of France.'

'So let's play this out,' Sam said. 'Booth and the other escapees from the *Dolphin* take with them the Adelise coins, then meet up with Bowen. They then hijack the *Speaker* and head for Zanzibar, where they . . . what? Bury their booty on Chumbe Island? Dump it in shallow water for later recovery?'

'Or maybe the *Speaker* never got away,' Remi added. 'Maybe the stories are wrong. Maybe she was sunk in the channel.'

'Half a dozen of one, six of the other,' Selma replied. 'Either way, the coin you found is from the Adelise lot.'

'The question is,' Sam said, 'does our bell belong to the *Speaker*?'

Chapter 4

Zanzibar

The storm that had closed over the island in the early-morning hours had moved on by dawn, leaving the air crisp and the foliage around their bungalow glistening with dew. Sam and Remi sat on the rear porch overlooking the beach and shared a meal of fruit, bread, cheese, and strong black coffee. In the trees around them, hidden birds squawked.

Suddenly a pinkie-sized gecko scaled the leg of Remi's chair and skittered across her lap and onto the table, where it navigated the dishes before retreating down Sam's chair.

'Wrong turn, I guess,' Sam remarked.

'I have a way with reptiles,' Remi said.

They shared one more cup of coffee, then cleaned up, packed their backpacks, and walked down to the beach, where they'd grounded the cabin cruiser. Sam tossed their backpacks over the railing, then gave Remi a boost.

'Anchor?' she called.

'Coming.'

Sam squatted beside the auger-shaped beach anchor, wriggled it free, then handed it up to Remi. She disappeared, and he could hear her feet padding along the deck, and then a few seconds later the engines growled to life and settled into a sputtering idle.

'Slow back,' Sam called.

'Slow back, aye,' Remi replied.

When Sam heard the propeller begin to churn, he leaned hard against the hull, dug his feet into the wet sand, coiled his legs, and shoved. The boat eased back a foot, then another, then floated free. He reached up, snagged the lowermost railing with his hands, then swung his legs up, hooked his heel on the gunwale, and climbed aboard.

'Chumbe Island?' Remi called through the open pilot-house window.

'Chumbe Island,' Sam confirmed. 'Got a mystery to solve.'

They were a few miles northwest of Prison Island when Sam's satellite phone trilled. Sitting on the afterdeck, sorting through their gear, Sam picked up the phone and pressed Talk. It was Selma. 'Good news, not so good news,' she said.

'Good news first,' Sam said.

'According to Tanzania's Ministry of Natural Resources regulations, the spot where you found the bell is outside sanctuary boundaries. There's no reef there, so no protection necessary.'

'And the not so good news?'

'Tanzanian maritime salvage law still applies – "No extraordinary excavation methods." It's a gray area, but it sounds like you're going to need more than Ping-Pong paddles to free that bell. I've got both Pete and Wendy looking into the permit process – discreetly, of course.'

Boyfriend and girlfriend Pete Jeffcoat and Wendy

32

Corden – tan and fit blond Californians with degrees in archaeology and social sciences, respectively – worked as Selma's apprentices.

'Good,' Sam said. 'Keep us posted.'

After a brief stop at the Stone Town docks to refuel and gather the day's provisions, it took another leisurely ninety minutes' cruising down the coast and picking their way through the channels of Zanzibar's outer islands before they reached the bell's GPS coordinates. Sam went forward and dropped anchor. The air was dead calm and the sky a cloudless blue. As Zanzibar sat just below the equator, July was during winter rather than summer, so the temperature wouldn't climb above the low eighties. A good day for diving. He hoisted the white-stripe-on-red diver-down flag on the halyard, then joined Remi on the afterdeck.

'Tanks or snorkel?' she asked.

'Let's start with snorkel.' The bell was sitting in ten feet of water. 'Let's get a good look at what we're up against, then regroup.'

As it had been the day before and was ninety percent of the time in Zanzibar, the water was stunningly clear, ranging in shade from turquoise to indigo. Sam rolled backward over the gunwale, followed a few seconds later by Remi. Together they hung motionless on the surface for a few seconds, letting the cloud of bubbles and froth dissipate, then flipped over and dove. Once they reached the white sand bottom they turned right and soon reached the lip of the bank, where they performed another pike dive and followed the vertical face to the bottom. They stopped, knelt in the sand, and jammed their dive knives into the bottom to use as handholds.

Ahead they could see the edge of the Good-bye Zone. The previous night's storm had not only ramped up the current in the main channel but had also churned up a lot of debris, so thick it looked like a solid gray-brown wall of sand. This at least would keep the sharks away from the shallows. The downside was they could feel the draw of the current from where they hovered.

Sam tapped his snorkel and jerked his thumb upward. Remi nodded.

They finned for the surface and broke into the air.

'You feel that?' Sam asked.

Remi nodded. 'Felt like an invisible hand was trying to grab us.'

'Stick close to the bank.'

'Got it.'

They dove again. On the bottom, Sam checked the readout on his GPS unit, oriented himself, then pointed south down the bank and signed to Remi: *30 feet*. Resurfacing, they swam that way in single file, Sam in the lead, one eye on the GPS, one eye on his position. He stopped again and pointed an index finger down.

Where the bell had jutted from the bank there was now nothing but a barrel-shaped crater. Anxiously they scanned left and right. Remi saw it first, a curved indentation in the bottom, ten feet to their right, connected to another indentation by a curved line like a sidewinder's trail. The pattern repeated. They followed it with their eyes until, twenty feet away, they saw a dark lump jutting from the sand. It was the bell.

It took little imagination to piece together what had happened: Throughout the night the storm-driven waves had scoured the bank, slowly but steadily eroding the sand around the bell until it tumbled from its resting place. From there the surge had rolled the bell along its mouth, physics, erosion, and time doing their work until the storm passed.

Sam and Remi turned to each other and nodded excitedly. Where Tanzanian law had forbidden them to use 'extraordinary excavation methods,' Mother Nature had come to the rescue.

They swam toward the bell but had only covered half the distance when Sam reached out a halting hand to Remi's arm. She had already stopped and was staring ahead. She'd seen what he'd seen.

The bell had come to a stop at the lip of the precipice, with the waist, shoulder, and crown embedded in the sand and the sound ring and mouth jutting into empty space.

Back on the surface, they got their breath. Remi said, 'It's too big.'

'Too big for what? To move?'

'No, to belong to the *Speaker*.'

Sam considered this. 'You're right. I didn't notice.'

The *Speaker*'s displacement was listed as four hundred fifty tons. According to standard measures for the era in question, her bell wouldn't have weighed more than sixty pounds. Their bell was bigger than that.

'Curiouser and curiouser,' Sam said. 'Back to the boat. We need a plan.'

*

They were ten feet from the boat when they heard the rumble of diesel engines approaching from behind. They reached the ladder and turned around to see a Tanzanian coast guard gunboat a hundred yards away. Sam and Remi climbed onto the Andreyale's afterdeck and shed their gear.

'Smile and wave,' Sam murmured.

'Are we in trouble?' Remi whispered through her smile.

'Don't know. We'll soon find out.' Sam continued waving.

'I've heard Tanzanian jails are unpleasant.'

'Every jail is unpleasant. It's all relative.'

Thirty feet away, the gunboat came about and drew parallel to them, bow to stern. Sam now saw it was an upgraded 1960s-era Chinese Yulin-class patrol boat. They saw Yulins several times on each of their trips, and Sam, ever interested, had done his homework: forty feet long, ten tons; three-shaft, two six-hundred-horsepower diesel engines; and a pair of twin 12.7mm deck guns fore and aft.

Two sailors in jungle fatigues stood on the afterdeck and two more on the forecastle. All bore shoulder-slung AK-47s. A tall black man in crisp whites, clearly the captain, stepped from the cabin and walked to the railing.

'Ahoy,' he called. Unlike Sam and Remi's previous encounters with the coast guard, this captain was grim-faced. No welcoming smile or pleasantries.

'Ahoy,' Sam replied.

'Routine safety check. We will board you now.'

'Be our guest.'

The gunboat's engines gurgled, and the Yulin angled

closer until its bow was ten feet away. The engines went back to idle, and the Yulin glided to a stop beside them. The sailors on the afterdeck tossed tire bumpers over the side, then reached down, grabbed the Andreyale's railing, and pulled the boats together. The captain vaulted over the railing and landed catlike on the Andreyale's afterdeck beside Sam and Remi.

'You are flying the diver flag, I see,' he said.

'Doing a little snorkeling,' Sam replied.

'This boat is yours?'

'No, a rental.'

'Your papers.'

'For the boat?'

'And diving certificates.'

Remi said, 'I'll get them,' then trotted down the steps into the cabin.

The captain asked Sam, 'What is your purpose here?'

'On Zanzibar or here specifically?'

'Both, sir.'

'Just on vacation. This seemed like a nice spot. We were here yesterday.'

Remi returned with the documents and handed them to the captain, who first examined the rental agreement, then their diving certificates. He looked up and studied their faces. 'You are Sam and Remi Fargo.'

Sam nodded.

'The treasure hunters.'

Remi said, 'For lack of a better term.'

'Are you hunting treasure on Zanzibar?'

Sam smiled. 'That's not why we came, but we try to keep our eyes open.' Over the captain's shoulder, behind the tinted windows of the Yulin's cabin, Sam saw a shadowed figure. It appeared to be staring at them.

'Have your eyes seen anything on this visit?'

'A coin.'

'You are aware of Tanzanian law regarding these matters?'

Remi nodded. 'We are.'

From the Yulin, a knuckle rapped once on the window.

The captain looked over his shoulder, said to Sam and Remi, 'Wait here,' then climbed back over the railing and stepped into the Yulin's cabin. He reappeared a minute later and jumped back down.

'The coin you have found – describe it.'

Without hesitation, Remi said, 'Round, copper, about the size of a fifty-shilling piece. It's badly pitted. We haven't been able to make anything of it.'

'Do you have it with you?'

'No,' said Sam.

'And you say you are not hunting for any shipwrecks or specific treasure?'

'That's correct.'

'Where are you staying on Zanzibar?'

Sam saw no point in lying. They would double-check the answer. 'A bungalow on Kendwa Beach.'

The captain handed back their papers, then tipped his cap to them. 'Good day.'

And then he was back over the rail and inside the Yulin's cabin. The gunboat's engines rumbled, the sailors pushed off, and the gunboat came about and steered west toward the channel. Sam took two long strides, ducked into the cabin, and reemerged with a pair of binoculars. He lifted them to his eyes and trained them on the Yulin. After twenty seconds, he lowered the binoculars.

'What?' Remi asked.

'There was someone in the cabin giving orders.'

'The knock on the window?' Remi said. 'Did you get a look at him?'

Sam nodded. 'Not black and not in uniform. He looked Hispanic – maybe Mediterranean. Thin, hawk nose, thick eyebrows.'

'What kind of non-Tanzanian civilian would have the power to order about a coast guard gunboat and her crew?'

'Someone with deep pockets.' As much as they loved Tanzania and Zanzibar and their people, there was no arguing that corruption was common. The majority of Tanzanians made a few dollars a day; military personnel, only slightly more. 'Let's not get ahead of ourselves, though. Right now we don't know anything. Just curious, Remi: Why'd you lie about the coin?'

'Gut reaction,' Remi replied. 'You think I should have – '

'No. I had the same instinct. The Tanzanian coast guard has two Yulin gunboats to cover the central coast, the main channel, and Zanzibar. I got the impression they were specifically looking for us.'

'Me too.'

'And as safety checks go, that one was worthless. Didn't ask about life preservers, the radio, or our dive gear.'

'And when was the last time we met a Tanzanian official that wasn't all smiles and geniality?'

'Never,' Sam replied. 'About the Adelise coin – '

Remi unzipped the side pocket of her dive shorts, withdrew the coin, and held it up with a smile.

'That's my girl,' Sam said.

'You think they'll search the bungalow?'

Sam shrugged.

'So, put it all together and what's it mean?' Remi pondered.

'No idea, but we're going to watch our step from here on out.'

Chapter 5

Zanzibar

For the next hour they sat on the afterdeck, sipping ice-cold water and enjoying the gentle rocking of the Andreyale and listening to the waves lapping at the hull. Within the first thirty minutes of the Yulin's departure, it appeared twice more, a mile out, cruising first north to south, then south to north. It had not returned.

'Can't help but worry the bell's tumbled over the edge,' Remi said. 'I can see it in my mind's eye.'

'Me too, but I'd rather risk that than have them come back while we're in the middle of raising it. Let's give it another twenty minutes. Worst case, we can probably still get to it.'

'True, but at a hundred fifty feet, things start getting dicey. Getting down there wouldn't be so hard. Finding it might be.' As massive as the bell was, after bouncing down a hundred-fifty-foot slope it could end up almost anywhere, like a dropped child's marble that's lost in the dining room but ends up under the refrigerator in the kitchen. 'And once we find it, getting it up to the surface is a different can of worms altogether. Better dive gear, compressor, lift bags, winch . . .'

Sam was nodding. There would be no chance of hiding that level of activity from curious or prying eyes. Simply renting the equipment in Stone Town – even anonymously – would set the rumor mill in motion. By day's end there would be onlookers both on the shoreline and in boats offshore – including, perhaps, the Yulin gunboat and her mysterious passenger.

'Let's hope it doesn't come to that,' he said.

They moved the Andreyale to within thirty feet of the bell's location. Sam went over the side and wedged the anchor behind a rock outcropping, and then, back aboard, they uncoiled the hundred feet of solid-braided three-quarter-inch anchor rope they'd purchased earlier in Stone Town. They looped the rope over the port and starboard rear gunwale cleats, then secured the loop in the center with a screw-link D ring. The remainder of the coil they tossed over the stern. Two minutes later they were in their snorkel gear and finning along the surface, dragging the rope behind them.

To their mutual surprise, they found the bell where they'd left it, perched on the edge of the precipice, but they immediately found the situation was more precarious than they'd anticipated. The sand beneath the bell's mouth was eroding before their eyes, wisps of sand and chunks of rock being ripped away by the current.

Remi fed the end of the rope through the D ring on her dive belt, then handed it to Sam, who did the same, then clamped the rope's screw-link D ring between his teeth.

They finned to the surface, grabbed a half dozen lung-fuls of air, then dove again.

Sam signaled to Remi: *Pictures*. If the worst came to pass and they lost the bell, pictures would at least give them a chance at identification. As Remi started shooting, Sam finned forward until he could see over the edge. The slope was not quite vertical but rather sixty or sixty-five degrees. Not that it mattered. As Remi had earlier guessed, the bell's weight surpassed that of the *Speaker* by twenty or thirty pounds. If the bell decided to go over the edge, the slope's angle would slow its descent only slightly.

And then, as if on cue, the sand beneath the bell gave way. The crown tipped upward, hovered for a split second, then the bell began sliding, mouth first, down the slope.

On an impulse he immediately regretted, Sam coiled his legs, gave a sharp dolphin kick, and followed the bell over the edge. He heard, fleetingly, Remi's muffled scream of 'Sam!' and then it was gone, replaced by the rush of the current. Sand peppered his body like a thousand bee stings. Tumbling now head over feet, Sam reached out in what he hoped was the direction of the bank. The out-stretched fingers of his right hand struck something hard, and he felt a sharp pain shoot through his pinkie finger. Ignoring the pain, he could feel the bell picking up speed now, the bulldozer-like effect of the mouth losing to the physics of momentum. His eyesight began to swim as his lungs began consuming the last molecules of oxygen. His heart pounded in his head like cannon fire.

Working from feel alone, he slid his hand up the bell's waist, then over the head. His fingers found the opening of the crown. He lifted his left hand up to his mouth, grabbed the D ring, and fed it through the crown. He curled it around the line and then, using his thumb, spun the screw link closed.

The bell jerked to a stop. The rope let out a muffled

twang. Sam lost his grip, and he began sliding downward, hands slapping at the bell's surface, fingers scrabbling for purchase. There was nothing. Then, suddenly, a ridge slid beneath his palm. He felt another stab of pain in his pinkie finger. The bead line, he thought. His curled finger-tips had landed on the bead line just above the mouth of the bell. He reached up with his other hand, gripped the line, then chinned himself upward, both legs kicking against the draw of the current until the anchor line came into view, a braid of pure white in the swirl of sand. He grabbed it. He felt fingers touch the back of his hand. Out of the gloom a face appeared. Remi. His eyesight was sparkling now and dimming at the edges. Remi pulled her-self down the anchor line, reached down, clamped onto his right wrist, and tugged.

Instinctively Sam latched onto rope and began climbing.

Ten minutes later he sat in the deck chair, eyes closed and head tilted back into the sun. After two minutes of this he brought his head level again and opened his eyes to find Remi sitting on the gunwale watching him. She leaned forward and handed him a bottle of water.

'Feeling better?' she asked gently.

'Yes. Much. Pinkie finger's jammed, though. Smarts.' He held it up for inspection; the digit was straight but swollen. He curled it and winced. 'It's not broken. Nothing a little athletic tape won't cure.'

'Nothing else wrong?'

Sam shook his head.

'Good, glad to hear it,' said Remi. 'Sam Fargo, you're a dummy.'

44

'Pardon me?'

'What were you thinking, going after that thing?'

'I just reacted. By the time I realized what the hell I was doing it was too late. In for a penny, in for – '

'A one-way trip to the bottom of the ocean,' Remi countered with a scowling shake of her head. 'I swear, Fargo . . .'

'Sorry,' Sam said. 'And thanks for coming to get me.'

'Dummy,' Remi repeated, then got up, walked over, and kissed him on the cheek. 'But you're my dummy. And you don't need to thank me – but you're welcome anyway.'

'Tell me we still have it,' Sam said, looking around. 'Do we still have it?' He was still a tad woozy. Remi pointed off the stern where the anchor line, taut as piano wire, arced down into the water.

'While you were taking your catnap, I dragged it off the slope. It should be resting about five feet from the edge.'

'Nicely done.'

'Don't get too excited. We still have to raise it.'

Sam smiled. 'Have no fear, Remi. Physics is our friend.'

Before they could apply Sam's idea, however, they had to exercise some brute force. With Sam's newly damaged pinkie wrapped in duct tape, he stood in the stern taking up slack in the anchor line while Remi reversed the Andreyale's engine and followed his hand signals until they were almost directly above the bell. He uncoiled the line from the cleats, took up the remainder of the slack, then looped and locked down again.

Sam called, 'All ahead slow. Nice and easy.'

'You got it.'

Remi eased the throttle forward a quarter inch at a time. Sam, leaning over the stern, his face mask in the water, watched the bell's progress as it bulldozed through the sand. When it was twenty feet from the edge of the precipice, he called: 'All stop.' Remi throttled down.

Sam settled the mask over his face and dove down to examine their prize. He resurfaced a minute later. 'Looks good. Not much barnacle growth, which means it's probably been embedded in that bank for quite a while.'

Remi extended her hand and helped Sam aboard. She asked, 'Damage?'

'None that I could see. It's thick, Remi – probably closer to eighty pounds.'

She whistled softly. 'Big boy. Okay, by standard measure that'd make the ship ... what, a thousand tons displacement?'

'Between that and twelve hundred. Much bigger than the *Speaker*. The proximity of the Adelise coin and the bell is pure coincidence.'

With the bell no longer in danger of dropping into the channel, they disconnected and steered the Andreyale north a hundred yards, then eased their way through the inlet at the island's ankle and emerged in the stiletto lagoon.

Only a half mile wide and long, the lagoon was actually a mangrove swamp. Jutting from the water were a couple dozen 'floating islands': mushroom caps of earth sitting atop buttresses of exposed, gnarled mangrove roots. Ranging in size from standing-room-only to a double garage, all were covered in thick weeds, and most supported miniature forests of scrub trees and bushes. At the southern end of the swamp was a narrow beach, and beyond that a copse of coconut palms. It was eerily quiet, the air dead still.

'Now, this isn't something you see every day,' Remi murmured.

'Any sign of the Mad Hatter or Alice?'

'No, knock wood.'

'Let's get moving. Daylight's burning.'

The made their way through the floating islands, dropped anchor just off the beach, and waded ashore.

'How many are we going to need?' Remi asked. With one hand she deftly curled her auburn hair off her neck and snapped a rubber band around it, making a neat topknot.

Sam smiled. 'It's like magic, how you do that.'

'We are a wondrous species,' Remi agreed with a smile and wrung the water from her shirttails. 'So, how many?'

'Six. No, five.'

'And you're sure we couldn't get what we need in Stone Town and sneak back here?'

'You want to risk it? Something tells me that gunboat captain would be only too happy to arrest us. If he thinks we were lying to him . . .'

'True. Okay, Gilligan, let's make your raft.'

They had no trouble finding plenty of downed trees but a harder time finding ones of a manageable size. Sam identified five candidates, all roughly eight feet long and about as big around as a telephone pole. He and Remi dragged

47

each log down to the beach, where they arranged them in a row.

Sam went to work. The construction was simple enough, Sam explained. He grabbed a nearby piece of driftwood and inscribed the plan in the sand:

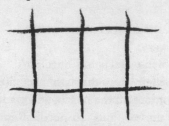

'Not exactly the *Queen Mary*,' Remi observed with a smile.

'For that,' Sam replied, 'I'd need at least four more logs.'

'Why the protruding ends?'

'Two reasons: stability and leverage.'

'For what?'

'You'll see. Right now I need some line – a few dozen six-foot lengths.'

Remi saluted. 'As you command.'

After an hour's work, Sam straightened up and stared at his creation. His narrowed eyes told Remi her husband was running equations in his head. After a minute of this, Sam nodded. 'Okay. Should be buoyant enough,' he proclaimed. 'With about twenty percent in reserve.'

With the raft in tow, they slipped back through the inlet to the island's western side and headed south along the coast until they were again over the bell's resting place. Using the gaff hook, Sam maneuvered the raft around to the landward side of the Andreyale and secured it to the cleats.

'My gut tells me we're due for another drive-by,' Sam said, sitting down in a deck chair. Remi joined him, and together they drank water and watched the water until, thirty minutes later, the Yulin appeared to the north, a half mile out.

'Good call,' Remi said.

The Yulin slowed to a walking pace, and from their afterdeck Sam and Remi could see a figure in a white uniform standing on its afterdeck. Sun glinted off binocular lenses.

'Smile and wave,' Sam said.

Together they did just that until the figure lowered its binoculars and disappeared into the cabin. The Yulin came about and began heading north. Sam and Remi waited until it disappeared around the curve of the island, then went back to work.

With the already prepped anchor in one hand, Sam donned his fins and mask and rolled over the side. After a bit of wrangling, he centered the raft over the bell. He knotted the end of the anchor line to the far side of the raft, dove at an angle until the line was taut, then jammed the anchor's flukes into the sand.

Back on the surface, he caught the line Remi tossed to him, then looped it over the raft's center beam, dove down, and clamped the D ring onto the bell's crown. A minute later he was back on the afterdeck, where he secured Remi's line to both cleats.

Hands on his hips, he appraised the setup.

Remi smiled sideways at him. 'You're very pleased with yourself, aren't you?'

'I am.'

'You should be. My intrepid engineer.'

Sam clapped his hands together once. 'Let's do this.'

With Remi at the wheel, Sam called, 'Slow ahead.'

'Slow ahead,' Remi repeated.

The water beneath the stern turned to froth, and the Andreyale eased forward a foot, then two. The cleated line began rising from the water. With a muffled squelch-pop, the rope cinched down on the raft's crossbeam.

'Looking good,' Sam called. 'Keep going.'

The raft began moving, closing the distance to the stern.

'Come on,' Sam muttered. 'Come on . . .'

On the far side of the raft the anchor line quivered with tension as it negated the Andreyale's drag on the raft. Sam donned his mask, bent over the side, and stuck his face in the water. Twelve feet below, the bell was hovering a few inches off the bottom.

Remi called, 'How're we doing?'

'A thing of beauty. Keep going.'

One careful foot at a time they lifted the bell until finally the crown broke the surface and thunked into the crossbeam.

'Slow to idle!' Sam ordered. 'Just enough to hold position.'

'Idling!' Remi replied.

Sam grabbed the six-foot length of line from the deck

and dove over the side. Three strokes brought him to the raft. Five loops through the bell's crown and a bowline knot over the crossbeam, and the bell was secure. Sam lifted his hands triumphantly, like a cowboy who'd just roped a calf.

'Done!' he called.

The Andreyale's engines sputtered and went silent. Remi walked onto the afterdeck, smiled, and returned her husband's thumbs-up.

'Congratulations, Fargo,' she called. 'Now what?'

Sam's smile dropped away. 'Not sure. Still working it out.'

'How did I know you were going to say that?'

Chapter 6

Zanzibar

In truth, there was nothing to work out. They didn't dare tow the bell back up the coast to their bungalow. They needed a safe place to stash it while they made some decisions and arrangements.

While they both recognized their encounter with the Yulin might be a molehill they'd built into a mountain, they'd also come to trust their instincts, and on this issue Sam's and Remi's gut reactions were in agreement: Neither the Yulin's initial visit nor its repeated appearances were happenstance. Also, her captain's questions were variations on a theme: Were the Fargos looking for something specific? This suggested someone – perhaps the shadowy figure hiding in the Yulin's cabin – was concerned that something of note was at risk of discovery. Was it the bell or the Adelise coin, or something else entirely?

'The question is,' Sam said, 'do we want to wait and see what they do or shake the tree a little bit?'

'I'm not fond of sitting on my hands.'

'I know. Me neither.'

'What did you have in mind?'

'Behave like we're people with something to hide.'

'We are people with something to hide,' Remi replied.

'A two-hundred-pound ship's bell suspended from a homemade raft.'

At this, Sam laughed. His wife had a knack for cutting to the heart of a matter. 'If we're not blowing all of this out of proportion, they – whoever they are – have probably already searched the bungalow.'

'And found nothing.'

'Right. So they'll watch and wait for us to come home.'

Remi was nodding, smiling. 'We don't come home.'

'Right. If they come looking for us, we've got confirmation the game's afoot.'

'Did you say "the game's afoot"? Really?'

Sam shrugged. 'Thought I'd try it out, see how it plays.'

'Oh, Sherlock . . .' Remi said, rolling her eyes.

With the bell and raft in tow, they retraced their course through ankle inlet and to the mangrove lagoon. Nightfall was only a couple hours away. They spent an hour of this time tooling around the lagoon's perimeter looking for a suitable hiding spot for the raft, which they found along the eastern shoreline where a cluster of cypress trees were growing diagonally from the bank. Using the gaff, they eased the raft beneath the overhanging branches, then Sam dove in and tied it off to one of the trunks.

'How's it look?' Sam called from behind the screen.

'Can't see a thing. They'd have to get in there to find it.'

They returned to the mouth of the inlet, where Sam used a dead line to catch four small red snappers, then they returned to the lagoon and waded ashore to the beach. Remi, who had the better filleting skills, cleaned and prepped the snapper while Sam collected wood for the fire. Before long the fillets were sizzling and, as the sun dropped behind the coconut palms, they were eating.

'You know, I think I like roughing it,' Remi said, flaking off a piece of fish and putting it in her mouth. 'To a degree, that is.'

'I understand.' He did. Remi was a trouper; she'd never withered before a challenge and had stood side by side with him in mud and snow, under gunfire and pursuit, and she rarely failed to find a bright side. For all that, however, she also loved her comforts. As did he. 'Once we get things settled with our mystery bell, we'll head over to Dar es Salaam, get a suite in the Royal, drink gin and tonics on our balcony, and bet on the cricket matches.'

Remi's eyes lit up. The Moevenpick Royal Palm was Dar es Salaam's only five-star hotel. She said, 'You're singing my song, Sam Fargo.'

'But first,' he replied, looking at the sun and checking his watch, 'we need to get ready for our guests.'

With the arrival of nightfall, the lagoon came alive with the trilling of crickets. In the trees along the shorelines and in the shrubbery atop the floating islands fireflies winked at them. Sam had steered the Andreyale between two of the bigger floating islands and dropped anchor with the bow facing west. The sky was clear, a black backdrop sprinkled with pinpricks of light and a half-moon surrounded by a hazy, prismatic ring.

'Could rain tomorrow,' Sam observed.

'Does that wives' tale apply to the Southern Hemisphere?'

'Guess we'll find out.'

They sat on the afterdeck sipping coffee in the dark and watching the insect light show. From their position they could see both the mouth of the lagoon and the beach, where they'd erected a makeshift A-frame tent from a canvas tarp they'd found in a storage locker. Behind the canvas came the faint yellow glow of a lantern, and, a few feet outside the tent, was a small bonfire. Sam had enough coconut palm logs to keep embers glowing all night.

Remi yawned. 'Long day.'

'Go below and get some sleep,' Sam said. 'I'll take the first watch.'

'You're a doll. Wake me in two hours.'

A peck on his cheek, and she was gone.

The first two watches were uneventful. Nearing the end of the sixth hour, shortly before three A.M., Sam thought he heard the faint rumble of engines in the distance, but the sound faded. Five minutes later it returned, this time louder and closer. Somewhere to the north. Sam scanned the mouth of the lagoon through binoculars but could see nothing save ripples on the water's surface where the current surged through the inlet. The engines faded again. No, not faded, Sam corrected himself. Died. As if they'd been shut down. He lifted the binoculars to his eyes again.

A minute passed. Two minutes. And then, at the four-minute mark, a shadow appeared in the inlet. Like a bulbous shark's snout, the object seemed to float a few feet above the surface. Moving at less than a walking pace, the Zodiac raft glided noiselessly from the inlet and into the mouth of the lagoon. Thirty seconds later another Zodiac appeared, followed by a third. In single file they drifted for fifty feet before turning in formation to starboard and entering the lagoon proper.

On flat feet, Sam ducked down the ladder, stepped to the bunk, and touched Remi's foot. Her head popped up from the pillow. Sam whispered, 'Company.' She nodded once, and within seconds they were back on the afterdeck and sliding over the gunwale into the water. On impulse, Sam reached back over the side and grabbed their only possible weapon, the gaff pole, from its bracket.

Having already rehearsed their plan, it was a short ten-second breaststroke to the nearest floating island. With Remi in the lead, they wriggled their way between the exposed mangrove roots and picked through the maze until they reached a hollow in the center. Their earlier inspection of the cavity showed it to be three feet in diameter and almost eight feet tall, rising to the underside of the earthen mushroom cap. Around them, rattail roots and vines drooped and curled. The air was heavy with the tang of mold and loam.

Through the tangle of roots they could see the Andreyale ten feet to their right. So close they were almost hugging, Sam and Remi rotated themselves until they could see the mouth of the lagoon. At first, there was nothing. Dark, moonlit water and silence.

Then a faint, almost imperceptible hum.

Sam put his lips to Remi's ear. 'Zodiac rafts with electric trolling motors. Moving very slowly.'

'Zodiacs probably mean a mother ship,' Remi whispered back.

Her point was well made. While Zodiacs could manage Zanzibar's coastal waters, most trolling motors had limited range and a top speed of four to five knots. Whoever their visitors were, they'd launched from somewhere nearby. Remi's guess of a larger boat seemed the most likely scenario.

Sam said, 'You left the goodies out for Santa?'

She nodded. 'They'll have to look around a bit, but everything's there.'

Two minutes passed before the first Zodiac appeared, two hundred yards away and to their right. The second appeared, at the same distance but to the left. A few moments later, the third slid into view, coming down the center of the lagoon. None showed a speck of light, but in the gray moonlight Sam and Remi could see a single silhouetted figure sitting in the stern of each raft.

Three Zodiac rafts, traveling in a line abreast with neither a spoken word nor a flashlight among them . . . These were not tourists on a nocturnal water safari.

'You see any weapons?' Sam whispered.

Remi shook her head.

For the next few minutes they watched as the trio of Zodiacs weaved their way between and around the floating islands until they were fifty yards from the Andreyale. The figure in the middle Zodiac raised his hand, made a strange gesture, and the other two Zodiacs responded by coming about and converging on the Andreyale.

Sam tapped on Remi's shoulder to get her attention, then jerked his thumb downward. Together they submerged until only their eyes and noses were above the surface.

The middle Zodiac – the leader's boat, it seemed – reached the Andreyale first, gliding up to the bowsprit, and the leader grabbed onto the rail with one hand. Now in profile, the man's face was visible. The gaunt face and hawkish nose were unmistakable. Here was the mystery man from the Yulin.

As if flying in formation, the other two Zodiacs slid down the port and starboard sides of the Andreyale and came together at the stern. Within seconds both men were over the rail and standing on the afterdeck. The one closest to Sam and Remi's hiding spot reached up to his shoulder, grabbed something, and lowered his hand. Moonlight glinted off steel. A knife.

Remi's hand found Sam's underwater and squeezed. He squeezed back. In her ear he whispered, 'We're safe.'

The two men disappeared into the cabin, then reemerged a minute later. One of them leaned over the gunwale and signaled to Hawk Nose, who gestured back, then pushed off, brought his Zodiac about, and headed for the beach. Once there he too drew a knife. Moving slowly but steadily, he padded up the beach to Sam and Remi's lantern-lit tent. He peeked inside, straightened up, then scanned the beach and the coconut palms for half a minute before returning to the Zodiac. Two minutes later he was aboard the Andreyale with the other two.

For the first time, one of the group spoke. Hawk Nose muttered something in Spanish, and the other two ducked back into the cabin. The Andreyale began rocking. Cabinet doors opened and slammed shut. Glass broke. Through the portholes came the glow of flashlights moving about. After five minutes of this, the two men reappeared on the afterdeck. One of them handed Hawk Nose a small object, which he examined briefly before tossing it back down the cabin's ladder. It pinged down the steps. The second man handed Hawk Nose a yellow legal pad. Hawk Nose studied it, handed it back. The other man produced a digital camera and flashed a picture of the page in question. The legal pad was tossed back into the cabin.

In Remi's ear Sam whispered, 'Hook, line, sinker.'

Hawk Nose and his companions climbed back into the Zodiacs and pushed off. To Sam and Remi's surprise the group didn't head for the inlet but rather began a search of the lagoon, starting with the shorelines. Flashlights skimmed over the banks and through the trees. As one of the Zodiacs drew even with the bell's hiding place Sam and Remi held their breaths, but the boat never slowed and the flashlight never wavered.

Finally the trio reached the mouth of the lagoon and finished their examination of the shoreline, but instead of heading for the inlet they turned again, formed a line abreast, and started checking the floating islands, flashlights scanning each mangrove buttress before moving to the next.

'This could be bad,' Sam muttered.

'Very bad,' Remi agreed.

The drawn knives had told Sam and Remi everything they needed to know: Whoever these men were, they had no compunction about using violence. Had Sam and Remi been either aboard the Andreyale or in the tent, they would be dead now.

'Head back to the Andreyale?' Remi suggested.

'If they decide to board her again, we'll be trapped.'

'I'm open to suggestions.'

Sam thought for a moment, then said, 'How about two birds with one stone?' He explained his plan.

'Risky,' said Remi.

'I'll make it work.'

'Okay, but only if there's no other way.'

'Agreed.'

They watched the progress of the Zodiacs. If they continued on their current paths, the one to their right would reach their hiding spot in less than two minutes. The other two were ahead by half a minute. With luck, they'd finish their searches first and turn back toward the mouth.

'Cross fingers,' Sam said to Remi.

'Already there,' she replied and kissed him on the cheek. 'For a little more luck.'

Sam ducked underwater and pulled himself back through the root system and into open water. Doing his best to keep all three Zodiacs in view, he maneuvered himself around to the back side of the roots. Thirty seconds later, to his left, Hawk Nose and his partner slid into view. Each man scanned his final floating island, then turned and headed back toward the inlet. The last Zodiac was still on course, forty feet away.

'¡Apúrate!' Hawk Nose called. Hurry up!

Sam's target raised a hand to acknowledge the order.

Thirty feet away . . . twenty feet.

Sam kept moving, pulling himself clockwise around the mangrove roots. He stopped, peeking around the edge. The Zodiac was ten feet away. Sam watched, waited until the nose of the Zodiac disappeared around the opposite side, then glanced back up the lagoon. The other two Zodiacs were a hundred yards away and still moving.

Sam took a deep breath, ducked under with the gaff pole, kicked twice, pulled himself around the roots, and let his eyes pop above the surface. The rear of the Zodiac was five feet away, moving slowly, the driver sitting with one hand on the motor's throttle as he leaned sideways and scanned the mangrove with his flashlight. Sam did a half kick with his feet and closed to within a foot of the Zodiac. He reached out, gently placed his left hand on the rubber side, then raised the gaff from the water, cocked it back, and flicked it forward as though casting a fishing lure. The gaff's steel tip caught the man on the side of his head, just above the ear. He let out a gasp, then slumped over the side, his head drooping in the water. Before Sam could make another move, Remi was there, lifting the man's head and rolling the body back into the Zodiac. Sam looked over his shoulder. Hawk Nose and his partner were two hundred yards away now.

'Yaotl!' Hawk Nose's voice echoed over the water.

'Hurry,' Sam said to Remi, then climbed aboard the Zodiac and took a seat at the motor. 'Stay on the port side. I'll drag you back to the Andreyale.'

Remi swam around and grabbed the oar hook with two fingers. Sam revved the motor, and the Zodiac glided out from behind the mangrove. Sam found the man's – Yaotl's – flashlight where it had fallen, picked it up, and aimed it at the other two Zodiacs, which come to a halt. Sam flashed the beam twice and raised a casual hand, praying it would be enough. He held his breath.

Nothing from the Zodiacs. Ten seconds passed. And then the double wink of a flashlight followed by a raised hand. 'Yaotl . . . ¡Apúrate!'

Sam guided the Zodiac to the Andreyale's stern, using the length of the boat to hide their movements. Remi climbed aboard, and together they rolled Yaotl over the gunwale. He landed with a thump on the afterdeck.

'Now what?' Remi asked.

'Tie him up, hands and feet to the cleats, and search him. I've got to catch up with my new friends.' Remi opened her mouth to protest, but Sam interrupted: 'I need my mask and the binoculars.' She went into the cabin with both items and traded them for Sam's gaff. 'Don't worry, Remi, I'll keep my distance.'

'And when you can't any longer?'

'I'll have a terrible mishap.'

He gave her a wink, revved the engine, and motored away.

Hawk Nose and the other man had continued on. By the time Sam reached the midpoint of the lagoon, they were turning west into the inlet. Sam mentally recalled the twists and turns of the inlet, did a few quick calculations, and kept going. Fifty feet from the entrance, he slowed to idle and listened. No sound of the other motors. He revved up, kept going, and made the turn. A hundred yards ahead the other two were moving single file through the inlet. Beyond them, about a half mile away, Sam could see the inlet widening into Chumbe Island's shoals. He lifted the binoculars to his face and scanned the channel. Nothing was moving, and no lights were visible within ten miles – save one. A mile to the south-west, a single white light hovered thirty feet off the water – the international signal for a boat at anchor. The boat itself was bow on, rake stemmed, with a gleaming white superstructure, clearly a luxury yacht. The mother ship, perhaps?

Hawk Nose and his partner veered left and disappeared from view momentarily. Time to prepare for the mishap: Sam throttled down, veered left, and let the Zodiac ground itself on the sand. A quick glance around gave him what he needed: a dagger-shaped rock. He grabbed it, shoved the Zodiac back into the inlet, jumped aboard, and took off again.

So far Sam's luck was holding. Aside from a few backward glances to make sure 'Yaotl' was following, neither Hawk Nose nor his partner slowed to let him catch up. The remainder of the transit took ten minutes, and soon enough Sam could see the other two Zodiacs jostling as they moved into the shoals.

'Come on, guys, show me where you're going,' Sam muttered.

Now clear of the shoals, Hawk Nose and his partner veered left and headed toward the yacht. Two minutes later Sam was himself in the shoals, but he put on a few more degrees left rudder, steering the Zodiac nearly parallel to the bank in which they'd found the bell. Onshore, landmarks began looking familiar. He was within twenty yards of the precipice. It was time.

He grabbed the rock from between his feet, leaned over the side, stabbed the tip into the rubber sidewall, and heaved backward. He repeated the process twice more until he'd created a ragged eight-inch gash. He tossed the rock over the side and checked the progress of the other two Zodiacs: they were a few hundred yards out into the main channel and still heading for the yacht.

It took only twenty seconds for Sam's sabotage to take effect. The Zodiac began slowing, shuddering and wallowing as water gushed into the sidewall. He gave the throttle one last twist, then let out what he hoped would sound like a panicked scream, then rolled over the side.

He ducked underwater, settled the mask over his face, blew it clear, then clamped the snorkel's mouthpiece between his teeth. He went still now, floating with just his eyes and the tip of the snorkel above the surface.

His scream had done the trick. Hawk Nose and his partner had reversed course and were heading at top speed toward the rapidly deflating Zodiac, which was now drifting twenty yards to Sam's left – and directly over the precipice. When the rescuers were fifty yards away, flashlights blinked on and began scanning the surface.

'Yaotl!' Hawk Nose called. 'Yaotl!' The other man joined in.

Sam had been hyperventilating his lungs for the past minute. Now he took one final deep breath, ducked beneath the surface, and finned toward the bank. He was there in ten kicks. He turned so Hawk Nose and the other were on his right, then begin finning north along the bank, occasionally glancing back to check the location of the flashlight beams. Both Zodiacs had converged on the remains of the third.

'Yaotl!' Sam heard through the water. Then again, this time more strident: 'Yaotl!'

Sam kept swimming. Behind him, the deflated raft was being dragged from the water and into one of the Zodiacs. Sam stopped, held still. He felt the ache of oxygen depletion in his lungs and a tingle of panic in his neck. He quashed it and remained still.

After what seemed like minutes but was no more than thirty seconds, the Zodiacs revved up, came about, and headed back into the channel.

Sam finned for the surface.

Chapter 7

Zanzibar

Twenty-five minutes later when Sam climbed back aboard the Andreyale, he found Remi sitting in a deck chair casually sipping a bottle of Kenyan Tusker beer. Their guest, Yaotl, lay like a defeated game fish on the deck, back bent, wrists bound to his feet, these in turn knotted to the nearest cleat. He was still unconscious.

'Welcome back,' she said, handing him a beer. 'How'd the mishap go?'

'They seemed to have bought it. How's he?'

'Bad lump on the side of the head, but he's breathing fine. Aside from an ugly headache that'll last a day or two, he'll survive. He was well armed. She nodded to two objects lying at her feet: one was the knife they knew about, the other a semiautomatic pistol. Sam hefted it.

'Heckler and Koch P30. Nine millimeter, fifteen-round magazine.'

'How in the world do you know . . .'

Sam shrugged. 'No idea. I store trivia. Can't help it. Unless I'm mistaken, this isn't a civilian gun. They're only sold to law enforcement and military.'

'So our guest here is, or was, either a cop or a soldier?'

'Or someone with back-channel influence. Did you find anything else on him?'

'Not so much as pocket lint. No wallet, no identification. And his clothes and shoes are local. I checked the tags.'

'Professionals, then.'

'Seems so,' Remi said. 'As for the cookies we left for Santa . . .'

'We saw what they thought of the Adelise coin. Tossed it away like a penny. But the ginned-up notepad was another story.'

Before setting the stage for their guests, Sam and Remi had decided there were five possibilities the mystery man, 'Hawk Nose,' was interested in: one, the Adelise coin; two, the bell; three, the Fargos themselves; four, something he was worried they might find; or five, nothing – the molehill/mountain scenario.

Their ruse had ruled out numbers one and five and seemed to rule in numbers two, three, and four. Sam and Remi had filled the notepad mostly with nonsensical scribbles and numbers, save one area: a side-view diagram of a ship's bell and below it a time (2:00 P.M.), a place (Chukwani Point Road), and a phone number provided by Selma that, when called, would be answered by Mnazi Freight & Haul. If Hawk Nose took this bait, they could be reasonably certain his interest lay with the bell.

This, of course, raised the questions of how Hawk Nose had learned about the bell. Sam and Remi had told no one except Selma. Since Hawk Nose hadn't paid his visit before they'd raised the bell using Sam's raft, could it be attributed to someone having spotted the bell as they moved it to the lagoon? But, then again, they'd seen no one in the area, either onshore or offshore.

'It'll be dawn soon,' Sam said. 'Let's gather our booty

and find a place to lie low until we can find us some different accommodations.'

'And him?' Remi asked, nodding to Yaotl.

'We'd better move him inside. Don't want him getting broken, do we?'

Once Yaotl was secure in the cabin, they raised anchor and crossed the lagoon to where they'd hidden the bell raft. After towing it closer to the beach, Sam jumped over the side and maneuvered it until the bell was floating a foot off the bottom.

'Leverage . . .' Sam muttered to himself. 'Remi, I need the hatchet from the toolbox.'

She collected it and handed it down. Sam then waded ashore and disappeared into the trees with a flashlight. Remi listened as he moved about in the darkness: twigs breaking, the thunk of wood striking wood, a few hushed curses, then a few minutes of chopping. Five minutes later he returned carrying a pair of palm saplings, each eight feet long and four inches across. Into each end he had chopped a notch. He handed the poles to Remi, then climbed aboard.

'Care to share your plan?' she asked.

Sam gave her a wink. 'Don't want to spoil the fun. We're going to need daylight, though.'

The wait was short. Ten minutes after they watched the first yellow-orange tinges of sunrise over to the east, they went into action. Sam untied the raft, jumped into the water, and rotated the raft so the side with the three protruding logs were facing the beach. He straddled the outer log, causing it to sink six inches, and called, 'All back slow!'

'All back slow,' Remi replied.

The engines rumbled to life. The Andreyale backed up until the transom bumped into the raft. 'Keep coming!' Sam called. Between his weight and the Andreyale's horsepower, the protruding logs dipped beneath the surface and began burrowing into the sand. The water beneath the Andreyale's stern turned to froth. When the logs were embedded a foot into the sand, Sam called, 'All stop!'

Remi throttled down and walked to the stern. Sam ducked under the raft and emerged in its center beneath the transom. 'I'm going to push up on this crossbeam, and you're going to pull,' he said.

'Got it.'

Working together they manhandled the log onto the gunwale with the protruding ends jutting over the afterdeck.

Remi stood back and wiped her hands. 'I think I see where you're going with this.' She recited, '"Give me a lever long enough and a fulcrum on which to place it – "'

'" – and I shall move the world,"' Sam finished. 'Archimedes.'

Using the hatchet, Sam chopped a notch into each end of log resting on the gunwale. Next he picked up one of the saplings, handed it to Remi, then grabbed his own.

'Now the trick part,' Sam said.

Each of them placed the notched tip of a sapling into the corresponding notch on the log, then braced the other end against the port and starboard cleats respectively.

'Care to do the honors?' Sam asked.

'Where are you going to be?'

'In the cabin with you. If those saplings let go, we don't want to be anywhere near them. Slow back, if you will.'

Remi engaged the throttle and eased the Andreyale backward. Slowly the front edge of the raft began rising. The saplings trembled and bent like a pair of bows being drawn. The logs groaned. Inch by inch the bell rose from the water until its mouth was even with the gunwale.

'Hold here,' Sam said. 'Steerageway only.'

He grabbed the remainder of the anchor line and padded onto the afterdeck, his eyes darting from one trembling sapling to the other. At the transom he leaned out, knotted the line around the bell's crown, then backed into the cabin, uncoiling line as he went.

'All back slow,' he murmured.

Remi leaned back and whispered in his ear, 'If we drop that thing through the deck, I'm pretty sure we're going to lose our deposit.'

Sam chuckled. 'We've got Triple A.'

The Andreyale eased backward. The saplings kept bending, creaking. Gingerly, Sam took up the slack in the line. The bell slid over the gunwale, bounced on the lip, and started swinging.

'Sam . . .' Remi warned.

'I know,' Sam muttered. 'Hold it here. Easy . . .'

He spun around, darted down the ladder, and emerged ten seconds later carrying a mattress. In a double-handed bowler's motion, he slid the mattress down the deck to the transom.

'Gun it!' he called.

Remi jammed the throttle to its stops. Sam heaved back

on the line. Like overlapping gunshots, the saplings snapped and twirled away. With a dull thunk the bell crashed into the mattress, rolled onto its side, and went still.

Chapter 8

Zanzibar

'We lost a man,' Itzli Rivera said into the phone.

'Oh?' President Quauhtli Garza replied. Even from ten thousand miles away his disinterest was palpable.

'Yaotl. He drowned. His body was lost in the channel. He was a good soldier, Mr. President.'

'Who gave his life for a greater cause. It's fitting. In Nahuatl, Yaotl means "warrior," you know. He will be greeted by Huitzilopochtli and reside for eternity in Omeyocan,' Garza replied, referring to the Aztec god of war that kept the sun moving in the sky, and the most sacred of the Aztecs' thirteen heavenly realms. 'Is that not reward enough?'

'Of course, Mr. President.'

'Itzli, please tell me that's all you have to report.'

'No. There is more. The Fargos may have found something. A ship's bell.'

'What do you mean "may have found"?'

'We searched their boat. On a pad of paper we found a diagram of a ship's bell.'

'Describe it. Is it the right one?'

'The drawing was generic. They may not even know what they have. Either way, it appears they're going to try to get it off the island. Next to the diagram was a notation about a freight company and a time. The pickup location is just south of Zanzibar's airport.'

'That can't happen, Itzli. That bell can't leave the island. The Fargos' investigation needs to end here and now.'

'I understand, Mr. President.'

'You know where they'll be and when they'll be there. We'll have all our bad eggs in one basket.'

'That's one pampered ship's bell,' Remi said.

Standing across from her on the shaded cobblestone patio, Sam nodded. For the last hour they had been swaddling the bell in sheets soaked in a warm solution of water and nitric acid. Now it sat, draped and steaming, in the center of a slowly expanding slick of gray-green marine growth dissolved by the acid.

'How long until we swap?'

Sam checked his watch. 'Ten more minutes.'

Three hours earlier, after dismantling the raft and scattering the parts, they'd left the mangrove lagoon and headed south along the coast past Fumba Point into Menai Bay. With Remi at the wheel, Sam called Selma and brought her up to speed and then explained what they needed. Forty minutes later, as they were rounding Zanzibar's southern tip, Selma called back.

'It's a little smaller than your bungalow, but it's secluded, and the agent promised to leave the keys under the mat. You're paid up for the week.'

'What and where?'

'A villa on the eastern side of the island, two miles north of the Tamarind Beach Hotel. The awning over the porch is red-and-green striped. There's an old stone quay on the beach.'

'You're a wonder, Selma,' Sam said, then hung up and dialed again, this time Abasi Sibale's home phone number. Without a question, Abasi agreed to meet them on the villa's beach with his pickup truck. Upon seeing the ship's bell sitting on the Andreyale's afterdeck, he merely smiled and shook his head. 'Someday,' he said, 'you will come to our island and have a perfectly boring time.'

'I'll go check on our guest,' Sam now said.

'I'll make sure our bell doesn't get away,' Remi replied.

'If it tries, let it.'

'Gladly.'

They were both tired, and this bell, having both resisted their efforts and attracted some dangerous attention, had become the enemy. Their outlook would improve with sleep and some answers, which would hopefully come after a couple more hours of nitric-acid swaddling.

Remi smiled. 'Leave the gun.'

Sam smiled back and walked across the patio and through the French doors. The villa Selma had rented for them was just under two thousand square feet and Tuscan style, with faded mustard plaster walls, climbing vines, and a red tile roof. The interior was decorated in a mishmash of contemporary and craftsman. Sam walked to the back bedroom, where their visitor, Yaotl, was bound hand and foot to a four-poster bed. Yaotl saw Sam and lifted his head.

'Hey, what's going on? Where am I?'

'Depends on who you ask,' Sam replied. 'As far as your

friends are concerned you're either floating facedown somewhere between here and Mombasa or making your way through a shark's digestive system.'

'What does that mean?'

'Well, after we knocked you out – '

'I don't remember that . . . How did you do that?' He sounded slightly amazed.

'I snuck up on you then hit you with a big stick. Now your friends think you've been dead about . . .' Sam checked his watch. 'Six hours.'

'They won't believe it. They'll find me.'

'Don't bet on it. What kind of name is Yaotl?'

'It's my name.'

'Are you hungry? Thirsty?'

'No.'

Sam chuckled. 'There's no crime in admitting it.'

'Just do what you're going to do. Get it over with.'

'What exactly do you think we're going to do to you?' asked Sam.

'Torture me?'

'If that's your first guess, you must keep some nasty company.'

'Then why did you take me?'

'I'd hoped you'd be willing to answer some questions for us.'

'You're American,' Yaotl said.

'How could you tell? My winning smile?'

'Your accent.'

'And I'm guessing you're Mexican.'

No response.

'And based on the gun you were carrying and how you

and your partners moved, you're either current or former military.'

Now Yaotl's eyes narrowed. 'You're CIA.'

'Me? No. I have a friend who is, though.'

This was true. During his time at DARPA Sam had undergone covert operative training at the CIA's Camp Perry facility, the hope being that by seeing how field operatives work DARPA's engineers could better supply their needs. Going through the program at the same time was a CIA case officer named Rube Haywood. He and Sam had become friends and remained close ever since.

'And that friend has friends,' Sam added. 'In places like Turkey and Bulgaria and Romania . . . I think they call it "rendition." You've heard of rendition, I'm sure. Grim-faced guys in black jumpsuits shove you aboard a plane, you disappear somewhere for a few weeks, then come back with an aversion to electricity and power drills.'

The rendition part was, of course, a bluff, but Sam's presentation had the desired effect: Yaotl's eyes were gaping, his lower lip trembling.

Abruptly, Sam stood up. 'So, how about some food. Is bread okay?'

Yaotl nodded.

Sam fed him a half loaf of chapati bread and a liter of mineral water from a sports bottle, then asked, 'About that friend of mine . . . should I call him or will you answer a few questions?'

'I'll answer.'

Sam took him through the basics: his full name; the names of his partners, including Hawk Nose; who they worked for; had they come to Zanzibar looking for him and Remi; what were they supposed to accomplish; the name of their mother ship . . . Most of the questions Yaotl could answer only partially. He was simply a civilian contractor, he claimed, a former member of Mexico's Special Forces Airmobile Group, or GAFE. He'd been recruited four days earlier by a man named Itzli Rivera, aka Hawk Nose, also a former member of GAFE, to come to Zanzibar and 'find some people.' He'd been given no further background, nor had Rivera explained why Sam and Remi had been targeted. Nor was he sure whether Rivera was working for himself or someone else.

'But you saw him on the phone several times, correct?' Sam asked. 'Did it sound like he was reporting in?'

'It's possible. I only overheard parts.'

Sam questioned him for another ten minutes, at the end of which Yaotl asked, 'What will you do with me?'

'I'll let you know.'

'But you said you wouldn't — Hey, wait!'

Sam left the room and rejoined Remi on the patio. He recounted his conversation with Yaotl. She said, 'Sam . . . electricity and power drills? That's mean.'

'No, doing it would be mean. I just planted the seed and let his imagination chew on it for a while.'

'Yaotl said four days ago, right? He got the call from Rivera four days ago?'

'Yes.'

'That was our first day on the island.'

Sam nodded. 'Before we found the bell.'

'Then it's us they're interested in.'

'And the bell, perhaps. Our ruse with the legal pad clearly got their attention.'

'But how did they know we were here?' Remi asked, then answered her own question: 'The BBC interview right after we landed?'

'Could be. Let's put it together: Rivera and whomever he's working for find out we're here. They got worried we might find something and they came to investigate.'

'It's a big island, though,' Remi replied. 'They'd have to be awfully paranoid to think we'd stumble onto whatever they're worried about. Even if it's something as big as our bell, it's a proverbial needle in a haystack.'

'The interviewer asked us where we were planning on diving. We told her Chumbe Island. Maybe that was the magic phrase.'

Remi considered this. 'And, like it or not, we've got something of a reputation. We've had some great luck finding treasure that didn't want to be found.'

Sam smiled. 'You call it luck. I call it – '

'You know what I mean.'

'So it's the combination of us, Zanzibar, and Chumbe Island that got their attention.'

They went silent for a minute, each examining their what-if scenario from various angles. Finally Remi broke the silence: 'Sam, our friend inside . . . his name is Yaotl, his boss's name is Itzli, and the third is named . . .'

'Nochtli.'

'And they're from Mexico?'

'So he said.'

'Those aren't Spanish names.'

'So I guessed.'

'I'll have Selma do some double checking for me, but I'm almost certain those are Nahuatl in origin.'

'Nahuatl?'

'Aztec, Sam. Nahuatl was the language of the Aztecs.'

They stood in silence for the next ten minutes, watching the steam rise from the sheet draped around the bell. Sam checked his watch and said, 'Time.'

Using his fingertips, Sam uncoiled the sheet from around the bell, then dragged it away and piled it at the edge of the patio. He turned back to see Remi kneeling before the bell.

'Sam, you need to see this.'

He walked around to her side and leaned over her shoulder.

Though still heavily mottled, the nitric acid had removed enough patina that they could make out the lettering engraved in the bronze:

O P H E L I A

'Ophelia,' Remi repeated in a whisper. 'What's Ophelia?'

Sam took a deep breath, let it out. 'I have no idea.'

Chapter 9

Zanzibar

'Can't you two just have a normal, uneventful vacation?' Rube Haywood asked over the speakerphone.

'We have plenty of those,' Remi replied. 'But we only call you on the abnormal ones.'

'I don't know if I should feel complimented or offended,' Rube muttered.

'The former,' Sam said. 'You're our go-to guy.'

'What about Selma?'

'Our go-to gal,' Remi shot back.

'Okay, so let me see if I've got this straight: You found a diamond-shaped coin that once belonged to the governess of a French commune on some island near Madagascar but was stolen by a pirate. Then you found a ship's bell belonging to some mystery ship. Then a gunboatful of Mexican mercenaries with Aztec names showed up and tried to kill you. And now you've got one of the bad guys tied up in your spare bedroom. Is that the gist of it?'

'That about covers it,' Remi said.

'With three minor corrections,' Sam added. 'The Adelise coin has nothing to do with it, we don't think, and Selma's double-checking the Aztec angle. As for the name *Ophelia*, we don't think it was the original. First of all, the engraving is very rough, not professionally done. Second, once we were able to clear away more of the muck we picked up a couple engraved letters beneath *Ophelia*, an *S* and two *H*s.'

'I feel like I'm on one of those practical-joke shows,' Rube said. 'Okay, I'll play along. What can I do to help you?'

'First, take our guest off our hands.'

'How? If you're thinking about all that rendition business, Sam, I – '

'I was thinking you pull some strings in the Tanzanian Ministry of Home Affairs and have the police detain him.'

'On what charges?'

'He's got no passport, no money, and he was carrying a weapon.'

Rube went silent for a moment. 'Knowing you two as I do, I'm guessing you not only want him out of the way but want to see who shows an interest in him.'

'It had crossed our minds,' Sam replied.

'You still have the gun?'

'Yes.'

'Okay, let me make some calls. What else?'

'He claims his boss's name is Itzli Rivera, former Mexican army. It'd be nice to know more about him and the yacht they were using. He claims it's home-ported out of Bagamoyo. The *Njiwa*.'

'Spell it.'

Remi did so. 'It's Swahili for "pigeon."'

'Oh, good. Thanks, Remi. I've always wondered what the word for pigeon was in Swahili,' Rube said.

'Somebody's cranky.'

'What are you going to do with the ship's bell?'

'Leave it here,' Sam replied. 'Selma booked the villa anonymously and wired cash. Not much chance of them finding it.'

'I already know the answer to this, but I feel obligated to ask: Any chance of you two just taking the bell and going home?'

'We might do just that,' Sam replied. 'We're going to do a little more research and see where it takes us. If nothing pans out, we'll head home.'

'Miracle of miracles,' Rube said. 'You two be careful. I'll call you when I have info.' He hung up.

Remi said to Sam, 'We're going to have to get him something extra-special for Christmas.'

'Right about now I can guess what he's wishing for.'

'What's that?'

'A new, unlisted phone number.'

They took the Andreyale south to Uroa Village, found a ramshackle hardware store, gathered what few supplies they needed, and were back at the villa before noon. Remi left Sam with his hammer and nails and wooden planks and went inside to check on Yaotl, who was sound asleep. She found a couple cans of clam chowder, heated them up, and took the bowls out to the patio. Sam was nailing the last two planks into place.

'What do you think?' he asked.

'As a box, Sam, it's wonderful.'

'It's supposed to be a crate.'

'Crate, box, whatever. Sit down and eat.'

*

Half a mile from the end of Chukwani Point Road, Itzli Rivera pulled the rented Range Rover onto the shoulder, then down into the ditch and up the other side into the trees. The terrain was rugged and heavily choked with scrub brush, but the Rover's four-wheel drive handled it easily. He turned southwest toward the clearing on Chukwani Point.

'Time?' he asked Nochtli.

'Just after one.'

An hour before the Fargos were set to meet the truck from Mnazi Freight & Haul. Plenty of time to find a vantage point that provided not only a good line of sight but also an easily accessible route to cut off any escape attempt.

'I see the clearing,' Nochtli said, binoculars lifted to his eyes.

'There's something there.'

'What?'

'See for yourself.'

He handed the binoculars to Itzli, who focused them on the clearing. Sitting in the middle of the dirt road was a wooden crate. Tacked to the side of the crate was a cardboard sign. 'There's something written on it,' he said, then zoomed in. After a moment he muttered, '¿Qué madres . . . ?'

'What?' asked Nochtli. 'What does it say?'

'"Merry Christmas."'

Itzli drove through the trees, down into the ditch, and back up the side into the clearing. He stopped the Rover and walked over to the crate. He nudged it with his toe. It was empty. He ripped off the cardboard sign and flipped it over. Written in block letters was a message:

LET'S MEET AND TALK ABOUT BELLS.
NYERERE ROAD CRICKET GROUNDS.
BENCH, SOUTHWEST CORNER.
4:00 P.M.

Chapter 10

Zanzibar

Sam saw Itzli Rivera appear at the northern side of the cricket grounds, walking through the trees bordering the parking lot. Behind him, another man was walking east through the lot, but Sam could not make out his face. The purposefulness of his stride made him stand out. This would be Nochtli, Sam thought.

In the middle of the field, a pickup cricket match of teenagers was under way. Their laughter and shouts echoed across the park. Rivera strolled down the sidewalk on the west side of the grounds and stopped before the bench on which Sam sat.

'You came alone,' Rivera said.

Seeing Rivera up close and in daylight immediately altered Sam's measure of the man. While Sam had never doubted Rivera's prowess, his chiseled face and sinewy build suggested a rawhide-like toughness. His black eyes regarded Sam impassively – an expression Sam suspected rarely changed, whether Rivera was eating a sandwich or murdering another human being.

'Have a seat,' Sam said amiably despite the flutter of fear in his belly. He felt like he was hand-feeding a great white shark.

Rivera did so. 'This is your meeting,' he said.

Sam didn't reply. He watched the cricket match. A minute passed. Rivera broke the silence. 'Your prank with the crate – amusing.'

'Something tells me you didn't laugh, though.'

'No. Where is your wife, Mr. Fargo?'

'Running an errand. You can signal your friend to stop circling the grounds. He won't find her.'

Rivera considered this for a few moments, then lifted his hand off the back of the bench and made a fist. Across the park, Nochtli stopped walking.

'Let's talk about our problem,' Sam said.

'And what do you imagine that problem is?'

'You think we have something you want.'

'Tell me exactly: What do you think you have?'

Abruptly, Sam stood up. 'I enjoy the occasional verbal joust as much as the next man, but not today.'

'All right, all right. Sit down, please.'

Sam did so. Rivera said, 'The people I work for have been looking for a shipwreck. We believe it was lost in this area.'

'Which ship?'

'The *Ophelia*.'

'Tell me about it.'

'A steam-sail passenger ship. It was believed to be sunk in these waters in the 1870s.'

'That's all you know about her?'

'More or less.'

'How long have you been looking for her?'

'Seven years.'

'Actively?'

'Yes, actively.'

'In and around Zanzibar?'

86

'Of course.'

'I'm assuming you have salvage experience or else they wouldn't have hired you.'

'I have experience.'

'The people you work for . . . what's their specific interest?'

'I'd rather not say.'

'Something of monetary value, I assume?' Sam asked. 'Something the *Ophelia* carried in her hold when she went down?'

'That would be a safe assumption.'

'And you think whatever we may have found belongs to the *Ophelia*.'

'It's a possibility my employers would like to explore.'

Sam nodded thoughtfully. For the past few minutes Sam had been trying to get Rivera to commit himself, to make statements he and Remi could then use in doing their own research.

Sam said, 'This must be one hell of a prize you're after. You bribe the captain of a Tanzanian gunboat to first intimidate, then surveil us; then, when night falls, you sneak into the lagoon and board our boat with knives drawn.'

This caught Rivera off guard. He took a deep breath and let it out with a frustrated sigh.

Sam said, 'We watched the whole thing.'

'From where?'

'Does that really matter?'

'No, I suppose not. Please accept my apologies. My friends are ex-soldiers. Some habits are hard to break. The excitement of the job got the better of them. I've already chastised them.'

'All three of them.'

'Yes.'

Of course, Sam didn't buy Rivera's *mea culpa*, but he said, 'Fair enough. What was your plan? To steal whatever you think we found?'

'At that point we didn't know what you'd found.'

Sam paused for a long ten seconds, then said, 'I can't decide if you think we're idiots or if you've got a short-term-memory problem.'

'Pardon me?'

'You're sitting here because of the sign I left on the crate. You found that crate because of the notations we left next to a diagram of a bell you found on our boat. You think we found a ship's bell. Why not just come out and say it?'

'Consider it said, then.'

'I can tell you this: The bell we found doesn't belong to the *Ophelia*.'

'You'll forgive me if I don't take your word for it.'

'Will I?' Sam asked.

'I'd like to inspect the bell myself.'

'The same bell you and your men would have killed us for had we been aboard our boat? I'm going to have to decline.'

'I've been authorized to offer you a finder's fee should the bell turn out to be the one we're looking for.'

'No, thanks. We've got all the money we can use.'

'Take me to the bell, let me inspect it, and my employer will donate fifty thousand dollars to a charity of your choosing.'

'No.'

Rivera's eyes turned cold, and he let out muffled growl. 'Mr. Fargo, you're making me angry.'

'They have pills for that.'

'I prefer a different approach.' Rivera lifted his shirttail to expose the butt of a pistol, a Heckler & Koch P30 – just like the one they took off Yaotl, Sam saw.

'We're leaving now,' Rivera muttered. 'Don't make a scene or I'll shoot you dead. We'll be gone before the police are even notified.'

'The police,' Sam repeated. 'As in the police in that station house across the road behind us?'

Rivera glanced over Sam's shoulder. His mouth tightened, the muscles of his jaw pulsated.

Sam said, 'You should have done your homework. I realize it's an old schoolhouse, but how hard would it have been to check? I'm sure this is embarrassing for you.'

'*¡Cabrón!*'

Sam's grasp of Spanish slang was slim, but he suspected Rivera had just called his parentage into question. He said, 'If you look a little closer, you'll see a man and woman sitting on a bench near the station's steps.'

'I see them.'

Sam pulled out his phone, hit Speed Dial, let it ring twice, then hung up. A moment later Remi Fargo turned on the bench, faced the cricket grounds, and gave a single wave.

'The man she's talking to is a Tanzanian police superintendent from Dar es Salaam.'

'Police can be bought. Just as naval officers can be bought.'

'Not this one. He happens to be a close personal friend of the FBI's legal attaché in the U.S. Embassy.'

'You're bluffing.'

'Right now my wife may or may not be telling the superintendent about a man named Yaotl who tried to break into our vacation home last night. He was armed with a gun identical to the one you're carrying and had no passport.'

Rivera's brows knitted together. 'The accident . . . the raft. That wasn't Yaotl.'

Sam shook his head.

'How did you do it?'

'I took a few theater classes in college.'

'It doesn't matter. He won't talk. Even if he does, he knows nothing.'

'Just your name and appearance.'

'Both of those can be changed. Give me the bell and return my man to me, and you'll never be troubled again.'

'Let me think about it. I'll call you by day's end tomorrow. If you bother us before then, I'll call our superintendent friend. Care to tell me where you're staying?'

Rivera smiled grimly and shook his head. 'No, I would not.' He recited his phone number. 'I expect to hear good news.'

Sam stood up. 'You can expect anything you like.'

He turned and walked away.

Sam walked across the street to the police station. Remi wrapped up her conversation with the superintendent with a warm handshake and a thank-you. The man gave Sam a nod and a smile, then strode away.

'Lovely man, Huru,' Remi said. 'Told us to give his regards to Rube.'

'What did you tell him?' Sam asked, sitting down beside her.

'That we thought someone had tried to break into our house last night. He said to call him personally if we have any more trouble. How did your chat with the human skeleton go?'

'As can be expected. He claims he's been working for some deep pockets who've been looking for the *Ophelia* for years. Problem is, he claims to know almost nothing about her pedigree.'

'He tried to wing it,' Remi said. 'He thought he could bluff you.'

Anyone who spends even a modicum of time chasing shipwrecks finds themselves well versed in every facet of a vessel's history. That Rivera feigned ignorance about the *Ophelia* told Sam and Remi that the ship was vitally important to Rivera and his employer.

'Did he mention the hidden engraving?'

'No. That could be telling. It's another thing an experienced hunter would know. He didn't mention it because he's hoping we missed it.'

'Any hint as to what specifically they're after?'

'He implied it was something in the *Ophelia*'s hold. Treasure of some kind. Even offered us a finder's fee.'

'How very kind of him. Where does this leave us?'

'Rivera claimed he had salvage experience, which may or may not be true, but he also claimed his patrons have been actively looking for the *Ophelia*.'

In the world of treasure hunting, an active search is a

specific beast that involves mounting expeditions – getting wet and dirty while laying out grids, doing magnetometer passes, picking through muck and slime. Not to mention the dry but no less daunting research work: interviewing relatives, scouting locations, and sitting in dusty old libraries looking for the slightest clue as to the target's possible location.

'If Rivera's been at it that long,' Remi said, 'there'll be public records, news stories, permits . . .'

'My thought exactly. We find those, we get a better idea of what Rivera and his people are really after.'

They sat under the shade trees outside the police station for ten minutes as Sam watched Rivera and his partner leave the cricket grounds parking lot, then overtly make a circuit around the police station. Sam and Remi gave them a parting wave on the last pass.

Once sure they weren't returning, Sam and Remi walked east to an open-air market, where they gathered food and necessities and walked the labyrinthine alleys while watching for signs of pursuit. Finding none, they walked three blocks north to a rental-car agency. Their reservation, a 2007 Toyota Land Cruiser, was waiting for them. Forty minutes later they were back at their Uroa beach villa.

Sam's phone trilled as they were walking up the driveway. Remi gestured for the bag of groceries he was carrying and continued into the villa. Sam checked the caller ID: Rube.

'Morning, Rube.'

'Early, early morning. How did your meeting go?'

'Fine. Huru told us to say hello.'

'A good man, Huru. Did you turn your guest over to him?'

'Not yet,' Sam replied, then recounted his conversation with Rivera. 'We already called Selma. She's working on shipwreck databases for the area. Tomorrow we're going over to the university for a little homework.'

'Well, I know I already said this once, but be damned careful. I did some digging into Itzli Rivera. The military stuff you already know, but he was also in their defense department's intelligence section. He retired about eight years ago and went private. Here's the kicker: According to the chief of station in Mexico City, Rivera's been arrested six times by the Policía Federal but never indicted.'

'What charges?'

'Burglary, bribery, blackmail, murder, kidnapping . . . And all related to national-level politics.'

'So he's a hatchet man.'

'A militarily trained hatchet man. It's a distinction to keep in mind. Nobody can pin down who he works for.'

'How'd he beat all the charges?'

'The usual: witness recantation either by change of mind or change in corporeal status, as in sudden and unexpected death.'

Sam chuckled. 'Yes, Rube, I get it.'

'The rest is pretty standard stuff: mislaid evidence, technicalities, etcetera.'

'Safe to say Rivera's got a heavyweight in his corner.'

'A heavyweight with a fetish for shipwreck artifacts. What're you going to do with the bell?'

'We haven't decided yet. The truth is, I don't think they

really care about the bell itself. Whether they're after the *Ophelia* or the ship belonging to the mystery engraving, it doesn't change where we found the thing. That's what's got them worried . . . Well, that and the fact that we aren't willing to leave it alone.'

'Maybe it's not about something they're looking for,' Rube said, 'but rather something they don't want anyone else to find.'

'Interesting,' Sam said.

Rube continued: 'That charitable donation business . . . He wanted you and Remi and the bell together in one place. Why not just accept an e-mailed picture of the bell? And if all they wanted was to find the *Ophelia*, why not hire you? Everyone knows how the Fargos work: A large percentage of the find goes to charity and nothing to you personally. Sam, I think this is about hiding something, not finding something.'

Chapter 11

University of Dar es Salaam

The university's central campus sat northwest of the city center on a hill. Having called ahead, Sam and Remi found the library's director, Amidah Kilembe, a beautiful black woman in a fern-green pantsuit, waiting to greet them on the steps.

'Good morning, Mr. and Mrs. Fargo. Welcome to our facility.'

Pleasantries were exchanged as Ms. Kilembe took them up the steps and through the main doors, at which point she gave them a walking tour of the building, which eventually took them to the third-floor reference area. The décor was a mixture of Old World colonial and traditional African: dark furniture and paneling that glowed from decades of polishing surrounded by splashes of colorful Tanzanian art and artifacts. Save a few of the library staff, the building was empty. 'It's a school holiday,' Ms. Kilembe explained.

'We're sorry,' Sam said. 'We thought – '

'Oh, no, no. For the staff it is a regular workday. In fact, as chance would have it, you've chosen the perfect day to visit. I myself will be assisting you.'

'We don't want to impose,' Remi said. 'I'm sure you have other . . .'

Ms. Kilembe smiled broadly. 'Not at all. I have read of,

and enjoyed, several of your exploits. I will, of course, keep my silence about what we discuss here today.' She touched an index finger to her lips and winked. 'If you'll follow me, I have a quiet room set aside for you.'

They followed her to a glass-enclosed room, in the center of which sat a long walnut table and two padded chairs. Before each chair sat a twenty-inch Apple iMac computer.

Ms. Kilembe saw their surprised expressions and chuckled. 'Three years ago Mr. Steve Jobs himself visited the campus. He saw that we had very few computers and all of them old, so he made a generous donation. We now have forty of these wonderful machines. And broadband Internet!

'Very well. I will let you get started. First, I will bring you coffee. I have you both set up with guest log-ins for the catalogues. Most of our materials have been digitized back to 1970. Those that have not been will be in our basement archives area. You tell me what you need, and I will bring it. So, good hunting!'

And then Ms. Kilembe was gone, pulling the door shut behind her.

'Where do we start?' Sam wondered aloud.

'Let's check in with Selma.'

Sam double-clicked the iChat icon on the screen and typed in Selma's address. The computer's iSight camera turned green and in ten seconds Selma's face appeared on the screen.

'Where are you?' she asked.

'University of Dar es Salaam.'

Behind Selma, Pete and Wendy were sitting at the worktable. They waved.

Remi said, 'We're getting ready to dig in. Do you have anything for us?'

'The last search is finishing now.'

On-screen, Pete walked across to a computer workstation, tapped the keyboard a couple times, then called, 'Coming over to you, Selma.' Sam and Remi watched as Selma studied the document, her eyes darting across the screen.

At last she said, 'Not much there. We checked all the major shipwreck databases and found only eighteen sites in the waters around Zanzibar. We even extended the grid fifty miles on all compass points. Of the eighteen, fourteen are identified, and only one of those comes even remotely close to the assumed same time frame as the *Ophelia*.'

'Go on.'

'The *Glasgow*. Commissioned in 1877 after the Sultan of Zanzibar lost his "fleet" to the 1872 storm. It was delivered in the summer of 1878, but the Sultan was unimpressed, so it sat abandoned and unused at anchor off Zanzibar until the Anglo-Zanzibar War of 1896, when the British sunk her with naval gunfire.

'In 1912 the wreck was reduced to her bottom frames by a salvage company, and the majority of the pieces dumped at sea. In the seventies, the *Glasgow*'s engine block, propeller shaft, some crockery, and a few nine-pound shells were found on the site.'

'Where's the site?' Remi asked.

'About two hundred yards off the Stone Town beach. In fact, you were within sight of it at the restaurant the other night.'

'So about fifteen crow's miles from where we found the *Ophelia*'s bell,' Sam said. 'So scratch the *Glasgow*. What else?'

'Four of the wrecks in the database are unidentified. One is sitting in the Pangani River thirty-five miles to the north; the next two are in Tanga Bay fifty miles to the north; the last one is sitting off Bongoyo Island in Dar es Salaam's Msasani Bay. As far as I can tell, none of them is any deeper than thirty feet.'

'Thirty feet of clear water,' Sam added. 'We'll check with area dive shops. Chances are, someone's identified them but never bothered to say anything. Probably nothing more than dive attractions now.'

'Sorry I came up empty,' Selma said.

'You didn't,' Remi replied. 'Ruling out is just as important as ruling in.'

'Two other things. Mrs. Fargo, you were right about those names, they are Nahuatl, traditional Aztec names. For what it's worth, it's been something of a trend in Mexico City for the last few years – '

'The Mexica Tenochca Party,' Remi finished. She saw Sam's confused expression, then added, 'The current president is an über-nationalist, a pre-Spanish invasion nationalist. Aztec names, history courses taught in schools, religious observances, art . . .'

'In addition to everything else, Rivera and his pals are political zealots,' Sam replied drily. 'Just what we need.'

'What else, Selma?'

'I studied the pictures of the bell you sent. I assume you noticed the clapper?'

'You mean that it's missing?' Sam asked. 'We noticed.'

Sam disconnected, then turned to Remi. 'So, newspapers?'

She nodded. 'Newspapers.'

Sam and Remi were believers in the pyramid theory of research: Start with the top of the pyramid, the specific, and work your way down to the base, the general. The first search terms they tried were *'Ophelia,'* 'wreck,' and 'discovered.' Not surprisingly, all they got were stories Selma had covered. Next they tried 'famous,' 'shipwrecks,' and 'Zanzibar' and got the expected results: fluff stories about the *Glasgow* and the *El Majidi*, another ship belonging to the Sultan of Zanzibar that had been lost during the 1872 hurricane, and the HMS *Pegasus*, sunk in 1914 following a surprise attack by the German cruiser *Königsberg*.

Ms. Kilembe returned with a carafe of coffee and two mugs, asked if they needed anything, then disappeared again.

Remi said, 'We forgot Chumbe Island, Sam. We're assuming the BBC interview brought Rivera here . . .'

'Right.' Sam combined the previous search terms with 'Chumbe Island' and got zero hits. He tried again with the terms 'diving,' 'artifact,' and 'discovery.' He scrolled through the stories, then stopped. 'Huh,' he muttered.

'What?'

'Probably nothing, but it's curious. Two months ago a British woman named Sylvie Radford was found murdered in Stone Town. An apparent mugging gone wrong. She'd come to do some diving off Chumbe. Listen to this: "According to the woman's parents, Ms. Radford had been having a wonderful diving vacation, having already found several artifacts, including what she thought might be part of a Roman-style sword."'

"'A Roman-style sword,'" Remi repeated. 'Interesting. Her words or the reporter's, do you think?'

'I don't know. Either way, it's a pretty specific description. Most laypeople would just say "sword."'

Remi leaned closer to the screen, then jotted down the reporter's name. 'It might be in her notes.'

Sam started tapping the keyboard again, this time with some urgency. Into the search box he entered 'southern,' 'Zanzibar,' 'diving,' and 'death' and set the time frame from present day to ten years earlier. Dozens of stories appeared on the screen.

'Let's split them up,' Remi said, then typed the terms into her own search box. 'Start with the oldest?'

Sam nodded.

In years ten through eight, four deaths were linked to their search terms. In each case, however, independent eyewitness reports confirmed they were accidental: one shark bite, one diving mishap, and two vehicle accidents, both involving alcohol.

'Here,' Remi said. 'Seven years ago. Two people, both tourists on diving vacations.'

'Where exactly?'

'It just says the southwest coast of Zanzibar. One of them was killed by a hit-and-run driver. The other one fell down some steps in Stone Town. No alcohol involved, no witnesses.'

'Six years ago,' Sam said, reading from the screen, 'two dead. One suicide, one drowning. Again, no witnesses.'

And so it went with year five up to the present day: tourist divers, most of them spending time near or around Chumbe Island, dying in strange accidents or muggings gone wrong.

'I count five,' Remi said.

'I've got four,' replied Sam.

They were silent for a few moments.

Remi said, 'Has to be a coincidence, right?' Sam simply stared at his screen, so Remi said, 'Otherwise, what are we saying? Rivera and whoever he works for have been murdering divers that show an interest in Chumbe Island?'

'No, it can't be that. They would number in the hundreds . . . the thousands. Maybe it's the people who declare their finds. Or take them to local shops for identification. If we're right about this, these people have to have something else in common.'

'They told someone about what they found,' Remi offered.

'And it was the right kind of artifact, something to do with the *Ophelia*. Or the ship with the blotted-out name.'

'Either way, if she'd sunk off Chumbe, artifacts would be washing up on the beach. Every monsoon there would be debris just sitting on the bottom waiting for someone with a Ping-Pong paddle to come along.'

'True,' said Sam. 'But there are plenty of people who find something and never mention it. They go home and put it on their mantel as a souvenir. In fact, that describes most casual treasure divers: They find something, make a minor effort to identify it, but if it's not something obviously "treasure-ish" they treat it as a keepsake . . . "Our week in Zanzibar."'

'This is a huge leap we're talking about, Sam.'

'I just remembered something: Rivera said he's been looking for the *Ophelia* for seven years.'

'About the same time the strange deaths started.'

'Exactly. I need to call Rube. We need to find out how good Tanzanian immigration and customs are at record-keeping.'

Sam made the call and explained their request to an incredulous but willing Rube Haywood, who said, 'So your theory is that Rivera was in Zanzibar around the time all the deaths would have taken place?'

'It's worth a shot. Even if the records don't show he was here every time, he may not have traveled under his own name.'

'I'll look into it. Wouldn't hold your breath.'

Sam thanked him and disconnected.

A few minutes later Ms. Kilembe knocked on the door and peeked her head inside. 'Do you need anything?'

They thanked her and declined. She was turning to leave when Sam asked, 'Ms. Kilembe, how long have you been with the library?'

'Thirty years.'

'And how long in this area?'

'All my life. I was born in Fumba, on Zanzibar.'

'We're looking for anything on a ship called *Ophelia*. Does that name mean anything to you?'

Ms. Kilembe furrowed her brow. After ten seconds of thought, she said, 'I assume you've been to the Blaylock already?'

'The Blaylock?'

'The Blaylock Museum in Bagamoyo. There's a charcoal sketch there of a ship. Unless my memory fails me, the ship's name is *Ophelia*.'

Chapter 12

Bagamoyo

Of the two cities within easy reach of Zanzibar, Dar es Salaam and Bagamoyo, the latter was Sam and Remi's favorite. With a population of thirty thousand, Bagamoyo is a microcosm of both traditional African and colonial African history without the big-city bustle of Dar es Salaam and its two and a half million inhabitants.

Founded by Omani nomads in the late 1700s, Bagamoyo has at times been home to Arab and Indian traders of ivory and salt, Christian missionaries, slave traders, the German East Africa colonial government, and big game hunters and explorers bound for Morogoro, Lake Tanganyika, and Usambara.

'Here's something we didn't know,' Remi said, reading from the guidebook as Sam drove. 'David Livingstone, in all his years in Africa, never visited Bagamoyo – at least not alive. He was brought to Bagamoyo after he died and was laid out in the Old Church Tower, now called Livingstone Tower, to wait for high tide so they could ship his body to Zanzibar.'

'Interesting,' Sam said. 'I'd always assumed he'd used Bagamoyo as a staging area just like everyone else. Okay, we're on the outskirts. Where'd Ms. Kilembe say the museum was?'

Remi plucked the Post-it note from inside the guidebook and read: 'Two blocks from the old German *boma*, a fort.'

'Which one? There are two, I think the guidebook said.'

Remi flipped over the note. 'That's all she wrote. Guess we'll have to check them both.'

They found the first a few hundred yards north of three of Bagamoyo's biggest tourist attractions: the crocodile farm, the Kaole Ruins, and a five-hundred-year-old baobab tree. They parked on the dirt road before the crumbling whitewashed fort and got out. A teenage boy walked by with a donkey on a lead. He smiled broadly and said, *'Jambo. Habari gani?'* Hello. How are you?

In halting Swahili, Sam replied, *'Nzuri. Unasema kiingereza?'*

'Yes, I speak little English.'

'We're looking for the Blaylock Museum.'

'Oh, yes, Crazy Man House.'

'No, I'm sorry, the Blaylock Museum.'

'Yes, same thing. Other *boma*. One kilometer up. Livingstone Cross, yes?'

'Yes. *Asante sana*,' Sam replied.

'You're welcome, bye-bye.'

With a click of his tongue, the boy continued on with his donkey.

'Your Swahili is improving,' Remi remarked.

'Just don't ask me to order food. You won't like what we get.'

'What did he mean "Crazy Man House"?'

'Guess we'll find out.'

They found the other *boma* with little trouble, following glimpses of its whitewashed battlements until they reached its crushed-shell parking lot. Here there were more locals going about their business, selling food and sundries from storefronts and awning-covered carts. Sam and Remi got out and began walking, looking for a sign that read either 'Blaylock' or 'Crazy Man.' After twenty minutes of fruitless searching, they stopped at a vendor's cart, bought two ice-cold bottles of cola, and asked for directions.

'Yes, Crazy Man House,' the man said. He pointed west down a narrow dirt alley. 'Two hundred meters there, find wall, then thick trees. Turn right, find path, find place.'

'Asante sana,' Remi said.

'Starehe.'

As promised, they found a waist-high mud-brick wall before a grove of acacia and wild lavender. They turned right and, twenty feet down, came to an opening in the wall. On the other side, a winding path took them through the grove to a white picket fence, beyond which stood an old schoolhouse, long and narrow, with a butter yellow exterior and heavy shutters in dark blue. A black-on-white hand-painted sign above the porch steps read BLAYLOCK MUSEUM AND CURIOS-ITY SHOP. The last three words were clearly written in a different hand, as though added later as an afterthought.

A bell above the door tinkled as they entered. Hand-hewn support posts ran down the center of the space supporting rafters, from which hung dozens of poorly stuffed African birds in poses that Sam and Remi assumed were meant to represent midflight. Sitting on the rafters above their inanimate cousins were several animate pigeons. Their cooing filled the space.

The walls were dominated by wicker shelving units, no two sharing the same height or width or shade of wood. Spaced at intervals down the building's midline were eight rickety card tables covered with threadbare sheets. On both the shelves and card tables were hundreds of knick-knacks: wooden and ivory statuettes of giraffes, lions, zebras, dik-diks, snakes, and people; collections of knives ranging from the standard pocket variety to daggers carved from bone; hand-painted fetishes covered with feathers and bits of tree bark; hand-drawn maps on hide; charcoal pencil portraits and landscapes; compasses; water bags made from animal stomachs; and several models of Webley revolvers and bullets of varying sizes.

'Welcome to the Blaylock Museum and Curiosity Shop,' a voice called in surprisingly good English.

At the far end of the room was a lone card table they hadn't noticed. Sitting behind it was an elderly black man wearing a Baltimore Orioles baseball cap and a white GOT MILK? T-shirt.

'Thank you,' Remi replied.

Sam and Remi walked over and introduced themselves.

'I am Morton,' the man replied.

'Forgive us, but what exactly is this place?' Sam asked.

'It is the Blaylock Museum and Curiosity Shop.'

'Yes, I know, but to whom is it dedicated?'

'The greatest unsung African explorer to ever grace the shores of the Dark Continent,' the man replied. Clearly, he'd delivered this pitch many times. 'The man to whom hundreds owe their lives and the lives of their grandchildren: Winston Lloyd Blaylock, the Mbogo of Bagamoyo.'

'The "Mbogo of Bagamoyo,"' Sam repeated. 'The Buffalo of Bagamoyo?'

'That is correct. The Cape buffalo.'

'What can you tell us about him?' Remi asked.

'Mbogo Blaylock came from America to Bagamoyo in 1872 to seek his fortune. He stood four inches over six feet, weighed twice as much as the average Tanganyikan man at the time, and had shoulders as wide as the *mbogo* for which he is named.'

'Is that him?' Sam asked, pointing to a grainy black-and-white daguerreotype on the wall above Morton. It showed a tall, broad-shouldered man in Hemingwayesque safari clothes. In the background were a dozen Maasai warriors kneeling with *assegai* spears.

'That is him,' Morton confirmed. 'The complete history of the Mbogo is available in this fine leather-bound volume.'

Morton swept his hand toward a wicker shelf on the right-hand wall. Remi walked over and lifted one of the books from the stack. The cover was not leather but rather Naugahyde, crudely stapled into place. Glued to the front was a reproduction of the wall photo.

'We'll take two,' Sam said, and brought their purchases back to the card table. As he was paying Remi asked, 'We were told we might find something about a ship here. The *Ophelia*?'

Morton nodded and pointed to a three-by-five-foot framed charcoal sketch of a steam-sail ship. 'The hunt for the *Ophelia* was Mbogo Blaylock's first great adventure. It is all in the book. I wrote the index myself. It took me three years.'

'That's true dedication,' said Remi. 'How did you come to . . . be here? Did your family know Mr. Blaylock?'

For the first time since they entered, Morton smiled. Proudly. 'My family is Mbogo Blaylock. I am second cousin to Mbogo's great-grandson.'

'Pardon me?' Sam asked. 'You're related to Winston Blaylock?'

'Of course. Doesn't it show?'

Sam and Remi didn't know how to respond. After a few moments Morton slapped his knee and laughed. 'Got you, yes?'

'Yes, you did,' Sam replied. 'So you're not – '

'No, that part is true. The resemblance is difficult to see, however. You may see my birth certificate if you wish.' Before they could answer, Morton produced it from a lockbox beneath the card table. He unfolded it and slid it across to them. Sam and Remi leaned over to study it, then straightened up.

'That's amazing,' Remi said. 'So he married? Took a Tanzanian wife?'

'Back then it was still called Tanganyika – before the Germans came, you see. And no, he did not take a wife. But he did take six concubines and had many children. That, too, is in the book.'

Sam and Remi exchanged dumbfounded glances. Sam asked Morton, 'What happened to him?'

'No one knows. He disappeared from here in 1882. His grandson claims he was chasing a treasure.'

'What kind of treasure?'

'That is a secret he shared with no one.'

'Some people in town called it the – '

'Crazy Man House,' Morton said. 'It's not an insult. The word doesn't translate well into English. In Swahili, it doesn't mean crazy so much as . . . free-spirited. Wild.'

'All these artifacts belonged to him?' Remi asked.

'Yes. Most he killed, made, or found with his own hands. Others are gifts and offerings. Offer a fair price, and I will consider it.'

'I don't understand. You're selling his belongings?'

'I have no choice. I am the last of Mbogo Blaylock's descendants. At least that is still here. My two children live in England. They are going to school. I'm sick and not long for this world.'

'We're very sorry to hear that,' Sam said. 'May we look around?'

'Of course. Ask questions if you have them.'

Sam and Remi walked away. She whispered, 'You think it's all true? The picture does look an awful lot like Hemingway.'

'Why don't you call Ms. Kilembe and ask.'

Remi went outside, returned five minutes later, and walked over to Sam, who was staring at a walking staff mounted on the wall.

'She says it's all legitimate. The museum's been here since 1915.' Sam didn't respond. He remained still, his eyes fixed on the staff. 'Sam? Did you hear me? Sam, what's so fascinating?'

'Do you see anything unusual about it?' he murmured.

Remi studied it for a few moments. 'No, not really.'

'Look at the head . . . the metal part with the rounded end.'

She did. She cocked her head, squinted her eyes, then: 'Is that . . . ?'

Sam nodded. 'A bell clapper.'

They stared at it for another long ten seconds, then Sam turned to Morton and said, 'How much for all of it?'

Chapter 13

Zanzibar

'Pardon me?' Selma said over the speakerphone. 'Say that again. You want what shipped back here?'

From the passenger seat of their Toyota Remi said, 'Not the whole museum, Selma, just the contents. In all it should weigh about . . .' She looked to Sam, who said, 'Five to seven hundred pounds.'

Selma said, 'I heard.' She sighed. 'Who do I – '

'The owner's name is Morton Blaylock. We're putting him up in the Moevenpick Royal Palm in Dar es Salaam while you two make arrangements. By this afternoon he'll have an account set up at Barclays. Wire thirty thousand dollars to him from our business account, then another thirty when everything's packed up and on its way to you.'

'Sixty thousand dollars?' Selma said. 'You paid him sixty thousand? Do you know how much that is in Tanzanian shillings? It's a fortune. Did you haggle with him at least?'

'He wanted twenty,' Sam replied. 'We talked him up. Selma. He's a dying man and he's got grandkids to put through college.'

'Sounds like a con man to me.'

'We don't think so,' Remi replied. 'The staff's seven feet tall, made of black ironwood, and topped with the bronze clapper from the *Ophelia*'s bell.'

'Is this pull-a-joke-on-Selma day?'

Sam replied, 'You'll see it for yourself. Morton's including it in the first shipment from the museum. We're also FedExing you a copy of Blaylock's biography. We need you to work your magic on it. Dissect it, cross-reference every name, place, and description . . . You know what to do.'

'I haven't heard you two this excited since you called from that cave in the Alps.'

'We are excited,' Remi replied. 'It appears Winston Blaylock spent a good portion of his adult life chasing a treasure, and, unless we're wrong, it's something Rivera and his boss don't want us to find. Blaylock could be our Rosetta stone.'

Sam turned the Land Cruiser onto the road leading to their villa, then slammed on the brakes. A hundred yards away through the windshield they saw a figure walk across the patio and disappear into the bushes.

Remi said, 'Selma, we'll have to call you back,' then hung up. 'Is it them, Sam?'

'It's them. Check out the patio. The bell's gone.'

Ahead and to the right, the figure emerged from the bushes bordering the beach and began sprinting toward the waterline, where a twenty-seven-foot Rinker power-boat sat alongside the quay across from their Andreyale. A half mile out the yacht *Njiwa* sat at anchor. Standing on the Rinker's afterdeck were two figures. Between them was the *Ophelia*'s bell.

'Damn it!' Sam muttered.

'How did they find us?' Remi said.

'No idea. Hold on!'

He punched the gas pedal. The tires bit into the dirt, and the Land Cruiser lurched forward. Sam watched the speedometer climb past fifty, then swung the wheel left, then right, aiming the hood squarely at the brush-covered berm.

'Oh, boy . . .' Remi said. She pressed her hands against the dashboard and her head against the rest.

The berm loomed before them. The Land Cruiser tipped backward. Sky filled the windshield, then they were tipping forward again, soaring through the air, the engine roaring as the tires spun freely. The Cruiser crashed to the earth. Sand peppered the windshield. Sam jammed the accelerator to the floorboard, and after a momentary groan of protest the engine responded and they were again moving forward, albeit at half speed as the tires struggled to find purchase in the dry sand.

Ahead, the running figure had nearly reached the quay. He glanced over his shoulder, saw the Land Cruiser, and stumbled. It was Yaotl.

'Guess he didn't like our hospitality,' Sam called.

'Can't imagine why,' replied Remi.

Yaotl was back on his feet. He charged up the quay's steps, taking them two at a time, then dashed toward the waiting Rinker, where Rivera and Nochtli were waving their arms, urging him on.

Sam kept going, jostling the wheel and trying to feel his way to firmer ground. The quay was fifty yards away. Yaotl reached the Rinker and jumped aboard. Thirty yards to go. Nochtli moved to the driver's seat and settled behind the wheel. Smoke burst from the exhaust manifold.

Quite casually, Rivera stepped past the panting Yaotl,

gave him a clap on the shoulder, then stepped to the transom. He stared at the approaching Land Cruiser for a
moment, then raised his hand as if to wave.

Sam muttered, 'Son of a — '

Remi said, 'He's got something.'

'What?'

'In his hand! He's holding something!'

Sam slammed on the brakes. The Land Cruiser slewed
sideways and shuddered to a halt. Sam shifted the transmission into reverse, his foot ready to move from the
brake to the accelerator.

His eyes never leaving theirs, Rivera smiled grimly, then
reached up, pulled the pin on the grenade, turned, and
tossed it into the Andreyale. Ahead of a rooster tail of
water, the Rinker shot away from the quay and headed for
the *Njiwa*.

With a dull crump, the grenade exploded. A geyser of
water and wood splinters shot upward and rained down
on the quay. The Andreyale settled lower in the water,
then slowly disappeared beneath the surface in a cloud of
bubbles.

After backing the SUV over the sand and dunes to the road,
they watched Rivera and his men tool out to the *Njiwa*.
Within minutes the anchor was weighed, and the yacht got
under way, heading south down the coast.

'I'd started to grow attached to that bell,' Sam muttered.

'And you don't like losing,' Remi said. When Sam shook
his head, she added, 'Me neither.'

Sam leaned sideways across Remi's lap and retrieved
the H&K P30 from the glove box, then said, 'I'll be right

back.' He climbed out, walked down the road to the villa, then slipped inside. He emerged two minutes later and gave Remi the OK sign. She scooted into the driver's seat and pulled the Toyota into the driveway.

'Did they toss the house?' she asked, climbing out.

Sam shook his head. 'But I know how they found us.'

He led her through the villa to the guest room where they'd been keeping Yaotl. Sam walked to the headboard and pointed to the loop that had been secured around their guest's left wrist. It was stained a dark reddish brown. The remaining three loops had been untied.

'That's blood,' Remi said. 'He worked his way free.'

'Then called Rivera,' Sam added. 'I'll give him this much: He's got a high tolerance for pain. His wrist must be raw down to the bone.'

'Why didn't they ambush us?'

'Hard to say. Rivera's no dummy. He knows we've got Yaotl's gun and didn't want to risk attracting the police.'

'I think we're a secondary concern. They got what they came for. Without that, all we've got is an interesting story. Sam, what in the world can be so important about that bell?'

Erring on the side of caution, they agreed the villa was no longer safe. They packed what few belongings were left inside, got back into the Toyota, and drove eight miles south to Chwaka, a small town whose only claim to fame seemed to be that it was home to the mysteriously named Zanzibar Institute of Financial Administration. They found a beachfront restaurant with air-conditioning and went inside. They asked to be seated in a quiet area near an aquarium.

Remi pointed out the window. 'Is that . . . ?'

Sam looked. Two miles offshore they could see the *Njiwa*, still steaming south at a leisurely pace. Sam grumbled a curse under his breath and took a sip of iced water.

'Well, what do you want to do about it?' Remi prodded.

Sam shrugged. 'I can't decide if my ego is just bruised because they stole something we worked so hard to get. That's not much of a reason to put ourselves back in their gunsights.'

'It's more than that. We know how badly they don't want people to know about the bell or the ship it was attached to. They probably murdered for it. They're going to either destroy it or dump it in the deepest part of the ocean, where it'll never be found again. It's a piece of history, and they're going to treat it like garbage.'

Sam's phone rang. He said, 'Selma,' to Remi, then answered and tapped the Speakerphone button. As was her way, Selma jumped in without preamble: 'That bell you've got is an interesting find.'

'Had,' Sam replied. 'We don't have it anymore.' He explained.

Remi said, 'Tell us anyway, Selma.'

'Do you want the fascinating news or the astounding news first?'

'Fascinating.'

'Wendy used her Photoshop wizardry skills and ran the pictures through some filters or something. Most of what she said was Greek to me. Under all that marine growth there's engraved writing.'

'What kind?' asked Sam.

'We don't know for sure. There are bits of symbology,

some words in Swahili, a smattering of German, pictographs, but not enough of any one of them to make sense. From the looks of it, most of the bell's interior is covered with it.'

'Okay, now astound us,' Remi said.

'Wendy was also able to pull a few more letters from the name beneath the *Ophelia* engraving. In addition to the first two – *S* and *H*, and the last one, *H*, she was able to pull two letters from the middle: a pair of *N*s separated by a space.'

As Selma had been talking, Remi had grabbed a napkin from the holder, and she and Sam were working the anagram.

Selma continued: 'We fed the letters and arrangement into an anagram program and cross-matched the results against our shipwreck databases and came up with – '

'*Shenandoah,*' Sam and Remi said in unison.

Chapter 14

Zanzibar

The Confederate States ship *Shenandoah* had long fascinated Sam and Remi, but they'd never had the time to explore the mysteries behind the saga. Now it appeared fate had handed them a bronze invitation in the form of a ship's bell.

A 1,160-ton steam cruiser, *Shenandoah* was launched at the Alexander Stephen & Sons shipyard in River Clyde, Scotland, in August of 1863 under the name *Sea King*. Iron-framed, teak-planked, and black-hulled, *Sea King* was fully rigged for both sail and auxiliary steam power, designed as cargo transport for the East Asia tea trade routes. Tea hauling did not lie in her future, however.

A year after her commissioning, in September 1864, *Sea King* was covertly purchased by agents of the Confederate Secret Service, and on October eighth she sailed with a full complement of merchant sailors, ostensibly headed for Bombay on her maiden trading voyage. Nine days later *Sea King* rendezvoused near the island of Madeira, off the African coast, with the steamship *Laurel*, which had been lying in wait. Aboard *Laurel* were the officers and the nucleus of the *Sea King*'s new crew, all loyal and experienced sailors, either Southerners or sympathetic British citizens. Their captain was Lieutenant James Iredell

Waddell, a forty-one-year-old North Carolinian and graduate of the United States Naval Academy.

The *Laurel*'s cargo of naval guns, ammunition, and general stores were quickly transferred aboard *Sea King*, whose dumbfounded and angry crew were given the option of joining this new expedition at higher wages or being transferred to the *Laurel* and subsequently deposited on Tenerife, an island in the Canary Archipelago off the coast of Morocco. In the end, however, Waddell was only able to enlist enough of *Laurel*'s seamen to bring the newly commissioned commerce raider *Shenandoah* to half her normal sailing complement. Despite this, *Shenandoah* left the Madeira Islands on October twenty-first and set about her task of destroying or capturing Union ships wherever she found them.

Through the fall of 1864 and into the winter of 1865 *Shenandoah* sailed through the South Atlantic, around the Cape of Good Hope, and into the Indian Ocean and across to Australia, destroying and capturing Union-flagged merchant vessels before setting her sights on the Union's Pacific whaling grounds, sailing north from New Guinea into the Sea of Okhotsk and the Bering Sea.

In the nine months *Shenandoah* sailed under the Confederate flag as a warship, she accounted for the destruction of some three dozen enemy ships. On August 2, 1865, some four months after Lee's surrender at Appomattox, *Shenandoah* learned of the war's end by the passing British barque *Barracouta*. Captain Waddell ordered *Shenandoah* disarmed, then set a course for Liverpool, England, where he and *Shenandoah*'s crew surrendered in November 1865. The following March she was sold through intermediaries to Sayyid Majid bin Said al-Busaid, the first Sultan of Zanzibar, who renamed her *El Majidi*, after himself.

For Sam and Remi it had always been this part of the *Shenandoah*'s history that they found so intriguing. There were three accounts of *El Majidi*'s final disposition. One had her being scuttled in the Zanzibar Channel shortly after being damaged in the 1872 hurricane; the next, her sinking six months later while being towed to Bombay for repairs; the last, her going down in November of 1879 after striking a reef near the island of Socotra on the way home from Bombay.

'This raises more questions than it gives answers,' Sam said. 'For starters, was it Blaylock or someone else who renamed her *Ophelia*?'

'And why was she renamed?' Remi added. 'And why is there no record of her anywhere?'

'And the biggest question: Why did we find the bell at all?'

'What do you mean?' asked Remi.

'After Waddell surrendered the *Shenandoah*, wouldn't she and everything aboard her have been the property of the Union?'

'Including the bell.'

'Including the bell,' Sam echoed.

'Maybe the Union sold her to the Sultan of Zanzibar, lock, stock, and barrel.'

'Could be. But that was in 1866. The *El Majidi* didn't sink for another six or thirteen years, depending on which account you go with. Hell, the Sultan named the ship after himself. Does he sound like someone who would hang on to a bell with another ship's name on it?'

'No, he doesn't. Maybe whoever refitted her just tossed the bell overboard. For the sake of expediency.'

Remi was the devil's advocate of the couple. She often did her best to poke holes in their thinking; if after going through the 'Remi Gauntlet' the theory remained afloat, they then knew they were on to something.

Sam considered this. 'Possible, but I'm trying to put myself in the shoes of the Sultan's shipfitter. He's probably not the wealthiest of guys – overworked and underpaid. Unsurprisingly, the Sultan demands the ship meet his royal standards, including a shiny new bell. What would this shipfitter do with a ninety-pound, solid bronze bell?'

'Sell it,' Selma chimed in.

'Let's put a pin in that,' Remi said. 'It seems safe to assume Blaylock himself came across the bell at some point. If it was still attached to the vessel, he either bought it or stole the ship, then changed the name to *Ophelia*. If the bell had been discarded by the Sultan, it means Blaylock salvaged the bell, blotted out the *Shenandoah* name, and engraved it with *Ophelia*.'

'And did what with it? Stared at it?'

'The charcoal sketch at the museum suggests he saw that ship as the *Ophelia*.'

Sam snapped his fingers. 'We're overthinking this. Remi, boot up your laptop. Selma, e-mail us pictures of the *Shenandoah* and the *El Majidi*.'

As they were waiting, Sam plugged his camera into Remi's laptop, and she called up the photo they'd taken of the *Ophelia* sketch. 'No Wi-Fi signal,' Remi said.

Sam stood up and walked around, checking beneath nearby tables. 'There are Ethernet plug-ins,' he said, then walked toward the hostess. He returned two minutes later with an Ethernet cable, which he first plugged into Remi's laptop, then into the closest plug. 'It's dial-up Internet, but it should do,' Sam said.

Over the phone, Selma said, 'Images on the way.'

It took four minutes for the JPEG images to load. Remi arranged the pictures on her screen, and they spent a few minutes rotating and zooming and playing with colors until they were certain. 'Same ship,' Remi said.

'I agree,' Sam agreed. 'Blaylock's *Ophelia* is also the *Shenandoah* and the *El Majidi*. The question is, at what point in the time line did Blaylock appear and why are there no records of any of this?'

'Clearly, Rivera and his friends are interested in our bell. But is it the bell itself or the ship or ships it had once been attached to?'

'There's only way to find out,' Sam said. 'We have to steal it back before Rivera destroys it or loses it.'

They immediately realized that, like many things in their line of work, this task was much easier said than done. Sam rummaged around in his pack and came up with a pair of binoculars. He stood up and aimed them out the window. After thirty seconds, he lowered the binoculars. 'She's still headed south, about to slip behind Pingwe Point. Still in no big hurry.'

'They know they've got us beat.'

Sam grinned. 'Never say die.' He picked up his phone and dialed Rube Haywood.

'Sam, I was just about to call you,' Rube said.

'Great minds. I hope we're on the same wavelength.'

'I have information on the yacht, the *Njiwa*.'

'Bless you.'

It belongs to a guy named Ambonisye Okafor. One of the ten richest men in the country. You name a Tanzanian export, and he's got a major stake in it: cashews, tobacco, coffee, cotton, sisal, precious gems, minerals . . .'

'How did a hatchet man like Rivera get hooked up with someone like Okafor?'

'Hard to say, exactly, but I did a little digging. In the last five years, the Mexican government has sharply increased its importation of Tanzanian goods, most of it from companies controlled by Ambonisye Okafor. That tells me Rivera has powerful friends in Mexico City. Sam, you two aren't up against a few mercenaries. You're up against a government and a Tanzanian millionaire with a whole lot of influence.'

'Trust me, Rube, we're not going to ignore that, but right now all we want is to get back that bell – '

'What does that mean?'

'They stole it. All we want is to get back the bell and head home.'

'That may be easier said – '

'We know. What else can you tell us about the *Njiwa*?'

'It's one of two yachts Okafor owns. This one is home-ported on Sukuti Island, about thirty miles south of Dar es Salaam as the crow flies. Okafor has a vacation estate there. Owns the whole island.'

'Of course he does.'

Over the years Sam and Remi had found one of the most common traits among megalomaniac millionaires was their aversion to fraternization with the 'great unwashed masses.' Owning a private island was an exceedingly effective way to accomplish this.

Rube said, 'I don't have to ask what you're going to do next, do I?'

'Probably not.'

'Okay, but I'm going to throw in my obligatory "Be careful."'

'We'll call you when we can.'

Sam disconnected and recounted the conversation to Remi. After a few moments' thought, she said, 'Can't hurt to check it out. On one condition.'

'Name it.'

'That discretion will trump valor. If we get in over our heads – '

'We'll retreat.'

'Of course, we're assuming the *Njiwa* is headed to Sukuti.'

Sam nodded. 'If she's not, we're probably out of the game. If she is, we need to get to the bell before they do something nasty to it.'

Chapter 15

Tanzania

The *Njiwa*'s negligible head start quickly became insur-
mountable as Sam and Remi came up against Tanzania's
geography. Where road travel along the coast and in
between population centers was fairly easy, they realized
navigating off the beaten path would be a nightmare. The
only passable road heading south from Dar es Salaam was
the B2, which ran the length of southern Tanzania, never
straying closer than ten miles from the coast until it reached
Somanga Village, ninety miles south of Sukuti Island. After
realizing they would neither reach their destination by road,
nor before the *Njiwa*, they mentally regrouped. Now aware
Rivera had some powerful friends on his side, they decided
to err on the side of slight paranoia. If Rivera was playing
the worst-case-scenario game, he might assume they'd take
up pursuit from Zanzibar or Dar es Salaam, and, having
come to the same conclusion about road travel as they had,
he would expect them to arrive by boat.

By nightfall, after half a dozen fruitless phone calls,
they found a bush pilot who agreed to take them from the
Ras Kutani airstrip outside Dar es Salaam to Mafia Island's
airstrip the next morning. From there it would be a half
day's boat ride north to Sukuti Island, a detail they left in
Selma's expert logistical hands.

Such was Africa, the Fargos knew. Though they'd heard the term 'African mile' before, this was the first time they'd experienced it firsthand. What elsewhere would have been a thirty-mile jaunt down the coast had turned into a convoluted hundred-fifty-mile journey.

With a night to kill, Sam kept his promise and booked them into the Presidential Suite at the Moevenpick Royal Palm overlooking the ocean. Following an afternoon in the hotel's spa, they shared a late dinner in L'Oliveto, the hotel's Italian restaurant.

'It feels like we've been away from civilization for months,' Remi said across the table.

'You don't look it,' Sam replied. Ever resourceful, Remi had found a simple but elegant Zac Posen 'little black dress' in the hotel's boutique.

'Thank you, Sam.'

The waiter arrived, and Sam gave him their wine selection.

Sam said to Remi, 'I saw you were reading Blaylock's biography at the spa. Any revelations?'

'It's slow going. It wasn't written by Blaylock, I can tell you that much. Unless his grasp of English was tenuous at best. I'm guessing Morton penned it. But from what source? One thing that struck me: There's no mention of Blaylock before he arrived in Africa. It begins the day he set foot in Bagamoyo. No personal details about his life up to that point.'

'Interesting. How's the index?'

Remi shrugged. 'What you'd expect. I'm sure Selma, Pete, and Wendy will have more luck with it. I did check for any mention of the bell or the *Ophelia*. There was nothing.'

'Odd. If he's the one that took the time to inscribe all the hieroglyphics on the bell, you'd think it would at least warrant a mention. Sounds like a man trying to hide a secret.'

'A big secret,' Remi added. 'So big the Mexican government may have been murdering people over it for the last seven years.'

The airport shuttle dropped them off at the Ras Kutani shortly after dawn. Aside from a few maintenance people moving about in the morning fog, the airstrip was quiet and devoid of life. As the shuttle pulled away, a figure emerged from the mist and approached them. He wore safari khakis, calf-high jungle boots, and a baseball cap emblazoned with the U.S. Army Rangers insignia. He had close-cropped black hair and a thick mustache.

'Ed Mitchell,' he said without preamble.

'Sam and Remi Fargo,' Sam replied. 'You're American.'

'More or less. Expatriate, I guess you'd call it. That all you got?' he said, nodding to Sam and Remi's backpacks. They'd left the majority of their baggage with Vutolo, an old friend and the concierge at the Moevenpick.

'This is it,' Sam replied.

'Okay. I'm ready if you are.'

Mitchell turned and started walking. Sam and Remi followed him to a sturdy-looking but weathered Bush Air Cessna 182. Mitchell loaded their gear aboard, got them buckled into the backseat, and did a rote preflight check.

Within five minutes of arriving they were airborne and headed south.

'Diving?' Mitchell's voice said over their headsets.

'Pardon?' Remi replied.

'That's why you're going to Mafia, I assume.'

'Oh. Right.'

Sam said, 'Mr. Mitchell, how long have you been in Africa?'

'Name's Ed. Twenty-two years, I guess. Came here with RAND to do a radar installation back in '88. Fell in love with it and decided to stay. I flew Spads and Hueys in 'Nam, so bush flying seemed like a good fit. Set up shop and the rest is history.'

'Sounds familiar,' Remi replied.

'Which part?'

'Falling in love with Africa.'

'It has the tendency to get into your blood. Every few years I go back to the States to see friends, but I always end up coming back early.' For the first time, Mitchell chuckled. 'I guess that'd make me an Africa junkie.'

'What do you know about Sukuti Island?' Sam asked.

'Great diving. Prickly owner. A guy named Ambonisye Okafor. You thinking about going there?'

'Thinking about it.'

'We can fly over. He owns the island, not the airspace. It'd only cost us fifteen minutes or so.'

Mitchell made the course adjustment, and within a few minutes the island came into view out the left-hand window. 'Sukuti is actually part of the Mafia Archipelago and, depending on who you ask, they're part of the Spice chain along with Zanzibar,' Mitchell said. 'Big and little Sukuti

– the big one situated to the north, the little one to the south. See the little waterway between them? Since it's only fifty or sixty feet wide they're officially considered a single landmass. All in all, about five square miles. See the other one there, four miles to the south? That's North Fanjove.'

'And the long one sitting between them?' Remi asked.

'That's more atoll than island – a reef and sandbar. Doesn't really have a name that I know of. It's just so close to the surface that it looks solid. You can walk across it, but you'd be wading up to your knees.'

'Are those craters?' Sam asked, peering out the window.

'Yep. Back before World War One, German battleships and cruisers used to use Sukuti and Fanjove for target practice. In some places they punched holes straight down the water table. That's why Fanjove is so popular with cave divers. They rope down into the craters and explore. Every year three or four die doing it. Are you –'

'No,' Sam replied. 'Just regular diving.'

'Watch yourself. Okafor claims two miles all around Sukuti. He's got patrol boats and a few armed guards. He even tries to warn people away from Fanjove, but he's got no legal claim there. There's his house . . . there on the peak.'

Sam and Remi craned their necks to take a look. Ambonisye Okafor's island vacation home was a four-story Italian-style villa surrounded by a chest-high stone wall. Neatly groomed crushed-shell paths branched out from the estate like crooked wheel spokes.

If set sixty-five years earlier and dropped into the Pacific Ocean, Big Sukuti could have easily passed for a

Japanese fortress island during World War II. Shaped like a cone whose rear quarter had been cleaved down to the waterline, the island's southern, lower reaches were devoid of plant life, save the occasional scrub brush, and completely without cover save the occasional boulder. A half mile from the shore the moonscape gave way to a swath of rain forest that ended where the estate's grounds began.

'Replace that villa with a bunker complex, and you've got a smaller version of Iwo Jima,' Sam said. 'Keeping that jungle at bay probably requires a full-time maintenance staff.'

Two of the island's paths caught their attention. One led to a dock on the island's northwestern side. The *Njiwa* was tied up alongside the pier. Opposite her were two Rinker speedboats like those Rivera and his men had used during the theft of the bell. They could see several figures moving along the *Njiwa*'s deck, but at this altitude couldn't make out any faces.

The other significant path led to a clearing bordered by white-painted stones; in the center, more stones, these embedded in the earth, formed a giant *H*. A helicopter landing pad.

Remi said, 'Ed, is that a – '

'Yep. He owns a Eurocopter EC135. Top-of-the-line bird. Okafor doesn't drive anywhere if he can help it. A status thing, I suspect. Either of you fly?'

'I've got my single-engine,' Sam replied. 'I've taken helicopter lessons. I have ten hours in the cockpit. It's a tougher adjustment than I'd imagined.'

'Boy, you got that right.'

'I don't see many guards or fences down there,' Remi said. 'Odd for a man who enjoys his privacy.'

'He's got enough of a reputation that he doesn't need as much protection now. He prosecutes trespassers without mercy. Rumor has it, a few of them have even disappeared after pushing their luck.'

'You believe that?' Sam asked.

'I tend to. Okafor was a general in the Tanzanian army before he retired. Tough, scary guy. Seen enough?'

'Yes,' Sam replied.

The remainder of the flight was quiet, punctuated only by Ed's occasional utterances over their headsets as he pointed out landmarks and offered bits of African history. Just before seven-thirty they touched down on Mafia Island's gravel airstrip and taxied up to the terminal, a whitewashed building with dusky blue trim and a brick-red tin roof. Beside the building, a pair of uniformed immigration officials sat in the shade of a baobab.

As the engines wound down, Ed climbed out and retrieved their backpacks from the cargo compartment. He handed them his card, said, 'Safe travels, Fargos. Call me if you run into trouble,' then gave them a smile they could only describe as conspiratorial.

Sam smiled back. 'You know something we don't?'

'No, but I know adventure hounds when I see them. I'd say you two can handle yourselves better than most, but Africa is an unforgiving place. The number on my card is my satellite phone. I'll leave it on.'

'Thanks, Ed.'

They shook hands, then Ed turned and headed toward a Quonset hut whose window displayed a flickering red neon BEER sign.

They grabbed their backpacks and headed toward the terminal but were intercepted on the sidewalk by the two officials from under the baobab. After a cursory glance at their passports, the officials poked through their belongings, then stamped the passports and offered a 'Welcome to Mafia Island' in halting English.

'You need taxi?' one of the officials asked. Without waiting for a response, he raised his hand and whistled. From the turnaround outside the airport entrance, a rust-riddled gray Peugeot growled to life.

Sam said, 'Thank you but no. We'll find our own transportation.'

Hand still raised, the official looked quizzically at Sam. 'Eh?'

Sam pointed to the Peugeot and shook his head. '*La asante.*' No thanks.

The official shrugged, then waved off the taxi driver and said, '*Sawa.*' Okay. He and his partner walked back to the baobab.

'What was that all about?' Remi asked.

'They were in cahoots. At best, we get a padded fare; at worst, we get taken to a private alley and robbed.'

Remi smiled. 'Sam Fargo, where's your trust in humanity?'

'Right now, it's the same place as my wallet – well hidden.' While Mafia Island was a popular destination for extreme scuba divers, it was also a hub for the Tanzanian black market. Sam explained this to Remi.

She said, 'You're a font of trivia. Where did you come across this tidbit?'

'I downloaded the CIA World Factbook to my iPhone. Very handy. Come on, we'll walk. It's not far.'

'What's to stop us from getting mugged on the street?'

Sam lifted the tail of his shirt to expose the butt of the H&K.

Remi smiled and shook her head. 'Just go easy, Tex. No O.K. Corral reenactments, please.'

According to their maps, the Mafia Island airstrip bisected the island's largest town, Kilindoni, into north and south portions, the former situated more inland, the latter hugging the coast. That was where, Selma had told them, they would find the docks and the boat she'd rented for them.

Despite it being not yet eight in the morning, the sun shone brightly in a clear blue sky, and within minutes of leaving the airstrip both Sam and Remi were sweating. They felt eyes watching their every step, many of which belonged to curious children who paralleled their path, waving and smiling shyly at the white strangers who'd come to their village.

After twenty minutes of walking down hard-packed dirt roads lined with ramshackle huts that ranged in composition from tin to brick to cardboard, they arrived at the beach. Equally dilapidated boat sheds and warehouses lined the dunes overlooking the water. A dozen wood-plank docks jutted into the surf. Thirty to forty boats, from decades-old motor cruisers to skiffs to dhows, both sail driven and motorized, bobbed at anchor in the harbor. Near the waterline, clusters of men and boys worked, repairing nets, scraping hulls, or cleaning fish.

'I miss the Andreyale,' Remi murmured.

'Well, now that it's got a grenade hole in the center of the afterdeck, we own it,' Sam replied. 'Maybe we'll pull it off the bottom. We'll call it a souvenir.' He turned and scanned the row of buildings along the dune. 'We're looking for a bar called the Red Bird.'

'There,' Remi said, pointing fifty yards down the beach to a thatch longhouse fronted by a black-painted four-by-eight-foot plywood sign sporting a crow painted in bright red.

They walked that way. As they approached the wooden steps, a quartet of men stopped their animated conversation and looked at them. Sam said, 'Morning. We're looking for Buziba.'

For a long ten seconds none of them spoke.

'*Unazungumza kiingereza?*' Remi said. Do you speak English?

No response.

For the next two minutes Sam and Remi used their limited knowledge of Swahili to try to start a dialogue but to no avail. A voice behind them said, 'Buziba, don't be a jackass.'

They turned to see a grinning Ed Mitchell standing behind them. He had a Tusker beer in each hand.

'Are you following us?' Sam asked.

'More or less. We're probably the only three Americans on the island right now. Thought a little solidarity couldn't hurt. I know old Buziba here,' Ed said, nodding to the gray-haired man sitting on the top step. 'He speaks English. Playing dumb is his bargaining strategy.' Ed barked out a sentence in Swahili, and the other three men got up and wandered back inside the bar.

'Now, be a gentleman, Buziba,' Ed said. 'These are friends.'

The old man's dour expression dropped away. He smiled broadly. 'Friends of Mr. Ed are friends of me.'

'I told you not to call me that,' Mitchell said, then to Sam and Remi: 'He saw reruns of the TV show. He gets a laugh out of comparing me to a talking horse.'

Remi said to Buziba, 'Your English is very good.'

'Fair indeed, yes? Better than your Swahili, eh?'

'Without a doubt,' Sam replied. 'A friend of ours called you about a boat.'

Buziba nodded. 'Miss Selma. Yesterday. I have your boat. Four hundred dollars.'

'Per day?'

'Eh?'

Ed said something in Swahili, and Buziba responded. Ed said, 'Four hundred to sell. He gave up fishing last year; been trying to sell the thing ever since. The bar brings in plenty of money for him.'

Sam and Remi exchanged glances. Ed added, 'You'd probably pay that for two days' rental from anyone else here.'

'Let's see it,' Sam said.

The four of them walked down the beach to where an eighteen-foot aquamarine blue dhow sat atop a half dozen V-shaped sawhorses. A pair of young boys were sitting in the sand beside the dhow's hull. One was scraping while the other was painting.

Buziba said, 'Look. Inspect.'

Sam and Remi walked around the dhow, checking for signs of decay and disrepair. Sam poked the seams with his Swiss Army knife while Remi tapped the wood, sounding for rot. Sam walked to the stern, climbed up the ladder leaning against the transom, and stepped onto the afterdeck. He reappeared two minutes later and called down, 'The sails have got some rot.'

'Eh?' Buziba replied. Ed translated, listened to Buziba's response, then said, 'He'll throw in a new set for fifty dollars.'

Remi asked Sam, 'How's the cabin?'

'Cozy in the extreme. Not the Moevenpick, but we've seen worse.'

'And the engine?'

'Old but well maintained. Should give us six or seven knots.'

Remi walked to the transom and inspected the propeller and shaft. 'I'm betting the bearings could use repacking.'

Ed translated, listened, then replied, 'He says another fifty and he'll have it done in two hours.'

'Twenty-five,' Sam countered. 'He gives me the supplies and the tools, and I'll do it myself.'

Buziba jutted out his lower lip and stuck his chin in the air, thinking. 'Fifty. I add potable water and food for two days.'

'Three days,' Remi replied.

Buziba considered this, then shrugged. 'Three days.'

Chapter 16

Indian Ocean

'Okay, shut her down,' Sam called.

Remi turned off the ignition key and the dhow's engines sputtered out. Sam hoisted the sails, and they held their collective breaths for a few seconds until the canvas caught the wind and billowed out. The dhow's bow lifted slightly and the boat lurched forward. Sam crab-walked aft and dropped onto the afterdeck beside Remi.

'We have liftoff,' Sam said.

'Here's hoping we don't have to call Houston with a problem,' Remi said and handed him a bottle of water.

It was already midafternoon, and they were only five miles north of Mafia Island. While Remi's discerning eye had noticed the propeller shaft's bearing problem, it hadn't been until Sam had gotten it apart that they realized how much time the repair would require. As Remi supervised the boys in finishing up the maintenance and changing out the sails, Sam and Ed worked under the shade of a makeshift sheet awning.

Once done, Buziba and another dozen boys appeared and carried the dhow down to the waterline, where they tested the engine and took the dhow for a test drive around the harbor. An hour later, the dhow fully stocked with water, supplies, and food, Sam and Remi waved to Buziba and Ed and set out.

'How long until we get there?' Remi asked.

Sam got up, retrieved the chart they'd found inside the cabin, and unfolded it in his lap. He checked the readout of his handheld GPS unit and plotted their position. 'Another thirty-nine miles. We're doing about five knots . . . If we run all night, we'll get there shortly after midnight. Or we could find someplace to lie up tonight, then set out early and get there about dawn. There's an unnamed island about twelve miles south of Fanjove.'

'That's my vote. Without radar, we're asking for trouble.'

'Agreed. We wouldn't be able to see anything of Sukuti until daylight anyway.'

They sailed north for another five hours, caught a tail-wind for the last hour, and found the island just as the upper rim of the sun was dipping behind the horizon. Sam steered the dhow into a small cove and dropped anchor. Once the boat was secure, Remi ducked into the cabin for a few minutes, emerging with a lantern, a camping stove, and two cans of food.

'What can I serve you, *el capitán*? Baked beans or baked beans and franks?'

Sam pursed his lips. 'Choices, choices. Let's celebrate our not sinking. Let's have both.'

'A fine choice. And for dessert: fresh mango.'

The surprisingly comfortable double army cot, combined with the salt air and the gentle rocking of the dhow at anchor, lulled them into a deep, restful sleep. At four A.M. Sam's watch chimed, and they got up and moving, sharing a breakfast of leftover mango and strong black coffee before weighing anchor and setting out again.

They lost an hour of progress to sluggish predawn winds, but shortly before sunrise the air picked up and before long they were clipping north at a steady six knots that brought them within sight of North Fanjove Island by seven A.M. A half hour later they drew even with the atoll Mitchell had pointed out. Here they secured the sails, switched to engine power, and spent another nerve-racking forty minutes picking their way through the reefs until they reached the south side of Little Sukuti Island. Sam tooled along the coast until Remi spotted a mangrove-choked cove they hoped would shield the dhow from prying eyes. Following Remi's hand signals from the bow, Sam steered into the cove. He shut off the engine and let the dhow drift forward until the bow gently wedged itself between two mangroves jutting diagonally from the bank.

Having listened to the steady put-put-put of the dhow's engine for the last hour, the sudden silence was jarring. They stood still for half a minute, listening, until the jungle around them slowly came back to life with a cacophony of squawks and buzzes.

Remi secured the bowline to one of the tree trunks, then headed aft to join Sam on the afterdeck. 'What's the plan?' she asked.

'We're assuming the bell is still aboard the *Njiwa*. That's the best-case scenario. With any luck, we won't have to set foot on the island itself. Either way, we have to wait for nightfall. For now, I say we do a little reconnaissance and have a little picnic.'

'Reconnaissance and a picnic,' Remi repeated with a smile. 'Every woman's dream date.'

Unlike its larger alter ego, Little Sukuti Island was all mangrove swamp and jungle, save a lone jagged peak that, on the vertical, was no more than five hundred feet above the ocean's surface, but, as Sam and Remi had learned many times, a five-hundred-foot ascent on rough winding trails could turn into a three- or four-hour hike.

By ten A.M., already sweating profusely and covered in bug bites and mud, they emerged from the swamp and pushed their way into the jungle. With Sam in the lead, they pushed north until they came across what they were looking for: a stream. Water meant animals and animals meant game trails. It took them only a few minutes to find one heading northwest toward the island's summit. Shortly before one in the afternoon, they broke free of the jungle and found themselves at the foot of the escarpment.

'That's a relief,' Remi said, staring upward.

The rock face was manageable, fifty feet tall, no steeper than fifty degrees, and with plenty of crags and cracks they could use for foot- and handholds. After a short water break, they headed upward and were soon nestled in a little rock alcove beneath the peak. They each pulled a pair of binoculars from their packs, rose up, and looked around.

'Thar she blows,' Sam muttered.

A mile away and a hundred feet below them was Oka-for's home. Painted a butter yellow with stark white trim, it sat in a near-perfect circular clearing of reddish brown dirt. At this distance they could make out details they'd missed from the air. As Sam had predicted, a trio of men in green coveralls were working along the eastern side of the grounds, two hacking at the encroaching foliage with machetes, the third mowing a strip of lawn. The villa itself was massive, easily fifteen thousand square feet, with wraparound balconies on each floor. At the rear of the property was what looked like a radio antenna/satellite TV tower.

'Do you see that?' Remi asked.

'What?'

'On the roof, eastern corner.'

Sam pointed his binoculars where Remi had indicated and saw a pair of Big Eyes naval binoculars mounted on a tripod.

'Well,' Sam said, 'the bad news is to the southwest they can see anything coming ten miles away. You see the coaxial cable attached to the housing?'

'I see it.'

'It's for remote control and monitoring, I'm guessing. Probably from a control room in the house. The good news is, I don't think they're night-vision capable.'

They continued panning their binoculars, moving down the slope to the helicopter pad. At the edge of the white stone perimeter a lone man in khaki coveralls sat in a lawn chair; leaning against his left thigh was an AK-74 assault rifle.

'He's asleep,' Remi said.

'That, and the missing helicopter tell us the boss is away.' Sam panned his binoculars again. After a moment he said, 'I've got movement on the *Njiwa*.'

'I see it,' Remi replied. 'There's a familiar face.'

There was no mistaking Itzli Rivera's gaunt, ropy frame and sunken face. He stood on the yacht's foredeck, a satellite phone to his ear. After a minute of listening he nodded, checked his watch, said something into the handset, and disconnected. He turned aft, cupped his hands to his mouth, and shouted something. Ten seconds later Nochtli and Yaotl came jogging through the arch on the port-side weather deck and stopped before Rivera, who spoke to them for a few minutes before they rushed off again.

'Looked like Rivera was passing on some orders from on high. Let's hope it's about the bell.'

'Our bell,' Remi corrected him with a smile.

'I like the way you think. Let's do a guard count.'

They spent the next fifteen minutes doing just this and came up with four: one at the helicopter pad, one patrolling the road to the dock, and two strolling around the villa's perimeter. Unless they missed someone, it appeared no guards were watching the island's approaches.

'We can't forget Rivera and the other two stooges,' Sam said. 'They're probably staying aboard the boat. If so, we might have to find a way to get them off.'

'That won't be easy. Based on how much trouble they've gone to get the bell, they're probably sleeping beside it.'

They spent the remainder of the afternoon drawing a detailed map of the island and enjoying their ersatz picnic of fruit, nuts, and bottled water. Shortly after five, they heard a faint chopping sound to the east. They focused their binoculars, and soon enough the sound took the shape of a helicopter. Ambonisye Okafor's

Eurocopter EC135, jet-black with tinted windows, swept over the island and did a slow circuit, as though the man aboard were surveying his kingdom, before stopping in a hover over the pad and touching down. The guard on duty was already standing at attention, spine erect, an AK-74 held at port arms. As the rotors spooled down, the Eurocopter's side door opened and out stepped a tall, lean African man in a crisp white suit and mirrored sunglasses.

'Fun's over,' Sam said. 'Dad's home.'

'Clearly our host went to the Idi Amin school of fashion,' Remi said. 'I'd be willing to bet his closet is packed with clones of that outfit.'

Sam smiled behind his binoculars. 'Then again, who's going to risk telling him he's a cliché?'

Okafor strode across the pad and snapped off a salute to the guard. As he reached the path, an electric golf cart pulled to a stop before him. He climbed in, and the cart headed up the hill toward the villa.

Sam said, 'Now we'll see if Okafor's return stirs up any action.'

After another ten minutes the cart returned down the hill, turned onto the dock road, and stopped beside the *Njiwa*. Rivera strode down the gangplank and got into the passenger seat, and the cart returned to the villa, where Rivera disappeared inside. He emerged twenty minutes later, and the golf cart returned him to the *Njiwa*. Sam and Remi kept their focus on the yacht. Five minutes passed, then ten, then twenty. There was no movement on the decks; no reaction to Rivera's meeting with Okafor.

'That was underwhelming,' Remi said, looking sideways at Sam. 'I can see the gears turning in your head. You have a plan of attack?'

Over the years Sam's and Remi's complementary personalities had molded the planning of the dicier parts of their adventures: Sam would develop the plan, and Remi would play devil's advocate, running the plan through her steel-trap mind, until they decided it workable and would minimize the likelihood that they'd find themselves in over their heads. So far, the system had worked well, though the water frequently reached their chins.

'Almost,' Sam said. He lowered his binoculars and checked his watch. 'We better start back down. It'll be nightfall in four hours.'

The return leg of the hike was easier going, partially because they weren't fighting gravity and partially because they'd already blazed the trail. Back at sea level, they circumnavigated the mangrove swamp to the south, turned north again at the beach, then swam the last quarter mile. They were nearing the mouth of the cove when Remi stopped swimming and said, 'Quiet. Listen.'

Sam heard it a few moments later, the faint rumble of a marine engine somewhere to their right. They turned to see a Rinker speedboat coming around the headland a hundred yards away. One man was behind the wheel; a second stood behind him, scanning the shoreline through a pair of binoculars.

'Deep breath!' Sam said to Remi.

Together they gulped a lungful of air, then curled under the water and dove. Six feet beneath the surface they leveled off and began stroking toward the cove. Arm outstretched, Sam reached the bank a few seconds before Remi. He curled his fingers around the roots jutting from the mud, then turned, grabbed Remi's hand, and pulled her in. Sam pointed above their heads where a tangle of dead brush floated on the surface. Together they let themselves float up. They broke into the air and looked around.

'You hear the engine?' Sam whispered in Remi's ear.

'No . . . Wait, there they are.'

Sam looked in the direction of Remi's nod. Through the twigs he could see the Rinker sitting still in the water about fifty feet away. The engine coughed once, sputtered, then went dead. The driver tried again but got the same result. He pounded his fist on the wheel. His partner stepped to the stern, knelt down, and lifted the engine hatch.

'Engine trouble,' Sam whispered. 'They'll move on soon.'

It was either that, they both knew, or these two would have to call for a tow, which meant Sam and Remi wouldn't be going anywhere for a while.

'Cross fingers,' Remi replied.

Aboard the Rinker, the second man turned and said something to the driver, who tried the engine again. It coughed and died.

'Spark plug,' Sam muttered. In the corner of his eye he saw Remi's head move, slowly leaning backward until her face was pointing upward. Sam slowly turned his head, looked at her, and followed her gaze. He found himself staring into a pair of beady brown eyes. Not six inches away, the eyes blinked once, then narrowed slightly. It took a moment for Sam to realize what he was seeing.

'Monkey,' he whispered to Remi.

'Yes, Sam, I noticed.'

'Capuchin?'

'Colobus, I think. Juvenile.'

From the direction of the Rinker they heard the engine turn over again. This time it caught, sputtered, then settled into a steady idle. Above them, the colobus jerked its head up at the noise, its tiny hands clamping down on the branches. It looked back down at Sam and Remi.

Remi cooed, 'Easy, little – '

The colobus opened its mouth and began shrieking and shaking the branches so wildly that leaves rained down on them.

Sam lowered his head and peered through the brush pile. Aboard the Rinker, both men were standing up, rifles at the shoulder, muzzles aimed in their direction. Suddenly a crack. One of the muzzles flashed. The bullet zipped through the foliage above their heads. The colobus shrieked louder and flailed at the branches. Sam groped underwater, found Remi's hand, squeezed it.

She whispered, 'Are they – '

'I don't think so. They're looking for lunch.'

Crack! More shrieking and shaking.

Silence.

Sam could hear the colobus's hands and feet pattering away.

'They're turning our way,' Sam whispered. 'Get ready for a deep breath.'

Through the brush they watched as the Rinker's bow came around until it was pointed directly at them. It began gliding forward, slowly closing the gap. The second man was now standing beside the driver, rifle braced on the windshield's frame.

'Wait,' Sam rasped. 'Wait . . .' When the Rinker was fifteen feet away he said, 'Deep breath . . . under.'

They submerged together, each one clawing for handholds as they dragged themselves back first down the bank. When their feet sunk into the mud, they craned their necks back. On the surface, the Rinker's bow was shoving its way into the brush pile. Sam and Remi heard muffled voices, then the cracking of branches. Leaves fluttered down and dotted the surface.

Finally, after nearly a minute, the Rinker's propeller reversed and began churning. The boat began backing out. Sam and Remi waited until the bow swung around and the Rinker began moving away before resurfacing. They caught their breath and watched as the boat disappeared around the bend.

'They didn't get him, did they?' Remi asked.

Sam turned and smiled at her. 'That's my girl. Animal lover until the end. No, he got away. Come on, let's get out of here.'

Chapter 17

Sukuti Island

'There!' Remi called from the bow. 'All stop! Back slow.'

With his view blocked by the mast, Sam throttled to neutral, let the dhow drift a bit, then reversed and eased backward around the knob of shoreline they'd been following.

'That's good,' she called. 'They're about a mile ahead of us. Another ten minutes and they'll make the turn north.'

Forty minutes earlier, after beaching their dhow in the cove, they'd wasted no time in getting under way. Sam and Remi hoped the Rinker was on a route that would take it along Sukuti's southern coast and back to Okafor's docks, as their planned approach would take them around the northern side of the island. They were anxious to reach the relative safety of the inlet that separated Little Sukuti from Big Sukuti – providing that, too, wasn't on the Rinker's route.

While a straight shot along the southern coast would have been the quickest route to the docks, it would also have left them exposed to any observant eyes and ears. By following the inlet north and shadowing the coast around to the western side, they would be invisible to anyone not standing atop the escarpment.

They sat in silence, watching the sun on its slow downward arc to the horizon, until finally Remi checked her watch and said, 'Slow ahead.'

Sam started the engines and goosed the dhow's throttle, easing them from behind cover. On the bow, Remi lay on her belly with the binoculars trained along the coast.

'They're gone,' she said. 'We're clear.'

Sam shoved the throttle forward, and the dhow surged ahead. Another ten minutes passed. Remi called out: 'There it is.'

Sam leaned sideways over the rail until he could see, a couple hundred yards away, the mouth of the inlet. No more than fifty feet wide, the channel looked as much like a tunnel as it did an inlet, its banks overgrown with jungle and trees arcing over the water to form an impenetrable canopy, save a patch of ten-foot-wide sky down the center.

Sam eased the dhow's wheel to starboard. The bow came about.

Remi walked aft, ducked under the boom, and dropped to the deck beside Sam. 'Jungle Cruise,' she said.

'Pardon?'

'The inlet. Remember the Disney World Jungle Cruise? That's what this reminds me of.'

Sam chuckled. 'My favorite ride as a kid.'

'Sam, it's still your favorite ride.'

'True.'

Within minutes they'd closed to within a hundred yards of the inlet's mouth. They felt the dhow shudder beneath their feet, and it leapt ahead, picking up five knots in as many seconds.

'Good call,' Remi said to her husband.

Having already experienced the power of the current off Zanzibar, Sam had earlier worried about similar conditions here. Positioned as it was along the coast, with the tide surging from the south, the mouth of the inlet was a hydraulic vacuum, sucking ocean in from the south and spitting it out to the north.

Sam switched off the engine to save gas and gripped the wheel tighter. He said, 'The good news is, we probably don't have to worry about running aground. This current's digging a pretty deep trench in there.'

The dhow bucked to the side and the stern slipped sideways. Sam corrected first to starboard, then to port, and the bow realigned on the mouth of the inlet. With both hands clamped on the rail, Remi was leaning over the side, a smile on her face, auburn hair streaming behind her.

'How fast are we going?' she called.

'Ten, twelve knots,' Sam replied, laughing. This close to the water's surface it felt much faster. 'Better make your way forward. I'm going to need your eyes.'

'Aye, captain.' She made her way to the bow. 'Fifty yards to go,' she called. 'Steady on.'

To starboard Sam watched a four-foot wave crash over an exposed sandbar. 'Surge coming,' he warned Remi and turned the wheel a few degrees to meet it. The wave hit them on the starboard bow, pushing the dhow sideways. The bow started to swing around off course. Sam muscled the wheel hard to starboard, compensating until the surge passed and the bow found the line again.

'Looking good. Steady on,' Remi called. 'Twenty yards.'

Sam leaned over the starboard rail and looked down. The indigo water was thirty to forty feet deep, but six feet to the right he could see the white sand bottom through the turquoise water. He leaned to port and saw the same.

'We haven't got much room to spare,' Sam called forward. 'How does it look ahead?'

'Narrower still. Want a little drag?'

'Sure.'

Remi shimmied around on her belly, retrieved the Danforth anchor from its mount, tossed it over the bow, and let the line stream between her hands until she felt it skipping along the bottom. She hauled in a few inches of line and secured it to the pulpit rail. The dhow began slowing until they were moving in a jerk-and-surge fashion.

'Ten yards,' Remi called.

And then, as if the sun had suddenly been eclipsed, the dhow slipped inside the inlet. To the left and right, walls of green closed in around them; above, a ragged ribbon of blue sky. Sam looked aft and felt a surge of vertigo as the entrance to the inlet seemed to close like an iris door on a spaceship.

'Turn coming up,' Remi called. 'Forty-five degrees to starboard.'

Sam faced forward again. 'Ready when you are.'

'Three . . . two . . . one . . . Turn!'

Sam gave the wheel a quarter spin to port and held it.

'Starboard turn!' Remi shouted.

Sam spun the wheel again.

'Hold it there,' Remi ordered. A few seconds passed. 'Okay, start easing back to port. Keep going . . . more . . . Good. Steady on.'

As if on cue, the current died away until the dhow was skimming ahead at a walking pace. The inlet widened out slightly, leaving fifteen feet on both beams.

'Haul anchor,' Sam called. 'I think we're okay.'

Remi retrieved the Danforth and returned to the cockpit. From the banks came the sounds of the jungle easing into twilight: the plaintive squawks of parrots, the croaking of frogs, and the buzz of insects.

'It's so peaceful,' Remi said, looking around. 'A little spooky but peaceful.'

Sam grabbed the map from its compartment and unfolded it on the roof of the cabin. Remi clicked on a flashlight. Sam skimmed his index finger around the island. 'We need the circumference.'

Remi retrieved the dividers and walked them around the coastline, occasionally marking headlands and landmarks with a pencil. Once done, she scribbled some calculations in the margins, then said, 'Big Sukuti is nine miles, give or take. Little Sukuti, about five.'

Sam studied his watch for a moment. 'We'll reach the other mouth in twenty minutes. If that Rinker makes another patrol right away, it'll be passing the northern side of this inlet about twenty minutes after that. If it doesn't show up, it probably means no more patrols for the night or they're only doing them every few hours.'

'That's a big if,' Remi replied. 'If the latter, it means we might run into them somewhere along the coastline. We'd better hope we see them before they see us.'

Sam nodded. 'Do me a favor. Find every nook and cranny along the coast. We'll need to be ready to hide on a moment's notice.'

It took Remi ten minutes to finish the task. She said, 'There're plenty to choose from but no depth markings; I can only be certain of six or seven being deep enough for our draft.'

'We'll have to play it by ear.'

'So, about your master plan . . .'

'Wish I had one,' Sam replied. 'There're too many variables. We have to assume they'll be moving the bell sooner rather than later – either shipping it somewhere or dumping it somewhere. For that, they have three choices: one of the Rinkers, the *Njiwa*, or Okafor's helicopter. We'll start with the *Njiwa*. Whatever they do, that's where the bell will stay until they decide to move it. If they use a Rinker or the *Njiwa*, I say we put on our pirate hats and stage a hijacking.'

'And if it's the helicopter?'

'Same plan. We just put on our flying scarves.'

'Sam, my dear, you don't have much time logged on helicopters.'

'I think I can manage the four or five miles to the mainland. We'd be across the channel in six minutes – probably before they could even organize a posse. We find a secluded clearing somewhere, put her down, and – '

Remi smiled. 'Play it by ear?' Sam shrugged and smiled back. 'It's the best chance we have,' Remi agreed, 'but you've left out a lot of big, potentially disastrous ifs.'

'I know – '

'For example, what if we're spotted? We'll be outgunned and outmanned.'

'I know – '

'And, of course, the biggest if: What if the bell's already been moved?'

Sam paused. 'Then the game's over. If we don't intercept it here, it's gone for good. Remi, we're a democracy. If it's not unanimous, we don't go.'

'I'm in, Sam, you know that. On one condition, though.'

'Name it.'

'We take out some insurance.'

The sun was setting by the time the mouth of the inlet came into view: a rough oval of golden orange light at the end of the tunnel. When they were ten feet away, Remi steered the dhow toward the right-hand bank and jostled the throttle until the overhanging limbs draped over them. Standing atop the cabin, Sam manhandled the thicker branches around the mast and boom until the dhow was nestled against the bank. He crawled forward to the pulpit and peeked through the foliage.

'Got a perfect view,' he called back.

The sun had dropped behind Big Sukuti, casting the western half of the island, including the inlet, in twilight. Sam added, 'If they're doing another circuit, they'll be here in fifteen or twenty minutes.'

'I'm going to pack our gear and do some scrounging.'

Remi went below. Sam could hear her moving about in the cabin. She returned to the cockpit, sat down, and began humming 'Summer Wind' by Frank Sinatra. They got through 'Hotel California' by the Eagles, 'In the Midnight Hour' by Wilson Pickett, and were halfway through 'Hey Jude' by the Beatles when Sam raised his hand for silence.

Ten seconds passed.

'What is it?' Remi asked.

'Nothing, I guess. No, there . . . Hear it?'

Remi listened for a few moments, then there it was, the faint rumble of a marine engine. 'The pitch sounds right,' she said.

'It's coming from the northwest. Our guest may be en route.'

Of the scenarios they'd considered – a delayed second patrol, meeting the Rinker along the northern coast, or an immediate patrol that would pass before they headed out from the inlet – the third was ideal. By knowing the Rinker's route and its average speed, they could be reasonably sure of their foe's location at any given time. Barring the unforeseen, they would reach the docks long before the Rinker did.

Lying on his belly, binoculars raised, Sam kept his eyes focused on the headland a quarter mile away. The grumble of the engine grew in intensity until finally the Rinker's bow appeared. As expected, it was occupied by a driver and a spotter; also as expected, the boat turned southeast, following the coastline.

A spotlight glowed to life.

'We're okay,' he said, half to himself, half to Remi. 'They won't see us unless they're on top of us.'

'Odds?'

'Ninety-five percent. Maybe ninety.'

'Sam . . .'

'We're okay. Keep your head down and cross your fingers.'

The Rinker kept coming. It was now a hundred yards from the inlet and heading straight for them, the spotlight skimming along the bank and over the trees.

'Anytime, boys,' Sam muttered. 'Nothing to see here . . . Move along . . .'

The Rinker closed the gap to fifty yards.

Forty yards.

Thirty yards.

Sam took one hand off the binoculars, slowly reached backward, and grabbed the H&K from the thigh pocket of his cargo shorts. He brought the gun up and laid it on the deck beneath his shoulder. He flicked off the safety.

The Rinker was twenty yards away.

Sam whispered, 'Remi, you better get below.'

'Sam –'

'Please, Remi.'

He felt the dhow rock slightly as she crept down the ladder.

Sam lowered the binoculars. He wiped his right palm on his pant leg, then grabbed the H&K, extended it through the branches, and took aim on the shadowed form behind the Rinker's wheel. Sam let the scenario play in his head: driver first, then the spotlight, then the second man before he had a chance to take cover or return fire. Two shots for each, then pause and wait for signs of life.

The Rinker kept coming.

Sam took a deep breath.

Suddenly the Rinker's engine revved up. The bow rose up and pivoted to port, and within five seconds the boat disappeared from view.

Sam exhaled. He knocked twice on the cabin's roof. A few seconds later Remi whispered, 'Clear?'

'Clear. Check the map. How long until they clear the northern tip of Little Sukuti?'

There came the crinkle of paper in the darkness, followed by the scratching of a pencil. Remi said, 'It's a little over a mile. Twenty-five minutes and we should be okay.'

*

For safe measure, they let thirty minutes pass before shoving off and motoring out of the inlet. For the next forty minutes they glided along the northern shoreline, never straying more than fifty feet from the beach and never exceeding a quiet but frustrating three miles per hour.

Leaning over the map on the deck, penlight clamped between her teeth, Remi was walking the dividers. She looked up, took the penlight out of her mouth. 'The Rinker should be reaching the southern tip of Little Sukuti. We've got at least twenty minutes on them.'

They reached Big Sukuti's northern tip, paused there for a binocular scan of the coastline ahead, then set out again.

'The docks are less than a mile away,' Remi told Sam.

'What do you think? Stop at half a mile?'

'Sounds good.'

They covered the distance in twelve minutes. To port, the island's sloped moonscape rose from the beach to meet the rain forest. Sam slowed the dhow as Remi scanned the shoreline.

'This looks good here,' she said, then scrambled to the bow.

Sam turned to port, aimed the bow at the beach, and followed Remi's curt directions until she called, 'All stop.'

Sam throttled down, then collected their packs from the deck and met Remi at the pulpit. She lowered herself over the side, then Sam grabbed her wrists and lowered her the rest of the way. The water was waist-high. He handed down their packs.

'Come here,' Remi said.

'What?'

'Come here, I said.'

He smiled, then leaned his head over the side until she could crane her neck and kiss him on the cheek. She said, 'Be safe. No drowning allowed.'

'Noted. I'll see you in a few minutes.'

The next part of their plan turned out to be anticlimactic. Sam reversed the engines, brought the bow around, and took the dhow a few hundred yards off the coast, then turned off the engine and dropped anchor. He estimated there was fifty feet of water beneath the keel. He went below and opened each of the dhow's five scuttle valves. When the water reached his calves, he went topside and dove over the side and began swimming. Five minutes later he stood up in the shallows and waded ashore to where Remi was waiting.

Together they watched the dhow settle into the water and sink from view.

Sam gave it a salute, then said, 'Ready?'

Remi nodded. 'Lead on.'

Chapter 18

Big Sukuti Island

With Sam in the lead they walked in silence for fifteen minutes, keeping to the harder wet sand until they came upon a twenty-foot-high rock outcropping bisecting the beach. Sam scaled up the slippery rocks, found a flat spot below the ridge, and peeked over. After a few seconds he turned and motioned for Remi to join him.

Together they poked their heads above the rocks. A few hundred yards down the beach they could see the dock jutting into the water. On one side the *Njiwa* was still moored, her interior cabin lights glowing yellow through sheer curtains; opposite her, both Rinkers were tied up as well. There was no sign of either the driver or passenger.

'They must have cut a few corners to get back so quickly,' Remi said.

'They probably move at a pretty good clip along the southern side. With the Big Eyes we saw on the roof earlier, nobody's going to be sneaking up from that direction.'

'And at least we know where everyone is,' Remi added. 'I don't see any activity. You?'

'Nothing. We've got two choices, by land or by water.'

'There's too much loose rock on the slope and no cover,' Remi said.

'Agreed. Water it is.'

'How're we getting aboard the *Njiwa*?'

Sam zoomed his binoculars until he could see the yacht's companion ladder. While it was less than five feet tall, its head was attached to the deck right in front of the cabin's sliding door.

'Not by the ladder,' Sam said. He thought for a moment. 'Back on the dhow I saw a sea anchor in the cabin – '

Remi reached over her shoulder and patted the backpack. 'In here. Improvised grappling hook?'

'You read my mind. We hook the stern rail and shimmy up.'

They climbed back down to the sand, then waded into the surf and set off, perpendicular to the beach, in a quiet, energy-efficient breaststroke. Once they'd covered fifty yards, they turned south, parallel to the beach, until they drew even with the dock. They stopped and treaded water.

'Movement?' Sam asked.

'I don't see any.'

'Head for the Rinker.'

They set out again, arms sweeping them forward, their eyes scanning the dock area for movement. Soon they reached the Rinker's transom. They took a moment to catch their breath, listening and looking. From the *Njiwa*'s cabin they heard muffled voices, then a pounding sound. Silence. More pounding.

'Someone's hammering,' Sam whispered. 'Touch that engine.'

Remi touched the Rinker's outboard with the back of her hand. 'Cold. Why?'

'This one will have more gas. Wait here. Time for our insurance policy.'

He took a breath, ducked under, and swam alongside the first Rinker to its twin at the head of the dock. He grabbed the gunwale, chinned himself up, and looked around. No movement. He boosted himself over the side onto the deck, then crawled forward to the driver's seat. He checked the ignition. Not surprisingly, the keys were missing. He rolled onto his back, opened the maintenance hatch beneath the dashboard, and wiggled inside. He clicked on his penlight and studied the wiring bundle.

'Just like old times,' Sam muttered. Five months earlier he'd found himself doing the same thing with another speedboat on a lake in the Bavarian Alps. Luckily, like that boat's, this Rinker's wiring was simple: ignition, wipers, navigation lights, and horn. Using his Swiss Army knife, Sam severed each wire, taking as much length as he could. He rolled them into a tight ball and tossed it over the side, then wriggled back out and closed the hatch. He crawled back to the gunwale, did a quick check, then rolled back into the water and returned to Remi.

'Okay, if all goes well, this'll be our getaway boat. We grab the bell, disable the *Njiwa* if we can, then bring the bell back here – '

'How?'

'I'll manage it somehow. We'll worry about the hernia later. We bring the bell back here and slip away before anyone knows what's happened.'

'And if all goes unwell? Never mind; I already know. We play it by ear.'

They stroked around the dock to the *Njiwa*'s stern and

immediately realized the yacht was bigger up close. The stern rail was ten feet above the waterline. Remi fished the dhow's sea anchor from her backpack. Sam examined it.

'Too short,' he whispered into her ear, then gestured for her to follow. They stroked back to the Rinker's transom. 'Time for Plan B,' Sam said. 'I'll try the ladder.' Remi opened her mouth to speak, but he pushed on. 'It's the only way. If I jump from the dock, it'll make too much noise. Get into the Rinker and be ready to take off.'

'No.'

'If I get caught, run.'

'I said – '

'You run and get back to civilization and call Rube. He'll know what to do. With you missing, Rivera will assume you've contacted the authorities. He won't kill me – not right away. He's too smart for that; dead bodies are more trouble than they're worth.'

Remi frowned and gave him a withering stare. 'Let's call all that Plan C. Plan B is you don't get caught. We're up to our chins, Sam.'

'I know. Keep a sharp eye out. I'll signal you when it's clear. If I raise my hand and spread my fingers, it's safe to come; a raised fist, stay where you are.'

He took off his shirt and shoes, stuffed both in his backpack, and handed the pack to Remi.

'What're you doing?' she asked.

'Clothing drips and shoes squeak.'

'Sam, have you been taking commando classes on the side?'

'Just watching the Military Channel.'

He kissed her, then ducked beneath the surface, stroked

163

under the Rinker, and resurfaced under the dock. Another breath and another duck brought him alongside the *Nji-wa*'s white hull. He stroked forward beneath the companion ladder, then paused. He could hear muffled voices coming from the cabin. Two men, perhaps three. He strained to catch any words or isolate the voices but failed. He boosted himself onto the dock, laid flat, waited and listened, then got up and crept up the ladder. Below the top rung he paused, poked his head up, saw nothing, and crawled onto the deck. He stood up and pressed himself against the bulkhead.

The sliding door opened. A rectangle of yellow light angled onto the deck. Heart in his throat, Sam did a rapid sidestep along the bulkhead and around the corner to the forecastle, where he froze and took a few calming breaths.

He heard the clump of footsteps on the deck. The door slid shut again, followed by footsteps clanging down the companion ladder. Sam stepped forward, peeked aft and saw nothing, so he took another step and peeked over the rail. A figure was walking down the dock. At the end of a dock, in a small clearing, sat a green gas-powered Cushman flatbed cart and, directly behind it, a white golf cart. Ahead of them, the trail curved up and away toward the helicopter pad and the main house.

The figure leaned over the Cushman, removed a rake and a pair of shovels, and tossed them into the brush beside the path.

'Making room for cargo,' Sam muttered to himself.

He turned toward the Rinker, raised a 'Stay put' fist for a few seconds, then ducked down and waddled back to the bulkhead.

Footfalls clicked on the wooden dock, then back up the ladder, followed by the sliding door opening and closing. Three minutes passed. The door slid open again. More clomping now. Multiple feet. Grunting. Something heavy sliding across the deck . . . Sam peeked around the corner and saw three men in the light from the cabin door: Rivera, Nochtli, and Yaotl. Between them sat a crate roughly the size of the dummy crate Sam had created on Zanzibar.

Yaotl, the biggest of the three, backed down the ladder in front of the crate while Rivera and Nochtli shoved it forward. Sam drew back into the shadows and listened as they manhandled the crate down the ladder to the dock. Sam crab-walked to the rail and peeked over.

Nochtli and Yaotl were moving down the dock, each gripping one of the crate's rope handles. Rivera walked a few paces behind. The trio reached the clearing. The crate was placed onto the Cushman's flatbed.

Rivera began speaking in Spanish. Sam caught only snippets: '. . . take it . . . helicopter . . . there shortly.'

The Cushman's engine started. Tires crunched on the shell path. After a few seconds the engine faded and died away. Sam risked a peek over the railing. Rivera was striding down the dock toward the ladder. Sam backed away and took cover against the bulkhead. Rivera climbed the ladder and went into the cabin.

Sam considered his options. He had little desire to tangle with Rivera, a trained and accomplished killer, but as soon as the man reached the helicopter it would lift off with the bell aboard. More important, whatever he and Remi did next would be easier with Rivera out of the equation. The H&K was out of the question, Sam knew, because the noise could attract the attention of the other guards. He'd have to do it the hard way.

He took a deep breath and crept aft along the bulkhead to the sliding door. He took a few moments to mentally rehearse his actions, then reached out, pressed his thumb against the door's handle, and shoved. With a hiss, the door slid open.

From inside, Rivera's voice: 'Nochtli? Yaotl?'

Sam took a half step backward, balled up his right fist, and cocked it over his shoulder.

A shadow blocked out the cabin's light.

Rivera's nose appeared from behind the doorjamb, followed by his chin and eyes. Sam lashed out with a straight punch, aiming for Rivera's temple, but the man's reflexes kicked in, and he twisted his head sideways. Sam's fist glanced off Rivera's temple. Wary of him recovering and grabbing whatever weapon he was sure to be carrying, Sam pivoted through the door. Out of the corner of his eye, Sam saw Rivera to the right. As predicted, Rivera was reaching for something behind his back.

Years of judo training took over. Instinctively, Sam assessed Rivera's posture and stance and saw the weak point: Still slightly stunned, Rivera was leaning against the bulkhead, trying to regroup, all his weight concentrated on his left foot. Sam ignored Rivera's weapon hand and instead lashed out with a Deashi-Harai – a Forward Foot Sweep – that caught him just below the left ankle. Rivera collapsed sideways and slid down the bulkhead, but still his weapon hand was coming around. Sam saw the gun in it, reached up, grabbed the wrist, and used the arm's momentum to slam Rivera's hand against the wall. Sam heard the crack of bone. The gun fell away and bounced across the carpeted deck.

Hand still clamped on Rivera's wrist, Sam took a big step backward, dropped his center of gravity and twisted his hips, whipping Rivera's body flat across the floor. Sam released the wrist and dropped onto Rivera's back. He snaked his right arm around the throat, going for a rear naked choke. Rivera reacted immediately, lashing backward with an elbow punch that caught Sam below the eye. His eyesight sparkled and dimmed. He turned his face away, felt another elbow crash into the back of his head. Sam breathed through it and curled his forearm, sliding farther across Rivera's throat. Using his legs as counterweights, Sam rolled left, taking Rivera with him. Then Rivera made his mistake: He panicked. He stopped throwing elbows and started clawing at the forearm around his neck. Sam extended the choke, clamped his right hand onto his left bicep, then squeezed while pressing his head forward, forcing Rivera's chin toward his chest and compressing his carotid arteries. Almost immediately Rivera's flailing weakened. Another second, and he went limp. Sam held on for three more beats, then let go and shoved Rivera aside. Sam got to his knees and checked the man's pulse and breathing: alive but in a deep sleep.

Sam took ten seconds to catch his breath, then climbed to his feet. He reached up and touched his cheekbone; his fingers came back bloody. He shuffled out the door, looked around to make sure all was clear, then held up five fingers. He returned inside.

Remi stepped through the door sixty seconds later. She

167

glanced at Rivera's motionless body, then to Sam, then dropped their backpacks. She strode to Sam and they embraced. She pulled away. She used her index finger to tilt his face sideways. She frowned.

'It looks worse than it is,' Sam said.

'How do you know what it looks like? You're going to need stitches.'

'My pageant days are over.'

Remi nodded to Rivera. 'Is he . . .'

'Just sleeping. He's going to be one angry man when he wakes up.'

'Then let's not be here. I assume we're going with the helicopter hijacking?'

'They were kind enough to load the bell aboard. It'd be rude to let that effort go to waste. The Rinker . . . Did you . . .'

'Jerked out the wires and tossed them overboard. What now? Tie him up?'

'No time. We've got surprise on our side. If anyone comes back looking for him, that's gone.' Sam looked around. He walked forward and opened a door, revealing a ladder leading upward. 'That'll be the bridge. Go up and do some damage to their communications.'

Remi said, 'Ship-to-shore phone and radio, right?'

Sam nodded. 'I'll go below and see if there're any bazookas lying around.'

'Pardon?'

'We're going to have company at the helicopter pad, and I doubt they'll be happy to see us. Something big and loud and scary might change their minds.'

Sam knelt down, retrieved Rivera's gun – another H&K

semiautomatic – and handed it to Remi. She examined it for a few moments, then deftly ejected the magazine, checked the ammunition, slid the magazine back into place, flipped on the safety, and shoved the H&K into her waistband.

Sam stared at her.

She said, 'Home and Garden Television.'

'Okay, then. We'll meet back here in two minutes.'

Remi headed up the ladder, and Sam went belowdecks. He ransacked each of the six sleeping quarters and found only one weapon, a .357 Magnum revolver. He went back up the ladder. Remi was waiting.

'How'd you do?' he asked.

'I ripped both handsets out of their sockets and tossed them overboard.'

'That'll work. Okay. Everyone's waiting for Rivera at the pad. With luck, it'll be Yaotl, Nochtli, the guard, and the pilot. Four people at most. We drive up and hope they don't get suspicious until it's too late.'

'And if there's a big party waiting for us?'

'We retreat.'

Chapter 19

Big Sukuti Island

'Okay, sit tight,' Sam said to Remi.

He brought the cart to a halt and set the parking brake. Ahead he could see the crest of the path. He walked forward until he could see over the rise. A hundred feet down the path was a clearing where the road forked up to the main house. To the right of the clearing, sitting under the glow of a pole-mounted sodium-vapor lamp, was the helicopter pad.

Sam walked back to the cart. Remi asked, 'How many?'

'I only saw three: the guard, Nochtli, and Yaotl, all standing together at the edge of the pad. They've all got AK-74s, but they're slung over their shoulders. As for the pilot, no sign. He's either at the house or sitting in the helicopter waiting.'

'No offense, Sam, but I hope it's the latter. If we convince him to fly us –'

'No offense taken.'

'What about the bell?'

'It's not on the Cushman. Looks like they've done the heavy lifting. I'll take the first three; you head straight for the helicopter. You ready?'

'As I'll ever be.' She crouched on the golf cart's floor and ducked her head beneath the fiberglass dashboard. She looked up at him. 'You don't look much like Rivera.'

'As long as we get close enough fast enough, it won't matter.'

Sam withdrew the .357 and the H&K from his pockets, tucked one each beneath a thigh, then released the parking brake and depressed the gas pedal. The cart eased forward, and within seconds they were over the crest and heading for the clearing. He resisted the impulse to jam the accelerator to the floorboards.

'Fifty feet to go,' he muttered to Remi. 'Still haven't seen us.'

At thirty feet, Yaotl looked up and spotted the cart. He said something to the other two. They turned around. All eyes were on the cart now.

'Still no reaction,' Sam said. 'Hold on tight. I'm going in.'

He stomped on the gas pedal, and the cart accelerated, covering the final twenty feet in a matter of seconds. Sam slammed on the brake, locking the parking mechanism, took his hands off the wheel, grabbed both guns, and jumped out before the trio, just outside the glow of the pole light. He raised both guns.

'Evening, gentlemen,' he said.

'It's you . . .' said Yaotl.

'Us,' Sam corrected.

Without a word, Remi climbed from the cart and joined Sam, who told the group, 'Everyone act natural. Nothing's changed. Just three guys hanging around. Big smiles, everyone.'

He and Remi had decided it was best to assume the pad was under observation from the Big Eyes binoculars on the main house's roof. To avoid arousing suspicion, Yaotl and the other two would have to keep their weapons until Sam and Remi were ready to leave.

'Remi, see what you can do about that light.'

Careful to stay at the edge of its glow, Remi stepped forward and studied the pole. 'No switch, but the cables are coming up from the ground. It looks like standard one-ten voltage.'

Sam said, 'Nice of Okafor to cut corners for us.' While two-twenty-volt lines carried enough juice to electrocute, one-ten lines carried only enough to cause a painful jolt. 'Do you think you can make it to the helo without being seen?'

'I think so. Be right back.'

She walked back down the road and ducked into some bushes alongside the helicopter pad. Thirty seconds later she appeared on the opposite side and, using the helicopter to screen her movements, sprinted to the pilot's door. With the pilot under her H&K, she retraced her course and returned to where Sam stood. The pilot was a short black man in dark blue coveralls. His expression was one of genuine fear.

Remi said, 'The crate's aboard, all strapped down.'

Yaotl asked Sam, 'Where's Rivera?'

'Napping.'

The guard moved his hand, trying surreptitiously to unsling his AK-74. Sam raised the gun and pointed it at his head. 'Don't,' Sam said, then added in Swahili: *'Usifanye hivyo!'* The guard stopped, let his hand drop.

'Remi, do you have them?'

'I have them.'

Sam stepped backward and motioned for the pilot to join him. 'What's your name?'

'Jingaro.'

'You're Okafor's pilot.'

'Yes.'

'Your English is good.'

'I went to missionary school.'

'I want you to fly the helicopter for us.'

'I cannot do that.'

'Yes, you can.'

'If I do, Okafor will kill me.'

'If you don't, I'll kill you.'

'Not in the same way he will. And perhaps my family, too. Please, I just fly for him, that's all. I'm not part of this. You see I don't have a gun. I just fly the helicopter.'

'Are you lying about your family?'

'No, it is the truth. I'm sorry I cannot help you. I do not like Mr. Okafor, but I have no choice.'

Sam studied Jingaro's eyes and decided he was telling the truth. 'Is the helicopter ready to fly?'

'Yes. Are you a pilot?'

Sam shrugged. 'On rotary, I'm not much past takeoff, hover, and touchdown.'

Jingaro hesitated, then said, 'This one is equipped with a hover coupler. On the far right side of the dash. It is labeled "H-V-C-P." As long as your flight level is steady, you can engage the coupler, and the craft will go into auto hover. Also, the rudder pedals are heavy. I like them that way. It is harder to overcompensate. Do not be afraid to step on them. Keep your airspeed below one hundred knots. She's much easier to handle.'

'Thanks.'

'You are welcome. Now hit me.'

'What?'

'Hit me. If Okafor suspects I – '

'I understand. Good luck.'

'And you.'

Sam cocked his hand back and slammed his palm on the tip of the pilot's nose. The blow wasn't enough to break bone, but blood began gushing immediately. The pilot stumbled backward and sprawled onto his back.

'Stay there,' Sam barked. 'Don't move. Remi, can you see the Big Eyes from there?'

She reached her hand behind her, withdrew the binoculars from her pack's side pocket, and aimed them at the house's roof. 'I see them. They're pointing to the south right now. Panning slowly this way. Another thirty seconds or so and they'll have the pad in sight.'

Sam looked at the guard. *'Unazungumza kiingereza?'* he said in Swahili. Do you speak English?

'Bit English.'

Sam pointed at the sheathed machete strapped to his belt and said, *'Kisu. Bwaga Ku.'* Knife. Throw it down. Sam pointed at his feet and barked, 'Now.'

The guard unclipped the machete and tossed it toward Sam, who picked it up. To the group he said, 'Here's the plan, everybody. We're going to walk to the helicopter. We'll go first, and you'll follow feet behind us, spread out in a line – '

'Why?' asked Yaotl.

'You'll be the sandbags if anyone starts shooting at us. Yaotl, make sure the other two understand.'

'You won't get away with – '

'Maybe not, but we're going to give it the old college try.'

'If we say no?' This came from Nochtli.

'Since you brought it up, you'll be the first one I shoot.'

Yaotl said, 'I do not think you will. Even if you do, the rest of Okafor's guards will be here in under a minute.'

'Probably so, but you won't be around to see it.' Sam took a step forward and leveled the .357 on Yaotl's chest. 'Remember your stay at our villa?'

'Yes.'

'We treated you decently.'

'Yes.'

'Well, we're all out of nice.' To punctuate his point, Sam raised the .357 so it was level with Yaotl's forehead. 'Care for some proof?'

Yaotl shook his head.

'Make sure the others understand the plan.'

Yaotl translated first to Nochtli, then to the guard in pidgin Swahili. Both men nodded. Yaotl said, 'Where will you go, Mr. Fargo? If you knew how to fly you wouldn't have been talking to the pilot. If you stop now and surrender – '

Sam interrupted. 'We've had enough of Nightmare Island. We're leaving, and we're taking our bell with us.'

'The bell . . . Is it so important you are willing to die for it?'

Remi spoke up. 'Is it so important that you murdered nine tourists for it? Sam, he's stalling us.'

Sam nodded. 'Keep an eye on them. I'm going to see about making those carts disappear. Yaotl, take the laces out of your boots and give them to me.'

Yaotl bent over, removed the laces, balled them up, and tossed them forward. Sam retrieved them and walked to the golf cart. Thirty seconds later, the steering wheel was locked down by one of the laces. Sam released the parking brake, braced his arms on the front bumper, and pushed the cart over the crest of the hill, where it started rolling on its own. After a few seconds it disappeared into the darkness. He then repeated the process with the Cushman, and returned to Remi's side.

'Ready?' he asked.

'A relative term, that.'

'I don't know how quickly we'll get a reaction once the light goes out, so let's be quick.'

Sam watched the Big Eyes on the roof until they moved toward the light pole. Remi stopped him. 'Hold on, Sam.' Then to Yaotl and the others: 'Turn around and face the helicopter.' The group complied. 'Now look up and stare at the light.' Again the group complied. She said to Sam, 'To ruin their night vision.'

Sam smiled. 'Yet another reason why I love you.'

Through his binoculars he watched the Big Eyes on the roof until they were pointed to the southwest, then strode forward, knelt beside the light pole, took a breath, and slammed the edge of the machete into the power line. There was a hissing pop and a shower of sparks. Sam jerked his hand back. The light went dark.

Remi asked, 'Are you all right?'

'Yes, but it got my attention. Okay, let's go.'

They separated, walking clockwise and counterclockwise until they were facing the group. 'Walk toward us,' Sam ordered.

Blinking and shaking their heads against the sudden loss of their night vision, Yaotl and the others started forward. With Remi in the lead and Sam walking backward, his H&K trained on the group, they began moving toward the helicopter.

'Twenty feet away,' Remi told Sam. Then, 'Ten feet.'

Sam stopped walking. 'Stop. Spread out,' he ordered. To Remi: 'I'm doing preflight.'

'I've got them covered.'

Sam tossed their packs into the cabin, then opened the pilot's door and climbed inside. Using his penlight, he scanned the controls and panels, doing his best to ignore the Eurocopter's dizzying array of options and concentrate on the essentials. After thirty seconds he'd found what he needed.

He flipped on the battery switch. The interior lamps and control panel glowed to life. Next he turned on the fuel pump, followed by the auxiliary power switch, which began the prestart of the turbine. After a few seconds of whining the turbine kicked in and began to spool up. The rotors begin turning, slowly at first but with increasing velocity as the rotor RPM gauge began climbing.

Sam leaned out the window and said to Remi, 'Collect their guns.'

Remi passed the order on to the group and, one at a time, each man stepped forward and tossed his weapon into the helicopter's cargo cabin. Using hand signals, she backed them up until they were just outside the helicopter's rotor radius.

In the cockpit, Sam saw the rotor RPM hit a hundred percent. 'Time to say good-bye,' he shouted to Remi.

'Gladly,' she yelled back and climbed aboard. With one eye trained on the group, she shoved the weapons into the safety webbing on the bulkhead.

'Grab ahold of something,' Sam called.

She wrapped her free hand around the webbing. 'Done!'

Sam tested the helicopter's cyclic control between his legs, then the collective stick at his side, gauging the blade pitch, then finally the antitorque foot pedals until he had a feel for them. He engaged the collective, and slowly the helicopter lifted off. He tested the cyclic, moving the helicopter first left, then right, then nose up and down.

Remi yelled, 'Sam, we've got a problem!'

'What?'

'Look right!'

Sam glanced out the side window. It took a few moments for him to register what he was seeing: Yaotl and the others were scattering across the pad as a dark rectangular shape bumped over the pad's rock-lined perimeter and headed toward the helicopter. It was the Cushman. Sam caught a glimpse of Rivera in the moon's pale glow hunched over the wheel.

'Nap time's over,' Remi called.

'I knew I'd forgotten something,' Sam shouted. 'The keys!'

He returned his attention to the controls, working the collective to gain altitude. In his haste he jerked the cyclic to the right and pressed the rudder pedal. The helicopter dipped right, and the tail spun around. He overcompensated. The helicopter dropped straight down, bounced off the pad, rose again. Sam risked another glance out the side window.

The Cushman was thirty feet away and closing fast. To one side a figure – Nochtli, it looked like – dashed across the pad and threw himself into the Cushman's cargo bed.

'Slow them down!' Sam called. 'Aim for the engine! Bigger target!'

In the back, Remi opened up with one of the AK-74s, firing controlled three-round bursts into the ground ahead of the Cushman, but got no result. She switched targets. Bullets pounded into the cart's front end, sparking off the bumper guards and shredding the fiberglass. Steam gushed from the engine compartment. The Cushman stuttered and began slowing, but not before it slid from view beneath the helicopter.

Sam lifted the collective, trying to gain altitude.

'I can't see them anymore,' Remi called.

Sam glanced out one side window, then the other. 'Where – '

Suddenly the helicopter lurched sideways and down, the open side door facing the ground. Remi's feet slid out from under her, and she skidded toward the opening. Instinctively, she released her grip on the AK-74 to latch onto the safety harness. The rifle slid down the deck, bounced off the bell's crate, and disappeared out the door.

'We lost an AK!' Remi called. A moment later a hand appeared in the opening, clawing at the deck for a handhold. Nochtli's head rose into view. 'And we've got a passenger!' Remi shouted.

Sam glanced over his shoulder. 'Kick him!'

'What!'

'Smash his fingers!'

Remi coiled her leg and lashed out, slamming her heel into Nochtli's pinkie finger. He screamed but held on. With a grunt, he heaved his upper torso onto the deck and reached for the tie-down straps attached to the crate. Remi curled her leg for a second strike.

From below came three overlapping cracks. Bullets thunked into the cabin's doorway.

'Sam!'

'I hear it! Hold tight, I'm going to try to shake him!'

Sam jerked the helicopter to the left and looked out both side windows, trying to locate the source of the gunfire. Below and to the right, Rivera stood in the cargo bed of the Cushman with Remi's fallen AK-74 tucked into his shoulder. The muzzle flashed orange. Sam's passenger's-side cockpit window spiderwebbed. He shifted the cyclic again, continuing to slide the helicopter left toward the trees at the edge of the pad. He pulled up on the collective to gain altitude.

In the cabin, Remi cocked her leg again and heel-kicked Nochtli in the thigh. Nochtli grunted and collapsed face-first onto the deck, shattering his nose. With one hand still entwined in the safety webbing, she reached over her head, groping for one of the weapons.

Sam looked left, saw the dark outline of the treetops looming before the window. A bullet tore through the passenger-seat headrest, zipped past Sam's chin, and punched through the windshield. He grunted and lifted the collective, but it was too late. Tree limbs scraped the belly of the helicopter. 'Come on, come on . . .' he grumbled. 'Remi, can you – '

'Little busy here!'

A branch snagged on the helicopter's tail boom, and the craft spun clockwise like a top. Alarms began blaring in the cockpit. Red and orange lights flashed on the dashboard. Sam worked the cyclic and collective, trying to compensate. Tree limbs slapped at the cockpit window.

Remi's hand touched the wooden butt of one of the AKs; she grabbed it, pulled hard, and it slid from the webbing. It stopped. She craned her neck back. The AK's front side was snagged on a strap. In the doorway, Nochtli was pushing himself upright. He hooked one of his knees over the edge of the doorway and began dragging himself toward Remi. Her hand slipped off the AK's butt; her fingers touched something metallic, tubular – a pistol barrel. She grabbed it, jerked it free of the webbing. Nochtli latched his free hand onto her ankle. Remi set her teeth and swung the pistol in a backhand. The butt caught Nochtli on the side of the chin. His head snapped sideways, and his eyes rolled back in his head. Still kneeling, he teetered for a moment, then tipped backward and disappeared through the doorway.

She called to Sam, 'He's gone!'

'You okay?'

She gulped a few breaths and replied, 'Shaken and stirred but still here!'

Bullets peppered the fuselage. Sam saw an opening in the canopy and worked the cyclic and rudder pedals, crabbing the nose around until it was pointed in the right direction, then nosed down and lifted the collective. With the shrieking of wood on aluminum, the helicopter lurched forward and into the clear. Now he lowered the collective and dropped the helicopter below the tree line. He stopped in a hover twenty feet above the slope, looked around for the H-V-C-P Jingaro had mentioned, and flipped it on. The helicopter shuddered slightly, slid sideways, dipped, then settled into a steady hover. The alarms and the flashing lights stopped. Sam tentatively took his hands off the controls and exhaled heavily. In the back, Remi scooted sideways and slid the door shut. The thumping of the rotors faded.

Sam turned in his seat and extended his hand between the gap. Remi grabbed his hand and pulled herself toward him. Sam asked, 'You okay?'

'Yes, You?'

He nodded. 'Let's get out of here. I think we've fully worn out our welcome.'

Chapter 20

Big Sukuti Island

They had just cleared the island's southern coastline when Sam realized Rivera's gunfire had caused more than cosmetic damage. The rudder pedals felt spongy, and the collective and cyclic were sluggish, responding to his commands with a slight delay.

'What do you think?' Remi asked, her face pressed between the seats.

'Hydraulics, maybe.' He scanned the gauges, looking for oil pressure, temperature, revolutions per minute . . . 'Engine's running a little hot, too, and the oil pressure looks dodgy.'

'What's that mean?'

'Nothing good.'

'How far to the beach?'

'Three miles, give or take.'

'We should assume Rivera isn't giving up.'

'I agree. Whether they call someone and how fast they respond is the question.'

'Or how fast they can get the Rinkers working again.'

'True. Let me see if I can get her settled down.'

Carefully Sam worked the controls, dropping both altitude and speed until they were a hundred feet off the water and moving at sixty knots – roughly seventy miles per hour. Below them, the sea was flat, calm, and black save the reflection of the helicopter's navigation strobes.

Remi said, 'Sam, they'll be able to track the lights.'

'Lights or no lights, they're tracking us through the Big Eyes. Once we cross the beach, I'll switch them off. Against the backdrop of the land we'll be invisible.'

'You're assuming they'll come after us.'

'Have to.' He did a quick scan of the gauges. 'The engine temperature's come down a little bit. But the oil pressure is still hinky. The controls are still soft.'

'Hydraulics, then.'

'At the very least. Any one of those can put us in the drink. All we need is another four minutes or so.'

'And a non-crash landing,' Remi added.

'And that.'

Slowly through the windshield they could see Africa's east coast turn from a dark smudge to identifiable bits of landmass: trees, white sand beaches, rolling hills, and rivers and streams zigzagging across the terrain.

A half mile from the beach Sam felt the cyclic jerk in his hand, followed by a thump-bang above their heads. The cockpit and cabin began shaking. An alarm shrieked. Yellow and red lights flashed.

'That's a tad ominous,' Remi said with a tight grin.

'Just a tad,' Sam agreed. 'Grab ahold of something. It's going to get bumpy.'

He lifted the collective and dropped the nose, pushing the helicopter past eighty knots. Through the windshield he saw the shoals slip beneath the fuselage, then the beach, then the black-green of the forest. He reached forward and flipped off the navigation strobes.

'There's a big sandbar ahead on the riverbank,' he called. 'Think you can manage the bell?'

'Define "manage"?'

'Shove it out the door.'

'That, I can do. What's the plan?'

'I hover. You, the guns, our packs, and the bell get off on the sandbank.'

'And you?'

'I'm going to put down in the river.'

'What? No, Sam – '

'You said it yourself: They're coming after us. If we can ditch this thing, they'll have nowhere to start looking.'

'Can you do it?'

'If I can get the rotors shut down quickly enough.'

'More ifs,' Remi replied. 'I'm beginning to hate ifs.'

'This'll be the last one for a while.'

'Uh-huh. I've heard that before.'

'When you're on the ground, find the thickest tree trunk around and get behind it. If the rotors don't spool down enough before she flips over, they'll tear free and turn into shrapnel.'

'Flip over? What do you mean – '

'Helicopters are top-heavy. As soon as she touches the water she's going to roll.'

'I don't like this – '

'The sandbar's coming up. Get ready!'

'You're infuriating, you know that?'

'I know.'

Remi mumbled a half curse under her breath, then turned around and released the tie-down ratchets around the crate. She crab-walked around it, braced her back against the bulkhead and her legs against the crate, and shoved it across the deck until it bumped up against the door.

'Ready,' she called.

Sam bled off airspeed and altitude until they were thirty feet off the sandbar and crawling ahead at fifteen knots. The helicopter was wobbling now; the earlier thump-bang had settled into an ominous three-second cycle that shook the fuselage from stem to stern.

'It's getting worse,' Remi said.

'We're almost there.'

Sam eased the helicopter downward a foot at a time.

'Check the distance,' he asked.

Remi slid the cabin door halfway open and poked her head out. 'Twenty feet . . . fifteen . . . ten . . .'

'Can you make that?' Sam asked.

'I may be well past my gymnastics days, but I can still do ten feet blindfolded.'

Sam flipped on the hover coupler. He took his hands off the controls. The helicopter lurched sideways, quivered, dipped, then steadied itself.

'Okay, go,' Sam called. 'Give me a wave when you're down and safe.'

Remi hunch-walked forward, stuck her head between the seats, kissed him, said 'Good luck,' then walked back and shoved the door the rest of the way open.

'Try to miss the skids,' Sam said.

Remi put her shoulder to the crate, took a deep breath, and shoved. The crate tumbled through the opening and disappeared. The guns went next. Remi gave Sam a final glance and jumped out. Ten seconds later Sam spotted her farther up the sandbar. She gave him a thumbs-up and dashed off into the darkness.

Sam counted to sixty to give her time to find cover, then grabbed the collective. He disengaged the hover coupler and seized the cyclic. He dipped the nose slightly and let the rotor blade's pitch angle ease him across the sandbar and over the river. When he reached a section that was both wide and deep enough for his purposes, he pulled the nose up and worked the collective into a hover.

He took one final look around. Once the helicopter submerged, the interior would be black. With no visual reference points, he'd have to escape by feel alone. He checked his seat belt to ensure he knew how to unhook it, then studied the cabin-door latch, then rehearsed his movements in his mind's eye.

He lowered the collective ever so slightly and felt the helicopter drop. He pressed his face against the door window. The skids were about five feet off the water. Close enough. Any closer, Sam feared, and he'd have a zero margin for error.

'Here goes everything,' Sam muttered.

He released the cyclic, shut off the engines, pulled the collective up to its stops to slow the blades, and grabbed the collective again. Sam felt his belly shoot into his throat. With a crash, the helicopter struck the surface. He was thrown forward against the restraints. He felt the helicopter tipping right, thought, *Collective!*, and jerked the control to the left. The effect was immediate. With the blades already fully pitched, the rotor assembly responded to Sam's command by angling to the left and shifting the helicopter's center of gravity. Water rushed up the windshield, horizontally at first, then diagonally as the helicopter pitched sideways. Sam tucked his chin to his chest, grasped the restraints with both hands, and set his jaw.

He felt a bone-shaking jolt. White light burst behind his eyes. Then nothing.

He awoke coughing. Water filled his throat. He jerked his head back, sputtered again, and forced his eyes open. Seeing only blackness, he felt a moment of panic. He squashed it, forced himself to breathe. He reached out, fingers extended, until he touched something solid – the tip of the cyclic. Gravity was pulling his head to the left. The helicopter was lying on its side; the river hadn't been deep enough for the helicopter to completely capsize. That was the good news. The bad news was that he could hear water gushing into the cabin behind him. Already the level had reached his face.

'Move, Sam,' he muttered.

He extended his right arm up, felt the upholstery of the passenger seat, and kept groping until his fingers found the safety belt. He latched on, then dipped his left hand beneath the water and punched the Release button on his restraints. He fell sideways, then brought his free hand up, joined it with his left hand, and chinned himself from the water until his knees reached the gap separating the cockpit from the cabin. Toes pointed, he shoved his legs through the opening and stretched to his full length until his feet touched the cabin's bulkhead. He let go of the restraints and slid the rest of the way into the cabin. Now that he was standing hunched over, the water was at his chest. He extended his arms upward, felt the cabin door, and traced its outline with his finger-tips. Water was spurting through the seams. He found the latch, tested it with slight downward pressure. It seemed operable.

'Deep breath,' Sam told himself.

He sucked in a lungful of air, shoved the latch down, and slid the door open. Water crashed onto his head. He stumbled backward and slid beneath the surface. He let the wave shove him against the cabin wall, using the momentum to coil his legs beneath him. The pressure subsided. He kicked off, arms spread before him, hands grasping at the doorframe and pushing, feet kicking –

His head broke the surface.

'Sam!' he heard. Remi's voice.

He opened his eyes and turned in the water, trying to get his bearings.

'Sam!' she called again.

He turned again, saw her standing on the bank waving at him.

' – diles!' she yelled.

'What?'

'Crocodiles! Swim!'

Sam did just that, pouring his last shred of energy into a sprint for the bank. He touched sand, shoved himself to his knees, then to his feet, then stumbled forward into Remi's arms. Together they slogged up the sand onto level ground before collapsing.

'Forgot about crocodiles,' Sam said a couple of min-utes later.

'Me too. I spotted them in the shallows about fifty

yards upstream. The commotion must have woken them up. Are you okay? Any broken bones?'

'Don't think so. How'd I do?'

Remi pointed toward the middle of the river. Sam focused on the spot, but it took several seconds for his eyes to adjust. All that remained visible of the helicopter was a branchlike shard of rotor blade jutting a half foot above the surface.

'The rest of the chunks went into the water.'

'Just as I planned,' Sam said with a weary smile.

'Planned?'

'*Hoped*. How's the bell?'

'Aside from a few cracks in the wood, the crate's surprisingly intact. I collected our packs and the guns. Let's find some cover in case we have visitors.'

Chapter 21

Wary of leaving telltale drag marks, they chose to leave the crate where it sat. Unintentionally, they'd dropped it in an ideal location – a dry rivulet near the riverbank. They covered it with scrub brush and then, using bundled foliage to obscure their tracks, they back-walked off the sandbar to solid ground and into a copse. A hundred feet inside the tree line they found a ten-by-ten-foot depression surrounded by fallen logs. It gave them a vantage point of not only the crate but the open ground down to the beach.

After probing the area with the muzzles of the rifles to drive off any snakes or sundry creepy crawlies, they settled into their bolt-hole. While Sam kept an eye out for visitors, Remi took inventory of their packs. 'Remind me to send a thank-you letter to Ziploc,' she said. 'Most everything is dry. The satellite phone looks okay.'

'How much battery life?'

'Enough for one call, maybe two.'

Sam checked his watch. It was just after two in the morning. 'It might be time to take Ed Mitchell up on his offer.' Remi fished Mitchell's card out of her pack and handed it over. Sam dialed.

A gravelly voiced Mitchell picked up on the fourth ring: 'Yeah.'

'Ed, it's Sam Fargo.'

'Huh?'

'Sam Fargo – your Mafia Island charter a couple days ago.'

'Oh, yeah . . . Hey . . .what the hell time is it?'

'About two. I don't have much time. We need an evac.'

'That's a word I ain't heard in a while. You in trouble?'

'You could say that.'

'Where you at?'

'On the mainland, about four and half miles due east of Big Sukuti,' Sam replied, then gave him a description of the area.

'You guys get around,' Mitchell said. 'Hang on a minute.'

Sam heard the sounds of paper crinkling, then silence. Mitchell came back on the line: 'You know you're sitting smack-dab in the middle of crocodile hell, don't you?'

'We do now.'

'Can't get a fixed wing in there. I'll have to use a helo. That'll take a little doing.'

'We'll make it worth your while.'

'I know you will, but that's not my worry. I probably won't get there until just after sunrise. Can you hang on?'

'We'll have to,' Sam said.

'Are folks going to be shooting at me when I get there?'

'No guarantees.'

There was ten seconds of silence, then Mitchell chuckled. 'Ah, what the hell. Life's a daring adventure or nothing at all.'

Sam laughed at this. 'It is indeed.'

'Okay, keep your heads down. I'll be there at first light. Just in case I've got some competition at the LZ, I'll drop blue smoke so you don't shoot at me.'

Sam disconnected. Beside him, Remi said, 'Here, drink.'

Sam turned, took a deep gulp from the canteen, then accepted a piece of beef jerky. He recounted his conversation with Mitchell. Remi said, 'That man's on our permanent Christmas list. So he'll be here in another four or five hours.'

'With luck.'

They sat in silence, chewing for several minutes. Sam checked his watch. 'It's been forty minutes since we left the island.'

'You don't think they – '

Sam held up his hand. Remi went quiet. After a few moments, she said, 'I hear them. Two of them, somewhere offshore.'

Sam nodded. 'Hard to tell, but it sounds like the Rinkers. We'd better assume so.'

'How far inland are we?'

'A quarter mile, maybe a little more.'

They listened for a few more minutes. The sound of the engines rose in volume, then suddenly went silent. 'They're ashore,' Sam said.

They checked their weapons: two AK-74s, one with a full magazine, the other missing the dozen or so rounds Remi had fired at the Cushman; the .357 Magnum; and the H&K P30. Whether these would be enough should a firefight erupt was an unknown. They'd been lucky so far with Rivera and his men, but neither Sam nor Remi were under any illusion: In a head-to-head contest, they had little chance of besting Special Forces soldiers.

'Let's get comfortable,' Sam said.

'And invisible,' Remi added.

After shoving their packs under a rotting log and covering them with loam, they did the same for themselves, lying lengthwise, head-to-head, so that each of them could see the approaches from the beach. Sam handed Remi a handful of mud to cover her face, then smeared some on his own.

'Promise me something, Sam,' Remi said, slathering herself.

'A suite at the Moevenpick?' he guessed.

'I was going to say a hot shower and a big breakfast, but since you offered I've been composing a list . . .'

Peering through a gap between the logs, Remi spotted a speck of light a few hundred yards to the east. She tapped Sam on the shoulder, mouthed, *Flashlight*, and pointed. The flashlight beam seemed to float through midair, disappearing and reappearing through the trees as the owner picked his way inland.

'I'll say this much for Rivera,' Sam whispered, 'he's like a dog with a bone.'

'He's probably said the same thing about us but in less congenial language. Are we waiting until we see the whites of their eyes?'

'No, we're crossing fingers they don't even wander this way.'

'Why wouldn't they?'

'In Africa, darkness and forest equals predators.'

'I could have done without that tidbit.'

'Sorry.' As if on cue, somewhere in the distance they heard the deep-throated huff-huff-huff of a big cat. It was a sound they'd both heard before, but either on organized safaris or from the safety of a lodge. Here, in the open and alone, the sound was chilling.

Sam whispered, 'It's a long way off.'

Soon a second flashlight joined the first; then a third and a fourth. The men were moving in a line abreast like flushers leading a hunting party. Soon the party was close enough that Sam and Remi could see the figures behind the flashlights. Not surprisingly, each man appeared to be carrying an assault rifle.

Another five minutes brought the group to the sandbar, where they converged. One of the men – Rivera, perhaps – appeared to do most of the talking, gesturing first up and down the shoreline, then inland. They shined their flashlights along the bank and over the water. Twice the beams appeared to skim over the helicopter blade jutting from the water, but it generated no response. Suddenly one of the men pointed across the river. Almost in unison, each of the men unslung his rifle.

'They spotted our fanged friends,' Remi whispered.

Weapons up and ready, the group backed off the sandbar until they were on the scrub ground. They conferred for another minute, then separated, one pair walking downriver, the other upriver. This was the pair Sam and Remi watched closely; as the river abutted the copse's northern edge, the pair's path would take them within fifty feet of the hiding spot.

Sam whispered, 'I took a look as we flew in: The nearest crossing is a mile downstream. Now we'll see how determined they are.'

Clearly wary of what other dangers the river might hold, the two men kept a safe distance from shore, walking from left to right across Sam and Remi's field of vision until the river curved east and merged with the copse. Here they turned southeast, shining their flashlights along the tree line as they walked. Now only twenty yards away, their figures were more distinct. One of them was more distinct than the other: Tall and gaunt, he moved with the economical, purposeful gait of a soldier. It was Itzli Rivera.

Suddenly Sam felt clawed feet crawling over his ankle. Before he could resist the impulse, he kicked his foot. The unseen creature squealed and skittered off through the underbrush.

Rivera stopped suddenly and held up a closed fist, the soldier's universal hand signal for 'Halt!' His partner stopped in his tracks, and in unison they slowly dropped to one knee. The flashlights were doused. Each man's head began rotating, looking, listening. The flashlights popped back on again and began skimming over the trees, pausing occasionally here and there. Rivera looked over his shoulder and gestured something to his partner. Together they stood up, turned, and began picking their way into the trees, heading directly for Sam and Remi's hiding spot.

Sam felt Remi's hand on his shoulder. He reached up, gave it a reassuring squeeze.

Rivera and his partner kept coming. They were thirty feet away.

Now twenty feet. Ten feet.

They stopped, looked left and right, and flashlight beams probed the gaps between the logs around Sam and Remi. Twigs cracked. Rivera whispered something to his partner. Sam and Remi felt the log over their heads sink a couple inches. The tips of a pair of boots appeared at the edge of the log, and a flashlight beam swept over the depression.

Five long seconds passed.

The flashlight clicked off. The boots pulled back, followed by a double thump as Rivera dismounted the log. Slowly the footfalls faded.

Sam counted to one hundred, then slowly lifted his head until he could see through the gap. Silhouetted by the glow of their flashlights, Rivera and his partner were back at the tree line and moving south toward the sandbar. Sam watched them for another minute and turned his head so his mouth was closer to Remi's ear.

'They're moving off. We'll stay put in case they double back.'

For the next twenty minutes they remained still, wedged as tightly as possible in their bolt-hole, until finally they heard in the distance the Rinker's engines growling back to life.

Sam whispered, 'Just a little longer.' He gave it another five minutes, then rolled out from under the log. 'I'm going to have a look around.'

He crawled out of the depression and disappeared. He returned ten minutes later. 'They're gone.' He helped Remi out from her hiding spot.

She exhaled heavily. 'That bell better be worth it.'

'Another few hours and we're home free.'

Ed Mitchell was as good as his word, if not a little better. Just as the sun was peeking through the forest to the east they heard the thump of helicopter rotors. As a precaution Sam and Remi scrambled back into their bolt-holes, occasionally peeking out as the rotors grew louder. To the west they saw a yellow-and-white Bell helicopter sweep in over the beach and turn inland, following the course of the river. When the helicopter reached the sandbar, the pilot's door opened. A moment later, blue smoke began drifting over the ground.

Sam and Remi rolled out together and stood up. Sam asked, 'Ready for home?' Remi shook her head, and he chuckled. 'Right. Sorry. Hot shower and breakfast.'

An hour later, with the crate strapped safely to the Bell's deck, they touched down at the Ras Kutani airstrip. While Mitchell trotted off to collect his vehicle for the ride back to Dar es Salaam, Sam and Remi used the sat phone to place a long-overdue call to Selma.

'Where have you been?' their chief researcher said over the speaker. 'I've been sitting by the phone.'

'Is that your way of saying you were worried about us?' Remi asked.

'Yes, it is. Now, explain yourselves.'

Sam briefly recounted the last few days, ending with their recovery of the bell. Selma sighed. 'I wish I could say positively you haven't wasted your time.'

'What do you mean?' Sam asked.

'We got the first shipment from Morton's museum yesterday. In with the miscellanea we found what looks like a journal of sorts – Blaylock's journal, to be exact.'

'That's good news,' Remi said, then added tentatively, 'Right?'

'It would be,' Selma replied, 'if not for the fact that I'm pretty sure Winston Lloyd Blaylock, the Mbogo of Bagamoyo, was certifiably insane.'

Chapter 22

Goldfish Point,
La Jolla, California

Exhausted and wanting to hit the ground running when they got home, Sam and Remi spent the majority of the flights home sleeping and eating and generally trying to keep their minds off Selma's proclamation regarding Winston Blaylock. Their chief researcher wasn't prone to hyperbole, so they took seriously her suspicion which, if true, cast a pall on their efforts to recover the *Shenandoah*'s bell. Of course, while the bell was of significant historical value regardless, the cryptic inscription on the bell's inner surface and Blaylock's obsession with the ship (either under the guise of the *Ophelia*, the *Shenandoah*, or the *El Majidi*) had suggested to them a deeper mystery – one that had apparently prompted Itzli Rivera and perhaps someone in the Mexican government to murder nine tourists.

As promised, Pete Jeffcoat and Wendy Corden were waiting for them in the baggage claim area. Pete took their carry-ons. 'You look tired.'

'You should have seen us eighteen hours and a couple dozen time zones ago,' Sam replied.

'What happened to you?' Wendy asked, gesturing to Sam's swollen cheekbone and his taped finger. While the latter was now properly bandaged with medical tape, the cut on his cheekbone was crusty with Super Glue – a remedy Ed Mitchell swore was better than stitches.

'I burned a casserole, and Remi got mad,' Sam said. He got a light punch on the arm from his wife in return.

Remi said to Wendy, 'Boys being boys, that's what happened.'

'We're glad you're home,' Pete said. 'Selma's been pulling her hair out. Don't tell her I told you.'

The baggage carousel started turning, and Pete wandered off to collect Sam and Remi's luggage.

Sam asked Wendy, 'Any word on the bell?'

'It's en route. Should be halfway across the Atlantic by now. With luck, we'll have it the day after tomorrow.'

'Care to give us a hint why Selma thinks Blaylock is a fruitcake?'

Wendy shook her head. 'She's been up for almost three days straight trying to piece this together. I'm going to let her explain.'

Sam and Remi's home and base of operations was a four-story, twelve-thousand-square-foot Spanish-style home with an open floor plan, vaulted maple-beamed ceilings, and windows and skylights enough that they bought their Windex in ten-gallon buckets.

The upper floor held Sam and Remi's master suite, and below this, one flight down, were four guest suites, a living room, a dining room, and a kitchen/great room that jutted over the cliff. On the second floor was a gymnasium containing both aerobic and circuit training exercise equipment, a steam room, a HydroWorx endless lap pool, a climbing wall, and a thousand square feet of hardwood floor space for Remi to practice her fencing and Sam his judo.

The ground floor sported two thousand square feet of office space for Sam and Remi and an adjoining workspace for Selma, complete with three Mac Pro workstations coupled with thirty-inch cinema displays, and a pair of wall-mounted thirty-two-inch LCD televisions. On the east wall was Selma's pride and joy, a fourteen-foot, five-hundred-gallon saltwater aquarium filled with a rainbow-hued assortment of fish whose scientific names she knew by heart.

Selma's other love, tea, she approached with equal passion; an entire cabinet of the workroom was devoted to her stock, which included a rare Phoobsering–Osmanthus Darjeeling hybrid that Sam and Remi suspected was the source of her seemingly boundless energy.

In appearance, Selma Wondrash was eclectic in the extreme: She wore a modified 1960s bob, horn-rimmed glasses, complete with a neck chain, and a default uniform of khaki pants, sneakers, and a tie-dyed T-shirt.

As far as Sam and Remi were concerned, Selma could be as strange as she wished. There was no one better at logistics, research, and resource scrounging.

Sam and Remi walked into the workspace to find Selma leaning over the tank, writing something on a clipboard. She turned, saw them, held up a finger, then finished writing and set aside the clipboard. 'My *Centropyge loricula* is looking sickly,' she said, then translated: 'flame angelfish.'

'That's one of my favorites,' Remi said.

Selma nodded solemnly. 'So, welcome home, Mr. and Mrs. Fargo.'

Sam and Remi had long ago given up trying to convince Selma to call them by their first names.

'Good to be home,' Sam replied.

Selma walked to the long, maple-topped workbench that ran down the center of the room and sat down. Sam and Remi took the stools opposite her. Blaylock's massive walking staff was lying lengthwise on the table.

'You look well,' Selma said.

'Pete and Wendy disagreed.'

'I was comparing your current condition to how I imagined you over the past few days. Everything is relative.'

'True enough,' Remi said. 'Selma, are you stalling?'

Selma pursed her lips. 'I'm not fond of handing you incomplete information.'

Sam replied, 'What you call incomplete we call mysterious, and we love a good mystery.'

'Then you're going to love what I have for you. First a little background. With Pete and Wendy's help, I dissected, indexed, and footnoted Morton's biography of Blaylock. It's on our server in PDF format, if you want to read it later, but here's the condensed version.' Selma opened a manila folder and began reading.

'Blaylock arrived in Bagamoyo in March 1872 with nothing but the clothes on his back, a few pieces of silver, a .44 caliber Henry rifle, a bowie knife big enough to "chop down a baobab tree" stuck in his boot, and a short sword strapped to his hip.'

'Clearly, Morton had a creative streak,' Remi said. She looked to Sam. 'Do you remember the story we read about the murdered British tourist?'

'Sylvie Radford,' Sam finished.

'Remember what she found while diving?'

Sam smiled. 'A sword. It's a long long shot, but maybe what she found had once belonged to Blaylock. Selma. Can you . . .'

Their chief researcher was already jotting a note. 'I'll see what I can find out.'

'A short sword and a bowie knife could easily be confused. Maybe Morton got it wrong. Sorry, Selma, keep going.'

'Evidently, Blaylock terrified the locals. Not only was he a foot taller and wider than almost everyone, he wasn't prone to smiling. On his first night in Bagamoyo, half a dozen thugs got together and decided to separate Blaylock and his money. Two of them died, and the rest required medical attention.'

'He shot them,' Sam said.

'No. He never picked up his Henry, the bowie, or the sword. He fought with his bare hands. After that, no one bothered him.'

'Which was probably the point,' Sam replied. 'Doing that to six men while unarmed tends to create an impression.'

'Indeed. Within a week, he was serving as a bodyguard for a rich Irishman on safari; within a month, he'd started his own guide business. As good as he was with his hands, he was even better with the Henry. Where other European guides and hunters were using big-bore hunting rifles, Blaylock could take down a charging Cape buffalo – a mbogo – with one shot from his Henry.

'About two months after Blaylock arrived, he contracted malaria and spent six weeks on his back near death while his two mistresses – Maasai women who worked in Bagamoyo – nursed him back to health. While Morton never came out and said as much, Blaylock's brush with death seemed to have left him slightly . . . touched in the head.

'After the malaria Blaylock would disappear for months on end on what he called "vision quest expeditions." He lived with the Maasai, took concubines, studied with witch doctors, lived alone in the bush, hunted for King Solomon's mines and Timbuktu, dug fossils in Olduvai Gorge, followed the trail of Mansa Musa, hoping to find his staff of gold . . . There's even an anecdote that claims Blaylock was the one who found David Livingstone first. According to Morton's account, Blaylock sent a runner to Bagamoyo to alert Henry Morton Stanley; shortly after that the pair had their famous "Dr. Livingstone, I presume" moment near Lake Tanganyika.'

'So if we're to believe Morton,' Remi said, 'Winston Lloyd Blaylock was the Indiana Jones of the nineteenth century.'

Sam smiled. 'Hunter, explorer, hero, mystic, Casanova, and indestructible savior all rolled into one. But this is all from Morton's biography, right?'

'Right.'

'By the way, we're assuming Morton was named after *the* Morton – as in Henry Morton Stanley?'

'Right again. In fact, according to the family tree in the back of the book, all of Blaylock's direct descendants were named after Africa in some fashion – the places, the history, the larger-than-life characters . . .'

'If you got all this from the biography, what about the journal you mentioned?' asked Sam.

'I used the word "journal" for lack of a better term. In fact, it's a potpourri: diary, field sketchbook . . .'

'Can we see it?'

'If you'd like. It's in the vault.' Off the workspace, Selma had a temperature- and humidity-controlled archive area. 'It's in bad shape – insect-eaten, soiled, water-damaged pages stuck together. Pete and Wendy are working on the restoration. We're photographing and digitizing what pages we can before we start work on the damaged portions. There's one more thing: It appears the journal also served as Blaylock's captain's log.'

'Pardon me?' Remi said.

'While he never mentions the *Shenandoah* or the *El Majidi*, many of his entries clearly indicate he was at sea, on and off, for long periods. Blaylock does, however, mention Ophelia quite often.'

'In what context?'

'She was his wife.'

'That would explain his obsession, I suppose,' Sam said. 'Not only did he mentally rename the *Shenandoah*, he also carved Ophelia's name into the bell.'

'Ophelia is a distinctly un-African name,' Remi said. 'It had to be the name of his wife back in the U.S.'

Selma nodded. 'There's no mention of her in the biography. And he never speaks in detail about her in the journal – just little snippets everywhere. Whether he was simply yearning for her or it's something more, I don't know, but she was never far from his mind.'

'Are there dates in the journal?' asked Sam. 'Anything we can cross-reference with Morton's biography?'

'In both books, only months and years are used; in the journal, those are far and few between. We're trying to do some matching, but it's turning up discrepancies. For example, we found a time where in the biography he's trekking in the Congo, while according to the journal he's at sea. It's slow going so far.'

'Something doesn't add up,' said Sam.

'Just one thing?' Remi replied. 'My list is longer than that.'

'Mine too. But on the captain's log angle: If we're thinking Blaylock might have been at sea aboard the *Shenandoah* – *El Majidi*, I mean – then we've got a contradiction. By all accounts, after the Sultan of Zanzibar bought the *Shenandoah* in 1866 he all but abandoned her at anchor until she was destroyed either in 1872 or 1879. I think someone would have noticed her missing.'

'Good point,' Selma said, jotting down a note. 'Another point of curiosity: Sultan Majid died in October 1870 and was succeeded by his brother and bitter rival, Sayyid Barghash bin Said. By default, he became the owner of *El Majidi*. Some historians find it curious that Sayyid didn't change the ship's name, let alone keep it around.'

Sam added, 'Can we put together a time line of the *Shenandoah/El Majidi*? Be easier to visualize the events.'

Selma picked up the phone and dialed the archive room. 'Wendy, can you throw together a rough time line of the *Shenandoah/El Majidi*? Thanks.'

'We also need to find out more about Blaylock's life before Africa,' Remi said.

'I'm working on that as well,' said Selma. 'I reached out to an old friend who might be able to help.'

Wendy stepped out of the archive room, smiled at them, held up a *Just one second* finger, then sat down at one of the workstations. She tapped away at the keys for five minutes and said, 'On your screen.'

Selma used the remote control to find the new graphic:

✚ March 1866: *Shenandoah* sold to Sultan of Zanzibar.

✚ November 1866: *Shenandoah* arrives Zanzibar, renamed *El Majidi*.

✚ November 1866–October 1870: *El Majidi* spends most time sitting at anchor or on occasional merchant voyages.

✚ October 1870: First Sultan dies. Brother's reign begins.

✚ October 1870–April 1872: *El Majidi* presumed at anchor.

✚ April 1872: Hurricane damages *El Majidi*. Sent to Bombay for repair.

✚ July 1872: *El Majidi* reportedly sinks en route to Zanzibar.

✚ July 1872–November 1879: Six years' lost time. Disposition unknown.

✚ November 1879: En route to Bombay, *El Majidi* reportedly sinks near island of Socotra.

Sam said, 'We've got two seemingly reliable accounts of her sinking that contradict each other, and over six years where the *El Majidi* is unaccounted for.

'Selma, what's the earliest date in Blaylock's journal?'

'As best we can tell, August 1872, about five months after he arrived in Africa. On our time line, that's a month after the *El Majidi*'s first reported sinking and at the beginning of her lost years.'

'Six years,' Remi echoed. 'Where was she all that time?'

Mexico City, Mexico

Fifteen hundred miles to the south, Itzli Rivera sat in President Garza's anteroom waiting to be summoned, as he had been for the past hour.

Garza's executive assistant, a doe-eyed girl in her early twenties with glossy black hair and an hourglass figure, sat at her desk typing, her index fingers wandering over the keyboard and occasionally punching a key. Her expression was one of puzzlement. *As though she's trying to finish a master-level Sudoku puzzle*, Rivera thought. Clearly, the woman's administrative skills had not been a priority during the hiring process.

Hoping to kill some time, Rivera wondered if Garza had ordered the woman to take a Mexica name. If so, what would it be? As if on cue, President Garza's voice came over the intercom on the woman's desk, answering Rivera's question.

'Chalchiuitl, you may send Mr. Rivera in.'

'Yes, sir.'

She smiled at Rivera and gestured toward the door with one of her ridiculously long fingernails. 'You may – '

'I heard him, thank you.'

Rivera walked across the carpet, pushed through the

double doors, and closed them behind him. He strode to Garza's desk and stopped at semiattention.

'Sit down,' Garza ordered.

Rivera did.

'I was reading your report,' Garza said. 'Do you have anything to add?'

'No, sir.'

'Let me summarize, if you don't mind . . .'

'Go ahead, sir.'

'That was rhetorical, Itzli. You and your men, after being outwitted for days by these treasure hunters . . . these Fargos . . . You finally manage to take possession of the bell and transport it to Okafor's island, only to have it stolen out from under your noses.'

Rivera nodded.

'Not only did they steal back the bell, but they also stole Okafor's four-million-dollar helicopter.'

'And I lost a man. Nochtli fell from the helicopter and broke his neck.'

President Garza waved his hand dismissively. 'You were vague about how the Fargos managed to get aboard the helicopter at all. Can you elaborate? Where were you when all this was happening?'

Rivera cleared his mouth and shifted nervously in his seat. 'I was . . . unconscious.'

'Pardon me?'

'The man, Sam Fargo, attacked me aboard Okafor's yacht. He surprised me. He clearly has some martial arts training.'

'Clearly.' Garza rotated his chair and gazed out the window. He drummed his fingers on his desk blotter for a minute, then said, 'We have to assume they're not going to give up. That could work in our favor. If they're as clever as they seem, we know they'll be visiting at least one of the areas we've already searched.'

'Agreed.'

'Start reaching out to your contacts – immigration officers, airport employees, anyone who will alert us when the Fargos appear.'

'Yes, sir. I'll start with Antananarivo. Anything else?'

Garza stared hard at his underling. 'You mean, are there going to be any repercussions for your failure?'

'Yes, sir.'

Garza chuckled humorlessly. 'What are you expecting, Itzli? Something from the movies, perhaps? For me to pull out a pearl-handled revolver and shoot you? Or open a trapdoor beneath you?'

Rivera let himself smile.

Garza's expression went cold. 'For now, you're still the best man for the job. The best I have, in fact. Now I want you to prove that my faith isn't wasted. Ideally, that would involve Sam and Remi Fargo ending up dead.'

'Yes, Mr. President, thank you.'

'One more thing before you go: I want to make memorial arrangements.'

'For Nochtli,' Rivera said. 'Yes, sir, I – '

'No, no, for the other one – Yaotl. It seems he and his wife died in a car accident this morning.'

Rivera felt the hair on the back of his neck stand up. 'What?'

'Sad, isn't it? He lost control and drove his car off a cliff. They were both killed instantly.'

'They had a child, a five-year-old.'

Garza pursed his lips as though weighing the question. 'Oh, the girl. She's fine. She was at school at the time. I suppose we'll have to find her new home. You'll see to that as well?'

'Yes, Mr. President.'

Chapter 23

Library of Congress, Washington, D.C.

Their first lead into Winston Blaylock's life prior to his arrival in Africa came in the form of an old friend of Selma's, Julianne Severson, who'd taken over the Library of Congress's Special Collections Division after Selma's departure.

Severson met Sam and Remi at the Second Street researcher's entrance of the Jefferson Building. The other two buildings that made up the library's campus, the Adams and the Madison, sat a block to the east and the south respectively.

After shaking hands, Severson said, 'It's a pleasure having you, Mr. and Mrs. Fargo – '

'Sam and Remi,' said Remi.

'Wonderful. I'm Julianne. I've been a fan of yours for quite some time. You probably don't realize this but your adventures spark a lot of interest in history, particularly among children.'

'Thank you, Julianne,' Sam replied.

She handed them a pair of laminated badges attached to neck lanyards. 'Reader identification cards,' she explained with a shrug and a smile. 'All part of the CSP, Collections Security Program. Ever since nine/eleven, the protocols are much more strict.'

'We understand.'

'If you'll follow me . . .' They started walking. 'I'll be helping you personally while you're here . . .'

'That's kind of you,' Remi said, 'but we don't want to take up your time.'

'Nonsense. The library runs smoothly on its own; my assistant will handle anything that comes up.' Severson turned up a marble stairway, and Sam and Remi followed. 'How much do you know about the library?'

'We've visited several times, but never as researchers, believe it or not,' Remi replied.

The tour alone was a breathtaking experience, Sam and Remi knew. The oldest federal institution in the country, the Library of Congress was founded in 1800 and located in the Capitol Building until 1814, when British troops lit the building on fire and destroyed the library's core collection of three thousand volumes. A year later, Congress voted to reestablish the LOC and purchased Thomas Jefferson's personal library of some six thousand books.

The library's collection had since grown significantly: 33,000,000 books and printed materials, 3,000,000 recordings, 12,500,000 photographs, 5,300,000 maps, 6,000,000 pieces of sheet music, and 63,000,000 manuscripts – in all representing almost 500 languages – some 145,000,000 items altogether on 745 miles of bookshelves.

'It almost seems more a cathedral than a library,' Remi said. 'The architecture is . . .'

'Awe-inspiring?' Severson finished.

'Exactly. The marble floors and columns, the arches, the vaulted ceilings, the artwork.'

Severson smiled. 'I think Selma once referred to this place

as "part cathedral, part museum, part gallery, with a little bit of library thrown in for good measure." I suspect grandeur was foremost on the Congress's collective mind in 1815. After the British sacked everything, I imagine there was a "we'll show them" mentality during the reconstruction.'

'Bigger, better, more ostentatious. Architectural nose-thumbing, if you will,' Remi said.

Severson laughed.

'Are we going to the Main Reading Room?' Sam asked.

'No, we're going to the second floor – Rare Book and Special Collections. The Main Room is hosting a tour for local elementary schools. It's going to be a bit wild in there today.'

They reached a door numbered 239 and walked through. 'If you want to take a seat at the worktable, I'll man the workstation. While our catalogue has gotten more user-friendly over the years, it might be easier if I do the legwork.

'Okay, Selma e-mailed me some of the documents and gave me a little bit of background: Winston Lloyd Blaylock, wife named Ophelia, believed to be in the United States prior to March 1872. Anything else?'

'We have a rough physical description,' said Remi.

'Everything helps.'

'Six feet four inches tall, around two hundred fifty pounds probably.'

'Also, he carried a .44 caliber Henry rifle,' Sam added. 'As I understand it, those weren't very common.'

'Certainly not as common as Winchesters, Remingtons, or Springfields. The Henry wasn't standard-issue during the Civil War, but many Union soldiers used their own money to buy one. The government did, however, issue them to scouts, raiding parties, and Special Forces units. The Confederate soldiers hated the Henry. It could hold sixteen rounds, and a trained soldier could fire off twenty-eight in a minute. Back then, that was as close to a hand-carried machine gun as you could get. Do we know if Blaylock was adept with it?'

'According to our source, he was a crack shot.'

Severson nodded. She started typing, and for the next five minutes there was silence save for the clacking of the keyboard's keys and the murmur of 'Fascinating' or 'Interesting' from Severson. Finally she looked up.

'I have a service record here, a microfiche copy from the National Archives. Two sources, actually: the CMSR, or Compiled Military Service Record; and Publications M594 and M861, which are the "Service of Military Units in Volunteer Union Organizations" for both the Union and the Confederacy.'

'Any mention of Blaylock?'

'I've got fifty-nine entries, in fact. Since Blaylock carried a Henry rifle, let's start with the Union list first.' Severson started typing again. 'The problem is, many of the abstract entries list only the first name, middle initial, and last name. I've got several W. Blaylocks, and two W. L. Blaylocks. The first one has an attachment, a medical record. Did your Blaylock have any wounds?'

'Not that we know of.'

Smiling, Severson tapped the screen, clearly excited by what she'd found. 'Right leg amputated at field hospital during the battle of Antietam. Guess that rules him out, huh? Oh, sorry, that sounded morbid, didn't it?'

'It's okay,' Sam said. 'You and Selma share the same love of research. We're used to it.'

'Okay, here's the other entry. Well, this is interesting. This Blaylock was detached from the Union Army in September 1863, but there's no reason listed. He wasn't transferred or wounded. Just detached.'

'What does that mean?' Remi asked.

'I'm not sure. Let me see if I can find more than an abstract on him.'

Fifteen minutes later Severson again looked up from her workstation. 'Got it! A full service record. This might be your man: William Lynd Blaylock.'

'That's close,' Sam said. 'Conspicuously close.'

'His physical description is close as well: six feet four inches, two hundred ten pounds.'

'It wouldn't be hard to gain thirty or forty pounds after leaving the army,' Remi observed.

Severson was frowning. 'Parts of the record are missing. I've got early details of his training and unit assignments, promotions, campaigns he was involved in, evaluations . . . But after 1862 his assignments are all listed as "supplementary service."'

'That sounds very James Bond-ish,' said Remi.

'You're not far off,' Severson replied. 'When it comes to Civil War-era records, the term "supplementary service" is usually associated with guerrilla units – what we'd call Special Forces today.'

Sam said, 'Like Loudoun Rangers, Quantrill's Raiders, the Kansas Jayhawkers . . .'

Severson nodded. 'Right. Combine that with this

Blaylock's mysterious detachment from the Union Army in 1863, and I think you're looking at a soldier turned spy.'

The afternoon wore on as Severson sat at her workstation typing, jotting notes, and occasionally sharing her progress with Sam and Remi. At four P.M. Severson stopped and looked at her watch. 'Oh, my, time flies. It's almost closing time. There's no reason you should have to sit here for this. Why don't you go back to your hotel and have dinner? I'll call you if I find anything. Correction: *When* I find something.'

'Please, Julianne, you go home as well,' Remi said. 'I'm sure you have other plans.'

'Nope. My roommate will feed my cat, and I'll grab dinner here.'

Sam said, 'We can't – '

'Are you kidding? This is like going to Disney World for me.'

'That sounds familiar,' Remi said with a smile. 'Are you sure you and Selma aren't related?'

'We're part of a secret society: Librarians-in-Arms,' Severson replied. 'You two go and let me do my thing. I'll be in touch.'

As they did every time they stayed or passed through Washington, Sam and Remi had booked the Robert Mills Suite at the Hotel Monaco. Twenty minutes after leaving the Library of Congress their taxi slowed before the Monaco's red-awning-covered steps. The doorman had the door open a moment after the car stopped rolling. Sam and Remi got out.

The Monaco, once the U.S. General Post Office Building and now a registered National Historic Landmark, is located in Washington's nineteenth-century neighborhood known as Penn Quarter, within walking distance of the Mall, the Smithsonian American Art Museum, the J. Edgar Hoover Building, the U.S. Navy Memorial, and enough five-star restaurants to keep a gourmand enraptured for years.

'Welcome, Mr. and Mrs. Fargo,' the doorman said. He walked to the rear of the cab and collected their luggage from the trunk. 'I'll have your bags brought up immediately. If you'd like to step inside, I believe you'll find the concierge is expecting you.'

Ten minutes later they were in their suite. Still fatigued from their African odyssey, they took an hour-long nap, then showered, dressed for dinner, and walked down to the street. They found the Monaco's restaurant, the Poste Moderne Brasserie, around the corner on Eighth Street through a carriageway portal set into the building.

After a glance at the wine list and menu, they settled on a bottle of 2007 Domaine de la Quilla Muscadet – a zesty, crisp wine from the Loire Valley – arugula salad with basil, mint, and parmesan, and steamed bouchot mussels in white wine, saffron, mustard, and garlic confit. As was visiting the Monaco itself, the choice of fare was something of a tradition for the couple.

Remi took a sip of wine. She closed her eyes and let out a sigh. 'I have a confession, Sam. I love adventure as much as the next gal, but there's something to be said for good food and a warm bed with clean sheets.'

'You'll get no argument from me.'

Remi's iPhone chimed. She checked the screen, then set it aside. 'Selma. She found another Aztec symbol in Blaylock's journal.'

Before leaving for Washington, they'd asked her to focus her search on anything that remotely resembled the Miquiztli glyph. For Selma's reference, Remi had downloaded from the Internet a high-resolution image of the twenty-four-ton Aztec Calendar, the Sun Stone, on display in Mexico City's National Museum of Anthropology.

'That makes four symbols so far,' Remi said.

'Any discernible pattern? Any annotations near the symbols?'

'None. She's says they're isolated.'

'At some point you're going to have to give me a primer on all things Aztec.'

'I'll see what I can do. There aren't many ancient peoples with a more complex history and culture. Even after a full semester of it, I felt like I'd barely scratched the surface. Every symbol has multiple meanings and every god multiple identities. It doesn't help that most of the historical accounts are biased toward the Spanish.'

'Victors write the history,' Sam said.

'Sadly true.'

Sam took a sip of wine. 'It seems a safe bet that Rivera and whoever he's working for share an obsession with Blaylock – even separated by a hundred forty years. Don't ask me how, though. The Aztec angle can't be a coincidence. Or are we too close to the forest?'

'I don't think so, Sam. It's the one common denominator that links Blaylock, the ship, the bell, and Rivera. The question is, where do the middle two fit into it?'

The waiter appeared with their salads.

Sam said, 'We still don't know how Rivera got interested in the *Shenandoah* in the first place. Hell, we don't even know if it *is* the *Shenandoah*. Aside from *Ophelia*, which is Blaylock's own invention, the ship had two other names: the *Sea King* and *El Majidi*. We're not only dealing with *what* but also *when*.'

'What if they stumbled onto something to do with Blaylock – another journal or some letters, for example. Worse still, what if Selma's right and Blaylock's bout with malaria left him insane, and the doodling in his journal is pure fantasy?'

'In other words,' Sam said, 'we could all be on a wild-goose chase.'

After dinner they shared a wedge of strawberry-rhubarb pudding cake and finished with two cups of decaf Ethiopian coffee. They were back in their room shortly before nine. The message light on the telephone was blinking.

Remi said, 'I knew I forgot something: I didn't give Julianne our cell phone numbers.'

Sam dialed into the hotel's voice-mail system and turned on the speaker. 'Sam, Remi, this is Julianne. It's about eight-thirty. I'm going to go work from home, but I'll be back at the library by six tomorrow morning. Come by around eight. I think I've found something.'

Chapter 24

Library of Congress

They arrived at the researchers' entrance at seven forty-five and were met by a security guard, who checked their credentials then escorted them to the Special Collections Room on the second floor. They pushed through the door and found Julianne Severson sitting at her workstation, head resting on the desktop. She was wearing the same clothes as the day before.

As the door clicked shut, she jerked upright and looked around. She saw them, blinked rapidly a few times, then smiled. 'Morning!'

Remi said, 'Oh, Julianne, please don't tell us you never went home.'

'I almost did. I meant to, really, but I was following a thread that turned into another and another . . . You know how it goes.'

'We do,' Sam replied. 'If it helps, we brought a Venti Starbucks dark roast and bagels and cream cheese.'

He held up the box. Severson's eyes widened.

After gulping down half the coffee and most of a bagel, Severson wiped her lips, ran her fingers through her hair, and joined Sam and Remi at the worktable. 'Better,' she said. 'Thanks.' Beside her was a manila folder stuffed with printouts and a yellow legal pad covered in notes.

'Before we're done here I'll of course print out all the reference material I've found, so right now I'll just give you the highlights.

'The good news is, everything I found had long ago been declassified and is now open source. I spent the night connecting dots, using private archives, university collections, War and Navy Department documents, Secret Service records, nonfiction books and periodicals . . . You name it, I checked it.'

'You've got our full attention,' Sam said.

'First let me show you a picture of my Blaylock. Tell me if it matches yours.'

She pulled a photo from the folder at her elbow and slid it across the table. On her iPhone Remi pulled up a scanned version of the Blaylock photo they'd found in the Bagamoyo museum. Severson's version showed a tall, broad-shouldered man, in his late teens or early twenties, wearing a Union Army officer's uniform. Sam and Remi compared the photos.

Sam said, 'That's him. In ours he's older, a little grayer and weathered, but it's the same man.'

Severson nodded and took back the photo. 'The man you know as Winston Lloyd Blaylock was in fact named William Lynd Blaylock: born in Boston in 1839, graduated from Harvard two years early at the age of nineteen with a degree in mathematics – specifically, topology.'

'Which is?' Remi asked.

Sam replied, 'It's spatial mathematics – curved surfaces, deformed areas. The Mobius strip is a good example.'

'Then it's no surprise Blaylock had a thing for the Fibonacci spiral. Sorry, Julianne, go on.'

'A month after he graduated, he was hired by the War Department.'

'As a cryptologist,' Remi predicted.

'Right. By all accounts Blaylock was a genius. A prodigy.'

Sam and Remi looked at each other. Given the references to the Fibonacci sequence and the golden spiral they'd found in Blaylock's journal, they'd wondered if there were more to the journal than met the eye. Namely, hidden messages or codes. Over the years they had learned many things about those who hide and hunt treasure, but one lesson stood above all: People will go to extraordinary lengths to keep their obsession from prying eyes. If this were true in Blaylock's case, he would likely use the method he knew best – mathematics and topology.

Severson continued: 'A few days after Fort Sumter was attacked in April 1861, Blaylock quit his job and joined the Union Army. After initial training he emerged as a second lieutenant and was immediately thrown into the fray, fighting throughout July and August in several battles: Rich Mountain, Carrick's Ford, First Bull Run. Apparently he proved himself much more than your average math nerd. He was promoted to first lieutenant and acquired a chestful of medals for gallantry.

'The following spring, in 1862, he was transferred to the Loudoun Rangers and served under Samuel Means, who was in turn under the direct aegis of Secretary of War Edwin Stanton. Sam, as you already mentioned, the Loudoun Rangers were the equivalent of a modern-day

Special Forces. They worked in a small unit, behind enemy lines, living off the land, conducting raids, sabotage missions, and intelligence gathering. They were a tough bunch.

'Shortly before the Rangers were absorbed into a regular army unit in 1864, Secretary Stanton tapped Blaylock and a few others for recruitment into the Secret Service. A few months after that Blaylock surfaced in Liverpool, England, under the name Winston Lloyd Babcock, where he worked undercover for a man named Thomas Haines Dudley.'

Sam said, 'Lincoln's spymaster.'

'You know him?' Severson asked.

'I've read a few books where he's featured. He was Quaker, as I recall. U.S. Consul in Liverpool. He ran the Secret Service spy network in the UK.'

Severson added, 'He had almost a hundred agents, all of whom were dedicated to stopping the covert flow of supplies from Great Britain to the Confederacy. While England was officially neutral during the war, there were a great many Southern sympathizers, both in and out of the government. Care to guess what Blaylock's primary assignment was?'

Remi answered; both she and Sam had been reading between the lines. 'The reflagging of merchant ships for Confederate Navy use,' she said.

'Right again,' replied Severson. 'Specifically, Blaylock ran a cell that was focused on a ship called the *Sea King* — later known as the CSS *Shenandoah*.'

'The one that got away,' Sam said. 'Not only that but got away and spent the next nine months wreaking havoc with Union shipping until after the end of the war.'

Severson continued: 'For Blaylock it was a personal and professional disaster.'

'Professionally?' Sam repeated. 'Was he reprimanded? Relieved of duty?'

'I found no evidence of that. In fact, quite the opposite. Thomas Haines Dudley was an avid supporter of Blaylock. He wrote several glowing evaluations of him. In an 1864 letter to the chief of the Secret Service, William Wood, he called Blaylock "one of the finest agents I have had the pleasure to have in my employ." I suspect Blaylock simply took the failure so personally that it impacted his work. Two weeks later he boarded a ship in London for the return voyage home. When he got there he discovered that his wife, Ophelia, had died while he was in transit. In a bit of tragic irony, she'd been killed during a raid by a Confederate guerrilla band known as Mosby's Rangers – one of the very units Blaylock had fought against during his time in the Loudoun Rangers.'

'My God,' Remi whispered. 'That poor man. Do we know whether Ophelia had been the target? Did Mosby and his men seek her out because of her husband?'

'It doesn't appear so. By all accounts she was simply in the wrong place at the wrong time.'

'So not only did Blaylock come home in disgrace, but he came home to find the love of his life snuffed out,' Sam said. 'Remi, I'm starting to think the malaria was only part of his mental problems.'

'I agree. It's understandable.'

'As is his obsessive personality,' Severson added. 'Selma e-mailed me the ship sketch he did. To rename a ship after a woman . . .That's true love.'

Remi asked, 'Julianne, did they have children?'

'No.'

'What happened after he got home?'

'There's not much to tell. I found only one record of him. In 1865 he was hired by a newly founded school called the Massachusetts Institute of Technology. It appears Blaylock settled back into civilian life as a math teacher.'

'Until March 1872, when he resurfaced in Bagamoyo.'

'And four years after the *Shenandoah* was sold to the Sultan of Zanzibar,' Remi said, then added wryly, 'a mother of all coincidences. Unless Blaylock's grief had turned to rage. The *Shenandoah* got away on his watch and his wife died in the process. If he was actually insane, he may have somehow come to blame the *Shenandoah* for his loss. It's a stretch, but the human mind is a mysterious thing.'

'You may be right. Only Blaylock could answer that,' Severson said. 'But I can tell you this much: I don't think he went to Africa on a whim. I think he was sent there.'

'By whom?' Sam asked.

'Secretary of War William Belknap.'

Remi and Sam were silent for several seconds as they absorbed this information. Finally Sam said, 'How do you know this?'

'I don't know, with certainty,' Severson replied. 'At this point my case is circumstantial and based on private letters between Belknap, Secretary of the Navy George Robeson, and the director of the Secret Service, Herman Whitley.

'In a November 1871 letter to both Belknap and

Robeson, Whitley cites a recently received intelligence report. He doesn't mention the source, but there were three lines that jumped out at me. First, intelligence reports that "suggest apostles of Captain Jim following in his footsteps"; second, 'our man in Zanzibar playing us for the fool'; and third, "I have it on good authority the anchorage in question is frequently empty."'

Remi said, '"Our man in Zanzibar" could be Sultan Majid II.'

'And "Captain Jim" could be the *Shenandoah*'s captain, James Waddell,' replied Sam. 'Whitley's choice of language is interesting: "apostles." A man like him wouldn't have risen to his position without a firm grasp of language. An apostle is a firm believer, someone dedicated to following a leader's example. As for the empty anchorage . . .'

'That could refer to where the Sultan had supposedly abandoned the newly renamed *El Majidi*,' said Remi.

'I agree.'

'There's more,' Severson replied. 'In a letter that followed a few days later, both Belknap and Robeson encouraged Whitley to contact "our Quaker friend" – Thomas Haines Dudley, I'm guessing – and ask if he might have any agents that could investigate the "vessel in question." Six weeks later Whitley replied. According to "the Quaker's sources," the vessel in question was spotted, but not at its anchorage. It was in Dar es Salaam, returning to port – and I quote – "fully-rigged for sail, steam, and cannon, and crewed by skilled sailors of Caucasian descent."'

Sam and Remi were silent for ten seconds. Finally Sam said, 'Unless I'm seeing something that's not there, I'd say

Captain Waddell's "apostles" remanned the *Shenandoah* for war.'

'The best part's yet to come,' Severson said, 'In that same letter Whitley informs Belknap and Robeson that he's ordered the Quaker – Dudley – to dispatch his best man to investigate the situation in Dar es Salaam.'

'And we know who Dudley considered his best agent – Blaylock.'

'Who arrives in Bagamoyo a couple months later,' Remi added.

'It seems to fit, but you said it yourself, Julianne: It's all circumstantial at this point.'

'I haven't finished cataloging all the letters, but in the interim I think I know someone who can help. How do you two feel about a trip down to Georgia?'

Chapter 25

Savannah, Georgia

After listening to the remainder of Julianne Severson's presentation and her hunch about where they might unravel the next portion of Blaylock's story, Sam and Remi booked an early-afternoon flight out of Dulles. They touched down in Savannah shortly before three.

While Sam stood at the Hertz counter and made arrangements for a car, Remi checked her voice mail. Car keys in hand, Sam walked up to her.

'Selma got the bell this morning,' Remi announced.

Sam smiled and let out an exaggerated sigh. 'I have to admit, after all we went through to get that thing, I had visions of it falling off the plane and dropping into the ocean.'

'Me, too. She says it's in great condition. She called Dobo; he's coming to pick it up.'

Alexandru Dobo – who preferred to be addressed only by his last name – was a full-time surfer/beach bum, part-time restoration expert, and their go-to guy for projects beyond their expertise. As the former curator of Romania's Ovidius University's Architecture, Restoration and Conservation Department and the primary consultant for Constanta's Romanian Navy Museum and the National

History and Archaeology Museum, Dobo had yet to encounter an artifact he couldn't restore.

As Selma was herself from Romania's next-door neighbor, Hungary, she and Dobo liked to both reminisce and quarrel about the 'old country.'

'She said he's going to work on it throughout the night,' Remi added.

'What, the surf's bad?'

'Terrible.'

'How're they doing on the journal?'

'All she said was "still working."'

In Selmaspeak that meant slow but steady progress that could be imperiled by any further questions.

'She also mentioned the spiral and the Fibonacci sequence. They're finding both of them repeated everywhere. Like a mantra. What an interesting man, Blaylock.'

Sam jingled the keys and said, 'Let's get moving.'

'What did you get?'

'Cadillac Escalade.'

'Sam . . .'

'Hybrid.'

'Okay.'

For Sam and Remi, Savannah epitomized Southern charm and history – it was in every turn of her shaded oak- and Spanish moss-lined streets; in her cherry blossom-filled squares and around her well-tended monuments; dripping from balconies and stone walls in the form of hydrangea and honeysuckle; and in the facades of the pillared Greek Revival plantation houses and the sprawling neoclassical estates. Even the buzz of cicadas was part of

Savannah's charm. In fact, it was their love of Savannah that led them to accept Severson's travel suggestion without question. When pushed for a hint, the librarian had merely smiled and said, 'I think you'll find something familiar there.'

Despite the heat, they kept the Escalade's tinted windows rolled down so they could admire the scenery. With one hand on her fluttering beach hat, Remi asked, 'Where exactly are we going?'

'Whitaker Street, near Forsyth Park. Very close to the Heyward House, I think.'

The former summer house of a onetime plantation owner and one of the signatories of the Declaration of Independence, Heyward House was just one of the many landmarks in the city's Bluffton's National Register Historic District. A stroll in Bluffton was a stroll through history.

They parked on the east side of Forsyth Park under a sprawling oak and walked a block south to a taupe-colored house with mint green shutters. Sam checked the address against the one Severson had given them.

'This is it.'

A hand-painted sign above the porch steps said in flowing cursive: MISS CYNTHIA'S MUSEUM AND GALLERY.

As they mounted the steps, a bony, white-muzzled coonhound lifted its head from the mat on which it was lying, let out a single howl, then put its head back down and went back to sleep.

The front door opened, revealing a wizened woman in a white skirt and pink blouse standing behind the screen door. 'Afternoon, folks,' she said in a melodic Georgia drawl.

'Good afternoon,' Remi replied.

'Bubba is my doorbell, you see.'

'He's good at it,' said Sam.

'Oh, yes, he takes his job very seriously. Please, come in.'

She unlatched the screen door and pushed it open a few inches. Sam opened it the rest of the way, then followed Remi through.

'I'm Miss Cynthia,' the woman said and extended her hand.

'Remi – '

'Fargo, yes. And you would be Mr. Sam Fargo.'

'Yes, ma'am. How did you – '

'Julianne told me to expect you. And I don't get many visitors, you see, so it was a safe guess. Please, come in. I'm making tea.'

In an unsteady yet strangely elegant shuffle, she led them into what Sam and Remi could describe as a parlor. The heavy ornate furniture, lace curtains, and velvet-covered settees and chairs could have been taken straight from the set of *Gone with the Wind*.

Sam asked, 'Miss Cynthia, how do you and Julianne know each other?'

'I try to make it up to Washington once a year. I love its history. I met Miss Julianne about five years ago during a tour. I guess she found my pestering questions endearing, so we stayed in touch. Whenever I find a new piece I can't identify, I call her for help. She's been here to visit. Excuse me while I check on our tea.' She disappeared through another door and returned two minutes later. 'It's steeping. While we're waiting, let me show you what you came to see.'

She led them back out of the parlor, across the foyer, down a short hall, and through a door into a spacious, sunlit room painted snow white.

'Welcome to Miss Cynthia's Museum and Gallery,' she said.

Much like in Morton's Museum and Curiosity Shop in Bagamoyo, Miss Cynthia had assembled a plethora of artifacts – these all related to the Civil War – from musket balls and rifles to uniform patches and daguerreotypes.

'I collected all of this with my own hands,' Miss Cynthia said proudly. 'On battlefield sites, garage and estate sales . . . You'd be surprised what you find if you know what you're looking for. Oh, my, that sounded very wise, didn't it?'

Sam and Remi laughed. Remi said, 'It did indeed.'

'Those bits come to you now and again as you age. Well, you can look around at your leisure later, but let me show you this.'

Miss Cynthia walked to the room's northern wall, which was packed from floor to ceiling with framed photographs and sketches. She stood before it, lips pursed, as she scanned her eyes back and forth.

'Ah, there you are.'

She hobbled to the corner, reached up, and took down a black-framed four-by-six-inch image. She shuffled back and handed it to Sam.

A grainy daguerreotype showed a three-masted wooden ship sitting at anchor.

'My God,' Remi breathed. 'It's her.'

'Remi, look at this.' Sam brought the picture closer to their faces.

In the photo's lower right-hand corner, etched in faded ink, was a single word: Ophelia.

Five minutes later in the parlor, teacups in hand, they were still staring, dumbfounded, at the photograph. Sam said, 'How did you . . . ? Where . . . ?'

'That Julianne has quite a memory – eidetic, I think it's called.'

'Photographic memory.'

'Yes. She spent hours in my museum. This morning she sent me a pencil sketch through the e-mail whatsahoozit and asked me to compare it to mine. I assume the sketch was yours?'

'Something tells us it's more yours than ours,' Remi replied.

Miss Cynthia smiled, waved her hand. 'I told Julianne the two could be twins, despite the difference in media. The same right down to the inscription.'

'Ophelia.'

'Yes. Sadly, we never knew much about her.'

'Pardon me?' said Sam.

'My apologies. I'm getting ahead of myself. You see, William Lynd Blaylock was my great-great-great – I'm not sure how many "great"s, but he was my uncle.'

Miss Cynthia smiled sweetly and took a sip of tea.

Sam and Remi exchanged glances. Remi pursed her lips, thinking, then said, 'You're a Blaylock?'

'Oh, no, no. I'm an Ashworth. So was Ophelia until she married William. After Aunt Ophelia was killed, my great-

great – my grandmother Constance stayed in touch with William. It was never more than a friendship, of course, but I imagine there was some fondness there. He wrote her often, starting a few months after he got back from England and all the way until the end. Around 1883, I think.'

'The end,' Sam repeated. 'You mean his death?'

'Oh, I don't know. In fact, no one knows what became of him. I'm simply talking about the last letter he sent Grandmother Constance.' Miss Cynthia's eyes brightened. 'Goodness, there are dozens of them, with the most wonderful postmarks and stamps from all over. He was quite the character. Always on some kind of adventure or quest. As I understand it, Grandmother Constance was worried that he was a bit touched in the head. She took all his stories with a grain of salt.'

'You mentioned letters,' Remi said. 'Do you still – '

'Oh, yes, certainly. They're in the basement. Would you like to see them?'

Sam, not trusting himself to speak, merely nodded.

They followed her through the kitchen and down a set of narrow steps near the back door. Predictably, the basement was dark and dank, with rough stone walls and a veined concrete floor. Using the light streaming down the stairs, Miss Cynthia found the light switch. In the center of the basement a single sixty-watt bulb glowed to life. The walls and floor were stacked with cardboard boxes of all sizes and shapes.

'You see the three shoe boxes there?' Miss Cynthia said. 'Beside the Christmas-tree box?'

'Yes,' said Sam.

'That's them.'

Back in the parlor, Sam and Remi opened the boxes and were immediately relieved to find the letters had been divided and stored in gallon-sized Ziploc baggies.

Sam said, 'Miss Cynthia, you're our hero.'

'Nonsense. Now, I have one condition,' she said sternly. 'Are you listening?'

'Yes, ma'am,' said Sam.

'Take care of them and bring them back when you're done.'

'I don't understand,' Remi replied. 'You're letting us – '

'Of course. Julianne said you were decent people. She said you were trying to find out what happened to Uncle Blaylock in Africa – or wherever he ended up. It's been a mystery in our family for a hundred twenty-seven years. It would be nice to have it solved. Since I'm too old for that kind of adventure, at least I can hear about it later from you. Providing you promise to come back and tell me everything.'

'We promise,' Sam said.

Chapter 26

'Pete, Wendy, get these into the vault and do a quick assessment,' Selma said. She slid the shoe boxes across the worktable, and her assistants picked them up and disappeared into the archive chamber.

Unsure of the Blaylock letters' condition, Sam and Remi had resisted temptation and refrained from opening the Ziplocs before they got home.

'A fruitful trip, it seems,' Selma said.

'Your friend Julianne is one of a kind,' Remi said.

'Tell me something I don't know. If I'm ever hit by a bus, she should be your first call for a replacement.'

'Before or after we call 911?' Sam said.

'You're a funny one, Mr. Fargo. This Ashworth woman . . . she seemed genuine?'

'She did,' replied Remi. 'Between Blaylock's journal and Morton's biography we should be able to definitively prove or disprove the letters' bona fides.'

Selma nodded. 'While Pete and Wendy are working with those, care to see what progress we've made on the journal?'

'Can't wait,' said Sam.

The three of them sat down at the worktable facing the nearest LCD screen, and Selma used the remote to scroll into their server. She located the file she wanted and double-clicked it. It filled the screen:

'Wow,' Sam murmured. 'That's a busy mind. Could be the thoughts of a genius or a nut.'

'Or someone who did a lot of daydreaming,' Remi said. 'But in this case Blaylock doesn't strike me as the fanciful type. He was a type A personality before the term was coined.'

Selma said, 'This is a fairly representative page. Some have nothing but writing, but the majority are a mishmash of notes and drawings, some freehand and some probably done with a template or drafting tools.'

'Clearly the image in the upper left-hand corner is a hand-drawn map,' Sam said. 'And some text in the middle of it . . . "Great green jeweled bird." To the right of that, some more text – can't make it out – then some geometric symbols in the corner. Have you tried enlarging the text?'

Selma nodded. 'I had Wendy work on it – she's the graphics wizard. The more we enlarged it, the fuzzier it got.'

'What's at the bottom right? Was "Orizaga" there?

Selma, have you seen that elsewhere?'

'The name? In many places.'

Remi stood up and walked closer to the screen. 'In the middle, on the left and right . . . "Leonardo the Liar" and "63 great men." Between them, these numbers here . . . '1123581321.' Boy, talk about cryptic.'

'The bottom right is clearly a bird of some kind,' Selma added.

'The "great green jeweled bird"?' Remi suggested.

'Could be. As for two images in the middle – the one that looks a little like a cave painting and the arc below it – they've appeared on dozens and dozens of pages so far.'

The three fell silent, staring at the screen for several minutes. Eyes narrowed, Sam stood up and walked to screen and tapped the number sequence Remi had pointed out. 'I must be more tired than I thought,' he said. 'These numbers are the Fibonacci sequence.' Knowing his wife didn't share his love of math, Sam explained: 'When added together, the sum of the first two digits equals the third digit. You add the third and fourth digit together and get the sum of the fifth digit, and so on.' He walked back to the worktable and scribbled on a pad:

$$1 + 1 = 2$$
$$1 + 2 = 3$$
$$2 + 3 = 5$$
$$3 + 5 = 8$$

'You get the idea,' he said. 'It's also the basis of what's known as the golden ratio, or the golden spiral, or even the Fibonacci spiral. Here, I'll show you.' He walked to one of the computer workstations, did a quick Google search, and double-clicked a thumbnail. It filled the screen:

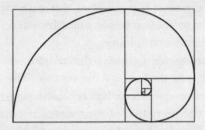

'You simply build a grid with whatever Fibonacci numbers you choose and overlay it with an arc,' Sam said. 'Your first box could be an inch square or a foot square. Anything.'

'That's what's on the journal page,' Remi said. 'A Fibonacci spiral.'

Sam nodded. 'Part of one, at least. The spiral is central to a lot of sacred geometry theories. You see the spiral in nature – the way shells form, in the buds of flowers. The Greeks used the spiral in a lot of their architecture. Even Web designers and graphic artists use it to create layouts. There've been scientific studies that show the golden spiral is inherently pleasing to the eye. No one's exactly sure why.'

'The question is,' Remi said, 'why was Blaylock obsessed with it? What else can it be used for, Sam?'

'Anything to do with geometry, really. I read that the NSA uses the Fibonacci sequence and the spiral in cryptography, but don't ask me how. That's far outside my wheelhouse. Selma, are there any more images that repeat?'

In response, Selma picked up the phone and dialed the archive vault. 'Pete, do you remember image twelve-alpha-four? Right, that's the one. How many repeats so far? Have you digitized it yet? Good, put it on the server, will you? I want to show it to Mr. and Mrs. Fargo. I'll hold.' A few moments later: 'Thanks.'

Selma hung up, grabbed the remote, and used it to scroll back into the server's file system. 'The image we've named twelve-alpha-four has repeated nine times so far, usually in the margins but sometimes as a central image. Here it is. Wendy worked her magic and plucked it off the page. It's still pretty messy.' On the screen, Selma moved the pointer over a thumbnail and double-clicked it. The image enlarged:

'Looks like a skull,' Sam said.

'My thought as well,' replied Selma.

Sam looked at Remi, who was staring at the image, her head cocked to one side, eyes narrowed. He said, 'Remi . . . Remi . . .'

She blinked her eyes and looked at him. 'Yes?'

'I know that expression. What's happening in your head?'

She didn't reply but shook her head absently. Without a

word she got up, walked to one of the workstations, and sat down. Her fingers began working the keyboard. Without turning she said, 'Just had a moment of déjà vu. Ever since we ran into Rivera and his men, their names have been stuck in my head. Why Aztec names? I thought it was just an oddity. I did a semester of Ancient Mesoamerican Studies at B.C., so I knew I'd seen that image before.' She tapped a few more keys and murmured, 'There you are . . .'

She turned in her seat and pointed at the TV screen. 'It's called Miquiztli. In Nahuatl, the Aztec language, it represented death.'

Chapter 27

'That's more than a little ominous,' Sam said after a moment.

'It also doubled as the symbol for the afterlife. It's all about context. Selma, do we have others?'

'Yes, three.' Selma brought them up on screen:

Remi peered at them for a few moments, then said, 'Do we have images we can use to compare?'

Selma picked up the phone to check.

Remi went on: 'Unless I'm wrong, they're all Aztec, too. The one on the right is Tecpatl, which represents flint, or obsidian knife; the middle one is Cipactli, or crocodile; the last one is Xochitl, or flower. It represents the last day of the twenty-day month.'

Sam asked Selma, 'And these were isolated like the first one? No annotations?'

Selma was off the phone. 'None. Wendy's uploading some clean images onto the server now.' Selma used the pointer to back out of the current image files until she found the new ones.

They were labeled 'Flint,' 'Crocodile,' and 'Flower'.

'They look like a match to me,' Selma said.

'Me too,' replied Sam. 'Remi, all of these are from the Aztec calendar, correct? It might be useful to see the whole thing.'

'I have the one Remi downloaded for me,' Selma said. She scrolled around the screen, found the correct file, and double-clicked it:

'Now, *that's* a calendar,' Sam muttered. 'How in the hell did they make sense of that?'

'Patience, I would imagine,' Remi replied. 'The symbols we've found so far all belong to the month ring. It's the fourth one from the edge.'

'No wonder the one in Mexico City's so big. How big exactly?'

'Twelve feet in diameter and four feet thick.'

'It'd have to be that big for anything to stand out. It's fascinating.'

'More so when you realize it's over five hundred years old. Three hundred of those it spent buried under the main square. Workers found it while doing repair work on the cathedral. It's one of the last vestiges of Aztec culture.'

The three of them went silent.

Selma's cell phone rang. She answered, listened, then said, 'We'll be here. Bring it to the side gate. I'll have Pete meet you.' She disconnected and told Sam and Remi, 'Dobo's on his way with the bell.'

'That was fast,' said Remi.

'Feels like Christmas morning,' Sam replied.

Twenty minutes later Pete Jeffcoat and Dobo came through the workroom's side door, one pushing and the other pulling a chest-high wheeled enclosure constructed of two-by-fours; hanging inside it was the *Shenandoah*'s bell. Aside from a few darkened patches, the tarnish and barnacles were gone, swept away by Dobo's magic. The bronze exterior fairly glowed under the workroom's halogen pendant lights.

Standing arms akimbo in his denim coveralls and white T-shirt, Dobo surveyed his handiwork. 'Nice, yes?'

'Beautiful work, Dobo,' said Sam.

If not for his frequent and easy smiles, Alexandru Dobo would have looked sinister, with his bald pate and thick, drooping mustache. He was, Remi had once observed, a Cossack lost in time.

'Thank you, my friend.' He clapped Sam on the back. Sam took a steadying step, then one more – away from Dobo. 'You see inside?' the Romanian asked. 'See inside! Pyotr, help.'

Dobo and Pete unlatched the bell from its hook, lifted

it free, turned it upside down, then returned it, mouth up, to the cage. 'Look, look!'

Sam, Remi, and Selma stepped forward and peered into the bell's interior. Remi sighed. After a few moments Sam said, 'Wish I could say I was surprised.'

'Me too,' replied Remi.

Carved haphazardly into the bell's bronze interior were dozens, perhaps hundreds, of what appeared to be Aztec symbols.

After a few moments Sam muttered, 'All aboard the Blaylock crazy train.'

Sam and Remi gathered their team around the work-table, and over the next few hours, and a pair of family-sized pies from Sammy's Woodfired Pizzas, they mulled over the mystery before them. The crux of the issue, they decided, could be summed up in two questions:

1. Did Blaylock's apparent mental instability cast into doubt all they'd found?

2. Were Rivera and his people on a fool's quest based on Blaylock's influence, or on other evidence?

Clearly Rivera was either searching for something or trying to keep something hidden, something that was probably Aztec in origin.

Pete Jeffcoat said, 'If you're right about the tourists they murdered, then it seems clear they're trying to hide something. It's hard for me to believe they'd do that just because of Blaylock. Wouldn't they have been asking the same questions about the guy that we are?'

'Good point,' Sam said.

'If that's the case,' Wendy said, 'then maybe Blaylock wasn't insane; maybe he was just eccentric, and there was something to his Aztec obsession.'

'As well as his fixation on the ship,' Selma added.

Remi said, 'Okay, let's take that as a given. How and why we don't know, but Blaylock became obsessed with the *Shenandoah*, or *El Majidi*; at some point after that, his mind turned to all things Aztec. Before we go any further, we need to find out when that happened and what caused it.'

Sam asked Pete and Wendy, 'How're we doing on Miss Cynthia's letters?'

'Another hour or so, and we should have them all examined,' Wendy replied. 'Another two hours to scan them and have the computer do an optical character recognition search. After that, we'll be able to easily sort them by date and search by key word.'

Sam smiled. 'Got any big plans tonight?'

'I guess we do now,' Pete replied.

Accustomed to how her husband's brain worked, Remi was not surprised to awaken and find him sitting up at the edge of the bed, Apple iPad propped on his knees. The nightstand clock read 4:12 A.M.

'Lightbulb moment?' she asked.

'I was thinking about chaos.'

'Of course you were.'

'And how most mathematicians don't believe in it. They

know it exists – there's even chaos theory – but I think secretly they all believe in underlying order. Even if it's not obvious.'

'I can buy that.'

'Then why would Blaylock go to all the trouble of randomly carving Aztec glyphs on the bell's interior? And why the bell?'

Remi said, 'I assume that's a rhetorical question.'

'I'm working through it. Did you read this poem from Blaylock's journal?'

'I didn't know there was one.'

'I just found it. Pete and Wendy just uploaded it,' Sam said, then recited:

> *In my love's heart I pen my devotion*
> *On Engai's gyrare I trust my feet*
> *From above, the earth turns, my day is halved*
> *Words of Ancients*
> *words of Father Algarismo*

'Not bad for a mathematician,' observed Remi.

'I wonder if he used the bell because it's durable, unlike paper. I also wonder if he used it because of its shape.'

'You've lost me.'

'The first line of his poem – "In my love's heart I pen my devotion" – he's got to be talking about his wife, about Ophelia, which is what he renamed the *El Majidi*.'

Remi caught on. 'And a ship's bell could be considered the heart of the ship.'

'Right. Now, the second line, "On Engai's gyrare I trust my feet." In Swahili, *Engai* is one of the spellings for the

Maasai's version of "God," and *girare* is Latin for "gyre"; it's a synonym for vortex or spiral.'

'As in the Fibonacci spiral. God's pattern in nature.'

'That's what I was thinking. Blaylock was using the spiral to guide himself. Put the lines together and maybe you've got Blaylock inscribing the bell with the source of his devotion – his obsession – and using the Fibonacci spiral as some kind of encoding technique.'

'And since by the time he made the inscriptions his wife was dead and he'd found the *Shenandoah*, his "devotion" was something else altogether,' said Remi. 'What about the gyre? How exactly would that fit in?'

'Picture a golden spiral.'

'Okay.'

'Now picture it superimposed on the interior of the bell, starting at the crown and spiraling downward and outward toward the mouth.'

Remi was nodding. 'And wherever the spiral intersects a symbol it means . . .' She shrugged. 'What?'

'I don't know. Something to do with the last three lines of the poem, maybe. I'm still working on that. All I know is that two of the most frequently repeated items in his journal are the Fibonacci spiral and Aztec symbols. If he's hiding something, they're probably involved.'

They got up, made a carafe of coffee, and headed down to the workroom. Selma was asleep on a cot in the corner. The overhead halogen lights were dimmed. Pete and Wendy sat at the worktable, laptops open, the screens' glow illuminating their faces.

'Coffee, guys?' Sam whispered.

Wendy smiled, shook her head, and nodded toward the collection of Red Bull cans on the table.

'We're almost done,' Pete said. 'Those Ziploc bags must have done the trick. It's just a guess, but I'd say the letters have been protected in one way or another for most of their life.'

'You got them all?' Remi asked.

Wendy nodded. 'Aside from some illegible spots here and there. We'll have everything uploaded and sorted in a couple hours.'

'Sam's got a hunch he wants to play,' Remi said.

'We're all ears,' replied Wendy.

Sam explained his theory. Pete and Wendy considered it for a few moments, then nodded in unison. 'Plausible,' Pete said.

'Ditto,' Wendy added. 'Blaylock was a mathematician. Those guys love order within chaos.'

From across the room Selma's scratchy voice said, 'Buy what?'

'Go back to sleep,' Remi said.

'Too late. I'm up. Buy what?'

She got off the cot and shuffled to the worktable. Remi poured her a cup of coffee and slid the mug down the table. Selma palmed it, took a sip. Sam re-explained his spiral/bell/symbol theory.

'It's worth a shot,' Selma agreed. 'The crown of the bell would be the likely place to start the spiral, but how do we know how big it is? And you're assuming it would unravel and end at the bell's mouth. What if it doesn't?'

Sam smiled wearily. 'Killjoy.'

*

The group began brainstorming. At the top of their list was the question of scale. A Fibonacci spiral could be built to any scale. If Blaylock was in fact using a spiral, he would've used a reference size for the first box in the grid. They tossed around ideas for an hour before realizing they were getting nowhere.

'It could be anything,' Sam said, rubbing his eyes. 'A number, a note, a doodle . . .'

'Or something we haven't even seen yet,' Remi added. 'Something we've overlooked.'

Across the table, an exhausted Pete Jeffcoat laid his head down on the wood and stretched his arms before him. His right hand struck Blaylock's walking staff, which rolled off the edge and clattered to the floor.

'Damn!' Pete said. 'Sorry.'

'No problem.' Sam knelt down to retrieve the staff. The bell clapper had torn free of its leather bindings and was hanging by a single thong. Sam picked them up together. He stopped and peered at the head of the staff. He frowned.

'Sam?' said Remi.

'I need a flashlight.'

Wendy pulled out a storage drawer and handed an LED across to Sam, who clicked it on and shone it onto the staff's head. 'It's hollow,' he muttered. 'I need some long-handled tweezers.'

Wendy retrieved a pair, handed them over.

Gingerly, Sam inserted the tips of the tweezers into the opening, wriggled them around for a few seconds, then began withdrawing them.

Grasped between the pincers was a corner of parchment.

Chapter 28

'Oh, sure,' Sam muttered. 'It couldn't have been something easy. Like a map with a big X on it.'

Wary of damaging the remainder of the parchment, or anything else that might lie hidden inside Blaylock's walking staff, Pete and Wendy had taken it into the archive vault for extraction and triage preservation.

Ten minutes later a digital image of what Sam had grabbed with his tweezers appeared on the workroom's LCD screen:

Pete came out of the vault. He said, 'We had to reduce it. The map's actual dimensions are roughly six inches wide by ten long.'

'What about those notations along the coast?' Sam asked.

'Once we get the map digitized, Wendy's going to work

her Photoshop magic and try to clean them up. Based on their placement and the capital *R* suffix, they're probably river names – in French, by the looks of it. The partial word in the upper left-hand corner – "runes" – might be something we can work with, too.

'There's another notation,' Pete continued. 'See the arrow I superimposed?'

'Yes,' Remi replied.

'There's some microwriting overtop that little island. We're working on that as well.'

The archive vault door opened, and Wendy emerged carrying a rectangle of parchment sandwiched between two panes of Lexan clear polycarbonate.

'What's this?' Remi asked.

'The surprise behind door number two,' replied Wendy. 'This was rolled up at the bottom of the staff.'

She laid the pane on the worktable.

Sam, Remi, and Selma gathered around it and stared in silence for ten seconds.

Finally Remi whispered, 'It's a codex. An Aztec codex.'

*

Faced with two seemingly disparate artifacts, they divided forces. Pete and Wendy settled down at a workstation to identify the map, while Sam, Remi, and Selma tackled this new parchment.

Remi began. 'Codex is Latin for a "block of wood," but over time it became synonymous with any type of bound book or parchment. It's the model for modern book manufacturing, but before binding became common practice anything could be considered a codex – even a single piece of parchment or several folded together.

'You see, when the Spanish invaded Mexico in 1519 – '

Sam interrupted. 'Maybe now would be a good time for an Aztec 101 course?'

'Okay. Bear in mind, among historians there's a lot of debate about the Aztecs, from the trivial to the significant. I'll give you the condensed, middle-of-the road version.

'Aztec is the popular name for a group of Nahua-speaking peoples that some historians refer to as the Mexica – sounds like Meh-SHEE-kah – who migrated into central Mexico from somewhere to the north in the sixth century.'

'"Somewhere to the north" is rather vague,' Selma observed.

Remi nodded. 'Yet another source of controversy. I'll cover that in a minute. So the Aztecs continued their migration into the Valley of Mexico, displacing and absorbing other tribes – including some of their mythology and cultural practices. This went on until around the twelfth century. At the time, most of the power in the region was concentrated in the hands of the Tepanecs in Azcapotzalco. Fast-forward: power trades hands, alliances are made and broken, and the Aztecs are fairly low on the power ladder.

'Until 1323, when legend has it that the Aztecs were shown a vision of an eagle with a snake in its mouth perched atop a cactus. After a few more years of wandering, the Aztecs come across a swampy, barely inhabitable island in the middle of Lake Texcoco – which is mostly gone today; it sits beneath Mexico City. It's on this island they supposedly see the eagle/snake/cactus vision. They stop wandering and start building. They called their new city Tenochtitlán.

'Despite their new capital being as much marsh as it was land, the Aztecs pulled off an engineering marvel. Tenochtitlán occupied about five square miles on the west side of Lake Texcoco. They built causeways to the mainland, complete with rising bridges to accommodate water traffic; they built aqueducts to supply the city with fresh water; there were plazas and palaces, residential areas, and business centers all connected by canals. When the population got too big to feed with crops grown on the mainland, Aztec engineers created floating gardens called *chinampas* that could produce up to seven crops a year.

'This went on another fifty years or so until the late 1420s, when the Triple Alliance among Tenochtitlán, Texcoco, and Tlacopan was formed. All the tribes outside the alliance were subjugated as the alliance grew in strength. Then, slowly, over the next century, the Aztecs and Tenochtitlán rose to the top.'

'And then Cortés arrived,' Sam said.

'Right. In the spring of 1519. Within two years, the Aztec Empire was all but destroyed.'

'What's the rest of the controversy?' Selma said. 'About the Aztecs?'

'Where they came from – north or south, or from how far away. Many of the classical and pre-classical Meso-american cultures – the Toltecs, the Maya, the Olmecs – share similarities with the Aztecs. It's a chicken-or-egg situation. Was it simply a matter of cultural cross-pollination or was one of these peoples the precursor to all the rest? There are a lot of historians who think the Aztecs were Meso-america's true progenitors.'

Sam and Selma took all this in. Then Sam said, 'Okay, you were talking about codices . . .'

'Right,' Remi said. 'When Cortés invaded and the Aztec Empire collapsed, there were a lot of codices written, most of them by Jesuit and Franciscan monks, some by soldiers or diplomats, and even a few by Aztecs as dictated to others. Those are fairly rare and usually discounted – or at least they were until the last couple hundred years. Aztec codices tended to stray from the Spanish "party line," which was that Aztecs were savages and that their conquest was wonderful and dictated by God. You get the idea.'

'Again, victors write the history,' Sam said.

'You got it.'

Selma said, 'You're talking about the Codex Borboni-cus, the Mendoza, the Florentine . . .'

'Right. There are dozens. Usually they depict Aztec life either before, during, or after the Spanish conquest. Some are just tableaus of routine activities while others are meant as historical accounts of Cortés's arrival, of battles fought or ceremonies, and so on.'

Remi grabbed a magnifying glass from a drawer and

bent to examine the codex. She spent ten minutes poring over every square inch, then stood up and sighed.

'In theme, this one's a lot like the Boturini Codex. Allegedly, the Boturini was written by an anonymous Aztec author between 1530 and 1541, about ten years after the Aztecs fell. It's supposed to tell the story of the Aztecs' journey from Aztlán to present-day Mexico.'

'Aztlán?' asked Sam.

'One of the two mythical ancestral homes of the Nahua peoples, which include the Aztecs. Many historians disagree about whether Aztlán is a legend or an actual physical location.'

'You said two homes.'

'The other one's called Chicomoztoc, or Place of the Seven Caves. It's important in Aztec lore and religion. Take a look at our codex. You see the hollowed-out flower shape in the lower right-hand corner?'

Sam and Selma nodded.

'That's how Chicomoztoc is usually represented. But this one's a little different, I think. I'll have to do some comparisons.'

'If I'm reading this right,' Sam said, 'it's meant to represent a sea voyage. I assume the canoe is a metaphor?'

'Hard to say. But do you notice the comblike object on the side of it?'

'I saw it.'

'That's the glyph for the Aztec number one hundred.'

'People or vessels?'

'Given its placement, I assume the latter.'

'A hundred ships,' Sam repeated. 'Sailing from Chicomoztoc to . . . where?'

'Wherever that bird and the object below it live?' Selma offered. 'What is that? I can't quite make it out.'

'Looks like a sword,' Sam offered. 'Or a torch, maybe?'

Selma said, 'I don't know about that, but that bird looks familiar.'

'It should,' Remi replied. 'It's from Blaylock's journal. There's something else you should all recognize, too.'

Sam tapped the rough-brushed shape occupying the upper half of the codex. 'Also from Blaylock's journal.'

'A gold star for Mr. Fargo. And one more,' Remi said, handing him the magnifying glass. 'The inscription.'

Sam lifted the glass to his eye and bent closer to the codex. He recited, 'My Spanish isn't the best, but here goes . . . *"Dado este 12vo día de Julio, año de nuestro Señor 1521, por su alteza Cuauhtemotzin. Javier Orizaga, S.J."'* Sam looked up. 'Remi?'

'Roughly translated it says, "Given this twelfth day of July, the year of our Lord 1521, by His Highness Cuauht-emotzin. Javier Orizaga, S.J."'

'Orizaga . . . That's another tidbit from Blaylock's journal: "Was Orizaga here?"'

'Here, where?' Selma asked. 'Chicomoztoc?'

'Anyone's guess,' Remi replied. 'You're missing the real bombshell, though.'

Without another word, she walked over to a workstation, brought up the Web browser, and spent five minutes navigating through pages on famsi.org – the Foundation for the Advancement of Mesoamerican Studies. Finally, she turned in her seat.

'Obviously, the S.J. in Orizaga's name means "Society of Jesus." He was a Jesuit monk. The date, July 12, 1521, is twelve days after what the Spaniards called La Noche Triste, the "Sad Night." It marks their emergency withdrawal from the Aztec capitol of Tenochtitlán after Cortés and his Conquistadors massacred hundreds of Aztecs – along with their king, Moctezuma II – at the Main Temple, the Templo Mayor. It was a watershed moment for the Aztec Empire. In August of the following year Tenochtitlán was razed to the ground, and the Aztecs' last king, Cuauhtemotzin, was captured and tortured.'

'Cuauhtemotzin,' Sam repeated, then turned back to the codex for a moment. 'That's who Orizaga claims dictated this codex.'

Selma murmured, 'Cuauhtemotzin saw the handwriting on the walls. He knew his people were doomed and he wanted someone to know . . .' Selma's voice trailed off.

Remi nodded. 'If this codex is genuine, we may be looking at the last will and testament of the Aztec people.'

Chapter 29

Madagascar, Indian Ocean

'Africa again,' Sam muttered, pulling the Range Rover to a stop off the dirt road. He shut off the engine and set the parking brake. 'Had to be Africa.'

'Don't let the locals hear you say that,' Remi replied. 'We're three hundred miles off the African coast. As far as these folks are concerned, Madagascar's a world unto itself.'

Sam raised his hands in surrender. He knew she was right. Their marathon, San Diego–Atlanta–Johannesburg–Antananarivo route had given them plenty of time to read up on Madagascar.

They climbed out, walked to the rear of the Rover, and began gathering their gear.

The identity of the map inside Blaylock's walking staff had remained a mystery for only a few hours as Pete and Wendy scoured the vast cartographical databases the Fargos had acquired over the years. As it turned out, the map in question was but a section of a larger chart penned by a French explorer named Moreau in 1873, some twenty-three years after France's armed annexation of the island. The partial word in the upper left-hand corner was in fact *Prunes* – French for 'plums' – the name given by an explorer to a series of atolls along the coast.

From there Pete and Wendy had had little trouble match-ing up the river names and isolating the section of coastline in question.

What remained a mystery, however, was why Madagascar had been so important to Blaylock. It was a question Sam and Remi hoped to answer while Selma, the Wonder Twins, and Julianne Severson at the Library of Congress continued to dissect and analyze Blaylock's journal, his letters to Constance Ashworth, and the newly named Orizaga Codex.

For their part, aside from a current topographical chart, all Sam and Remi had to go on was a laminated copy of the Moreau map and an enlargement of the area around the miniaturized annotation – which they'd matched to Blaylock's handwriting – that Pete had dis-covered penned over a cove in the coastline. Having grown accustomed to Blaylock's penchant for thought fragments, they'd been unsurprised to find the jot con-sisted of only seven words:

1442 Spans 315°
Into the Lion's Mouth

The fourth-largest island in the world, Madagascar was in many ways a world apart. For instance, it was home to five percent of the world's plant and animal species. Of these, eighty percent were found nowhere else on earth: lemurs of every stripe and size, cave-dwelling crocodiles, carnivorous plants and spitting beetles, and giant centi-pedes, thirty-two species of chameleon, two hundred two species of birds, and an array of baobab trees that seemed plucked from the mind of a science-fiction movie director. And for all that, not a single endemic poisonous snake called the island home.

Madagascar's history was no less unique. While the island's official history began in the seventh century with Bantus using encampments along Madagascar's northern tip as trading posts for passing Arab merchants, archeological finds in recent decades had to probe deeper, suggesting Madagascar's first settlers had arrived from Sulawesi, in Indonesia, between 200 and 500 C.E.

Over the next eleven hundred years, Madagascar became the melting pot of Africa, populated mostly by Portuguese, Indian, Arabic, and Somalian settlers, until the Age of Exploration arrived and the scramble for Africa began. European colonial powers and pirates alike rushed to Madagascar, and the island saw a series of ruling dynasties until the late eighteenth century, when the Merina family managed, with the help of the British, to gain control of most of the island in a hegemony that ended almost a century later with France's invasion in 1883 and what became known as the Franco-Hova War. In 1896 France annexed Madagascar, and the Merina royal family was exiled to Algeria.

They gave their gear a once-over, then donned their packs before standing back to take in the scenery. The drive from the Antananarivo airport had taken them east on Route 2 and down from the central highlands that ran roughly north to south down the island's spine to where they stood, the coastal lowlands, a two-mile-wide ribbon of rain forest and ravine-laden terrain buttressed by fifteen-hundred-foot escarpments interlaced with waterfalls. At their back was the Canal des Pangalanes, a five-hundred-mile-long chain of natural and man-made lakes and coves connected by canals.

It was in this section of the Pangalanes that they hoped to find the spot Blaylock had indicated with his cryptic notation. From there it would be only a matter of pacing off 1,442 'spans' (which they assumed and hoped referred to Blaylock's staff) on a compass bearing of 315 and looking for a 'Lion's Mouth' into which they could leap or stare or whatever Blaylock had in mind. The problem was, Moreau, the author of the map, had clearly missed Cartography Day in Explorers' School. His sense of scale and distance was nearly nonexistent. Sam and Remi's exploration would have to be trial and error.

'It never sounded simple,' Remi now said, 'but looking at this place . . .' Her voice trailed off, and she shook her head in frustration.

Sam nodded. 'The land that time forgot.'

In the lead, Sam stepped off the road onto what resembled a game trail, which evaporated after a hundred yards, at which point he unsheathed his machete and began bushwhacking through the head-height brush. With every step, saw-toothed leaves nicked their exposed skin while spiked stems plucked at their clothing, frequently requiring them to stop to free themselves. After thirty minutes they'd covered a quarter mile, when a garage-sized clearing opened before them. Remi took a reading from their handheld GPS, looked around to get her bearings, then pointed. They set off again, Sam hacking a path while Remi navigated. Thirty minutes turned into an hour. Sweat beaded on their pinpricked skin, and their clothes became so saturated they might as well have just stepped from a swimming pool. Despite the blazing sun, each of them felt slightly chilled. After another thirty minutes, Sam stopped suddenly and held up his hand for quiet. He glanced back at Remi and tapped his nose. She nodded. Smoke. Somewhere nearby was a campfire.

Then, somewhere off to their left, came a rustling sound. Something was moving in the underbrush. They stood stock-still, barely breathing, trying to pinpoint the location. It came again but sounded farther away.

Suddenly a male voice called out, 'Are you good folks lost, by chance?'

Sam looked back at Remi, who shrugged. Sam called back, 'I wouldn't so much call it "lost" as "serendipitous exploration."'

The voice chuckled. 'Well, that's a first. If you feel like a break, I've got coffee on.'

'Sure, why not? Where – '

'Look to your left.'

They did so. A moment later the flaming tip of a branch jutted up from the undergrowth thirty feet away. 'If you keep going straight for ten or twelve more paces, you'll run into a game trail. It'll take you straight in.'

'On our way.'

Five minutes later they pushed their way off the trail into a clearing surrounded by dwarf baobabs. Strung between two of them was a netted hammock. In the center of the clearing, hemmed in by a pair of fallen logs for seating, a small campfire crackled. A mid-seventies man with silver hair and a goatee smiled up at them. His eyes were a mischievous green.

'Welcome. Have a seat.'

Sam and Remi shrugged off their packs and sat down on the log opposite the man. They introduced themselves.

The man nodded, smiled, and said, 'Everybody calls me Kid.'

Sam nodded at the revolver strapped to the man's hip. 'Because of that?'

'More or less.'

'A Webley?'

'Good eye. Model Mark VI, .455 caliber. Circa 1915.'

'Enough gun talk, boys,' Remi said. 'We appreciate the invitation. It feels like we've been out there for two days.'

'In Madagascar time, that's about two hours.'

Sam checked his watch. 'You're right.' Sam noticed what looked like a two-foot-high pyramid of dirt clods lying at the man's feet. 'May I ask . . .'

'Ah, these. Madagascar truffles. Finest in the world.'

'Never heard of them,' Remi replied.

'Most of them get sold to Japan. A thousand dollars a pound.'

Sam said, 'Looks like you've got a few thousand dollars sitting beside your boots.'

'Give or take.'

'How do you find them?' asked Remi.

'Smell, location, animal tracks. After ten years, it's more a feeling than anything else.'

'Ten years? Not out here the whole time, I hope.'

The Kid chuckled. 'No. Truffle season's only five weeks long. The other forty-seven weeks I've got a little place on the beach near Andevoranto. Do a little fishing, a little diving, a little hiking, and a lot of staring at sunsets.'

'Sounds wonderful.'

'It is indeed, madam. What's not wonderful, however, is the nice collection of scratches there.'

Sam and Remi glanced at the red crisscrosses on their arms and legs. The man reached into an old canvas backpack leaning against the log, rummaged around, and came out with an unmarked glass tube. He tossed it across to Remi.

'Local recipe,' the Kid said. 'Works miracles. Just don't ask what's in it.'

Sam and Remi dabbed the greenish, foul-smelling ointment on their scratches. Immediately the sting disappeared. Sam said, 'Smells a lot like animal urine and – '

The Kid smiled. 'I told you not to ask.' He poured them each a cup of coffee from the soot-burnished percolator sitting at the edge of the fire. 'So if you don't mind me asking, what're you folks doing out here?'

'We're looking for a spot that may or may not exist,' Sam replied.

'Ah, the siren song of lost lands. As it happens, imaginary places are one of my specialties.'

Sam reached into the side pocket of his pack, withdrew the Moreau map, and handed it across. The Kid studied it for thirty seconds, then handed it back. 'Good news, bad news. Pick your poison.'

'Bad news,' Remi replied.

'You're about eighty years too late. That area of the Pangalanes was swallowed up after an earthquake in 1932.'

'And the good news?'

'It's dry land now. And I can probably get you to within a few yards of the spot you seek.'

They finished their coffee, then the Kid kicked dirt over his fire and packed his gear, and the three of them set out with the Kid in the lead, Remi in the middle, and Sam trailing. The Kid required neither machete nor compass as he headed northeast, following trails that at first glance seemed like nothing more than gaps in the foliage. Despite his years, he moved at a steady, economical pace that told Sam and Remi their guide had spent more of his life out-of-doors than in.

After forty minutes of walking in companionable silence, the Kid called over his shoulder, 'This place you're looking for . . . What's so special about it?'

Remi glanced back at Sam with a questioning look on her face. Sam gave it a moment's thought, then replied, 'You strike me as an honest man, Kid. Am I wrong about that?'

The Kid stopped walking and turned around. He smiled.

'You're not wrong. I've kept more confidences than steps I've taken.'

Sam held his gaze for a few moments, then nodded. 'Lead on, and we'll tell you a story.'

The Kid turned around and started walking again.

Sam said, 'Have you ever heard of the CSS *Shenandoah*?'

After another hour the underbrush began to thin out, and they soon found themselves surrounded by savanna dotted with clusters of baobab. A mile to their left, the grassland again gave way to rain forest that rose to meet the escarpment, while to their right they could see the Canal des Pangalanes; beyond that, the blue of the Indian Ocean.

They stopped walking and took a water break. After a gulp from his canteen, the Kid said, 'So this Blaylock fella . . . He sounds like quite a character.'

Remi nodded. 'The problem is, we still don't know how much of his story is real and how much is malaria- and grief-induced fantasy.'

'That's the blessing and the curse of adventure,' the Kid replied. 'As far as I'm concerned, one should never miss the chance to take the road less traveled.'

Sam smiled and held up his canteen. 'Cheers to that.'

They clicked canteens.

'Why don't you two take a break. I'm going to do some scouting. I think we're close, but I need to do some checking around.'

The Kid dropped his pack and walked off through the knee-high grass. Sam and Remi plopped down on the ground and listened to the waves crashing on the beach. A cluster of rainbow-hued butterflies drifted across the tops of the grass, fluttered above their heads for a few moments, then continued on. From a nearby baobab a ring-tailed lemur hung upside down staring at them. After two minutes of this, he slowly climbed up and out of view.

Without a sound, the Kid reappeared behind them. 'Eureka,' he simply said.

It was a five-minute walk away. As they topped a small, steep-sided hillock, the Kid stopped and spread his hands.

'Here?' Sam asked.

'Here. After the earthquake the cove closed up and the water evaporated, leaving just the upper part of the island exposed. Eighty years of ocean silt and storms filled in the depression.'

Sam and Remi looked around. Thankfully, the hillock measured no more than four hundred square feet.

Remi said, 'I suppose we find the center point and start walking.'

The Kid asked, 'How many spans did Blaylock indicate?'

'Fourteen hundred forty-two. A little under two miles.'

The Kid checked the sky. 'In Madagascar time, that's three or four hours, most of it back in the rain forest. My recommendation: We settle in for the night.'

Chapter 30

Madagascar, Indian Ocean

They were up shortly after dawn. At the Kid's insistence, Sam and Remi wandered down to a tidal pool for a rinse off while he threw together a meal of truffles and cassava hash browns. They returned to camp just as the percolator was beginning to boil. Remi poured three cups while Sam helped the Kid serve.

'Probably should ask you,' the Kid said between forkfuls, 'how much do you know about the situation here?'

'You mean politically?' Sam replied. 'Not much, aside from what we read in the papers – a coup, a new president, and an angry ex-president in exile.'

'That's the short of it. What you don't know is the ex-president is back from exile. Rumor is he's back and has set up shop in Maroantsetra, up the coast. If he manages to put together enough men and guns, there'll probably be a civil war; if he doesn't, it'll be a massacre. Either way, it's not the best time to be a white face on the island. Around the cities you're okay, but out here . . .' The Kid shrugged. 'Might want to keep a sharp eye out.'

'For what?' asked Remi.

'Mostly guys with AK-47s riding around in pickup trucks.'

'So we should hope we see them before they see us.'

'That would be the idea. Even if not, if you look like you're more trouble than you're worth, they might move on. Whenever politics get stirred up like this, the underdogs sometimes look at kidnapping as an income-and-leverage opportunity.'

Sam said, 'With luck we'll be back in Antananarivo before nightfall.'

The Kid smiled. 'After you've found whatever there is to find.'

'Or find that there's nothing to find,' Remi added.

Shortly before eight they packed up their gear, trudged up the hillock, took a bearing on 315, then set out single file across the savanna with the Kid in the lead, Remi in the middle, and Sam bringing up the rear with his handheld GPS, which he'd calibrated to bearing/countdown mode: 1,442 spans of Blaylock's 7-foot-tall walking staff, which would equal 10,094 feet or 1.91 miles.

'Here's hoping Blaylock's staff hasn't shrunk or expanded in the last hundred thirty years,' Sam called.

'Or that he was no good with a tape measure,' Remi added.

They hadn't crossed half the savanna before their boots and pant legs were soaked with dew. By the time they reached the edge of the rain forest, the sun's lower rim had broken free of the eastern horizon; they felt its heat on their backs.

The Kid stopped before the wall of jungle, said, 'Wait a moment,' then walked the tree line, first north for fifty yards, then south. 'This way,' he called. Sam and Remi joined him. Not surprisingly, he'd found a trail.

Ten feet inside the trees the sun dimmed behind them, leaving only faint stripes and splotches on the foliage around them.

'Fifty-five hundred feet down, forty-six hundred to go,' Sam announced.

They walked on. Soon the grade increased as the terrain began its climb toward the highlands. The trail narrowed, first to shoulder width, then to a foot, forcing them to sidestep and duck in places. The razor-sharp leaves and prickly stalks returned with a vengeance.

The Kid called a halt. 'Do you hear that?' he asked.

Sam nodded. 'A stream. Somewhere to the left.'

'I'll be right back.' The Kid ducked off the trail and was swallowed by the forest. He returned ten minutes later. 'It's about thirty yards south. I think it'll roughly parallel your course. How far to go?'

Sam checked the GPS. 'Three thousand feet.'

'Nine thousand on the Madagascar scale,' Remi added with a game smile.

'The stream will be easier going. Just watch out for crocs.'

'You're kidding,' Remi said.

'Nope. You've heard of the Madagascar cave crocodiles?'

'We weren't sure if they were a wives' tale or not,' Sam replied.

'Not. Madagascar's the only place on earth that has them. See, alligators and crocodiles are ectothermic: They rely on the environment to regulate their body temperatures — sun for warmth, water and shade for cool. Our crocs don't need that. *National Geographic* was out here a few years ago to look into them, but it's still a mystery. Anyway, sometimes in the morning they'll use underground streams to come out to hunt before the sun gets too hot.'

'And we'll spot them how, exactly?' Remi asked.

'Look for logs floating in the water. If the log's got eyeballs, it's not a log. Make a lot of noise, look big. They'll take off.'

The stream was calf deep and sand bottomed, so they made rapid progress, slowly winding down the GPS's screen until it read 400 feet. The stream curved first south, then back north, then west again, before broadening out into a boulder-lined lagoon. On the west side of the pool a forty-foot-wide waterfall crashed onto a rock shelf, sending up a cloud of spray.

Sam checked the GPS. 'Two hundred feet.'

'Bearing?' Remi asked.

In answer, Sam pointed at the waterfall.

After a few moments of silence, Remi said, 'Do you see it?'

'What?' replied Sam.

'The lion's head.' She pointed at the point where the water tumbled off the rock ledge. 'The two outcrops are the eyes. Below them, the mouth. And the water . . . If you watch it long enough, some of the streamers look like fangs.'

The Kid was nodding. 'I'll be darned. She's right, Sam.'

Sam chuckled. 'She usually is.'

'Maybe your Blaylock isn't crazy after all.'

'We'll see.'

Sam dropped his pack, stripped to the waist, and donned a waterproof headlamp. He clicked it on, pointed the beam at his palm, and clicked it off.

'Just an exploratory probe, right?' said Remi.

'Right. Five minutes, no more.'

'Hold on a second,' the Kid said. He dug into his pack and came out first with a marine flare – 'Crocs hate these' – then another revolver, this one similar to his own Webley. 'Crocs hate these even more.'

Sam hefted the weapon, studied it. 'I don't recognize it. Another Webley?'

'The Webley-Fosbery Automatic Revolver. One of the first and only wheel-gun semiautomatics. Break-top design, .455 caliber, six rounds. Not much good past fifty yards, but whatever you hit goes down.'

'Thanks,' Sam said. 'Exactly how many Webleys do you have?'

'Last count, eighteen. Kind of a hobby.'

'Antique revolvers and rare truffles,' Remi replied. 'You are an interesting man.'

Sam shoved the flare into one of his shorts' cargo pockets, the Webley into the other, then began picking his way around the lagoon's edge, hopping from boulder to boulder and doing his best to avoid wet patches, a task that became harder the closer he came to the waterfall. When he was within arm's length of the cascade, he turned, gave a short wave to Remi and the Kid, then ducked into the deluge and disappeared.

Four minutes later he reappeared, hopped onto a nearby boulder, shook the water from his hair, then made his way back to the beach.

'There's a shallow grotto behind the falls,' he announced. 'It's about twenty feet deep and fifteen wide. It's clogged with backwash — branches, rotting logs, heaps of grass that've formed into a loose dam — but behind all that I found an opening. It's a horizontal gap, really, like a stone garage door that didn't close all the way.'

'There goes our streak,' Remi replied with a smile.

'Pardon me?' asked the Kid.

Sam said, 'So far on this particular adventure, we haven't had to go subterranean, which is rare, given what we do. Before there were barable doors and lockable vaults, if you wanted to keep something safe or a secret you had only two reliable choices: bury it or hide it in a cave.'

Remi added, 'Still pretty common today. Might have something to do with genetic memory: When in doubt, burrow.'

'So you've never had a completely aboveground adventure?'

Sam shook his head. Remi said, 'It's why we stay current on our climbing and spelunking skills.'

'Well, caves are far down my list of favorite places,' the Kid said. 'So if you don't mind, I'm going to let you two have all the fun. I'll mind the fort.'

Ten minutes later, armed with the appropriate gear, Sam and Remi returned to the waterfall and ducked behind it into the grotto. The sunlight dimmed behind the curtain of water. They clicked on their headlamps.

Sam stepped close to Remi and said over the rush, 'Stand to one side. I'm going to see if we've got any company. Be ready with a flare.'

Remi stepped to the other side of the grotto while Sam

selected a long branch from the dam pile and pulled it free. Systematically, he began probing the debris, jamming the branch's tip into holes and gaps and wiggling it about. He got no reaction; nothing moved. He spent another two minutes heel-kicking the larger logs, trying to illicit a response, but fared no better.

'I think we're okay,' Sam called.

They got to work, slowly dismantling the pile until they cleared a path to the rear wall. They knelt before the four-foot-tall gap. A shallow runnel trickled past their boots and across the grotto before joining the waterfall proper.

Sam jammed his branch into the opening and rattled it about. Again, nothing moved. He pulled the Webley from his pocket, leaned forward, pressed his face to the rock, and panned his headlamp from right to left. He straightened up and gave Remi the OK sign.

'Once more into the breach,' she yelled.

'We two, we happy two,' Sam answered in kind.

'Nothing like a little bastardized Shakespeare to set the tone.'

Chapter 31

Madagascar, Indian Ocean

Their entry was thankfully short. After five feet of hunched walking, they saw that the rock ceiling abruptly sloped upward and found themselves standing in an elongated oval cavern a hundred feet wide with a thirty-foot-tall, stalactite-riddled ceiling. Their headlamps weren't strong enough to penetrate more than thirty feet ahead, but from what they could see the space appeared to be loosely divided into 'rooms' by mineral columns that shone pearlescent gray and butter yellow in the beams of their lamps. The quartz inclusions in the walls winked and sparkled. The floor, a mixture of jagged rock and silt that crunched under their boots, was split by a narrow, winding creek.

'Seems like a natural place to start,' Sam said, and Remi nodded.

Using the creek's path as a guide, they began moving into the cave.

'Somewhat anticlimactic,' Remi said after a few minutes.

'I know. The day is young, though.'

Their last spelunking adventure had ended with not only the solution of the mystery of Napoleon's lost cellar but also a discovery that was helping rewrite parts of ancient Greek history.

They continued on, covering a hundred feet, then two hundred. Sam's headlamp picked out a wedge-shaped wall ahead from whose base the creek gushed. On either side of the wall, a tunnel curved back into darkness.

'Your pick,' Sam said. 'Left or right?'

'Right.'

They hopped over the creek and started down the right-hand tunnel. After twenty feet the floor sloped down, and they found themselves standing in calf-deep water. Sam shined his beam over the surface; there was a slight eddying current. They kept walking.

Remi stopped and put her index finger to her lips.

She clicked off her headlamp. Sam did the same.

Then, following ten seconds of silence, a sound: something moving in the darkness ahead. Like leather scraping against stone. More silence, then another sound: like a heavy wet towel striking rock.

Sam and Remi looked at each other and, in near unison, mouthed: *Crocodile*. The leather was scaled skin rubbing on rock; the wet towel, a heavily muscled tail slapping stone. Splashing.

Heavy feet plodded through water. Sam drew the Webley and pointed it into the darkness. Together, he and Remi clicked on their headlamps.

Twenty feet away and sloshing directly toward them was a crocodile snout; just behind the snout a pair of heavy-lidded eyes staring back at them. Farther back, at the edge of their headlamp beams, they could see a half dozen scaly bodies writhing about, eyes flashing, mouths agape, tails whipping.

'Flare,' Sam said.

Remi didn't hesitate. With a hiss, the tunnel filled with flickering red light. Remi lowered the flare to knee level and waved it before the oncoming crocodile, which stopped, opened its mouth, and let out a low hiss.

'The Kid was right,' she said. 'They don't care for it.'

'For now. Start backing up. Slowly. Don't turn your back on it.'

In lockstep, with Remi's eyes fixed on the approaching crocodile, they began retreating. Sam glanced over his shoulder. 'Another ten steps and we're at the ramp, then the narrow part.'

'Okay.'

'When we get there, plant the flare in the sand. We'll see how they like that.'

When they reached the spot, Sam patted Remi's shoulder. She knelt down, jammed the flare into the silt, then stood up and kept back-stepping, with Sam's hand still on her shoulder. Halfway up the ramp, the crocodile stopped six feet before the hissing flare. It scrabbled first to the left, then to the right, then stopped again. It let out another hiss, then backed down the ramp and into the water. After a few seconds it disappeared from view.

'How long do flares last?' Remi asked.

'That kind? Ten or fifteen minutes. With luck, long enough for us to check the other tunnel.'

'And if not?'

'Then we get to see how good I am with the Webley.'

Pausing to listen every ten paces or so, they proceeded down the left-hand tunnel. After forty feet the tunnel suddenly broadened out into a roughly circular chamber.

Remi's headlamp swept over a dark elongated object on the floor. They both started and backpedaled ten steps, their feet skidding in the sand.

Remi whispered, 'Was it – '

'I don't think so.' He took a deep breath and let it out. 'Enough to get my heart going, though. Come on.'

They moved forward until their beams again found the object.

'Looks like a rotted telephone pole,' Remi said.

And it did. But almost immediately Sam noticed what looked like a trio of wooden cross braces affixed to the pole, then bindings of some kind, mostly crumbled to dust but intact enough to retain their basic shape.

'It's an outrigger,' Remi whispered.

Sam nodded and kept panning his headlamp along the cross braces to a point where they merged with an elongated heap of partially rotten wood, this one a few feet longer than the 'telephone pole,' and four to five times its diameter.

'Sam, that's a canoe.'

He nodded. 'A big one. At least thirty feet long.' Together, they sidestepped around the craft to the other side, where they found a corresponding cross brace/outrigger setup. The body of the canoe was five feet wide, and four feet tall from keel to gunwale, with a tapered bow and jutting bowsprit and a squared-off stern. At midships, rising eight feet from the hull, was what looked like a shattered mast; the upper part, about ten feet long, lay on the ground, its end propped up on the gunwale. Ahead of the mast the hull was topped by a shallow, double-pitch roof.

'Sam, step back,' Remi whispered.

He followed her back a few paces. She pointed at the ground beneath the vessel. What they'd taken for simply a high point in the floor was in fact a two-foot-high platform constructed of carefully placed stones.

'This is an altar,' he said.

After a quick check on their anti-croc flare, which had burned down to the halfway mark, they got busy examining the outrigger, Remi taking in situ pictures for scale and design before moving in for close-ups. Using the tip of his Swiss Army knife, Sam took trace samples of the wood and the bindings.

'Everything's coated in some kind of resin,' he told Remi, sniffing the material. 'It's thick. At least an inch.'

'That would explain its remarkable condition,' she replied.

Sam stepped over the starboard side outrigger, walked to the gunwale, and peered inside the craft. Lying around the base of the mast was a mound of what he could only describe as decomposed canvas. Mottled brown and gray, the material had partially congealed into a gelatinous mass.

'Remi, you need to see this.'

She joined him at the gunwale. 'Big sail,' she said and began taking pictures.

Sam unsheathed his machete and, with Remi hanging on to his belt lest he fall in, leaned forward and gingerly slid the blade into the pile. 'It's like onion skin,' he muttered. He lifted free a tattered section of the material. Remi was ready with an empty Ziploc bag. As he slid the sample inside, it broke into three sections. Remi sealed the bag and walked back to her pack to deposit it with the other samples.

Sam stepped around to the stern. Jutting from the transom was a bulbous wooden object, like a gnarled football leaning forward on a kickoff tee. Like almost everything else about the outrigger, it took Sam several seconds and several tilts of his head before he realized what he was seeing. Remi came up behind him.

'Our mystery bird,' she said.

Sam nodded. 'From the Orizaga Codex and Blaylock's journal.'

'What did he call it? The "great green jeweled bird,"' Remi mused. 'Though I don't think this is what he was talking about.'

She took a dozen pictures of the carving with her digital camera.

'Let's check the bowsprit,' said Sam. 'When it comes to boats, these kinds of things often come in pairs.'

They walked to the bow. As Sam had guessed, the bowsprit also bore a carving, this one in better condition than its counterpart. In fact, the bowsprit itself was the sculpture: a serpent, its mouth agape, feathered plumes streaming backward from its head.

'Sam, do you know what this resembles?' Remi asked.

'No. Should I?'

'Probably not, I suppose. It's less elaborate and stylized, but it's the near spitting image of Quetzalcoatl, the Great Plumed Serpent God of the Aztecs.'

*

'Crazy like a fox,' Sam muttered after a few seconds.

'Pardon?'

'Blaylock. Crazy like a fox. Clearly, he hid the Moreau map and the codex together in his walking staff for good reason. He was obsessed with something all right, but it was about more than the *Shenandoah* or the *El Majidi*.'

'Maybe it started out with them,' Remi agreed, 'but somewhere along the line he must have found something, or learned something, that changed his focus. The question is, how did whoever brought this canoe here get it in the cave?'

'Unless there's another entrance beyond croco-ville down there, they must have dismantled it, brought it in through the waterfall, then reassembled it.'

'That's a lot of work. We're two miles from the beach, and it weighs a couple thousand pounds.'

'Sailors tend to get attached to their vessel, especially if it's seen them through rough seas and a long voyage. We might know more once we get these samples tested, but if we're buying into Blaylock's odyssey this could be an Aztec boat. Which would make it what? At least six hundred years old?'

'We're talking about rewriting history, Sam. There are no accounts of the Aztecs traveling beyond Mexico's coastal regions, let alone across the Pacific and around the Cape of Good Hope.'

'We're thinking at cross-purposes, my dear.'

'How so?'

'You're thinking west to east and the sixteenth century. I'm thinking east to west and much earlier than that.'

'You can't be serious.'

'Remi, you said it yourself: Historians aren't entirely sure where the Aztecs originated. What if we're standing in front of a Proto-Aztec migration ship?'

Chapter 32

Madagascar, Indian Ocean

Remi was about to open her mouth to reply when the crack of a gunshot echoed through the cave. To their left they heard something plunk into a stalagmite. They doused their headlamps and dropped to the ground. Perfectly still, barely breathing, they waited for more shots. None came. At the mouth of the right-hand tunnel the flare was sputtering, almost consumed. Red light flickered over the wall.

'Do you see anything?' Remi whispered.

'I think it came from outside. Wait here. I'll be right back.'

Sam got to his feet. Hunched over, he dashed to a mineral column, stopped to look and listen, then moved on, zigzagging from cover to cover until he was pressed flat against the wall beside the entrance. He drew the Webley and ducked into the entrance.

Crack!

A bullet struck the floor beside him and ricocheted off into the cavern. Hurrying now, he ran out into the grotto, then sidestepped left until he reached the spot where they'd entered. He fell to his belly and crawled between a pair of boulders until his head slipped beneath the cascade. Eyes squinted against the torrent, he peered ahead until the lagoon came into view.

Six men, all armed with assault rifles, stood on the beach. They were dressed in torn jeans, ratty T-shirts, and combat boots. To a man, each wore a white bandanna with red-dyed corners tied around his forearm. Two of them knelt beside Sam and Remi's packs, sorting the contents into piles. Sam scanned the lagoon area and surrounding trees but saw no sign of the Kid.

One of the men – the leader, Sam assumed, based on his mannerisms and the semiautomatic pistol he wore on his belt – barked something to the others, then pointed toward the waterfall. The five subordinates began picking their way around the lagoon.

Sam back-crawled, holstered the Webley, and hurried back into the cavern. He found Remi where he'd left her. He said, 'Six men, all armed – the rebels the Kid mentioned.'

'Did you see him?'

'No, I think he got away.'

'Good.'

'They're coming in to investigate. We've got a minute, maybe two.'

'How many?'

'Five.'

'Bad odds for a gunfight. I'd suggest we go down the other tunnel and look for an exit, but I'm not in the mood to be devoured.'

Sam grinned. 'I'm sure our visitors will share your sentiment. You look for a better hiding spot, and I'll go stir up some trouble. Be back in a flash.'

Sam dashed across the cavern, hopped the creek, then started down the right-hand tunnel. After snatching the flare from the sand he dashed down the ramp to the water's edge, stopped, and clicked on his headlamp. Twenty feet away he saw a jumble of scaly tails, clawed feet, and fanged snouts. He counted at least three crocodiles. They hissed and thrashed as the light panned over them.

'Sorry about the intrusion,' Sam murmured.

He cocked his arm and heaved the sputtering flare down the tunnel. His aim was true. The flare landed on the nearest crocodile's back, then bounced into their midst. The hissing and thrashing became frenzied. En masse, the crocodiles began scrabbling away from the flare and moving toward the ramp.

Sam doused his headlamp, turned, and ran. As he reached the creek he saw Remi's headlamp flash once near the far wall. He ran that way and found her hunched between a crescent of boulders. Just as he skidded to a stop and dropped to his knees he heard the echo of voices at the cavern entrance.

'Are the natives restless?' Remi whispered into Sam's ear.

'More like enraged. If that flare stays lit, our visitors should head straight for it.'

'And into an ugly surprise.'

'Let's just hope their surprise doesn't turn on us.'

It took less than a minute for their visitors to make their presence known. Having grown accustomed to the steady if muffled rush of the waterfall, Sam and Remi heard its pattern change as bodies moved through the cascade. This was followed by the sound of boots in the grotto, then whispered voices through the entrance and in the main cavern. The whispering stopped, followed by the barely perceptible scuffing of feet on stone.

Sam whispered in Remi's ear, 'One man. A scout.'

This was a watershed moment for their plan. If the scout decided to investigate the flare on his own, the crocodile reception would probably send him and his compatriots running. If, however, they came en masse, the reception and its resulting pandemonium could easily engulf Sam and Remi as well.

Sam and Remi sat still, listening. The sound of the footfalls went quiet. A single voice called out something. More silence. Then more footfalls, overlapping, moving through the entrance tunnel. Now the crunch of footfalls moving across the loose rock and sediment. The group was moving deeper into the cavern. With their eyes already well adjusted, Sam and Remi could plainly see the faint red flickering of the flare down the right-hand tunnel. How soon this group would see the light was the question.

Sam and Remi turned their heads this way and that, trying to triangulate the location of the party. Remi whispered, 'They're near the far wall.'

The crunch of footfalls stopped. A single voice called something in what Sam assumed was Malagasy, and while the word made no sense the inflection was one of surprised announcement, as in, Sam imagined: Look, a flare!

Whatever was said, it had the desired effect. The group continued, but their pace seemed more cautious. Soon, Sam and Remi saw the first figure move into the sputtering glow of the flare. Then a second. And so on. Until all five men had moved into view. One by one, the men started down the ramp. Boots splashed in water.

Sam whispered, 'Any second – '

A guttural scream echoed through the cavern.

' – now,' Sam finished.

The first scream was joined by a second, then shouting. Remi managed to catch one of the words, a curse. 'Someone's developed a bladder control problem,' she whispered.

Sam drew the Webley and propped the barrel on the rock before him.

Across the cavern came the sounds of splashes in the water, then boots pounding up the stone ramp. Then the first gunshots, tentative at first, then in full automatic, the pop-pop-pop bouncing off the cavern walls. The mouth to the right-hand tunnel blinked orange with over-lapping muzzle flashes; caught in the strobe light, men backing up, stumbling, scrambling back to their feet.

'I count five of them,' Sam whispered.

'Me too.'

Once back on level ground, the rebels turned and sprinted, most of them heading straight for the entrance. One, however, clearly panicked, rushed headlong across the cavern toward Sam and Remi's hiding spot. The man stumbled into the creek, fell, then crawled across to the other side. The man got to his feet, took a few steps toward Sam and Remi, then stopped and looked around.

Silhouetted by the flare, the man was a mere outline. Sam placed the Webley's front sight on the center point between the man's shoulders.

'Turn, damn you . . .' While both he and Remi had taken

lives before, neither enjoyed the feeling. Necessary or not, it was an ugly thing. 'Turn . . .' Sam murmured.

From the main entrance a voice called, *'Rakotomalala!'*

The man spun around, paused a moment, then sprinted toward the entrance. Sam lowered the Webley and let out a deep breath.

He and Remi waited until they heard the interruption of the waterfall again, then Sam got up and picked his way to the entrance and through to the grotto. He crawled back between the boulders and inched his head through the cascade until he could see the lagoon. So panicked was the group that none of its members had bothered with the boulders, had rather chosen to swim back. They were just now reaching the beach. Gesticulating wildly and shouting, they related the crocodile story to the head honcho, who glared at them for a few moments, then barked an order. The men gathered Sam and Remi's packs, and the group marched away in single file, heading downriver.

Sam watched until they disappeared around the bend, then waited another five minutes for good measure. He returned to Remi. 'They've moved on.'

'How can we be sure?'

'We can't, but we either move on now or wait for nightfall, and I'm not keen on staying. We've pushed our luck far enough with our reptilian hosts.'

Remi glanced toward the right-hand tunnel. The crocodiles had settled slightly, but the hissing and the overlapping thwap of tails told Sam and Remi the group was far from calm.

'Might be better to make a break now,' Remi conceded.

Something moved on the ramp, and slowly the elongated snout moved from the shadows. The mouth opened slowly, then closed, and the snout retreated back into darkness.

'Definitely better to make a break now,' Remi said.

Chapter 33

Madagascar, Indian Ocean

They took their time on the way out, pausing first in the grotto, then repeating Sam's peek through the cascade before sliding on their bellies through the boulders and into the lagoon. They stroked across to the beach and climbed from the water. While Remi wrung the water from her hair, Sam took off his boots and drained them.

Leaning forward, her head tilted to one side, Remi murmured to Sam, 'There's someone waving at us.'

'Where?'

Remi pointed with her eyes toward what looked like a pile of undergrowth from which was jutting a hand and forearm. The hand was holding a Webley Model Mark VI. It gesticulated wildly as though trying to warn them away.

Sam put his hand on the butt of the Webley in his waistband.

Crack!

A bullet thumped into the sand between his legs.

Sam froze, as did Remi, her hands still tangled in her hair. At the pile of undergrowth, the Kid's arm slowly withdrew into cover.

'Guess they doubled back,' Remi observed.

'Seems so. Did you happen to read the manners and etiquette section of the Madagascar guide?'

'I thought you did that.'

'Skimmed it.'

Slowly Sam raised his hands above his head and turned around. Remi did the same. Predictably, standing above the waterfall atop the lion's head were the six rebels. Standing near the ledge, arms akimbo, the leader called down, 'No move! Understand, no move!'

Sam nodded, called back, 'No move.'

Under the watchful eye of the lone sniper atop the lion's head, the other five rebels made their way down via some unseen trail in the rocks. Soon they were standing in a semicircle around Sam and Remi. The leader stepped forward, scrutinized Sam's eyes, then glanced over and gave Remi a foot-to-head once-over. The leader reached out, plucked the Webley from Sam's waistband, then lifted it up for examination.

'Good gun,' he proclaimed in his broken English.

'Good gun,' Sam agreed.

'You are who?'

'Sam.'

'Tolotra. Who is woman?'

A bit of Madagascar etiquette popped into Sam's head. Carefully he lowered his right hand and pointed to Remi, careful to keep the tip of his index finger curled back toward himself. 'My wife. Remi.'

Sam's gesture was not lost on Tolotra. He looked at Remi, then back to Sam, then nodded thoughtfully. Tolotra's next statement told Sam that his recognition of a

Madagascar custom wasn't going to be a get-out-of-jail-free card.

'Sam . . . Remi. Hostages now.'

One of the rebels drew two lengths of rope from his belt and stepped forward as if to bind Sam and Remi's hands. Tolotra waved the man off and said to Sam, 'You run, we shoot. No run. You promise?'

Evidently, Sam's bent index finger had done some good.

In response, Sam raised his right hand up, ceremoniously crossed his index and middle fingers, then nodded solemnly. 'Not on your life,' he said.

Beside him, Remi rolled her eyes. 'Oh, God.'

Tolotra studied Sam's gesture for a moment, then smiled and mimicked him. 'Not on your life.' Tolotra turned and showed the gesture to his men. 'Not on your life!'

'Not on your life!' the men cheered back.

Remi whispered, 'If any one of them has an English phrase book, we're dead. You know that, don't you?'

They were placed in the middle of a well-staggered, single-file group and marched away from the lagoon, passing within five feet of the Kid's hiding place, before turning onto a trail that paralleled the river. Whatever language advantage Sam and Remi might have had was offset by the bandits' hostage-wrangling skills. They were never under the guns of fewer than two men who always maintained a minimum ten-foot gap. Moreover, the group's navigation skills were on par with those of the Kids', and soon Sam and Remi had lost whatever landmarks to which they'd been clinging.

After walking for forty minutes, the jungle thinned, and the trail broke into sunlight. They were back on the savanna, Sam realized, but how far from the one he, Remi, and the Kid had used earlier that day he had no clue. The ocean was on their left, the forested escarpment on their right. They were heading south.

After another twenty minutes they were back in the jungle, this time following a fairly straight trail, so Sam was able to maintain his bearings.

'I think we're near the road,' he whispered to Remi.

'That's probably how they found us – they found the Rover. Have you seen you know who?'

'No, but he's out there.'

Walking at the head of the line, Tolotra turned around and barked, 'No talking!' He held up his crossed fingers as if to lend gravity to the order. Sam returned the gesture.

Remi murmured, 'How nice. You made a friend.'

'Hope I don't have to shoot him.'

'With what? An invisible rubber-band gun?'

'No, my Webley,' Sam grumbled, his eyes fixed on Tolotra. 'After I take it away from him.'

'No talking!'

Sam's guess about their location was right. A few minutes later Tolotra reached an intersection of trails and turned right. The grade increased until they were pulling themselves up using exposed roots and low-hanging branches. The terrain had no effect on the bandits' discipline, however; whenever Sam and Remi looked around, they found themselves staring down at least two rifle muzzles.

The trail leveled out and reached a set of natural root steps in the hillside. Sam and Remi reached the top and found themselves standing on a gravel road. A quarter mile to the south, a rusted white Chevy pickup truck sat on the shoulder; ahead of it, Sam and Remi's Range Rover. And looming above both, the Three Wise Men.

'Where now?' Sam asked Tolotra.

He and Remi were under no illusions. While their hands being unbound was an advantage, this was not a Hollywood movie. Without a major distraction, any attempt to get the jump on any of these rebels would not only fail but likely end with them dying. Their chances would only worsen once they were put in vehicles.

'Secret place,' Tolotra replied.

'You want ransom, yes?'

'Yes.'

'How do you know we're worth anything?'

Tolotra considered this for a moment as though sorting through his grasp of English. 'Packs, clothes, camera – all expensive. Car expensive.'

'It's a rental,' Remi said.

'Eh?'

'Nothing.'

Sam, still trusting his hunch that the Kid hadn't abandoned them, had been surreptitiously scanning their surroundings. Now, out of the corner of his eye, he glimpsed movement on the slope above the road. He saw a flash of silvery hair appear between a pair of boulders.

Sam said, 'We have gold.'

This had the desired effect. Those in the group that hadn't been paying attention to the conversation turned to face Sam. Tolotra took a step closer.

'Gold? Where? How much?'

The Kid's head popped up from behind the boulder. He caught Sam's eye, winked, pointed toward the vehicles down the road, then ducked from view again.

Sam looked to Remi. Her expression told him she'd seen the Kid. Sam said, 'How much do you think, Remi?'

'I don't know . . . a couple dozen double eagle coins.'

This was enough for Tolotra. Eyes narrowed, he nodded sagely. 'Where?'

'Our hotel in Antananarivo.'

'You give us coins, you go free.'

This was a lie, Sam assumed, but it was a step in the right direction. Even if the worst happened and the Kid was unable to intervene here, he and Remi would fare much better moving toward civilization than away from it. No doubt Tolotra's 'secret place' was good enough to keep them hidden from government forces. If, however, Tolotra's discretion overwhelmed his greed en route to Antananarivo, Sam and Remi would find themselves back to square one.

'We go now,' Tolotra announced.

Again the group fell into formation with Sam and Remi in the middle. Using their peripheral vision, Sam and Remi kept watch for the Kid, but there was no sign of him. Whatever the old truffle hunter had planned, they would have to be ready to react and improvise.

They drew even with the Chevy pickup truck and stopped. Sam and Remi's packs were tossed into the bed.

Sam whispered to Remi, 'Stay sharp.'

Tolotra and four of the others clustered around the tailgate and began conversing. The sixth man stood ten feet behind Sam and Remi, his rifle trained on their lower backs. Based on Tolotra's gestures, Sam assumed they were trying to decide how best to execute the drive into Antananarivo – essentially, the enemy's capital.

Remi was the first to realize the Kid's plan was unfolding. With her eyes, she guided Sam's gaze over the roof of the Chevy and up the middle Wise Man to the top. At first Sam saw nothing, and then, almost imperceptibly, a barrel-sized boulder began inching toward the edge.

Sam whispered, 'When I move, go for the Range Rover.'

Tolotra turned and glared at Sam. Sam shrugged and smiled apologetically.

Remi whispered, 'Okay.'

Atop the Wise Man, the boulder had reached the edge, where it stopped. Sam and Remi took a deep breath. Waited. The boulder wiggled forward, paused momentarily, then tipped over the edge and started falling. The pillar's face was a slope, angled slightly backward, and smooth save some bumps near the bottom. The combination of the face, gravity, and the boulder's kinetic friction kept it adhered to the face. The engineer in Sam knew that would end as soon as the boulder hit its first bump, at which point the boulder would become a stone artillery shell.

Knowing no Malagasy, Sam did what he hoped would cause the most panic: He let out a distinctly un-macho, high-pitched scream, pointed at the boulder, and shouted, 'Boulder!'

In unison, Tolotra and his men glanced up. Lacking the

advantage of the foreknowledge Sam and Remi had, everyone froze and stared in awe. Sam, having kept his eye on Tolotra for most of the hike and having rehearsed his actions, took two leaping steps forward, heel-kicked Tolotra in the back of the knee, and, as he fell, jerked the Webley-Fosbury from his waistband.

Behind him, Remi's guard screamed something that Sam assumed was 'Stop!,' which he further assumed would be followed by the guard drawing a bead on the fleeing Remi. Sam never gave him the chance. With the Webley now free, Sam latched his left hand onto Tolotra's collar and pistol-whipped him in the side of the head. Tolotra grunted and went limp.

Sam spun on one heel and dropped to his knees, putting Tolotra between him and four other men, two of whom were backing across the road, the other two scrambling around to the Chevy's opposite side. Sam's spin naturally brought the Webley around to point in the general direction of Remi's guard. As Sam had feared, the man was jerking the rifle up to his shoulder, the barrel tracking Remi as she sprinted toward the Range Rover.

Sam fired once, hitting the man on the sternum. Like a puppet whose strings had been cut, the man dropped straight down, dead. Sam wrapped his left forearm around Tolotra's throat, pulled him tighter, then shifted his aim toward the two rebels backing across the road. Both had their rifles trained on Sam, obviously trying to decide whether to risk the shot. Sam shifted the Webley's sights from one man to the next. On the other side of the truck, he could hear the other two men moving through the high grass along the shoulder.

Boom. The ground shuddered, followed by the snapping of limbs. Another shudder, like a giant was on the march. Sam felt it in his belly.

Remi shouted, 'Boulder's bouncing!'

'Where!'

'Coming your way!'

Boom. Closer this time.

On the other side of the truck the two rebels shouted.

'They're running!' Remi called.

The two in front of Sam did the same, turning and sprinting back down the road.

Boom.

'Hold tight, Sam! It's almost on you! Three . . . two . . . one . . .'

Sam curled into a ball. Above his head there came the wrenching of steel. Glass shattered. He felt the Chevy lurch to the side, shoving him and Tolotra over the gravel. A shadow passed overhead. Boom. The boulder struck the far side of the road, bounced once, then disappeared over the shoulder, bulldozing trees as it went. After another ten seconds the sound stopped. Sam looked up, glanced around.

Down the road, the four remaining rebels had stopped running. After a brief huddled conference, they started back toward Sam and Remi. Sam, having watched Tolotra pocket the Rover's keys, dug them out.

'Remi, better start the Rover,' he called.

He tossed the keys up the road, then pointed the Webley down the road and took aim on the four advancing rebels.

One of them stumbled sideways, clutched his thigh,

and crumbled to the road, followed a split second later by a basso pop. Though Sam had never heard that particular sound, he surmised it was the report of a .455 caliber bullet from a circa 1915 Webley Model Mark VI revolver.

The remaining three rebels stopped, whirled toward the Wise Men.

A second bullet struck, this one between the legs of the center man. He backed up a few steps, followed by the second man. The third man, however, was a slow learner. Half crouching, his eyes scanning the high ground, he slowly brought his rifle to his shoulder. He got a bullet in the left kneecap for his trouble. He screamed and toppled over.

From the direction of the Wise Men, a disembodied voice shouted something. The two still-armed rebels dropped their guns. Another shout. The able-bodied men helped their comrades to their feet, and the group began limping off down the road.

Sam shoved the unconscious Tolotra off him and climbed to his feet. Remi walked up. Together, they stared at what remained of the Chevy. Aside from the four twisted stumps that formed the cab, the pickup had been decapitated.

A voice called, 'Looking at it, you'd think that's exactly what I had planned.'

A figure emerged from the trees at the base of the Wise Men and began striding toward them.

'Didn't you?' Sam asked the Kid.

'I'll never tell.'

Remi said, 'You certainly know how to create a distraction.'

The Kid stopped before them. 'It was all Mother Nature, my dear. And the luck of the bounce, of course.'

'Thanks for not deserting us,' said Sam.

'Don't mention it.'

Sam hefted the Webley-Fosbury in his hand, appraised the weapon for a moment, then handed it to the Kid, who frowned and shook his head. 'She's yours now.'

'Pardon me?'

'Until today, she'd never been fired. It's a tradition, you see . . . Chinese, if I recall.'

Remi smiled. 'I think you're thinking of, "Save a life and you're responsible for it."'

The Kid shrugged. 'Either way, Mr. Fargo, she's yours now.'

'Thanks. I'll treasure it. What should we do with these two?' Sam asked, pointing to Tolotra and the dead man on the road.

'Leave them. The sooner you get to Antananarivo, the better.' The Kid read Sam and Remi's somber expressions. 'Don't give it a second thought. They would've killed you.'

'How do you know that for sure?' Remi said.

'In the last five years, there've been sixty-three kidnappings here. Ransom paid or unpaid, not one came back alive. Trust me, it was you or them.'

Sam and Remi considered this, then nodded. Sam shook the Kid's hand, then grabbed their packs from the truck's bed as Remi gave their savior a hug. They turned and headed toward the Range Rover.

'One more thing,' the Kid called.

Sam and Remi turned back. The Kid dug into his pack and came out with a small burlap bag. He handed it to them. 'Truffles for your troubles,' the Kid said. Then he crossed the road and disappeared into the brush.

Sam turned the burlap bag over in his hands. Stamped on the side in red ink was a logo – the letter *C*, and beside it, in smaller letters, *ussler Truffles*.

Remi said, 'That's nice of him. But what's an "ussler"?'

Chapter 34

Madagascar, Indian Ocean

They were almost halfway back to Antananarivo and approaching a village named Moramanga at the junction of Routes 2 and 44 when their satellite phone trilled. In the passenger seat, Remi answered. 'It's Rube,' she said after a moment, then put it on speakerphone.

'Hi, Rube,' Sam called.

'Where are you?'

'Madagascar.'

'Damn. I was afraid of that.'

Remi said, 'Something tells me it's not just a general dislike of Madagascar that's got you bothered.'

'Someone flagged your passports at the Antananarivo airport.'

'When?' asked Remi.

'A couple days before you arrived.'

'What exactly does that mean?' Sam asked. 'We weren't stopped when we went through immigration.'

'That's what's got me worried. If it was a government-level request, you would have been stopped there. In spookspeak, the flag you got is called a "note-and-notify." Somebody just wanted to know when you got there.'

'And it doesn't have to be someone in the government,' Sam said.

'In Third World countries, where the average annual income is a few hundred dollars, you can buy a note-and-notify for the price of a cup of coffee. And since Rivera's already shown he's got connections in Africa . . .'

'Understood,' Sam replied. 'Recommendations?'

'Assume somebody's actively looking for you; assume they'll find you. Don't go back to Antananarivo. Have Selma track down a private airstrip and a pilot who doesn't mind working for cash and won't bother with passports.'

Such was the downside of being who they were. While far from famous, Sam and Remi had something of a reputation in the adventurer/treasure-hunting community, and while naturally they had a few detractors, they were widely respected. Getting caught sneaking into and out of countries on false passports could potentially cause more trouble than it was worth: jail, expulsion, headlines, being labeled persona non grata, and, perhaps most important, the evaporation of invaluable contacts in the academic world. By playing it mostly aboveboard, Sam and Remi were often easy targets for anyone willing and able to bribe the right person in the right place.

Remi said, 'We know about the political situation. How does that affect things?'

'Badly. Stay near civilization and know where the police stations are.'

'That could be a problem. We're a little off the beaten path right now.'

'Why am I not surprised? Okay, give me a second.' The line went silent for two minutes, then Rube returned. 'Best guess puts the rebels about a week away from being ready for a major attack, but that doesn't rule out skirmishes. Most of the cities within fifty miles of Antananarivo should be okay. The bigger, the better. Head south if possible. The rebels are clustered in the north. The downside is – '

'Rivera and his goons will be thinking the same thing and looking in those places,' Sam finished.

'Right. Wish I could be of more help.'

'Rube, you're the best. Don't ever doubt it. We'll call when we're safe.'

Their next call went to Selma, who listened, asked a few questions, and said, 'I'm on it,' then hung up.

Now Remi studied the map as Sam drove.

'We've got two options,' she said after a few minutes. 'One, take one of the dozens of roads – and I use that term very loosely – that head generally south, or close to within a couple miles of Antananarivo. There's a two-lane blacktop that circles the city to the east and then links up with Route 7 heading south.'

'How do the unnamed roads look?'

'As you'd expect: dirt and gravel, at best.'

'Multiple choices make for a harder trail to follow,' Sam observed.

'And if we're aiming for Route 7, it'll add five or six hours onto our travel time. Which takes us well past nightfall.'

'My vote is blacktop,' Sam said.

'Seconded.'

'Different subject . . . The fact that Rivera flagged our passports here, of all places, means something.'

Remi was nodding. 'It's not hard to guess what that is. They knew there was something here to find. But is it the outrigger we found or something more?'

'We'll know that when we know what got them interested in Madagascar in the first place. My guess: They've been here before and didn't find what they were looking for.'

'Which begs the question: Where else have they been?'

The afternoon wore on. Past Moramanga, moving ever westward and upward, they passed mile after mile of rice paddies and drove through village after village, each one bearing a quaint name that Remi described as 'part Malagasy, part French, with a dash of Italian': Andranokobaka, Ambodigavo, Ambatonifody. . . .

Ten miles east of Anosibe Ifody the terrain began to change yet again, giving way to tropical forest interspersed with rugged brown hills that reminded Sam and Remi of Tuscany. Jagged escarpments, glowing brownish gold in the sun, rose above the treetops to the north and south. Shortly after three o'clock they stopped at a Jovenna gas station on the outskirts of Manjakandriana. Remi went inside for snacks and water while Sam pumped the gas.

Down the block, a white Volkswagen Passat police vehicle came around the corner and headed toward the gas station. Moving at a sedate twenty miles per hour, the Passat slowed as it drew even with the Range Rover. After a few more seconds the Passat sped up and continued down the block, where it pulled to the side of the road and parked. Through the rear window Sam saw the driver pluck something off the dashboard and bring it to his mouth.

Remi came out with four bottles of water and a few bags of pretzels. Sam got back in the driver's seat.

'You're wearing your frowny face,' Remi observed.

'It may be exhaustion or paranoia, or a combination of the two, but I think that police car is interested in us.'

'Where?'

'Down the block, under the awning with the old Coca-Cola sign.'

Remi checked the side mirror. 'I see him.'

'He slowed beside us, then parked and got on the radio.'

Sam started the engine. They sat in silence for a few minutes.

'What exactly are we doing?' Remi asked.

'Giving him a chance.'

Remi caught on: 'If it's official business, he'll stop us here. If not . . . "note-and-notify."'

'Right.' Sam put the Rover in gear. 'Time to play navigator again, Remi. We're backtracking.'

'To where?'

'Hopefully, nowhere. If he doesn't follow us, we'll turn around again.'

'And if he follows us?'

'Then we're on the run. We'll be needing one of those unnamed roads you mentioned.'

'We're on the run,' Remi announced a few minutes later. Facing backward, she'd been staring through the rear window since they'd left Manjakandriana. 'He's a mile back.'

'We've got some dips and turns coming up. Let me know each time you lose sight of him.'

'Why?'

'If we sprint while he's watching us he'll know we're running; this way we may be able to get some distance before he realizes it.'

'Tricky, Fargo.'

'Only if it works.'

'What if he tries to stop us?'

'I don't even want to think about it.'

For the next fifteen minutes Sam followed Remi's cues, flooring the gas pedal for a ten count when Remi said, 'Go!,' before slowing back down to the speed limit. Slowly but steadily, they put an extra half mile between them and the Passat.

'Are any of those roads not gravel or dirt?' Sam asked.

Remi studied the map. 'Hard to tell, but this one coming up looks a tad thicker than the others. So far on this map, that's usually meant blacktop of some kind. Why do you ask?'

'No dust trail.'

'From a quick turn,' Remi said. 'That could work both ways.'

Sam frowned. 'Good point. Tell me when the turn's coming up.'

For the next few minutes Remi matched passing roads and signs against the map's markings. 'Should be the next turn to the south.' She measured the distance with her fingernail. 'A quarter mile, give or take. Should be just over this hill.'

'How's our friend?'

'Hard to be sure, but it looks like he's picked up speed.'

They crested the hill and started down. Ahead, Sam

saw the turnoff Remi had indicated. Sam jammed the accelerator to the floorboard, and the Range Rover surged forward. Her eyes wide, Remi braced herself against the dashboard. A hundred yards from the turn, Sam switched his foot to the brake, pressing as hard as he dared without skidding, and brought the Rover down to sixty-five kilometers per hour, or forty miles per hour.

'Hang on,' Sam said, then slewed the wheel right. Despite the Rover's high center of gravity, the tires clung to the road, but Sam could see he'd overshot the turn. He eased the wheel left, then tapped the brakes and jerked the wheel right again. The Rover's tail whipped around. The driver's-side rear tire slipped off the shoulder. They felt the Rover tipping sideways. Sam resisted the impulse to correct right and instead steered into the skid, dropping the driver's-side front tire off the shoulder. Now even with each other, the two shoulder-side tires bit down together. Sam gunned it, jerked the wheel to the right, and the Rover vaulted back onto the road.

'Sharp right!' Remi called, pointing at a gap in the foliage off the shoulder.

Sam reacted instantly, braking hard. The Rover shuddered to a stop. Sam switched into reverse, backed up ten feet, switched back to drive and turned into the gap. Shadows engulfed them. Foliage scraped the car's sides. He eased forward a few feet until the bumper tapped a wooden cattle gate.

Remi climbed over the center console into the backseat and poked her head up so she could see out the side window.

Sam asked, 'Are we off the road?'

'Barely. He should be along anytime now.' Thirty seconds later: 'There he goes.' She turned around in the seat, slumped back, and exhaled. 'Can we sit here for a – '

From down the main road came the shrieking of brakes, then silence.

Sam and Remi froze.

In the distance an engine revved and tires squealed.

Sam groaned. 'You've got to be kidding me. Buckle up, Remi.'

The road, while in fact blacktop, was narrow and winding, with no centerline and with ragged shoulders. With the Range Rover at top speed, they gained a half mile before they heard the Passat skid into the turn behind them. As they rounded the next corner a sign flashed past.

Remi caught it: 'Narrow bridge ahead.'

Sam gunned the engine, eating up the straightaway before the bridge. On either side, the jungle seemed to close in around them. The green tips of branches lashed the side windows. Through the windshield, the bridge appeared.

'They call that a bridge?' Remi called.

Spanning a narrow gorge, the bridge was anchored to each bank by a pair of steel cables, but there were neither center stanchions nor support pylons. Fence-post-and-rope handrails lined each side. The bridge's surface was little more than parallel twelve-inch planks with nothing but air and the occasional crossbeam between them.

Fifty yards from the structure, Sam slammed on the brakes. He and Remi glanced out the side windows; there was nothing. No breaks in the foliage, no turnoffs.

Nowhere to hide. Beside them, a sign read, in French: SINGLE VEHICLE CROSSING ONLY. BRIDGE SPEED LIMIT – 6 KPH. Essentially, a walking pace.

Sam looked at Remi, who forced a smile. 'Like a Band-Aid,' she said.

'Don't think, just do it.'

'Right.'

Sam aligned the Rover's wheels with the bridge's planks, then stepped on the accelerator. The Rover rolled forward.

Behind them came the sound of tires squealing. Remi turned in her seat and saw the Passat skid around the corner, fishtail slightly, then straighten out.

'Ten to one he was counting on this bridge.'

'No bet,' Sam replied, fingers white on the steering wheel.

The Rover's front tires thumped over the bridge's first crossbeam and onto the planks. The wood groaned and creaked. The Rover's back tires crossed over.

'Point of no return,' Sam said. 'Is he slowing down?'

Still turned in her seat, Remi said, 'No . . . Okay, he is. He's not stopping, though.'

Sam depressed the accelerator. The speedometer needle rose past twelve kph.

Remi rolled down her window, stuck her head out, and looked down.

Sam called, 'Do I want to know?'

'It's about a fifty-foot drop into a river.'

'A lazy river, right?'

'Whitewater. Class 4 at least.'

'Okay, sunshine, enough narrative.'

Remi pulled her head back inside and took another look through the rear window. 'He's almost on the bridge. Clearly, the sign doesn't worry him.'

'Let's hope he knows more than we do.'

They crossed the halfway point.

A moment later they felt the Range Rover dip slightly. Now double loaded, the bridge began undulating like a jump rope being flicked vertically at both ends. While the movement was but inches, the differing weights and positions of the vehicles began to feed upon each other.

'Interference wave,' Sam muttered.

'Pardon?'

'Physics. When two waves of disparate amplitude combine – '

'Bad things happen,' Remi finished. 'I get it.'

The Range Rover was rising and falling erratically now, six inches in each direction, Sam estimated. Remi felt her stomach rise into her throat.

'Do we happen to have any seasickness pills?'

'Sorry, my dear. We're almost there.'

The bridge's opposite side loomed before the windshield. Twenty feet . . . ten. Sam set his jaw, waited for the Rover to begin its downward plunge, then goosed the accelerator. The speedometer shot past twenty-five kph. The Rover bumped over the last crossbeam and onto solid ground.

Remi glanced out the rear window. Her eyes went wide. 'Sam . . .'

He turned. Without the Rover's compensatory weight, the police Passat was absorbing all the motion. The bridge lurched upward, then dropped suddenly, leaving the car suspended for a split second. It was just enough. The Passat dropped but landed slightly off line. The driver's-side front tire dropped into the center gap. With a gunshotlike crack, the nearest crossbeam gave way. The Passat tipped sideways onto the driver's door and slipped farther into the rift. The forward third of the car, including the engine compartment, was now dangling in space.

Remi murmured, 'Oh, God . . .'

On impulse, Sam opened his door and got out.

'Sam! What are you doing?'

'For all we know, he's just a cop doing what he was ordered.'

'Or he'll happily shoot you when you walk up to his car.'

Sam shrugged, then walked back and opened the Rover's tailgate. He rummaged through his pack and found what he was looking for: a fifty-foot coil of quarter-inch utility paracord. Careful to stay on the Passat's 'up side,' he walked down the plank until he was even with the passenger-side door. Below him, the river rushed past, frothing and sending up plumes of spray. He crouched down and examined the chassis; the situation was more precarious than he'd anticipated. The only thing keeping the Passat from falling was the driver's-side rear tire, which was wedged between a plank and a crossbeam.

Sam called, 'Do you speak English?'

After a few moments' hesitation, the cop replied in a French-Malagasy accent, 'A little English.'

'I'm going to get you out – '

'Yes, thank you, please – '

'Don't shoot me.'

'Okay.'

'Repeat what I just said.'

'You are going to help me. I will not shoot you with my gun. Here, here . . . I will drop it out the window.'

Sam walked to the rear of the car and peeked around the bumper so he could see the driver's door. A hand holding a revolver appeared through the open window. The revolver dropped through the gap and tumbled into the mist below. Sam walked back to the passenger door.

'Okay, hang on.'

He uncoiled the paracord, doubled it up, knotted the loose ends together, then tied square knots at three-foot intervals down its length. Once done, he gave the bridge's side railing a test tug, then tossed one end of the paracord through the passenger window.

'When I say go, I'm going to pull, and you're going to climb. Understand?'

'I understand. I will climb.'

Sam looped his end of the paracord around one of the posts, gripped it with both hands, then called, 'Go!,' and started pulling. The car began rocking and groaning. Wood splintered. 'Keep climbing!' Sam ordered.

A pair of black hands appeared through the passenger window, followed by a head and face.

The Passat lurched sideways and slipped a foot. Glass shattered.

'Faster!' Sam yelled. 'Climb! Now!'

Sam gave the paracord one last heave, and the cop came tumbling out the window. He landed in a heap, his torso lying across the plank, his legs dangling in space.

Sam leaned forward, grabbed his collar, and dragged him forward. With a series of overlapping pops and cracks, the crossbeam gave way, and the Passat slid through the gap and disappeared from view. A moment later, Sam heard a massive splash.

Panting, the man rolled onto his back and looked up at Sam. 'Thank you.'

'You're welcome.' He began coiling the paracord. 'You'll forgive me if I don't offer you a ride.'

The cop nodded.

'Why were you following us?'

'I do not know. We were given an alert from the district commander. That is all I know.'

'How far did this alert go?'

'Antananarivo and outlying communities.'

'When did you last report in?'

'When I realized you had turned onto this road.'

'What did they say?'

'Nothing,' the cop said.

'Are there any main roads ahead that come from the north?'

The cop thought for a moment. 'Asphalt roads? Yes . . . three before the main road west to Tsiafahy.'

'Do you have a cell phone?' Sam asked.

'It was in the car.'

Sam said nothing, continued to stare at the cop.

'I am telling the truth.' The cop patted his front pockets, rolled over, did the same to his back pockets. 'It is gone.'

Sam nodded. He finished coiling the paracord, then turned and headed for the Range Rover.

'Thank you!' the cop called again.

'Don't mention it,' Sam called over his shoulder. 'I mean it. Don't tell them I helped you. The people who are paying your district commander will kill you.'

Chapter 35

Madagascar, Indian Ocean

'Do you really think they will?' Remi asked when Sam climbed back into the car and recounted the conversation.

'I don't know, but if he thinks so, he'll be more likely to keep his mouth shut. I hope.'

Remi leaned over and kissed Sam on the cheek. 'That was a good thing you did, Fargo.'

Sam smiled. 'Somebody probably offered him a month's salary to just follow a pair of tourists. Can't blame him for that. If we're going to get intercepted, the car will probably come from one of three blacktop roads he mentioned.'

'Agreed.' Remi unfolded the map and studied it a moment. 'Tsiafahy is south of Antananarivo on Route 7. If we can get there . . .'

'How far to the Tsiafahy turnoff?'

'Sixty kilometers – about thirty-seven miles. Another twenty west to Tsiafahy.'

Sam nodded and checked his watch. 'We might make it before nightfall.'

Almost immediately they realized their optimism was probably unwarranted. Past the bridge, the road continued to wind through the jungle, a mix of gentle bends and switch-backs that slowed their pace dramatically. They passed the first blacktop road intersection without incident and soon found themselves driving along a boulder-strewn river – the same one, they assumed, they'd crossed thirty minutes earlier.

'Next intersection coming up,' Remi announced. 'Two miles.'

Five minutes later Sam saw the intersection. Remi pointed through the windshield. 'I saw something . . . a flash of sunlight.'

'It's a bumper,' Sam said between his teeth. 'Duck. If we're not a couple, maybe . . .'

Remi scrunched down in her seat. As they drew even with the blacktop, Sam pressed himself back into the headrest and cast a glance out Remi's window. The vehicle, a dark blue Nissan SUV, was parked on the shoulder a few feet back from the intersection.

'What's happening?' Remi asked.

Sam glanced in the rearview mirror. 'He's pulling out . . . He's behind us.'

Remi sat up, grabbed the binoculars from the floor between her feet, and focused them through the back window. 'A driver and a passenger. The silhouettes look male. I see a Europcar rental sticker on the bumper.'

'All bad signs. Are they speeding up?'

'No, just keeping pace. You know what they say, Sam: For every rat you see . . .'

He nodded. If, in fact, this Nissan was pursuing them, the chances were good there would be a second and perhaps a third car up ahead.

'How far to the next blacktop road?'

Remi checked the map. 'Four miles.'

It took nearly ten minutes to cover the distance. A few hundred yards behind them, the Nissan was still matching their speed. Remi alternated between checking the map and studying their possible pursuers through the binoculars.

'What are you expecting them to do?' Sam asked with a smile.

'Either go away or raise the skull and crossbones.'

'Intersection's coming up. Should be around this next bend.'

Remi turned to face forward.

Sam took his foot off the gas, eased the Rover into the turn, then accelerated again.

'Sam!'

Fifty yards away, sitting broadside across the road, was a red Nissan SUV.

'There's your skull and crossbones!' Sam called.

He eased the Rover slightly left, taking the center of the road, and aimed the hood directly at the Nissan's passenger door. He stepped on the accelerator, and the Rover's engine roared.

'I don't think they're going to move,' Remi said, hands braced on the dashboard.

'We'll see.'

Remi glanced over her shoulder. 'Our tail has closed the gap.'

'How close?'

'A hundred feet and coming fast.'

'Hold on, Remi.'

With his thumb depressing the button, Sam lifted the emergency brake handle. In the space of two seconds the Rover's speed dropped by half. The Nissan's driver, seeing no brake lights to alert him, was slow to react. The Nissan loomed in Sam's rearview mirror. He jerked the wheel right, tapped the brakes, and the Nissan swerved left to avoid the collision. Sam glanced in his side mirror and saw the Nissan coming up alongside. He yanked the wheel left and was rewarded with a crunch of metal on metal. The red Nissan filled the Rover's windshield. Sam torqued the wheel hard right, swerved around the Nissan's bumper onto the shoulder, then drove back up onto the road.

'Cut it a little close there, Fargo,' Remi said.

'Sorry about that. Do you see the blue one?'

Remi checked. 'He's still there, about two hundred yards back. The red one's getting turned around.'

Within two minutes both Nissans were back on their tail and trying to close the gap. While the Rover's engine probably had more horsepower, the Nissan's lower center of gravity gave them the advantage on the corners. Slowly but steadily, the Nissans ate up the distance.

'Ideas?' Remi asked.

'I'm open-minded.'

Remi opened the map and began tracing her finger along their course while murmuring to herself. She pulled one of their guidebooks from the glove compartment, flipped pages, and continued murmuring.

She looked up suddenly. 'Is there a left turn coming up?'

'We're on it now.'

'Take it!'

Sam did as instructed, braking hard, then slewing the Rover onto the intersecting dirt road. A sign flashed past: LAC DE MANTASOA.

'Lake Mantasoa?' Sam asked. 'Are we going fishing?'

'They've got ferries,' Remi replied. She consulted her watch. 'Next one leaves in four minutes.'

Sam checked the rearview mirror. The two Nissans were skidding into the turn. 'Something tells me we're not going to have time to purchase tickets.'

'I figured you could pull off something tricky.'

'I'll see what I can do.'

The road devolved into a series of descending switch-backs bordered on both sides by steep embankments. The jungle canopy closed in above them, blotting out the sun. They passed a brown-painted sign with a yellow *P*, a car pictograph, and '50M.'

'Almost there,' Remi said. 'Let's hope for a busy lot.'

Sam brought the Rover through the last switchback, and the road widened into a small parking lot covered with diagonal white lines. To the right was a forested embank-ment; to the left, beyond a strip of well-manicured grass, was a river, this one flat and calm. There were eight cars in the parking lot. At the far end, sitting before a wall of trees, was a gazebo-like ticket hut. To the right of this was what appeared to be a service road blocked by a chain draped between two fence posts.

'I don't see the ferry,' Sam said, accelerating across the lot.

'It just left.' Remi pointed.

To the left of the ticket hut Sam saw a fan of froth on

the river's surface. He rolled down his window and they could hear the distinct overlapping chop of paddle wheels.

'They're here,' Remi said.

Sam glanced in the rearview mirror. The blue Nissan accelerated out of the last switchback, closely followed by the red one.

'I've got a tricky idea,' Sam said. 'Or a really dumb one.'

'Either way, it's better than sitting here.'

Sam slammed the gas pedal to the floor, swerved around the parked cars like a slalom racer, then bumped over the curb and onto the grass before the ticket hut. The tires slipped on the damp grass; the rear end fishtailed. Sam corrected, eased right, and aimed the hood at the entrance to the utility road.

'Cross your fingers those posts aren't buried deep,' he said. 'Here we go!'

Remi hunched down in her seat, braced her feet against the dashboard.

The Rover's bumper crashed into the chain. Sam and Remi were thrown forward against their seat belts. Sam's forehead bonked into the steering wheel. He looked up, half expecting them to be sitting still, but was instead greeted by the sight of tree branches whipping past the windshield. Remi checked the side mirror. Both entrance posts had been uprooted like rotten stumps.

'Are they following?' Sam asked.

'Not yet. They're both still sitting in the parking lot.'

'Good. Let them debate it.'

What Sam had thought was a service road was in fact little more than a rutted trail barely wider than the Rover. As in the parking lot, the right side was bordered by an embankment; to the left, through a veil of trees, was the riverbank. He gripped the steering wheel tighter and tried to keep the Rover from lurching off the path.

'You've got a knot on your forehead,' Remi said, touching the spot. 'What's the plan?'

'Get ahead of the ferry and race to the next landing. That's where you and your guidebook come in.'

She began flipping through it. 'It's less than thorough, I'm afraid.'

'There's no stop listed?'

Remi shook her head, then checked the map. 'And according to this, there's no road.'

'Interesting. We're on a road that doesn't exist going nowhere. Are our friends nonexistent as well?'

Remi glanced back and ducked her head this way and that to see through the trees. 'No, sorry, they're coming.'

'The ferry?'

'No, I don't . . . Wait! There it is! About two hundred yards behind us.' Her eyes brightened. 'It's a Mississippi-style stern-wheeler, Sam.'

The tract slanted upward and the ground grew more cratered until the Rover was bumping over exposed roots. At the top of the rise the ground flattened out. Sam slammed on the brakes. Twenty feet ahead stood a wall of trees; paralleling this, a hiking trail.

Sam said, 'The trail to the left . . .'

'Goes down to the river.'

Sam shifted the Rover into Park and pushed the tailgate button; the tailgate popped open. 'Take everything we've got.' They gathered their belongings, raced around to the back, and grabbed their backpacks.

Down the slope, the blue Nissan rounded a bend in the road and started climbing.

Sam handed Remi his pack. 'Can you manage these?'

'Yes.'

'Run.'

Remi took off. Sam returned to the driver's seat, switched the transmission into reverse, then jogged beside the Rover, steering, until the rear tires bumped over the lip of the slope. He slammed the door and jumped aside. The driver of the Nissan saw the Rover rolling toward him and slammed on the brakes. The transmission ticked as he switched into reverse. Behind him, the red Nissan came around the corner and skidded to a stop.

'Too late,' Sam said.

The Rover's back tires bumped over a bundle of exposed roots. The tail vaulted, then crashed down onto the Nissan's hood. The driver's door opened. Sam drew the Webley, crouched down, fired a round into it. The door slammed shut. Sam adjusted his aim, put a bullet through the red Nissan's hood for good measure, then turned and ran.

Sam caught up to Remi a minute later. They'd been mistaken; the trail didn't go down to the river but rather over it. Remi stood at the head of the footbridge. As Sam drew alongside her, she handed him his pack. Behind them, through the trees, voices called to one another in Spanish.

'Looks sturdier than the last bridge,' Remi said. The construction was remarkably similar – planks, crossbeams, ropes, and two suspension cables. To their left they could see the bow of the ferry coming around the bend, its funnel belching black smoke. Aside from a dozen or so people lining the rails and a few on the forecastle, the ship was empty.

'Come on,' Sam said, and took off in a sprint, Remi at his heels.

They stopped in the center of the span. The ferry was a hundred feet away. Sam looked back down the bridge. Through the trees he glimpsed movement, arms flailing. Someone was trying to climb the slope.

Remi was leaning over the handrail. 'The drop's too far.'

'To the forecastle, it is,' Sam agreed. 'See the upper deck behind the wheelhouse? It's fifteen feet, maybe less.'

'Why not the wheelhouse roof? It's only – '

'We're trying to stow away. Wave, Remi, attract attention!'

'Why?'

'Rivera's less likely to start shooting if he's got an audience.'

'Always the optimist.'

They started waving, smiling, hooting. People on the forecastle and along the rails saw them and waved back. The ferry's bow slid beneath the bridge.

'Ten seconds,' Sam told Remi. 'Hug your pack. As soon as you hit the deck, bend your knees and roll into it. Okay, up you go!' Sam helped her over the guardrail. 'Ready?'

Remi gripped his hand. 'You're coming, right?'

'Absolutely. When you're down, find some cover in case they start shooting.'

The wheelhouse roof disappeared beneath their feet, followed a moment later by the funnel. Black smoke billowed around them. Sam glanced left. Through the haze he saw Itzli Rivera skid to a stop at the head of the foot-bridge. Their eyes met for a moment, then Sam turned away, gave Remi's hand a squeeze, and said, 'Jump!'

Remi fell away into the smoke. Sam felt the bridge shiver beneath his feet with the pounding of footfalls. Rivera and his men were coming. Sam climbed over the railing, looked down. Through the gaps in the smoke he saw Remi on the deck, scrambling clear on her hands and knees.

Sam pushed off.

He hit the deck hard, bounced once off his pack, then rolled right. From out of the smoke Remi scrambled forward and latched onto his forearm. 'This way.' He followed her, crawling blindly until he bumped into what he assumed was the wheelhouse's aft bulkhead. They sat together, gulping oxygen until their heart rates returned to normal.

Now that they were past the bridge, the funnel's exhaust cleared. Fifty yards away, Rivera and three of his men stood at the bridge railing, staring down at them. One of the men reached for something in his belt and pulled out a semiautomatic pistol. Sam reached into his own belt, drew the Webley, held it above his head in profile, and gave it a waggle.

Rivera barked something at the man, who holstered his gun.

Sam said, 'Wave to the nice men, Remi.'

Chapter 36

Goldfish Point,
La Jolla, California

'Mysteries have been solved and enigmas fathomed,' Selma announced, walking into the workroom with Pete and Wendy trailing.

Still on Madagascar time, Sam and Remi sat at the worktable, each nursing a double espresso. As before, they'd slept through most of the transatlantic flight home, but still they were exhausted.

After jumping from the bridge onto the paddle-wheel steamer they decided to simply act the part of tourists and, after cleaning themselves up as best they could, strolled the decks and took in the scenery with their fellow passengers. Not only did no one ask to see their tickets, but they were served cocktails and a supper by white-coated stewards in the main salon. After having spent the day crawling through caves, wrangling crocodiles, fighting rebels, dodging falling boulders, and being chased through the Madagascar countryside, Sam and Remi relished the chance to simply sit and be pampered.

Two hours after they jumped aboard, the steamer docked at a pier jutting from a forested peninsula. Sam and Remi disembarked with everyone else and walked through a stone archway onto a well-groomed gravel path.

At the end of this they found a four-story mansion whose architectural style landed somewhere between antebellum plantation house and French country. A post-mounted plaque read HÔTEL HERMITAGE.

Dumbfounded at finding such a place in the middle of the Madagascan wilds, Sam and Remi lingered as the rest of the ferry's passengers proceeded through the pergola-covered lobby entrance.

Behind them a female voice said in flawless French, 'Welcome to the Hôtel Hermitage.'

Sam and Remi turned to see a smiling black woman in a blue skirt and a crisp white blouse standing before them.

Remi said, *'Parlez-vous anglais?'*

'Of course, madam. Can I be of assistance?'

Sam said, 'It seems we've gotten separated from our tour group. Might you be able to arrange transportation for us back to Tsiafahy?'

The woman smiled. *'Bien sûr.'*

An hour later they arrived in Tsiafahy. One call to Selma took them to a private hostel for the evening, and the next morning they were on a charter flight to Maputo, Mozambique.

Now Selma took a stool beside them. 'You two look tired.'

Sam said, 'Perhaps we didn't properly regale you with the details of our Madagascan adventure.'

Selma nodded and waved her hand. 'Crocodiles, rebels, boulders . . . Yes, I remember. Meanwhile, we've been hard at work unraveling the unravel-able.'

'That's not a word. Did we mention the bridge we – '

Remi intervened: 'Selma, you have our full, if not fully animated, attention.'

'Good. First things first: We sent your samples from the outrigger to the lab in Point Loma. We should have results in a couple of days. Remi, as you requested, I e-mailed your pictures of the outrigger and a scan of the Orizaga Codex to Professor Dydell. He said he'll have some preliminary thoughts sometime tomorrow.'

Remi saw Sam's questioning expression and said, 'Stan Dydell. My anthropology teacher at Boston College. Selma, did you – '

'I didn't give him any details. I simply said you wanted him to do a cursory examination. Moving on to the mysterious Mr. Blaylock,' Selma continued, 'Pete and Wendy and myself – '

'Mostly us,' Wendy said.

' – have read through most of Blaylock's letters to Ophelia's sister, Constance. Miss Cynthia was wrong: We think there was love between Blaylock and Constance – more on her part than his, though.'

'Why do you say that?'

'The first couple of letters Blaylock mailed from Africa were mostly travelogue. Blaylock is affectionate in a restrained way. He mentions that he wishes he could reciprocate Constance's feelings but that he was' – Selma consulted the legal pad before her – '"Afraid my grief over my dear Ophelia would turn to heartrending guilt." He talks a lot about his early days in Bagamoyo and even mentions "my mission" several times but doesn't go into detail.'

'Or so we thought,' Pete added.

'Right. After the initial ones, we noticed that each of Blaylock's letters contained random dots beneath characters within the text.'

Sam was nodding. 'A code: Pull out the marked characters and combine them in a hidden message.'

'Yes. But Blaylock, ever the mathematician, didn't make it that simple. I'll spare you the details, but he used the dates and page numbers to create a subtraction filter. For example, if the filter is a three, you take the letter *G*, subtract three characters, and get the letter *D*.'

'One of the first things we learned,' Wendy said, 'is that Constance Ashworth was working for the Secret Service. She was his conduit to the powers that be.'

Sam chuckled. 'I did not see that coming. How did you find out?'

'The hidden message in Blaylock's third letter read, 'Inform Camden ship in Bombay for repairs; crew, Maximilian men all, quartered Stone Town.'

'What are Maximilian men?' asked Remi.

Sam answered. 'After the Civil War ended, Emperor Maximilian I of Mexico opened his doors to Confederate soldiers who wanted to fight on. At the time, the U.S. was backing partisans who were trying to overthrow Maximilian. He offered the Confederates quid pro quo: Fight for me first, then we'll take on the U.S. government. Estimates vary on how many Confederates went down there, but it was enough that Washington was concerned. When you combine Dudley's report that white men were crewing the *El Majidi* with Blaylock's mention of Maximilian . . . It adds up to a rogue Confederate intelligence operation. Someone went down to Mexico, recruited some sailors, and dispatched them to Zanzibar where the *El Majidi* was waiting.'

'To what end?'

'To continue where the *Shenandoah* left off, I imagine. That ship did immense damage while she was active, and there were plenty of powerful factions in the Confederacy that swore to fight on regardless of the surrender.'

Wendy said, 'What confuses me is, how did they get access to the *El Majidi*?'

'Hard to say. One thing we do know is, the second Sultan of Zanzibar – the brother of the man who initially bought the *Shenandoah* – had no love for either his brother or that ship, and yet, when he had a chance to scuttle her after the 1872 hurricane, he didn't do it. In fact, he had her towed to Bombay and repaired at what was probably great expense.'

'Maybe this secret Confederate cabal had already purchased her, and the Sultan had no choice,' said Pete.

Sam's brows furrowed at this. He stood up and walked to one of the computer workstations, where he began typing. After a couple minutes he turned in his seat. 'Before he died, the first Sultan of Zanzibar had started to secretly crack down on the slave trade in his country. When his brother took over, the policy was reversed.'

Selma was nodding. 'So if, against all odds, the Confederacy rose again, the second Sultan would have a built-in market for his slave industry.'

'It's all speculation, of course, but the pieces seem to fit.'

'Okay, go back to Blaylock's first coded message,' Remi said. 'He mentions "Camden." Who's Camden?'

'Camden, New Jersey, is where Thomas Haines Dudley

was born,' Selma replied. 'We think it was Blaylock's nickname for him rather than an official code name. In fact, Dudley had his own moniker for Blaylock: Jotun.'

'It's from Norse mythology,' Wendy added. 'Jotun was a giant with superhuman strength.'

'Of course,' Sam said. 'Jotun. I don't know how I missed that.'

Remi lightly punched his arm. 'Smart aleck. Don't mind him, Wendy. Go ahead, Selma.'

'In another letter to Dudley via Constance, dated July 1872, Blaylock reported that the *El Majidi* – now redubbed *Shenandoah*, we presume – had returned to port with her crew already aboard. Blaylock suspects the repairs on the ship had been completed at least a month prior and that the ship and crew had been at sea since then.'

'Were there any unaccounted-for attacks or losses in the area during that time?' asked Sam.

'Dozens. For a long time the Indian Ocean was a bigger pirate haven than the Caribbean. But we weren't able to connect the *Shenandoah II* to any of the losses. It's at this point the story gets stranger. Blaylock ends his report with this line: "Have acquired reliable vessel and received Sharps."'

'As in Sharps carbines?' Sam asked; Selma nodded. 'Dudley must have arranged for them to be shipped to Blaylock.'

Selma went on. '"Nilo-Hamitic crew learning rapidly and overcoming fear of water; expect to be fit to give chase by month's end. Intend to catch them red-handed."'

'Nilo-Hamitic?' Sam repeated. 'Never heard of them.'

'I have,' Remi replied. 'Nilo-Hamitic is an outdated name for the Maasai tribe. It appears our mysterious Mr.

Blaylock recruited a guerrilla army of Maasai warriors to chase down the *Shenandoah II*.'

'Well, I'll give him this much,' Sam said. 'The man had a flair for the dramatic. According to Morton's biography of Blaylock, he lived with the Maasai for a while.'

'He did,' Selma replied. 'As far as we can tell from his letters, he explored the area inland from Bagamoyo and became friendly with some Maasai. That's how he started the recruitment.'

'Okay, so it's July 1872. The *Shenandoah II* has a new crew and she's prepped for battle. What then?'

'Most of what happened next we got from Blaylock's coded reports, and some of it we matched against what few dated entries we found in his journal.

'A couple weeks later, Blaylock and his crew put to sea in a boum – essentially, a large two-masted dhow – and begin hunting the *Shenandoah II*, which slipped out of port a few days ahead of them. This cat-and-mouse game goes on for a month. Blaylock hears a report that a ship matching the *Shenandoah II*'s description has sunk two U.S.-flagged cargo ships near the Gulf of Aden. According to our databases, two ships were sunk in that area around the dates Blaylock mentions; the losses were attributed to pirates.'

'Not far off the mark,' Sam observed.

'Though Blaylock isn't a seaman, he proves an able captain, and the Maasai an adept crew. Blaylock knows he doesn't dare attack the *Shenandoah II* either directly or at sea, so all through July and August he does his best to shadow her. He gathers intelligence reports and bides his time until the night of September sixteenth.

'He catches the *Shenandoah II* at anchor off Sainte Anne Island in the Seychelles, about thirteen hundred miles east of Zanzibar. Blaylock anchors his boum in a nearby cove, then he and his men go ashore, sneak across the headland, and, in true pirate fashion, swim out to the *Shenandoah* and take her by storm. Not a single shot is fired, but the Maasai, being the warriors they are, show little mercy. Of *Shenandoah II*'s crew of seventy-eight, only six survive – the captain, another officer, and four enlisted men.

'Blaylock's official report of the capture reaches the U.S. in November. He tells Dudley that he put the *Shenandoah II*'s survivors ashore on Sainte Anne Island.'

'Do we know what became of them?' Remi asked.

'Unfortunately, I found nothing. Blaylock then splits his crew between the boum and the *Shenandoah II* and sets off for the return voyage to Zanzibar. Three hundred miles east of the Seychelles, they encounter a storm, and the *Shenandoah II* sinks.'

At this, Sam and Remi leaned forward together. 'Sinks?' Remi repeated. 'How in the world – '

'Along with his report to Dudley, Blaylock includes a coded message for Constance.' Selma flipped a page on her legal pad and traced her finger down a couple lines. '"Having secured the *Shenandoah*, we promptly took inventory of her stores and goods. To my great surprise, in the captain's cabin I found a most remarkable item: a statuette of a great green jeweled bird consisting of a mineral unfamiliar to me and depicting a species I have never encountered. I must admit, dear Constance, I was entranced."'

Sam and Remi were silent as they absorbed this. Finally

Sam said, 'That explains the line in his journal – the great green jeweled bird.'

'And all the bird sketches,' Remi added. 'And maybe what we found in Morton's museum in Bagamoyo. Remember all the stuffed birds hanging from the ceiling, Sam? He was obsessed. What else did he say in the letter, Selma?'

'I'm paraphrasing, but here's the gist of it: He's done his duty for his country, not once but twice, and he lost his wife in the process. He admits he lied to Dudley about the *Shenandoah II*'s sinking. He begs Constance's forgiveness and tells her he intends to discover where the *Shenandoah II*'s crew found the jeweled bird and recover the rest of the treasure.'

'What treasure?' Sam asked. 'At that point, does he have any hint there's more to find?'

'If he did, he never jotted a word about it. At least not in plain text. Given the nature of his journal, it may all be hidden in there somewhere.'

'What about the *Shenandoah II*'s captain's log?' Remi asked. 'If Blaylock was assuming the previous crew had found the jeweled bird during their travels, the log would be a natural place to start.'

'He never mentions a log, but I agree with your assumption.'

Sam said, 'My guess: He transcribed whatever he found relevant in the captain's log to his own journal.'

'At any rate,' Selma continued, 'Blaylock continued to write Constance after the *Shenandoah II*'s capture, but his letters became more and more irrational. You can read them yourself, but it's clear Blaylock was descending into insanity.'

'And those are just the plain text portions of the letters,' Pete added. 'We've still got fourteen to decode.'

'If we're to believe all this,' Sam said, 'then Winston Blaylock probably spent the remainder of his life sailing the ocean aboard the *Shenandoah II*, scribbling in his journal, staring at his jeweled bird, and carving glyphs on the inside of the bell while looking for a treasure that may or may not have existed.'

'It may be even bigger than that,' Remi said. 'If the Orizaga Codex is genuine and the outrigger is what we think it is, somewhere along the way Blaylock may have stumbled onto a secret that was buried with Cortés and his Conquistadors: the true origin of the Aztecs.'

Chapter 37

'There are a lot of loose ends here,' Sam pointed out. He grabbed a nearby legal pad and pen and began writing:

✢ How/when did Morton obtain Blaylock's journal, his walking staff, and the Orizaga Codex?
✢ How/when did the *Shenandoah*'s bell end up buried off the coast of Chumbe Island? How did the clapper come off?

Sam stopped writing. 'What else?' he asked. Remi gestured for the pad, and he slid it over to her. She wrote:

✢ How much do Rivera and his employer know about Blaylock? How did they get involved? What are they after?
✢ How did Rivera know about Madagascar?

She slid the pad back to Sam, who said, 'I have an idea about one of these ... What are they after? We suspect Rivera works for the Mexican government, correct?'

'It's a safe bet.'

'We also know the current administration, President

Garza's Mexica Tenochca, came into office on a wave of ultranationalism – pride in Mexico's true, precolonial heritage and so forth. We also know Rivera and his goons all have Nahuatl-Aztec names, along with most of Mexica Tenochca's leaders and cabinet members. The "Aztec Groundswell," as the press called it, won them the election.'

Sam looked around the group and got nods in return.

'What if whoever Rivera works for knows the truth about the Aztecs? What if they knew long before the election?'

Remi said, 'We did find what might be nine tourist murders in seven years in Zanzibar. If our hunch about them is correct, the cover-up goes back at least that far.'

Sam nodded. 'If Blaylock truly found what we think he found, this could turn Mesoamerican history on its head.'

'Is that enough to kill for?' Wendy asked.

'Absolutely,' Remi replied. 'If members of the current government won the election based on a lie and the truth comes to light, how long before they're drummed out of office? Or even its leaders arrested? Imagine if after George Washington was elected America's first president, it was proven he was a traitor. It's a bit of an apples-to-oranges comparison, but you get the idea.'

'Then, potentially, we're talking about President Garza being directly involved in this,' Pete said.

Sam said, 'He certainly has the kind of horsepower that's been backing Rivera from the beginning. At this point, all we've got to go on is Blaylock's journal and letters. My gut is telling me the answers are hidden there.'

'Where do you suggest we start?' Selma asked.

'His poem. Do you have it?'

Selma flipped pages on her pad, then recited,

In my love's heart I pen my devotion
On Engai's gyrare I trust my feet
From above, the earth squared
From praying hands my day is quartered, the gyrare once, twice
Words of Ancients, words of Father Algarismo

'The first two lines we already figured out – he's talking about the bell and Fibonacci spirals. Now we just need to figure out the last four lines.'

They broke into groups. Selma, Pete, and Wendy worked on Blaylock's letters to Constance Ashworth, searching for any clues they may have missed, while Sam and Remi retreated to the solarium to pore over Blaylock's journal, which Selma had loaded onto their iPads.

Side by side, they reclined on chaise lounges partially shaded by potted palms and billowing ferns. The sun streamed through the skylights and cast dappled shadows across the tiled floor.

After an hour, Sam muttered, half to himself, 'Leonardo the Liar.'

'Pardon?'

'That line from Blaylock's journal: "Leonardo the Liar." Clearly Blaylock was referring to Leonardo Fibonacci.'

'Of the sequence-and-spiral fame.'

'Right. But why did he add "the liar"?'

'I meant to ask what that's all about.'

'The Fibonacci sequence wasn't discovered by Leonardo; he simply helped spread it around Europe.'

'So he lied about the discovery?'

'No, he never claimed credit for it. And Blaylock, being a mathematician, would have known that. I'm starting to wonder if the line was meant as a reminder to himself.'

'Go on.'

'According to my research, the sequence is most often attributed to a twelfth-century Indian mathematician named Hemachandra who – surprise, surprise – also authored an epic poem entitled *Lives of Sixty-three Great Men*.'

'Another line from Blaylock's journal.'

'Which was placed directly across from the Leonardo the Liar quote.'

'Certainly sounds intentional,' Remi said. 'But what's it add up to?'

'I'm not sure. I need to see that page again.'

Back in the workroom, Sam told Wendy, 'I just need to see the area around the "Sixty-three Great Men" line.'

'Can do. Hold on a moment.' At one of the workstations, Wendy opened the image in Photoshop, made some adjustments, then said, 'Done. It should be on your screen . . . now.'

Sam studied the image. 'Can you isolate and enlarge the area around the Sixty-three?' Thirty seconds later, the new image appeared. Sam scrutinized it for a moment. 'Too fuzzy. I'm mostly interested in the tiny marks above and below the Sixty-three.'

Wendy went back to work. A few minutes later Wendy said, 'Try this one.'

The new image resolved on the screen:

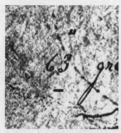

'I had to do a little color replacement, but I'm pretty sure the marks are — '

'It's perfect,' Sam murmured, eyes fixed on the screen.

'Care to share with the rest of the class?' Remi said.

'We've been assuming Blaylock used the Fibonacci spiral as some kind of encoding tool on the inside of the bell. The problem is, at what scale? The spiral's starting grid size can be anything. That's the piece we were missing. Now we have it.'

'Explain,' said Selma.

'Blaylock's line about Leonardo was meant as a pointer to the "Sixty-three Great Men" line. Look above and just to the right of the number three.'

'It's a quote mark,' Wendy said.

'Or the symbol for inches,' replied Pete.

'Bingo. Now look at the dash directly below the Sixty-three. It's a minus sign. If you move the inches symbol down and the minus sign up, you get this . . .' Sam grabbed a pad, scribbled something, and turned it around for everyone to see:

$$6'' - 3'' = 3''$$

'Blaylock is telling us the starting square in his spiral is three inches.'

They quickly realized the mathematics needed to re-create the spiral were beyond their grasp. Blaylock had devised his bell-spiral combination based on his expertise in topology. To solve it, the Fargos needed an expert of their own, so Sam took a page from Remi's book and called one of his former professors at Caltech. As it happened, George Milhaupt was now retired and living just seventy miles away on Mount Palomar, where he'd been playing amateur astronomer at the observatory since leaving the institute.

Sam's brief explanation of the problem so intrigued Milhaupt that he drove immediately to La Jolla, arriving two hours after Sam's call.

Milhaupt, a short man in his mid-seventies with a monk's fringe of white hair, followed Sam into the work space carrying an old leather valise. Milhaupt looked around, said, 'Splendid,' then shook everyone's hands. 'Where is it?' he asked. 'Where is this mystery?'

Not wanting to muddy the waters, Sam restricted his briefing to the *Shenandoah*, the bell, and the relevant portions of Blaylock's journal. When he finished, Milhaupt was silent for thirty seconds, pursing his lips and nodding thoughtfully to himself. Finally: 'I can't argue with your conclusions, Sam. You were right to call me. You were a good math student, but topology was never your strong suit. If you'll bring me the bell, your Fibonacci calculations, and a large sketch pad, then leave me alone, I'll lock horns with Mr. Blaylock and see what I come up with.'

Ninety minutes later, Milhaupt's scratchy voice came over the house's intercom system. 'Hello . . . ? I'm done.'

Sam and Remi and the others returned to the work space. Sitting on the table, amid dividers, pencils, flexible measuring tapes, and a pad covered in scribbles, was a sketch:

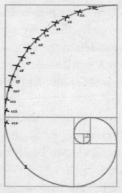

As though playing a slow-motion game of musical chairs, the group walked around the table, eyes fixed on the drawing, heads tilting this way and that, until finally Sam said, 'You've stumped us.'

'Do you see the *tr* notation in the upper right-hand

corner and the numerals near the curve at the bottom left?'

'Yes,' Sam said.

'That's my handwriting, of course, but they were also inscribed on the inside of the bell. I suspect it means "top right."'

Sam and Remi looked at him in surprise. 'We missed that,' Remi said.

'Don't feel bad. They were minuscule. Without my magnifying glass, I would have overlooked them, too. The *tr* notations were on the very edge of the bell's mouth.'

'You said "notations,"' Remi replied. 'As in plural.'

'There were two. I have a second sketch, but aside from the order of the symbols, each is identical to the other. When I saw the two *tr* notations, I assumed they were intended as both orientation points and end points for a pair of spirals. As to why there are two spirals . . . I suspect that answer is hidden in the rest of that poem of his. As you can see, each X mark is accompanied by a designator; each represents a different glyph. I have a legend with all this written down.'

'Amazing,' Sam said. 'Imagine the patience all this took.'

Milhaupt smiled and rubbed his hands together. 'And now I'd be happy to tackle Mr. Blaylock's poem.'

Selma read it aloud.

'Well, I agree with your assessment of the first two lines,' Milhaupt said. 'As for the other lines . . . I may have some ideas. First of all, this fellow's a very abstract thinker – which is especially strange for a mathematician.'

'He was a character,' Sam agreed. 'We also think he may have been a few sandwiches shy of a picnic.'

'Ah, I see. That puts things into perspective. Well, the third line – "From above, the earth squared" – suggests to me a pair of spirals that are to be viewed from overhead. The notations I found within the bell tend to validate that. Agreed?'

Everyone nodded.

'The fourth line – "From praying hands my day is quartered, the gyrare once, twice" – is a bit trickier, but as we're fairly certain about the overhead view issue, the "praying hands" may represent two hands of a clock, pointing toward midnight. I suspect the words "my day is quartered" mean Mr. Blaylock has divided his "clock" into four sections – midnight, three, six, and nine. And finally, following this logic, the line "the gyrare once, twice" probably means we're to rotate our first spiral to the three o'clock position and the second spiral to the six o'clock position.'

Milhaupt demonstrated, rotating his sketches, the first on top with the open end of the spiral pointing to the right; the second below that, the open end of the spiral pointing downward. He looked at each member of the group in turn. 'Thoughts?'

No one spoke up.

'Me neither,' he said. 'How about the last line of the poem?'

Selma recited it:

Words of Ancients, words of Father Algarismo

Remi said, 'As for the first part – "Words of Ancients" – we have a hunch what Blaylock means.'

'You're referring to those Aztec glyphs inside the bell?' Milhaupt asked with a Cheshire smile. 'I have no idea of their translation, of course. I assume you do?'

Sam nodded. 'They're from the Aztec calendar – thirteen months, thirteen corresponding symbols.'

'Clearly Mr. Blaylock was absorbed with the Aztecs, yes?'

'"Absorbed" isn't the word we've been using,' Remi said.

Sam said, 'The second part of the line – "words of Father Algarismo" – has us stumped.'

'I am happy to say I have your answer. At last, my love of obscure mathematical history has come in handy. There is no Father Algarismo, you see. It's another one of Mr. Blaylock's tricks. Algarismo is the Portuguese derivation of the word "algorithm." Quite simply, it means digit.'

Remi said, 'Then, translated, the last line reads, "Words of the Aztecs combined with numbers." Sam, you're the cryptography guy. Is any of this ringing any bells?'

Sam nodded. 'Maybe. I seem to remember a page in his journal that was nothing but dots. Did I imagine that?'

'No, I remember it,' Wendy said. 'I'll find it.' She disappeared into the archive vault.

'I can see the gears turning in your head,' said Remi. 'What's going on?'

'I don't think we're meant to combine Aztec words with numbers. I think we're meant to translate them. For example, take the symbol for "flint" and replace the letters with corresponding numbers.'

Remi was jotting along on her pad:

$$6, 12, 9, 14, 20$$

'A simple substitution code,' said Milhaupt.

'Right,' Sam said. 'I think Blaylock's spirals are just window dressing. Look at the two rotated sketches. If you straighten out the ends of the spirals, you get a horizontal line of glyphs and a vertical line of glyphs.'

'Essentially a grid,' said Remi.

Wendy's voice came over the intercom. 'Sam, I found that page you mentioned. It's on the screen.'

Selma grabbed the remote and switched on the TV. As Sam had described, the page consisted of nothing more than groupings of seemingly randomly placed dots – row after row, column after column.

'How many clusters?' Sam asked.

Remi was already counting. 'One hundred sixty-nine. Thirteen down and thirteen across.' She smiled. 'Same number as your spiral grid idea, Sam. And the same number of months in the Aztec calendar.'

Milhaupt said, 'We have a winner. Now you just need to plug your dots into the grid and figure out what it all means.'

Having chased Blaylock's riddles for what seemed like months, Sam, now certain he was closing in on his quarry, attacked the 'Blaylock Dot Grid Mystery' with a gusto that took him through the evening and into the early-morning hours of the next day.

Translating the Aztec-Nahuatl glyphs first into their

Anglicized meanings and then into numbers was straightforward but time-consuming. Once done, he began plugging the dot clusters into their corresponding rows and columns until he had what looked like an LSD-inspired Sudoku puzzle on steroids. Next he began experimenting with various cryptographic methods, hoping to stumble upon something that clicked. Shortly before midnight, he found just that: a binary-type system where the dots' positions determined which numbers in the grid were used.

After hearing Sam's theory, Remi said, 'You've worked this out? Tested it?'

'I did. Aside from the "empty" clusters, they're all latitude and longitude coordinates. This is a map.'

Chapter 38

Goldfish Point,
La Jolla, California

Coffee in hand, Sam and Remi walked into the workroom at eight A.M. to find Selma, Pete, and Wendy standing before a six-foot-wide map of the Indian Ocean tacked to the wall with blue painter's tape.

Six hours earlier, at Pete and Wendy's urging, Sam and Remi had gone to bed, leaving them to plot the coordinates on a world map.

'Of the one hundred sixty-nine locations in Blaylock's grid, eighty-two of them were null,' Pete now explained. 'Of the remaining eighty-seven, fifty-three were located in the middle of the ocean, which left us thirty-four latitude and longitude points that matched up with land. That's what you see plotted here.'

The coordinates were marked by red pushpins connected by white string. In rough, the pins formed a giant inverted V that started near Madagascar, peaked 2,800 miles to the northeast at Sri Lanka, and ended off the central coast of Sumatra, 1,400 miles to the southeast.

'Where are the other pins?' Sam asked.

Selma replied, 'We pulled some out, most of them well inland. We wanted you to see this particular pattern first.'

Both Remi and Sam recognized the gleam in Selma's eyes. During the night, she, Pete, and Wendy had discovered something significant.

'Go on,' Remi prompted.

'After you got back from Madagascar and proposed the east-to-west Aztec migration theory, I started doing a little digging. In recent years a number of archeologists and anthropologists have been finding more and more evidence that the Malagasy people of Madagascar arrived there in the first or second century, having sailed there from Indonesia – specifically, the island of Sulawesi. I came across a map of the route the Malagasy were believed to have taken.'

Selma picked up the remote and powered up the TV across the room.

The route, depicted as a red line on a map of the Indian Ocean, from the Indonesian Archipelago to the east coast of Africa, was nearly identical to the one on the workroom's wall.

'Incredible' was all Sam could say.

'So Blaylock beat present-day experts to this theory by a hundred twenty or so years,' Remi said. 'That's impressive, but I don't – '

'There's more,' Selma said. Pete and Wendy got up on step stools, removed the pushpins, peeled back the tape, and pulled away the map. Beneath it was a second map, this one spanning from the east coast of Africa to South America. Like the first map, this one was covered in red pushpins connected by white string.

'These are all Blaylock's?' Sam asked.

'Yes.'

The pushpins began near the coastal city of Lumbo in Mozambique and proceeded across the waist of Africa to the west coast of Angola before island-hopping first up the coastline, then west across the Atlantic to the eastern-most bulge of Brazil, where they turned north and followed the coast of South America past Trinidad and Tobago and into the Caribbean Sea.

Remi asked, 'Are we to believe Blaylock visited all these places?'

Sam replied, 'He captured the *Shenandoah* in 1872, then went treasure hunting for his jeweled bird. Who knows how long he was at sea? It could have been decades, for all we know.'

'This looks familiar,' Remi said. 'Pete, Wendy, put the first map up beside this one, please.'

They did as she asked.

Remi stared at this configuration for almost a full minute before smiling faintly. 'Do you see it?' she asked.

'See what?' asked Sam.

In answer, Remi walked to one of the workstations. 'Wendy's been teaching me a little Photoshop. Let's see how good a learner I am. Everybody go sit down. This might take me a few minutes.'

With her upper body blocking the computer monitor, no one could see what she was doing. At the worktable, Sam leaned sideways on his stool, trying to get a peek.

'Forget it, Fargo,' Remi muttered.

'Sorry.'

Twenty minutes later, Remi turned in her seat and addressed the group. 'Okay. We all remember the Orizaga Codex?'

Everyone nodded.

'Remember the symbol spanning the upper half?'

More nods.

'Turn on the TV, Selma.'

'I'll be damned,' said Sam. 'We were staring at it the whole time. It wouldn't win any cartography awards, but all the big pieces are there. Remind me: When did the Malagasy arrive in Madagascar?'

'First or second century.'

'And when did the Aztecs first emerge in Mexico?'

'Sixth century.'

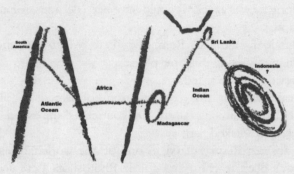

'The Malagasy blaze the first trail from Sulawesi, then a few centuries later, a bigger armada – a hundred ships if the Orizaga Codex is accurate – arrives in Madagascar, but they don't stop there. They keep heading west until they find Mexico.'

'The journey must have taken years,' Pete said. 'The walk across Africa alone would have lasted six months or more. If you figure, conservatively, eight people to an out-rigger, we're talking about as many as eight hundred people.'

'Sam said it before: an exodus,' Remi replied.

'How do we know they didn't go around Africa's southern tip?' asked Wendy.

'Two reasons,' Remi said. 'First, you'll notice that area doesn't appear on their map; second, they may have tried it, but I can't imagine anybody getting around the Cape of Good Hope in outriggers.'

'Those are some of the most unforgiving waters on earth,' Sam agreed. 'Here's the million-dollar question: On your map, where exactly does the big question mark fall?'

'You've got me. Indonesia's a big place. For Blaylock, it was probably where he thought he'd find his treasure. For the Aztecs, it was Chicomoztoc. When King Cuauhtemotzin dictated the codex to Orizaga, he was trying to show where his forefathers came from, but after centuries of having the story handed down through one generation of royalty to the next Cuauhtemotzin himself couldn't be more specific.'

Pete said, 'What I want to know is why they left in the first place.'

That question was at least partially answered two hours later when Remi's old professor, Stan Dydell, called Selma and requested a video conference. The group gathered around the TV in the workroom. Dydell's smiling face appeared on the screen. In appearance, he was the exact opposite of George Milhaupt: tall, thin, with a full head of salt-and-pepper hair.

'Good morning, Remi, nice to see you again.'

'And you, Professor.'

'And that man beside you would be Sam.'

'Nice to meet you, Professor.' Sam introduced Pete and Wendy.

Dydell nodded in greeting. 'My secretary is helping me with all this. You don't mind, do you? I think technology has outpaced me a bit.'

'Not at all,' said Remi.

'I imagine you're anxious to talk about your find, so I'll get right to it. First, let's talk about the photos you sent. The vessel itself isn't unique: canoe shaped, two outriggers, and a single mast. The size is impressive, however. Next: I'm probably not telling you anything you haven't already worked out for yourself, but the carving on the bowsprit looks remarkably like Quetzalcoatl, the Great Plumed Serpent God of the Aztecs.'

'Our guess as well.'

'We've talked about Quetzalcoatl,' Sam said, 'but what's the significance?'

'As in most Aztec myth systems, Quetzalcoatl plays an array of roles that depend on the period and the circumstances. In some cases, Quetzalcoatl was related to the wind, the planet Venus, arts, and knowledge. He was also the patron god of the Aztec priesthood. He was also believed to be responsible for the separation of the earth and sky, and an essential player in the creation of mankind.'

'That's a lot of hats to wear,' Sam remarked. 'And what about the other carving, the one on the stern . . .'

'Clearly it's a bird of some kind, but I don't recognize it. As for this parchment you have . . . It's a copy of the Orizaga Codex, but I'm guessing you already knew that, too.'

'Yes,' said Remi.

'Do you also know you may have the only known copy in existence?'

'No, we didn't.'

'In fact, until now it was believed there were no copies. Just the original. Here's the short story: Javier Orizaga, Society of Jesus, was said to have arrived in Mexico as part of Cortés's landing force. He carried with him a whole bevy of monks and such – presumably to help convert the savages.

'A few months after Orizaga penned his codex, he was ordered home by the powers-that-be. When he got back to Spain, his codex was confiscated by the Church. Orizaga was jailed and interrogated for two years, then released, having been denounced by the Church and the state. He left Spain and traveled to what is present-day Indonesia, where he remained until his death in 1556.'

'Indonesia again,' Sam murmured. Professor, do we know where exactly in Indonesia?'

'I'm not sure. I can check for you. This codex you have, Remi . . . Where did you find it?'

'In Africa.'

'Interesting. If it's genuine, it's an incredible find. Have you had it physically examined?'

'Not yet.'

'You'll have to do that eventually. For now, let's assume it's genuine. There are a number of things about it that are not just remarkable but potentially groundbreaking.'

Sam said, 'You mean that it was dictated to Orizaga by the last king of the Aztecs?'

'That and more. I have to admit, the upper part has me stumped. As for the lower part . . . Here's what strikes me:

The scene in the middle of the parchment clearly depicts a sea voyage of a great number of vessels. On the lower left side of the parchment is, I think, a depiction of the Aztecs' arrival in the area that would become their capital city of Tenochtitlán.'

Seeing their stunned expressions, Dydell chuckled and went on: 'Let me refresh your quintessential Aztec imagery. Legend has it that the Aztecs knew they'd found their homeland when they came across an eagle perched atop a cactus while eating a snake. The image on your codex is depicting essentially the same thing. The bird is different and the flora is different and there's no snake, but the theme is present.'

'Why wouldn't it be identical?' asked Sam.

'My guess: It's a case of what I like to call MDI – Migrational Displacement Iconography. It's a theory I've been toying with for some time. Essentially, it's this: As ancient peoples migrated, they tended to change their myths and imagery to suit their new geography. It's quite common, actually.

'If these Old World Aztecs – for lack of a better term – arrived in Mexico nine centuries before the Aztec Empire rose, it's perfectly reasonable to think their original iconography would have changed drastically – not to mention their appearance as they interbred with the locals.'

Sam and Remi looked at each other. Sam said, 'I can buy that.'

'Well, that's good, because that was the easy part,' Dydell said. 'The image in the lower right-hand corner, the one clearly meant to represent Chicomoztoc, is where the real wow factor is. How closely did you examine the image, Remi?'

'Not very,' she admitted.

'Well, there are a number of differences between the traditional depiction of Chicomoztoc and the one you have. First of all, there's no high priest at the entrance, and the faces you usually find clustered in each of the seven caverns are missing.'

'I can't believe I missed that.'

'Don't be hard on yourself. In class, we barely touched on Chicomoztoc. That aside, it is what's in the center of the cavern I find so fascinating. I took the liberty of enlarging the scan you sent me.' Dydell looked off camera and said, 'Gloria, would you mind . . . Okay, good, thanks.' He faced the camera again. 'This image is enlarged four hundred percent. Gloria says it should be on your screen now. Do you have it?' Dydell asked.

'We have it,' replied Sam.

'The first thing you'll probably notice is the creature between the two male figures in the middle of the cavern. The placement suggests it is a focus of reverence. The lower half of the creature appears to be Quetzalcoatl. The upper half, though, is hard to make out. It could be the tail, or something else altogether.'

Sam said, 'One of the figures is standing, the other kneeling. That has to mean something.'

'Indeed. It suggests supplication. Also, did you notice that the figure on the right is holding something?'

'It's the Nahuatl symbol for flint,' Remi said.

'Right you are. Normally, I would classify this scene as a sacrificial ceremony of some kind, but you have to remember that the Aztecs were highly metaphorical in their "written" language. Flint can also represent separation and the breaking of old ties.

'Now, here's the kicker: In traditional drawings of Chicomoztoc, you'll find two sets of footprints: one set going into the cave and one set going out. In your drawing, there is only one set.'

'And they're going out,' Sam said.

'When you combine all of this – the supplicant figure, Quetzalcoatl, the flint, the footprints – you get what I believe is a ceremony of exile. The figure on the left, along with all of his followers, was banished. Based on the rest of the codex, they left Chicomoztoc, boarded their armada, headed west, and ended up in Mexico to become what history considers the Aztec people.'

Remi asked, 'Professor, do we know what became of Orizaga's original codex? Did the Church destroy it or is it tucked away in some archive somewhere?'

'Neither, but I'm sure they'd intended that it never see the light of day. In 1992 the Church held an auction of old but generally mundane artifacts – letters, illustrations, etcetera. Apparently someone messed up, and the Orizaga Codex was included in the lot. It was purchased by a Mexican millionaire, I believe. A coffee magnate.'

'What was his name?' asked Sam.

Dydell hesitated, thinking. 'Garza. Alfonso or Armando, I can't remember which.'

They talked with Dydell for a few more minutes, then disconnected. As they often were, Sam and Remi were on the same wavelength. Almost in unison they said to Wendy, 'Do you think you can do something to clean up the – '

'I know . . . the Quetzalcoatl image. I'm on it.'

Next, Sam and Remi turned to Selma, but she was a step ahead of them, already seated at her computer, typing. 'Got it. Alfonso Garza, father of Cristián Garza. Currently known as Quauhtli Garza, president of Mexico and leader of the Mexica Tenochca Party.'

Sam and Remi shared a smile. 'That's where it all started,' he said. 'Just like Blaylock, Garza got ahold of the codex and caught the bug. It consumed him.'

Remi nodded. 'And took him somewhere he didn't expect.'

Thirty minutes later Wendy was done. 'I had to do some creative connect-the-dots, but I think I've got a fair representation of what it would've looked liked like originally.'

'There's a familiar face,' Sam said.

Remi nodded. 'Blaylock's bird.'

The day ended with a phone call that Sam and Remi, in their exhaustion, had forgotten they were expecting. Selma answered, listened for a few moments, then hung up and walked to her workstation. A minute later the laser printer started whirring. She walked back to the table with a sheaf of papers.

'The lab report on the samples you took from the outrigger.'

'Do the honors,' said Sam.

Selma scanned the sheets, then said, 'The wood is from a durian tree, native to Borneo, Indonesia, and Malaysia.'

'Score another point for Indonesia,' Sam said. 'There seems to be a trend developing.'

'The resin you scraped from the hull consisted of the sap from a subspecies of rubber tree, also found in Indonesia. Finally, the material you scooped from inside the hull ... They found traces of pandan leaf, rattan, and gebang palm.'

'Let me guess,' Remi said. 'All materials used in the construction of natural sail cloth?'

Selma nodded.

'And all native to Indonesia,' Sam added.

'You're batting a thousand,' replied Selma. 'Shall I book your flights now or wait until the morning?'

Chapter 39

Palembang, Sumatra, Indonesia

The tires crunched on gravel as Sam pulled the car off the road and coasted to a stop beneath the boughs of a kapok tree. A steady stream of compact cars and scooters whizzed past Sam's door, honking and swerving as though trying to beat a checkered flag.

'Okay, you win,' Sam said to Remi. 'But before I risk my life and step into this traffic to ask for directions, let me see the map one more time.'

While like most men, Sam prided himself on being equipped with a supernatural internal compass that kept him from ever being lost, he'd also learned to concede those rare times when that compass seemed to be in temporary disrepair. Now was one of those times.

Trying to conceal her smile, Remi handed him the map and sat quietly while Sam studied it. 'It's gotta be around here somewhere.'

'I'm sure it is.'

As was the case with many of Sam and Remi's revelations since finding the *Shenandoah*'s bell buried in the sand off Zanzibar, Winston Blaylock had, as the saying went, been there and done that. In this case, one of the latitude and longitude points they'd deciphered from his dot-grid system happened to fall where Javier Orizaga, S.J., had spent the final years of his life. It was no coincidence, they knew. Still, there were many questions unanswered.

Having spent years hunting for the origin of his 'great green jeweled bird' and discovering along the way the true story of the Aztec Empire, had Blaylock heard of Oriza-ga's codex and come here looking for a copy or had he found the codex elsewhere and deduced the location the same way Sam and Remi had? Similarly, what had brought Orizaga here: a quest for treasure or for the history of a people whose destruction he witnessed?

An hour after they'd ended their video-conference meeting with Professor Dydell, he'd called back with the name of the village Orizaga had called home the last two decades of his life: Palembang, Sumatra.

While Palembang, the 'Venice of the East,' might have been considered just a hamlet during the sixteenth century, today it was not only the oldest city in Indonesia, dating back to the seventh century, but also the biggest in southern Sumatra, boasting a population of 1.5 million.

Neither Sam nor Remi had any grand ideas about what, if anything, of value they'd find by investigating Orizaga's adopted homeland. However, all the hoops they'd jumped through since Zanzibar seemed to be leading them in one direction. Blaylock's quest, his journal, the maps, the codex, Orizaga himself, and now the lab report – all of it pointed toward an unknown location in Indonesia.

'It would have made our lives so much easier if Orizaga had left an address,' Sam said. 'It's a bit inconsiderate, really.'

'I'm sure if he'd known we were coming, he would have,' Remi replied. 'Did the woman at the last place say the house was red or green?'

'Green.'

Since arriving in Palembang the previous day, they'd visited six local museums or historians said to specialize in the pre–Dutch colonial period of the city's history. So far, none of the curators had heard of Orizaga, and each one had suggested Sam and Remi go to the city's administrative building and peruse centuries' worth of microfiche newspapers for any mention of their friend.

Sam traced his finger along the map, occasionally ducking his head so he could see the nearby street signs through the windshield. He folded the map and handed it back to Remi with a confident smile.

'I know where I went wrong.'

'In general or with the directions?'

'Funny lady.'

Sam put the car in gear, waited for a gap in traffic, then veered out and accelerated.

Twenty minutes of winding down backstreets brought them to an industrial park filled with warehouses. Behind this they were surprised to find a quiet, tree-lined residential cul-de-sac. The houses were small and old but well kept. At the end of the circle Sam pulled to a stop before what could have passed for a ranch-style house in Anytown, USA: kelly green with brown shutters and a white picket fence half hidden by red-flowering vines.

They walked up the path, mounted the porch steps, and knocked on the front door. They heard the click of footfalls on wood. The door opened to reveal a mid-fifties white man in crisp khaki pants and a button-down white shirt.

'Yes, good afternoon,' he said with an Oxford accent.

'We're looking for Sukasari House,' Remi said.

'You have found it, madam. How can I help you?'

'We're looking for someone – a monk – who may or may not have lived in this area in the sixteenth century.'

'Oh, well, is that all? I thought you'd come to try to sell me a vacuum or some pots and pans,' the man said with a wry smile. 'Please, come in.' He stepped back to let them into the foyer. 'My name is Robert Marcott.'

'Sam and Remi Fargo.'

'Follow me. I'll make some tea and then tell you everything I know about Indonesia in the fifteenth century.'

'Pardon me for saying this,' Remi said, 'but you don't seem surprised by our question.'

'I'm not. Here, come sit down. I'll explain.'

He ushered them into a study enclosed by floor-to-ceiling bookcases. The floor was covered with a Persian rug; on top of it were a few rattan furniture pieces around a coffee table. Sam and Remi sat on the sofa.

'I'll be just a moment,' Marcott said, then disappeared through a side door. They heard the clinking of china, then a kettle whistling. He came back in with a tea service, filled their cups, then sat down across from them.

'Who pointed you in my direction?' Marcott asked.

'A woman named Ratsami – '

'Lovely woman. Knows nothing about Sumatran history prior to the twentieth century.'

'She was under the impression this was a museum.'

'A bit of a language gap, I'm afraid: historian versus museum. While the official language here is Indonesian, dialects abound. I gave up trying to correct people. Ten years ago I wrote a book on Christianity in Indonesia. Evidently, it turned me into a museum.' Marcott got up, walked to a nearby shelf, retrieved a book, and handed it to Remi.

'*God in Java*,' she read.

'It could be worse. Almost was. My publisher wanted to call it *Jesus in Java*.'

Sam chuckled. 'You chose wisely.'

'I would have been inundated with people wanting to know the religious significance of coffee. It would have been a nightmare. At any rate, I came here to research the book, fell in love with the place, and stayed. That was fifteen years ago. You're looking for a monk, you said?'

'Yes, a man named Javier Orizaga, a Jesuit. He would have arrived here in the late 1520s, probably – '

'Ah, Orizaga. Fifteen twenty-eight,' Marcott said. 'He lived about two miles east of here, in fact. Of course, the hut is no longer there. I think it's a burger restaurant now.'

'What can you tell us about him?' asked Remi.

'What do you want to know?'

'How much time do you have?' Sam countered.

'Unlimited quantities.'

'Then tell us everything.'

'You're going to be disappointed. He was an interesting man and he worked hard to help the locals, but he was just one of thousands of missionaries that came here over the last half millennium. He opened a Bible school, helped at local hospitals, and spent a lot of time in rural villages trying to save souls.'

'Have you ever heard of the Orizaga Codex?' Sam asked.

Marcott narrowed his eyes. 'No, but, based on the name, I somehow think I should have. Am I about to be terribly embarrassed?'

'I don't see why,' Remi said. She gave Marcott the short version of the codex's history, leaving out the specifics about its content or origin.

Marcott smiled. 'Fascinating. Did this codex ingratiate him with the Church or was it the opposite?'

'The opposite.'

'Then it was sympathetic to the Aztecs. I wish I had known all this about him. I might have devoted a whole chapter to him. There was one interesting story, but it didn't really fit into the book so I left it out. He died in 1556, twenty-eight years after arriving here – or, at least, that's when he was last seen.'

'I don't understand,' Remi asked.

'The story goes that in November of that year, Orizaga announced to his followers and colleagues that he believed he'd discovered a sacred place in the jungle – he didn't say where exactly – and that he was going to find the . . . What was it?' Marcott paused, tapping his index finger on his lower lip. 'Oh, yes. He called it the seven caves or world of the seven caves. Something along those lines. He walked into the jungle and never came back. From what I understand, Orizaga was considered a bit of a nut.'

'There's a lot of that going around,' Sam said. 'So he walked into the jungle and just vanished?'

Marcott nodded. 'Never seen again. I realize it sounds very dramatic, but even today disappearances aren't uncommon. Five hundred years ago it was probably a daily event. The jungles here are unforgiving, even for someone as well traveled as Orizaga.' Marcott paused and smiled ruefully. 'Talking about the man, I find myself really wishing I'd devoted at least a few pages in the book to his story. Oh, well.'

'I don't suppose you still have your primary source material on him, do you?' asked Remi.

'No, I'm afraid not. But I can do better than that. I can take you to my source – providing he's still alive, that is.'

They followed Marcott in his twenty-year-old BMW to another residential area in Palembang's Plaju district. Here the roads were dirt, the houses no larger than six hundred square feet, with corrugated tin roofs, unpainted plank-wood exteriors, and mosquito netting windows. Beside almost every structure was a tiny vegetable garden and pens containing either chickens or goats.

Marcott pulled to a stop before one of the houses. Sam and Remi did the same and got out. Marcott said, 'He doesn't speak English and he's in his nineties, so be prepared.'

'Who are we meeting?'

'Apologies. Dumadi Orizaga. Before he died, Javier had ten children with a local woman. Dumadi is a direct descendent of Orizaga.'

'I thought he was a Jesuit,' said Remi.

'He was, but at some point he renounced his vows – including celibacy, obviously.'

'Maybe because of his ordeal with the Church,' Sam offered.

They followed Marcott up the path to a screen door made of two-by-fours and threadbare mosquito netting. After Marcott's fourth fist rap on the jamb, an old man in a white tank top shuffled into view. He was barely over five feet tall, and his face bore mostly Indonesian features with touches of Spanish thrown in.

Marcott said something to Dumadi in Indonesian or one of its dialects. The old man smiled and nodded and pushed open the door. The three of them stepped inside. The interior of the home was divided into thirds: a twenty-by-twenty-foot sitting area with four plastic lawn chairs and a cardboard-box coffee table, and two side rooms, one a bedroom/bathroom, the other a kitchen. Dumadi gestured for everyone to sit.

Translating as he went, Marcott introduced Sam and Remi, then explained that they'd come to Palembang to learn more about Orizaga. Dumadi said something.

'He wants to know why you're interested in him,' Marcott replied. 'They're very guarded about their family here, even after five hundred years. Ancestral veneration is a deeply ingrained tradition for Indonesians.'

Sam and Remi looked at each other. Never imagining they would find descendants of Orizaga, they hadn't discussed how to explain their mission.

'Let's tell him the truth,' Sam said. 'If the codex belongs to anyone, it's him.'

Remi nodded, reached into her carryall, and withdrew

a manila envelope. She flipped through the photos and papers inside, then withdrew the scan of the codex. She handed it across to Dumadi.

Sam said to Marcott, 'Tell him we think this belonged to Orizaga and that we believe it has something do with why he came here in the first place.'

Marcott translated. Staring at the scan in his hands, Dumadi nodded, but Sam and Remi could tell the old man had barely heard Marcott. The silence dragged out. Finally Marcott said something else to Dumadi, who laid the scan on the cardboard box, climbed to his feet, and shuffled off into the bedroom. He emerged a moment later carrying a frame. He stopped before Remi and handed it to her.

Drawn in stylized calligraphy, with filigreed edges and intricate swirls and flourishes, the original was far removed from the photo, but for Sam and Remi there was no mistaking what they were seeing: the picto-map from Orizaga's codex.

Dumadi pointed at the framed photo, then at the scan, and said something to Marcott, who translated: 'He doesn't recognize the bottom portion, but the top portion's been passed down through his family for centuries.'

'Why?' asked Sam.

Marcott asked, listened to Dumadi's response, then said, 'It's the Orizaga family coat of arms.'

'Does he know what it means?'

'No.'

'No one ever talked about what it might mean?'

'No,' Marcott replied. 'He says it's always been part of the family. He assumes it was important to Orizaga, and that's good enough for him.'

Sam flipped through Remi's manila envelope and withdrew Wendy's version of the Quetzalcoatl bird from the Chicomoztoc illustration. He handed it to Dumadi. 'Does that mean anything to him?'

Marcott asked, listened. He smiled and replied, 'Which part, the ugly snake or the bird?'

'The bird.'

Dumadi sat back down with a groan, then replied.

'It has no particular meaning to him,' Marcott said. 'It's just a bird. He's seen them in zoos.'

'Here?' Remi asked.

'He doesn't remember where, exactly. He saw one when he was a child. His father called it a helmet bird because of the bulge on the back of its head.'

Sam opened his mouth to speak, hesitated, then said, 'What is it? What's it called?'

'A *maleo*. Dumadi says he recalls they're much prettier than your drawing. Medium sized, black back, white breast, yellow skin around the eyes, and an orangish beak. Sort of like a colorful chicken.'

Dumadi said something to Marcott, who translated: 'He wants to know if this drawing has anything to do with Orizaga.'

'It does,' said Sam.

'It reminds him of a story about Orizaga. Would you like to hear it?'

'Yes, please,' Remi replied.

'Like most of their family stories, the details may have changed over time, but the gist of it is this: Near the end of his life, Orizaga was known by most of the people in

Palembang, and they were fond of him. They were also sure he was possessed by a mischievous spirit.'

'Why?' asked Sam.

Marcott listened. 'It's similar to what I told you back at my home. He wandered the jungles a lot, talking about caves and gods, and that he'd come here to find the home of the gods . . .You get the idea. No one was afraid of Orizaga; they suspected this mischievous spirit was having fun with a poor old man.

'The day Orizaga disappeared, he announced to everyone that he was again setting out to find his "god caves" and that he would know the place when he found a "hatchery of great birds."'

Chapter 40

Jakarta, Indonesia

'How sure are you about this, Selma?' said Sam.

He and Remi were sitting on their bed in their suite at the Four Seasons. The day before, shortly after leaving Dumadi's house and parting company with Robert Marcott, they'd boarded a Batavia Air charter at Palembang's Sultan Mahmud Badaruddin II Airport for the two-hundred-fifty-mile hop across the Java Sea to Jakarta. The Four Seasons seemed a decent place for a base of operations.

Selma said over the speakerphone, 'I confronted him. He admitted it.'

'That crafty SOB. I wonder if he's even got grandkids in London going to college.'

'Or if he's truly dying,' Remi added.

'Both are true. I checked. He's still a con man, in my book.'

Of the many unanswered questions and curiosities surrounding Sam and Remi's adventure, one had been plaguing Selma in particular: How had Rivera and his boss, President Garza, known the Fargos would be in Madagascar? What had prompted the note-and-notify bribe? Selma believed there were only two possibilities: Cynthia Ashworth, keeper of Constance Ashworth's letters, or Morton, proprietor of the Blaylock Museum and Curiosity Shop. These had been Sam and Remi's greatest sources for research material. Somewhere along the line, had Rivera and Garza tapped these sources as well?

Cloaked in her best 'bad cop' impression, Selma started with Morton, claiming she knew he'd sold Blaylock material to others and that if Morton didn't come clean she was going to take him to court. Morton broke down within two minutes, Selma said.

'He didn't know Rivera's name or how he'd come to know about the museum, but about five years ago he and a few of his goons showed up, asking questions about Blaylock and the *Shenandoah*. Morton says he didn't particularly trust Rivera, and he suspected they'd get rough with him if he didn't cooperate, so that night he moved all the important material out of the museum's storeroom and hid it in his home. Sure enough, the next morning he arrived at the museum to find it had been ransacked.

'Rivera showed up a few hours later, pleasant as can be. During the night Morton had scrounged up some of Blaylock's papers – pages from his journal, the original manuscript of the biography, random drawings and maps – '

'The Moreau Madagascar map,' Remi predicted.

'Yes. He'd seen the tiny writing on it and tore away that section and gave the bigger piece to Rivera. Morton says that seemed to satisfy Rivera. They completed the transaction, and Rivera left. Morton, being the clever fellow he is, figured Rivera wasn't quite done, so he moved the Blaylock material again, out of his home to another location.'

'And that night his house was burglarized,' Sam said.

'Right. Morton made it a point to stay out all night with friends. The ruse worked, he said. Rivera never returned.'

'And then we show up five years later, asking the same questions.'

'Why didn't he pull the same trick on us?'

'He said he liked you. And he wanted to retire and take care of his grandkids. When you offered sixty thousand instead of twenty, he decided to throw it all in and hold nothing back.'

'Then we don't know what Rivera knows, do we?' asked Remi.

'No,' Sam replied. 'By dumb luck, Morton sold him enough to send him down some paths and make some progress, but not enough to finish it. Now with us in the picture, Rivera and Garza can tag along to the end. We have to expect they're going to show up – if they haven't already.'

'Which brings me to my next point,' said Selma. 'We finished decoding the rest of Blaylock's letters to Constance. Care to guess the date of his last letter?'

'No,' replied Sam.

'Even the year?'

'Selma.'

'Eighteen eighty-three.'

Remi replied, 'That means he was out here chasing his treasure for eleven years. My God.'

'What about the letters in between?' Sam asked.

'There were only a few a year after Blaylock captured the *Shenandoah II*. As was his habit, the plain text part of the letters was mostly travelogue . . . the rakish man of adventure. In the letters, he duplicates almost all the tall tales from Morton's biography. They were window dressing. One of his coded messages to Constance suggests he was convinced Dudley and the others had discovered his lie about the *Shenandoah II* and were after him.'

'Were they?'

'Not as far as I can tell. And if they did know, they probably wouldn't have cared. The *Shenandoah II* was gone. She was no longer a threat. Blaylock had done his job.'

'Back to his last letter,' Sam prompted.

'Right. It's dated August 3, 1883, and was posted from Bagamoyo. I'll quote the relevant part directly:

> *'Have at last discovered the clue for which I've been praying. With God's help I will discover the foun-tainhead of my great green jeweled bird and collect my long-delayed reward. Sailing tomorrow for Sunda Strait. Expect 23–25 day voyage. Will write again as possible.*
>
> *'Yours,*
>
> *'W.'*

'You said the Sunda Strait, correct?' Sam asked.

'Yes.'

Sam paused. He closed his eyes for a moment, a half smile on his face. Remi asked, 'What is it?'

'Blaylock left Bagamoyo on August 3, 1883. Based on his estimated transit time, he would have arrived in the Sunda within a day or two of August twenty-seventh.'

'Okay . . .'

'The Sunda Strait was where the Krakatoa volcano was. August twenty-seventh was the day it exploded.'

Chapter 41

As history buffs, Sam and Remi were well familiar with the 1883 eruption of Krakatoa. The archipelago, which covers roughly eight square miles of ocean, sits almost dead center in the Sunda Strait between Java and Sumatra and consisted of three islands prior to the cataclysm: Lang, Verlaten, and Rakata – the largest island in the group and home to the three volcanic cones collectively known as Krakatoa. Having undergone three major eruptions in the centuries prior to 1883, Krakatoa was no stranger to turmoil.

On May twentieth, three months prior to the final explosion, a great slash appeared in the side of Perbuatan, the northernmost cone, and steam began venting, along with plumes of ash that rose twenty-two thousand feet into the atmosphere. The residents of the nearby towns and villages, having witnessed such activity before, paid little attention, and by the end of the month their disinterest seemed validated. Krakatoa settled and remained mostly quiet for the next month.

On June sixteenth the eruptions began again, blanketing great swaths of sea and land with jet-black smoke for nearly a week. When the haze cleared, massive ash columns could be seen streaming from two of Krakatoa's cones. Tides in the straits began running high, and ships at anchor had to strengthen their moorings lest they be beached.

Three weeks passed. Krakatoa's two cones were joined by the third, and soon ash began accumulating on nearby islands, in some places up to two feet thick, killing flora and fauna and turning once-lush forests into moonscapes.

The eruptions continued through the end of June and into mid-August. On the twenty-fifth of August, at one o'clock in the afternoon, Krakatoa went into its paroxysmal phase. Within an hour, a black cloud of ash had risen eighteen miles into the sky, and the eruptions were nearly continuous. Fifteen and twenty miles away, ships were bombarded by hot pumice stones the size of softballs. By early evening, as darkness fell over the strait, minor tsunamis were rolling ashore on Java and Sumatra.

The next morning, just before sunrise, Krakatoa went into its final death throes. A series of three eruptions, each one more powerful than the next, shook the area. So loud were the explosions that they were heard in Perth, Australia, two thousand miles to the southeast, and in the Mauritius Islands, three thousand miles to the west.

The resulting tsunamis, one for each eruption, radiated outward from Krakatoa at speeds up to one hundred twenty-five miles per hour, bulldozing their way onto the shores of Java and Sumatra and inundating islands as far away as fifty miles.

At 10:02, Krakatoa issued its final salvo with an explosion equal to twenty thousand atomic bombs. The island of Krakatoa tore itself apart. The erupting cones, having ejected all their magma, collapsed in on themselves, taking with them fourteen square miles of the island and gouging out a caldera four miles wide and eight hundred feet deep. The resulting tsunami wiped out whole villages, killing thousands within minutes. Trees were uprooted, and the land stripped of every scrap of vegetation.

Following on the heels of the massive wave came the pyroclastic flows, gargantuan avalanches of fire and ash that roared down Krakatoa's flanks and into the Sunda Strait. Traveling at eighty miles per hour and reaching temperatures in excess of twelve hundred degrees Fahrenheit, the surge boiled the ocean's surface below it, creating a cushion of steam that carried it thirty miles or more, charring or entombing everything in its path, manmade and natural alike.

Within hours of final explosion, what remained of Krakatoa fell silent. In the space of thirty hours, between 36,000 and 120,000 people lost their lives.

Chapter 42

Sunda Strait,
Java Sea, Indonesia

The loudspeaker in the corner of the patio cafe came to life: 'Attention, all ticketed passengers: The *Krakatau Explorer* will be departing the docks in five minutes. Please board via the aft gangway.' The message repeated in Indonesian, French, German, then once more in English.

Sam and Remi, sitting at a corner table beside a trellis covered in blooming bougainvillea, finished their coffee and stood up. Sam dropped a pair of five-thousand-rupiah notes on the table, and they stepped out from under the awning and onto the dock.

'Any sign of them?' Remi asked.

'No. You?'

'No.'

Earlier that morning, as the *Krakatau Explorer* tour van pulled out of the Four Seasons turnaround, Sam thought he'd caught a glimpse of Itzli Rivera, but they'd seen nothing more during the ninety-minute ride from Jakarta to the Carita Beach Resort docks. While riding in a van packed with other tourists wasn't Sam and Remi's preferred style of adventuring, they were keenly aware that if Rivera and his men were, in fact, here, being caught alone on a lonely road in the Javan rain forests could be disastrous.

Moreover, this boat tour of what remained of the Krakatoa volcano and the newly opened Krakatau Museum was not only a first step in following Blaylock's ill-fated trail – if there was one left to follow – but also an efficient way of drawing Rivera out and forcing his hand. The last thing the Mexican needed was to lose his quarry yet again. For Sam and Remi, it was akin to swimming with sharks: Better to have them in sight than wondering when they were going to swim out of the gloom and attack.

They joined the line of last-minute boarders at the aft gangplank, then boarded and chose a spot at the starboard rail. The *Krakatau Explorer* was a hundred-twenty-foot flat-bottomed skiff ferry with an oblong, pitch-roofed wheelhouse nestled high on the forecastle. The afterdeck, measuring eighty feet by forty feet, was divided into rows by blue-vinyl-covered bench seating.

Sam kept one eye on the docks while Remi scanned the other passengers; she estimated there were sixty aboard. 'Still nothing,' she said.

'Here too.'

On the dock, a pair of workers detached the gangplank and pulled it away from the ferry. A crewman on deck shut the gate. The mooring lines were singled up and hauled aboard. Three more crewmen appeared at the rail and pushed off the dock with poles. With a blare from the *Explorer*'s whistle, the engines started, and the ferry chugged away from the docks and headed west into the strait.

Three hours later an Indonesian-accented voice came over the intercom: 'Ladies and gentlemen, shortly the captain will be bringing the *Krakatau Explorer* around the island's headland for our approach to the museum.'

As promised, within minutes the ferry turned to port and headed east along the island's north shoreline. Passengers crowded the rail to stare up at the sheer, two-thousand-foot-high cliff – all that remained when the majority of the island collapsed into the sea.

The ferry pulled alongside the museum's dock, and the mooring lines were secured and the gangplank lowered. Sam and Remi disembarked and headed toward the main building. Anchored to the seabed at the western edge of the caldera, the five-thousand-square-foot museum was constructed of inch-thick tempered glass and white-painted steel crossbeams. According to the brochure Sam and Remi had picked up at the Four Seasons, the museum contained the single largest collection of Krakatoa memorabilia and source material in the world.

The inside was fully air-conditioned, the decor minimalist, with bamboo floors, taupe walls, and vaulted ceilings. The space was divided into sections by three-quarter walls that displayed period photographs, artwork, and illustrations, while freestanding platforms held artifacts that survived the disaster. Each section also contained a multimedia kiosk, complete with an LCD monitor and touch-screen controls.

Sam and Remi strolled around on their own until they were approached by one of the guides, a young Indonesian woman in an aquamarine dress. 'Welcome to the Krakatau Museum. May I answer any questions for you?'

*

'We're particularly interested in what ships might have been anchored in the strait at the time of the explosion,' Remi said.

'Certainly. We have an alcove dedicated to just that. This way, please.'

They followed the woman through several alcoves before arriving at one labeled THE MARITIME EFFECTS. Two of the walls were devoted to enlarged daguerreotype photos of the straits and surrounding bays and harbors. The third wall held copies of pages from ships' logs, newspaper accounts, letters, and illustrations. On the platforms in the center of the room was a collection of salvaged hardware, presumably from vessels caught in the explosion.

'How many ships were in the area at the time?' asked Remi.

'Officially, fourteen, but on any given day in 1883 there were hundreds of small fishing vessels and cargo boats sailing back and forth. Of course, it was easier to account for the ships because of insurance claims. Also, we were able to cross-reference captains' logs to account for all the vessels present.'

Standing before a plaque on the far wall, Sam asked, 'Is this a list of the ships and their crews?'

'Yes.'

'I recognize one of these names: the *Berouw*.'

The guide nodded. 'I'm not surprised. The *Berouw* is somewhat famous. She was a side-wheel steamer that was anchored in Lampung Bay fifty miles from Krakatoa. She was picked up by one of the tsunamis and carried several miles up the Koeripan River. The ship was found almost completely intact, but her entire crew was killed.'

'There are only thirteen names,' Remi said.

'Pardon me?'

'On this list. You mentioned fourteen ships, but there are only thirteen listed here.'

'Are you sure?' The guide stepped up to the plaque and counted the names. 'You're right. That's odd. Well, I'm sure it's an administrative error.'

Remi smiled. 'Thanks for your help. I think we'll wander around a bit.'

'Certainly. If you're so inclined, feel free to experiment with the kiosk. All of the documents in our collection – even those not on display – are available for viewing.'

Remi walked over to the wall of photographs where Sam was standing. She said, 'I was half hoping the *Shenandoah*'s name would be on the list.'

'Would a picture do?' Sam said.

'What?'

He pointed at the uppermost photo on the wall, a four-by-six-foot enlargement. The plate beside it read:

LOOKING NORTHEAST FROM THE DECK OF
BRITISH CARGO VESSEL *SALISBURY*,
ANCHORED ELEVEN MILES EAST OF KRAKATOA,
AUGUST 27TH, 1883.
SHOWN: PULAU (ISLAND)
LEGUNDI AND MOUTH OF LAMPUNG BAY

'Do you see it?' Sam asked.

'I see it.'

In the foreground of the photo against the backdrop

of Pulau Legundi was a square-rigged, three-masted clipper ship, her upper hull painted black.

'It doesn't mean anything,' Remi said. 'I'm sure there were plenty of ships of that era that looked identical to the *Shenandoah*.'

'I agree.'

'Let's find out. *Shenandoah* was two hundred thirty feet, twelve hundred tons, and rigged for battle. I guarantee you that a ship like that sails into the Sunda Straits, any captain or officer of the watch worth a damn is going to make note of it.'

They walked to the kiosk, played with the touch screen for a few moments, then began searching the museum's archives, which were organized and cross-referenced by subject, date, and key word. After an hour of trying various word combinations, Sam found an entry made by the captain of a German merchant ship named *Minden*.

He brought the translated text up on the screen:

26th August 1883, 1415 hours: Passed close astern by sail & steam clipper ship, identity unknown. Eight cannon ports observed on starboard beam. Vessel declined to return hail. Anchored on south side of Pulau Legundi.

Sam scrolled through a few more entries, then stopped again:

27th August 1883, 0630. Eruptions worsening. Nearly swamped by rogue wave. Have ordered crew to prepare for emergency departure.

'Here we go,' Sam murmured. He tapped the touch screen and another log entry filled the screen:

27th August 1883, 0800. Proceeding flank speed, course 041. Hoping to reach leeward side of Pulau Sebesi. Unidentified clipper ship still anchored south side of Pulau Legundi. Again refused hail.

Sam kept scrolling, then stopped. 'That's it. The *Minden*'s last entry. Could be her. The time frame is right; so is the description: eight cannon ports. The same number as the *Shenandoah*.'

'And if it was?' Remi replied. 'The *Minden*'s last entry was two hours before Krakatoa's final eruption. Whatever ship they saw probably made a run for it and either got clear or was overtaken by the tsunami or the pyroclastic flow.'

'There's one more possibility,' Sam replied.

'Which is?'

'She suffered the same fate as the *Berouw.* She was picked up and carried inland.'

'Wouldn't she have been found by now?'

'Maybe, maybe not.'

'Sumatra's a big island, Sam. Where do you propose we start?'

Sam pointed up at the picture again. 'The last place she was anchored.'

'Hello, Fargos,' a voice said behind them.

Sam and Remi turned around.

Standing before them was Itzli Rivera.

Sam said, 'We keep running into each other. Frankly, it's something we could do without.'

'I can arrange that.'

'As long as we help you finish what you haven't been able to on your own.'

'You read my mind.'

'The problem with that plan,' Remi said, 'is that it ends with you killing us.'

'It doesn't have to be that way.'

'Yes, it does,' replied Sam. 'You know it, and we know it. Even now we know enough about Garza's dirty little secret to topple his government. Compared to your other victims, we've got a mountain of information. You murdered a woman in Zanzibar just because she found a sword.'

'And eight others for much less, probably,' Remi added.

Rivera shrugged and spread his hands. 'What can I say?'

'How about, "Where's the tallest building I can jump off of?"'

'Here's a better question: Why don't you give me all your research, and I'll tell my boss I killed you?'

Remi said, 'After all we've been through together, you still think we're that gullible? You're a slow learner, Mr. Rivera.'

'You've been lucky so far. It won't happen again.'

Sam said, 'Let me see if I'm understanding you correctly: Option one, we give you everything we've got and you murder us; option two, we give you nothing and see how much farther our luck takes us.'

'When you put it that way, I can see your point,' Rivera replied. 'So let's change the terms: You give me what I want and I promise to kill you quickly and painlessly. Or we continue to play our cat-and-mouse game, and I will eventually catch you and torture your wife until you give me what I want.'

Sam took a step forward. He stared hard into Rivera's eyes. 'You need to learn some manners.'

Rivera pulled back his jacket a few inches to reveal the butt of a gun. 'And you need to learn some discretion.'

'So my wife tells me.'

'You're stubborn. Both of you. We're going to leave together right now. If you fight me or try to attract attention, I'll shoot your wife, then you. Let's go. I have a boat outside. We'll walk outside and – '

'No.'

'Pardon me?'

'You heard me.'

'I'm not bluffing, Mr. Fargo. I'll shoot you both.'

'I believe you'll try. Don't think I'll make it easy.'

'Nobody will stop me; I'll be gone before the authorities arrive.'

'Then what? Did you really think we'd come here carrying all our proof? You've really got a problem with underestimating people. You've searched our hotel room and found nothing, correct?'

'Yes.'

'All we've got with us is a few pictures, and they're nothing you haven't already seen. If you kill us here, everything goes public. By the time you get back to Mexico City, every news channel will be running the story.'

'You wouldn't be here if you had everything you needed. You don't have what Blaylock found or what he was after.'

'That makes two of us.'

'What you're forgetting is, I've dedicated myself to keeping this secret for almost a decade. You've been involved for a few weeks. Whatever you find, whatever story you tell, we'll spin it the other way. You know who I work for and you know how powerful he is. Even if you manage to survive, by the time we're done with you you'll be a pair of money-hungry, spotlight-seeking treasure hunters who created a fantastic lie for their own personal gain.'

'We'll still have our health,' Remi said sweetly.

'And our sense of humor,' Sam added. 'If you're so confident, why don't you go home and let the chips fall where they may?'

'I can't do that. I'm a soldier. I've got my orders.'

'Then we're at an impasse. Either shoot us or walk away.'

Rivera considered this for a few moments, then nodded. 'Have it your way. Remember, Mr. and Mrs. Fargo, I gave you a chance to make this easy. No matter what else happens, I'm going to make sure you die in Indonesia.'

Chapter 43

Lampung Bay, Sumatra

Sam eased back on the boat's throttles and brought the bow around until they were beam on to the wind. The boat slowed to a stop, then began rocking from side to side. A few hundred yards to port was Mutun, one of the dozens of tiny forested islands that lined both coasts of the bay; to starboard, in the distance, Indah Beach.

'Okay, one more time,' he said.

'We've been over this, Sam. Several times. The answer's still no. If you're staying, I'm staying.'

'So let's go home.'

'You don't want to go home.'

'True, but – '

'You're starting to make me angry, Fargo.'

And he knew it. When Remi started using his surname, it was a sign that her patience was wearing thin.

Following their encounter with Rivera at the museum, they'd caught the next ferry for the Sol Marbella landing, about fifteen miles from the Cartita Beach docks. While they waited for the ferry to get under way, Sam kept his eye on Rivera's speedboat until finally losing sight of it when it passed behind the Tanjung headland to the southwest.

Once back on the Javan mainland they hired a taxi to take them back to the Four Seasons, where they quickly packed, headed for the airport, and boarded the next Batavia Air charter across the straits to Lampung. They touched down shortly before nightfall and found a bayside hotel down the coast a few miles, where they called Selma.

The sooner they reached Pulau Legundi, the better, Sam and Remi reasoned. Though they'd half expected Rivera to turn up, his sudden appearance at the museum, combined with his menacing promise, drove home the point that they needed to move quickly. To that end, Selma worked her magic and arranged for a twenty-four-foot motorized *pinisi* – a type of narrow, flat-bottomed ketch – and all the necessary supplies to be waiting for them at the docks before sunrise. Now, nearing noon, they'd covered a third of the distance to Pulau Legundi.

Remi said, 'We've never let people like Rivera run us off before. Why should we start now?'

'You know why.'

She stepped up to him and laid a gentle hand on his shoulder. 'Drive the boat, Sam. Let's finish this together.'

Sam sighed, then smiled. 'You're a remarkable woman.'

'I know. Now, drive the boat.'

By late afternoon, what had merely been a smudge on the overcast horizon began to resolve into the island's lush green peaks and craggy coastline. Shaped like a jagged comma, the uninhabited Pulau Legundi was roughly four miles long by two miles wide. Like all the other islands in and around the Sunda Strait, it had once been blanketed by volcanic ash from Krakatoa. A hundred thirty years of wind and rain and an ever-patient Mother Nature had transformed the island into an isolated patch of thriving rain forest.

Just over twenty-four hours after leaving Jakarta, with the sun setting over the Legundi's peaks, Sam turned the *pinisi*'s bow in to a sheltered cove on the eastern shoreline. He gunned the engine and slid the bow onto a ten-foot-wide strip of white-sand beach, and Remi jumped out. Sam tossed down their packs and followed her. He secured the bowline to a nearby tree.

Remi unfolded the tourist map they'd purchased at the hotel – the best they could do in a pinch – and laid it on the sand. They crouched down. Before leaving the museum, Sam had studied a few digital maps on the kiosk and mentally marked the ship's position.

'From here it's less than a mile to the western side,' he said. 'As best I can tell, the *Shenandoah* – '

'Assuming it was her.'

'I'm praying it was her. My best guess puts her here, in this shallow bay. If we're using the *Berouw*'s fate as a model – '

'Yes, run that by me again.'

'According to accepted history, the *Berouw* was the only true ship to be pushed inland. Anything smaller was either driven to the bottom of the strait or instantly destroyed by the final tsunami. My theory is this: What made the *Berouw* different is that she was anchored at the mouth of a river.'

'A path of least resistance,' Remi said.

'Exactly. She was driven inland via a preexisting gouge in the terrain. If you draw a line from Krakatoa through the ship's anchorage and onto the island, you see a – '

Leaning closely over the map, Remi finished Sam's thought. 'A ravine.'

'A deep one, bracketed on both sides by five-hundred-foot peaks. If you look closely, the ravine ends below this third peak, a few hundred yards shy of the opposite shoreline. One mile long and a quarter mile wide.'

'What's to say she wasn't crushed into dust or shoved up and over the island and slammed into the seabed?' Remi asked. 'We're twenty-five miles from Krakatoa. The *Berouw* was fifty miles away and she ended up miles inland.'

'Two reasons: One, the peaks around our ravine are far steeper than anything around the river; and two, the *Shenandoah* was at least four times as heavy as the *Berouw* and iron-framed with double-thick oak and teak hull plates. She was designed to take punishment.'

'You make a good case.'

'Let's hope it translates into reality.'

'I do, however, have one more nagging detail . . .'

'Shoot.'

'How would the *Shenandoah* have survived the pyroclastic flow?'

'As it happens, I have a theory about that. Care to hear it?'

'Hold on to it. If you turn out to be right, you can tell me. If you're wrong, it won't matter.'

Within five minutes of breaching the tree line they realized Madagascar's forests didn't hold a candle to those of Pulau Legundi. The trees, so densely packed that Sam and

Remi frequently had to turn sideways to squeeze between them, were also entwined in skeins of creeper vines that looped from tree trunk to branch to ground. By the time they'd covered a hundred yards, Sam's shoulder throbbed from swinging the machete.

They found a closet-sized clearing in the undergrowth and crouched down for a water break. Insects swirled around them, buzzing in their ears and nostrils. Above, the canopy was filled with the squawks of unseen birds. Remi dug a can of bug repellant from her pack and coated Sam's exposed skin; he did the same for her.

'This could be a positive for us,' Sam said.

'What?'

'Do you see how most of the tree trunks are covered in a layer of mold and creepers? It's like armor. What's good for the trees could be good for ship planking.'

He took another sip from the canteen, then handed it to Remi.

'The going will get easier the higher we go,' he said.

'Define easier.'

'More sunlight means fewer creeper vines.'

'And higher means steeper,' Remi replied with a game smile. 'Life's a trade-off.'

Sam checked his watch. 'Two hours to sunset. Please tell me you remembered to pack the mosquito hammock . . .'

'I did. But I forgot the hibachi, the steaks, and the cooler of ice-cold beer.'

'This one time I'll forgive you.'

They pressed on for another ninety minutes, moving slowly but steadily up the western slope of the peak, pulling themselves along using exposed roots and drooping vines, until finally Sam called a halt. They strung their double-wide hammock between two trees, double-checked all the mosquito nets' seams, then crawled inside and shared a meal of warm water, beef jerky, and dried fruit. Twenty minutes later they fell into a deep sleep.

The jungle's natural symphony woke them just after sunrise. After a quick breakfast they were on the move again. As Sam had predicted, the higher they climbed, the more the foliage thinned, until they were able to move without the aid of the machete. At 10:15 they broke through the trees and found themselves standing on a ten-foot-wide granite plateau.

'That's what I call a view,' Remi said, shrugging off her pack.

Spread before them were the blue waters of the Sunda Strait. Twenty-five miles away they could see the sheer cliffs of Krakatoa Island and, beyond that, Java's west coast. They stepped to the edge of the plateau. Five hundred feet below them, at the bottom of a sixty-degree slope, lay the floor of the ravine. On either side of it were the peaks that formed its northern and southern walls. The ravine itself was more or less straight, with a slight curve as it neared the far shoreline a mile away.

Sam pointed at the patch of water visible beyond the ravine's mouth. 'That's almost exactly where she was anchored.'

'Let me ask you a question: Why didn't we start over there and just stroll up the ravine?'

'A couple reasons: One, that's the windward side of the

strait. I might be a tad paranoid, but I'd wanted us to have some cover from prying eyes.'

'And the second reason?'

'Better vantage point.'

Remi smiled. 'You were half hoping we'd find a mast jutting out from the canopy down there, weren't you?'

Sam smiled back. 'More than half hoping. I don't see anything, though. You?'

'No. Now might be the right time to tell me your theory: How would the *Shenandoah* have survived the pyroclastic flow?'

'Well, you probably know the scientific term for it, but I'm thinking of the Pompeii Effect.'

Pompeii, Italy, famous for having fallen victim to another volcano, Mount Vesuvius in 79 A.D., was also renowned for its 'mummies,' still-life casts of Pompeii's inhabitants in the final moments of life. Like Krakatoa, Vesuvius had unleashed an avalanche of blistering ash and pumice that rolled over the village, both charring and entombing virtually everything before it. Humans and animals unlucky enough to be caught in the open were instantly broiled alive and buried. As the bodies decomposed, the resulting fluids and gasses hardened the interior of the shell.

'I think that's the term for it, actually. The principle is a little different here, though.'

'That's what I'm counting on. Assuming the *Shenandoah* was driven here, she would have been waterlogged from the tsunami and blanketed in thousands of tons of soaked vegetation and trees. When the pyroclastic flow came, all the moisture would have flashed into steam and, hopefully, the blanket of foliage would have been charred instead of the ship.'

Remi was nodding. 'Then all of it was buried in several feet of ash and pumice.'

'That's my theory.'

'Why hasn't it been found already?'

Sam shrugged. 'Nobody's been looking for it. How many artifacts are eventually found just feet from where everyone's been excavating for years?'

'Too many to count.'

'Plus, the *Shenandoah* was only two hundred thirty feet long and thirty-two feet wide. That ravine is' – Sam did the calculation in his head – 'twenty-five times longer and forty times wider.'

'You're no dummy, Sam Fargo.' Remi looked down the slope before them. 'What do you think?' she asked. 'Straight down?'

Sam nodded. 'I think we can manage it.'

The going was slow but not particularly treacherous. Using the trunks of diagonally growing trees as makeshift steps, they picked their way down the slope and back into deeper jungle. The sun dimmed through the canopy, leaving them in twilight.

Sam called a halt for a water break. After a few gulps he wandered off along the hillside with a 'Be right back' over his shoulder. He returned a minute later with a pair of heavy straight sticks and handed the shorter of the two to Remi.

'A poker?' she asked.

'Yes. If she's here, the only way we're going to find her

is legwork. Likewise, if she's covered in a layer of petrified vegetation and ash, there are going to be gaps and voids. If we probe enough ground, we're sure to find something.'

'Assuming – '

'Don't say it.'

For the next six hours, as the afternoon wore toward evening, they marched side by side across the ravine floor and up and down hillocks, poking with their sticks and doing their best to keep to a north/south-oriented, switchback pattern.

'Six o'clock,' Sam said, glancing at his watch. 'We'll finish this line, then call it a night.'

Remi laughed wearily. 'And retreat to the lovely confines of our hammock – ' She stumbled forward and landed with an 'Umph!'

Sam strode over and knelt beside her. 'Are you okay?'

She rolled over, pursed her lips, and puffed a strand of hair from her cheek. 'I'm fine. Getting clumsy with exhaustion.' Sam stood up and helped her to her feet. Remi looked around. 'Where's my stick?'

'At your feet.'

'What? Where?'

Sam pointed down. Jutting two inches from the loam was the tip of Remi's stick. Sam said, 'Either that's a fantastic magic trick or you've found a void.'

Chapter 44

Pulau Legundi, Sunda Strait

Stepping carefully, they backed up a few feet and scanned the ground nearby. 'Anything?' Sam asked.

'No.'

'Hop onto that tree.'

'If we haven't fallen through yet, we probably won't.'

'Just humor me.'

Remi backed up until her butt bumped into the trunk, then turned and climbed onto the lowermost branch. Sam shrugged off his pack and laid it on the ground. Next, holding his stick parallel to the ground at waist height like a tightrope walker, he crept forward until he was standing over the tip of Remi's stick. He knelt down, placed his stick in front of his knees, then pulled Remi's free. He dug his headlamp from the thigh pocket of his cargo pants and shone the beam into the hole.

'It's deep,' he said. 'Can't see the bottom.'

'What do you want to do?'

'What I want to do is widen it and crawl down there, but it's almost dark. Let's set up camp and wait for daylight.'

They slept fitfully, passing the hours dozing and talking, their minds imagining what might lay only feet away from their hammock. Having both metaphorically and literally traced the same course Winston Blaylock followed during his quest, Sam and Remi felt as though they'd been hunting for the *Shenandoah* for years.

They waited until enough morning sun was filtering through the canopy to partially light their work, then ate a quick breakfast and climbed back up the hillock to the hole left by Remi's stick, this time equipped with a thirty-foot coil of nylon boating rope that had come with the *pinisi*.

Remi looped one end of the line twice around the nearest tree; the opposite end of the line Sam formed into a makeshift horse collar that he slipped over his shoulders and tucked under his armpits.

'Luck,' said Remi.

Sam paced over to the hole and knelt down. Carefully, he began jabbing with the stick, knocking chunks of loam and congealed ash into the unseen voids below, backing away on his knees as the hole widened. After five minutes' work, it was the size of a manhole.

Sam stood up and called over his shoulder, 'Have you got me?'

Remi grabbed the line tighter, took in the slack, and braced her feet against the trunk. 'I've got you.'

Sam coiled his knees and jumped a few inches off the ground. He did it again, a little higher. He paused and looked around.

'See any cracks?'

'All clear.'

Sam stomped on the ground once, then again, then six times in quick succession. 'I think we're okay.'

Remi tied off her end of the line and joined Sam at the

hole. He unraveled the horse collar and knotted it around the strap on his headlamp, then clicked the lamp on and started lowering it into the hole, counting forearm lengths as he went. The line went slack. At the bottom of the hole, the headlamp lay on its side. They leaned forward and peered into the gloom.

After a moment Remi said, 'Is that a . . . No, can't be.'

'A skeleton foot? Yes, it can be.' He looked up at her. 'Tell you what: Why don't I go first?'

'Great idea.'

After retrieving the headlamp, they spent a few minutes tying climbing knots in the rope, then dropped it back into the hole. Sam slid his feet into the opening, wiggled forward, and began lowering himself hand over hand.

Like a geologist examining an exposed cliff face, Sam felt as though he were descending through history. The first layer of material was regular soil, but passing two more feet the color changed, first to light brown, then a muddy gray.

'I'm into the ash layer,' he called.

Clumps and veins of what appeared to be petrified wood and vegetation began appearing in the ash.

His feet touched the bottom of the shaft he'd excavated from above. He kicked toeholds into the sides of the shaft and slowly transferred his weight to his legs until he was certain he was steady. Jutting from the side of the shaft was what they'd thought was a skeletal foot.

'It's a tree root,' he called.

'Thank God.'

'Next one will probably be the real thing.'

'I know.'

'Stick, please.'

Remi lowered it down to him. Using both hands, he worked the stick first like a posthole digger, then like a pot stirrer, knocking and scraping at the shaft until he was satisfied with the width. Plumes of ash swirled around him. He waited for the cloud to settle, then squatted on his haunches and repeated the process until he'd opened four more feet of shaft.

'How deep so far?' Remi called.

'Eight feet, give or take.' Sam lifted the stick up and slid it into his belt. 'We're going to have to evacuate this debris.'

'Hold on.'

A moment later, Remi called, 'Bag coming down.'

One of their nylon stuff sacks landed on his head; knotted to the drawstring was some paracord. Sam squatted down, filled the bag with the debris, and Remi hauled it up. Two more times cleared the shaft.

Sam began lowering himself again. Under the weight of the layers above, the mixture here had become more and more compressed until finally, at the ten-foot mark, the color morphed again, from gray to brown to black.

Sam stopped suddenly. He felt his heart lurch. He turned his head sideways, trying to aim the headlamp's beam at what had caught his eye. He found it again, then braced his feet against the shaft's sides to steady himself.

'I've got timber!' he called.

There were several seconds of silence, then Remi's faint voice: 'I'm dumbfounded, Sam. Describe it.'

'It's a horizontal piece about three inches thick. I can see eight to ten inches of it.'

'Three inches thick is too thin to be the spar deck.

Could it be the deckhouse roof? The only other raised structures were the stack, the engine-room skylight, the wardroom skylight, and the wheelhouse. Do you see any traces of glass?'

'No. I'm moving on.'

Again he reached the bottom of his excavation. They evacuated more debris, then he kicked out his toeholds and went to work with the stick. On his first strike, he heard the solid thunk of wood on wood. He did it again with the same result. He dug out the remainder of the shaft, then craned his neck downward, illuminating the bottom with his headlamp.

'I've got decking,' he shouted.

He lowered himself until his feet touched the deck. The wood creaked and bowed under his weight. After shoving debris to one side with his boot, he slammed his heel down and got a satisfying crack in reply. A dozen more stomps opened a ragged two-foot hole. The rest of the detritus plunged through the opening.

'I'm going through.'

Hand over hand, he lowered himself through the deck. The light from the surface receded and faded, leaving him suspended in the glow of his headlamp. His feet touched a hard surface. He tested his weight on it. It was solid. Cautiously, he released the rope.

'I'm down,' he called. 'Looks okay.'

'I'm on my way,' Remi replied.

Two minutes later she was beside him. She clicked on her headlamp and illuminated the hole above their heads. 'That has to be the deckhouse roof.'

'Which would make this the berth deck,' said Sam.

And a tomb, they quickly realized, panning their beams around the space. Running down each side of the space at sporadic intervals were twenty or so hammocks hanging from the overhead. All of the hammocks were occupied. The remains were mostly skeletal, save patches of desiccated flesh on whatever body parts weren't covered in clothing.

'It's like they simply lay down and waited to die,' said Remi.

'That's probably accurate,' Sam replied. 'Once the ship was buried, they had three choices: suffocation, starvation, or suicide. Let's move on. You choose.'

The only blueprints they'd seen for the ship had come from the original shipbuilder; they had no idea what, if any, changes either the Sultan of Zanzibar or Blaylock might have made to the interior layout. This berth deck seemed close to the original, but what about the rest of the ship?

Remi chose forward and started walking. The deck was almost pristine. Had they not come in the way they had, it would've been impossible to tell they were under fourteen feet of earth.

'Has to be the lack of oxygen,' Remi said. 'It's been hermetically sealed for a hundred thirty years.'

Their beams swept over a wooden column blocking their path.

'The foremast?' Remi asked.

'Yes.'

On the other side of this they found a bulkhead and two steps leading up into what had once been the petty officers' quarters; it had since been turned into a storage compartment for timber and sailcloth.

'Let's head aft,' Sam said. 'Providing Blaylock wasn't on deck when they got hit, I'm guessing he'd be in either the wardroom or his quarters.'

'I agree.'

'As much as I'd love to explore, I think this is one of those "discretion equals valor" moments.'

Remi nodded. 'This will take a full archaeological team and years of work.'

They walked aft, their footfalls clicking dully on the deck and their murmured voices echoing off the bulkheads. They stepped through the berth-deck hatch and found themselves facing another mast, this one the main; on the other side of this were a bulkhead and a ladder leading up to the main deck.

'Dead end,' Remi said. 'Unless we want to push through to the main deck and tunnel our way aft to the wardroom.'

'Let's call that Plan B. According to the blueprints, on the other side of this bulkhead are the coal bunkers, the upper level of the engine room, then the aft hold. The Sultan was known to deal in illicit cargo from time to time. Let's see if he made any covert adjustments to the layout.'

The bulkhead was six feet high and ran the width of the thirty-foot deck. Using their headlamps, Sam and Remi scanned the bulkhead from one side to the other. Directly below the spot where the ladder pierced the deck above, Remi spotted a quarter-sized indentation in one of the planks. She pressed her thumb into it and was rewarded with a *snick*. A hinged hatch swung downward. Sam caught it, then lowered it the rest of the way. On tiptoes, he peered into the opening.

'A crawl space,' he said.

'It's heading in the right direction.'

Sam boosted Remi through the hatch, then chinned himself up and followed. They headed aft, knees and hands bumping along the wood.

'We're over the coal bunkers, I think,' Sam said.

Ten more feet, and Remi said, 'Bulkhead coming up.'

They stopped. The sound of Remi's fingers tapping and probing the bulkhead filled the crawl space.

Snick.

'Eureka,' she said. 'Another hatch.'

She crawled through this opening and disappeared. Sam heard the clang of her feet hitting grated steel. He crawled to the hatch. Directly ahead was a stanchion; he grabbed it and used it to ease himself out.

They were standing on a railed catwalk. They walked to the edge and shined their headlamps down, illuminating shadowed shapes of machinery, girders, and piping.

They walked along the catwalk to the aft bulkhead, where they found a short ladder leading upward to yet another hatch; once through this hatch, they found themselves hunched over in the four-foot-tall aft hold.

Sam panned his light around, trying to orient himself. 'We're directly below the wardroom. There's got to be another – '

'I found it,' Remi called from a few feet away.

Sam turned to see her standing before a dangling ceiling hatch. She smiled. 'Crafty devil, the Sultan,' she said. 'Do you think this was for his harem?'

'I wouldn't put it past him.'

Sam waddled over and formed stirrups with his hands. 'Up you go.'

Once on the deck above, they found themselves standing in a thirty-foot-long corridor. At their backs was the *Shenandoah*'s third mast, the mizzen. Along the starboard side of the corridor were five doors. These would be officers' quarters.

Sam checked the first door. 'The head,' he whispered.

In turn, they checked the remaining doors. The second and third rooms were empty, but not so with the fourth and fifth. Lying faceup in each of the tiered bunk beds was a skeleton.

'Buried alive,' Remi murmured. 'My God, I wonder how long it took?'

'However long it took, it must have been a nightmare.'

At the end of the corridor, they turned right through another doorway and into the port-side corridor heading forward. One side was lined with more quarters. On the other, a single door led into the wardroom.

'Do you want to look?' asked Sam.

'Not particularly. It'll be more of the same.'

'One more room to check, then.'

They turned around. A few feet aft was a thick oaken door with heavy wrought iron hinges and a matching latch handle.

'Captain's quarters,' Sam said.

'My heart's pounding.'

'Mine too.'

'You or me?' Remi asked.

'Ladies first.'

Sam aimed his headlamp over Remi's shoulder, helping to illuminate her path. She stepped up to the door, placed her hand on the latch, and, after a moment's hesitation, depressed the thumb lever and pushed. Half expecting the clichéd creak of hinges, they were surprised when the door swung noiselessly inward.

From their research they knew the captain's quarters aboard the *Shenandoah* measured eighty square feet: ten feet long by eight feet wide. Compared to the officers' berths, and especially the enlisteds' bunk rooms, it was luxurious.

Sam and Remi saw him at the same time.

Directly ahead of them, facing the four mullioned stern windows, was a rocking chair. Jutting above the chair's headrest was a skull, bare save a few strands of whitish yellow hair and some bits of scabrous flesh.

Remi stepped across the threshold. Sam did the same. Headlamp beams focused on the figure in the chair, they paced forward, then circled around either side of the chair.

Winston Blaylock was dressed as they had imagined him for the past three weeks: calf-high boots, khaki pants, and a hunting jacket. Even as a skeleton, his stature was impressive: wide shoulders, long legs, barrel chest.

His hands were lying palms up in his lap. Cradled there, staring up at Sam and Remi, was a football-sized maleo statuette, its facets sparkling green in their flashlight beams.

*

409

Without a word between them, Sam gently reached down and lifted the maleo from Blaylock's lap. They stared at the man for another full minute, then searched the cabin. They found neither a logbook nor documents, save three sheets of parchment. Blaylock's neat scrawl covered both sides of each sheet. Remi scanned their contents.

'Three letters to Constance,' she said.

'Dates?' Sam asked.

'August fourteen, August twentieth, and . . .' Remi hesitated. 'The last one's dated September sixteenth.'

'Three weeks after the *Shenandoah* was buried here.'

They retraced their steps forward through the starboard corridor, down through the hatch, back through the engine room, and through the crawl space to the berth deck.

Remi climbed up through their excavated shaft, waited for Sam to secure the maleo to the end of the rope, then hauled it up to the surface. She dropped the line back down, and Sam went up.

Together, they collected an armload of twigs and small branches, then built a latticework over the shaft and covered it with loam.

'It doesn't seem right just leaving them down there,' Remi said.

'We'll come back,' Sam replied. 'We'll make sure that he's taken care of – that they're all taken care of.'

Each lost in his or her private thoughts, the climb back up to the plateau passed quickly. Three hours after leaving the *Shenandoah* they were picking their way down the trail

Sam had hacked. Remi was in the lead. Through the trees Sam glimpsed the white sand of the beach.

Their pinisi was gone.

'Remi, stop,' Sam rasped.

On instinct, he shrugged off his pack, unzipped the top pocket, grabbed the maleo, and tossed it into the brush. He donned his pack again and kept walking.

'What is it?' Remi replied, turning around. She saw the expression on her husband's face. She stiffened. 'What's going on?' she whispered.

From somewhere to the right, hidden in the trees, came Itzli Rivera's voice: 'It's called an ambush, Mrs. Fargo.'

'Step backward,' Rivera ordered. 'Five more feet, and you're on the sand. Mr. Fargo, there's a rifle trained on your wife. One more step, Mrs. Fargo.'

Remi complied.

'Drop your pack.'

Remi did so.

'Now you come forward, Mr. Fargo. Hands up.'

Sam walked down the trail and stepped onto the beach. To the right, Rivera stepped from the trees. To the left, another man, armed with an assault rifle, did the same. Rivera lifted a portable radio to his mouth and said something. Ten seconds later a speedboat glided around the peninsula and into the cove. Six feet from the beach, it stopped. On board were two more men, also armed with assault rifles.

'Did you find her?' Rivera asked.

Sam saw no point in lying. 'Yes.'

'Was Blaylock aboard?'

'Yes.'

Sam and Remi's eyes locked. Each one was expecting the same question to come next.

Rivera said, 'Did you find anything interesting?'

'Three letters.'

In Spanish, Rivera barked, 'Search them,' to the man behind Sam and Remi. He came forward, snagged each of their packs, and dragged them ten feet away. He searched each pack and found their iPhones and their satellite phone. He crushed each one under the butt of his rifle, then kicked the pieces into the water. Finally, he frisked Sam and Remi.

'Nothing,' the man reported to Rivera. 'Just the letters.'

'You can have them,' Rivera said. 'In trade, I'm going to take your wife.'

'The hell you are.' Sam took a step toward Rivera.

'Sam, don't!' Remi shouted.

The man behind Sam rushed forward and slammed the butt of his rifle into Sam's lower back just above the kidneys. Sam stumbled forward, dropped to his knees, then climbed back to his feet.

Sam took a calming breath. 'Rivera, you can – '

'Take you instead? No thank you.' He reached into his pocket, pulled out a cell phone, and tossed it to Sam. 'It's prepaid and untraceable, with three minutes of talk time left. You've got twenty-four hours to determine the location of Chicomoztoc.'

'That's not enough time.'

'That's your problem to solve. When you've got the location, dial star six-nine on that phone. I'll answer. At twenty-four hours and one minute, I'll kill your wife.'

Sam turned around to face Remi.

He said, 'Everything's going to be okay, Remi.'

She forced a smile. 'I know.'

Rivera ordered, 'Take her.'

At gunpoint, Remi was marched into the water to the boat. The two men aboard lifted her over the gunwale and shoved her down into one of the rear seats.

Sam turned back to Rivera, who said, 'Do I have to tell you not to involve the police or any of that nonsense?'

'No.'

'Your boat is anchored on the other side of the peninsula.'

'I'll hunt you down.'

'What's that?'

'If you hurt her, I'll spend the rest of my life and every penny to hunt you down.'

Rivera smiled thinly. 'I believe you'd try.'

Chapter 45

Twenty-two hours later, Southern Sulawesi

Sam's eyes scanned the gauges, checking airspeed, altitude, oil pressure, fuel ... As was everything else aboard the airplane, the few dashboard labels that hadn't worn off completely were in Serbian.

The Ikarus Kurir seaplane, painted an ugly shade of gray-blue, was sixty years old, a castoff from the Yugoslavian air force. The windows leaked, the engine knocked, the wheeled pontoons were badly dented, and the controls were so soft there was a two-second delay between the time he pushed the pedals and the plane responded.

He'd never been happier with a plane in his life.

A thousand miles east of Jakarta, the Ikarus had been the only seaplane available for rent, purchase, or theft – and, provided he didn't crash in the next hour, it would take him to Remi. Whether they stayed alive over the next few hours or days would depend largely on the credibility of the Hail Mary pass he and Selma had assembled.

As soon as Rivera's speedboat had disappeared from view, Sam had retrieved the maleo statuette, grabbed his pack, and sorted through their belongings, taking only the essentials. Blaylock's letters went into a Ziploc baggie. The swim back to the pinisi took just under seven minutes; the boat ride to the nearest civilization on the eastern coast of Lampung Bay, an excruciating ninety minutes. Once ashore and off the beach, he jogged a mile down a dirt road to a collection of Quonset huts on the outskirts of an industrial farm. He talked his way into the plant office and to a phone and called Selma, who listened, then said, 'It's not enough time.'

'I know that. It's all we have.'

'Should we call Rube?'

'No. There's nothing he can do in time. Have Pete and Wendy get me back to Jakarta.'

'On it.'

'Now, tell me where things stand. What do we know?'

'Virtually nothing.'

Five hours after he left Pulau Legundi, Sam touched down in Jakarta. He checked into the closest hotel with a Wi-Fi connection and a laptop to rent, then resumed his call with Selma.

'I don't care if we're right about the location,' Sam said. 'I just need to be able to sell it to Rivera and convince him we have to meet.'

'I could create evidence. Wendy could Photoshop something – '

'As a last resort.' Sam checked his watch. 'We're going to take six hours and work every angle we have. If we don't get anywhere, we'll go with your plan. Let's run through it: Orizaga wandered off, presumably looking for Chicomoztoc. Did he stay on Sumatra?'

'We don't know.'

'Both he and Blaylock were focused on the maleo. Orizaga said he'd know Chicomoztoc when he found a "hatchery of great birds." He had to have meant the maleo, agreed?'

'It seems likely.'

'Where are they found?'

'They're on the endangered species list. They're limited to Sulawesi and Buton islands.'

'How about five hundred years ago?'

'I don't know.'

'Have Pete and Wendy put together a list of maleo experts.'

'We don't even know if there is such a thing.'

'There are experts for everything. Ask about hatcheries, concentrations, migration . . . Okay, back to Sulawesi: It's where the Malagasy lived prior to migrating to Madagascar, and we found Blaylock's outrigger on Madagascar. That's two votes for Sulawesi. What do we know about Sulawesi prior to the sixth century?'

Sam heard the rustling of paper. Selma said, 'Human settlements as far back as thirty thousand years B.C. Believed to have been part of a land bridge between Australia and New Guinea – '

'More recent,' Sam said.

'As deep as I've been able to dig in the past few days, I've found very little until the sixteenth century, when the Portuguese arrived.'

'What about the language or the art? Any similarities to either the Aztecs or Blaylock's Proto-Aztecs?'

'Wendy's working on a search, but we're up against the same problem: Except for a few cities, Sulawesi is thousands of square miles of rain forest, dead volcanoes, and not much else. There are places on that island that have never been explored. There's very little Internet and even fewer online art collections. If we had a few weeks – '

'We don't. Just do your best. If you find something that looks or sounds even remotely Aztec, flag it.'

'Sam, you have to take a breath.'

'When I've got Remi back. Let's go back to the outrigger. You have the lab report. Remind me: What do we know about the materials used?'

'The wood used was durian. We know where it exists today. I'm working on where it might have grown before the sixth century. Same with the rest of it – the rubber tree, the pandan leaf, the gebang palm . . .'

'Let me guess: There aren't many experts on those either.'

'Not that I've been able to find.'

'How about Blaylock's letters?'

'We've decoded them all. Unless there's a code behind the code, there's nothing else there. That applies to his journal, too. How about the Constance letters you found on the *Shenandoah*?'

'They're not coded. The first two letters discuss the voyage to the Sunda Strait. The last was probably written shortly before he died. You can read it when we get home. He tells Constance he wished he'd come home to marry her.'

'So sad. How about the maleo statuette you found?'

'It could be emerald or jade or any number of other gems I'm not familiar with. I'll do a search for minerals endemic to Sulawesi, but I don't think it'll solve our problem. I'm going to need access to our server so I can look at everything from here.'

'Sure, give me ten minutes.'

'Good, thanks. What are we missing, Selma?'

'I don't know, Sam.'

'We're missing something.'

Three hours passed. Sam and Selma talked every twenty minutes, discussing progress, dissecting what they knew, and rehashing what they suspected.

At hour four, Selma called again. 'We've made a little progress. We found a book by a Norwegian botanist that discusses both the pandan leaf and gebang palm. I talked to him on the phone. He thinks that around the fourth and fifth century, both of them were heavily concentrated in the northern third of Sulawesi.'

'But not restricted to there.'

'No.'

'I just realized what we're forgetting.'

'What?'

'The codex. Remember the bush the maleo is sitting on?'

'Yes. Damn. How did I forget that?'

'Doesn't matter. Have Wendy do her thing: Enlarge the image, clean it up, and show it to the Norwegian.'

Sam hung up and returned to his laptop. As he had been on and off for the last three hours, he was scrolling through the gallery of images and scans they'd collected. There were dozens of Constance letters, hundreds of journal pages, the Orizaga Codex, the Fibonacci spirals . . . They all began to blur together.

He switched to Google Earth and continued his scan of Sulawesi, looking for anything that might ring the faintest of bells in his head. Minutes turned into an hour.

He zoomed in on a secluded bay on Sulawesi's north-eastern coast. As it seemed with every spot around Sulawesi, islets and atolls were scattered like confetti.

Sam stopped suddenly and tracked his finger backward, moving the map. He zoomed in again, paused, then zoomed some more. He squinted his eyes. Then smiled. 'A hollowed-out flower,' he muttered.

He was reaching for the phone when it rang. It was Selma: 'You were right, Sam, there are experts for everything. I heard back from a zoologist in Makassar. She claims up until the early seventeen hundreds, maleos were more migratory. Every year they would congregate in the north-east part of the island for a few months.'

On his laptop, Sam was switching between Google Earth and the photo gallery. 'Go on.'

'Also, I e-mailed a photo of the codex bush to a curator at the Cibodas Botanical Gardens in Jakarta. He thinks it could be a dwarf durian tree. I pressed him a little, and he thought it was probable the durian had migrated from east to west, which would have put it in Sulawesi about sixteen hundred years ago.'

'Fantastic,' Sam said absently. 'Can you get to Google Earth?'

'Hold on. Okay, I'm ready.'

Sam gave her a set of latitude and longitude points. 'Zoom in until that island fills most of your screen.'

'Done.'

'Does that shape remind you of anything? Imagine those erosion ridges deeper.'

'I don't see what . . . Oh!' Selma was silent for a few

beats. 'Sam, that looks like the Chicomoztoc illustration writ large.'

'I know.'

'It's just a coincidence. It has to be.'

'Maybe, but it's in the northeast part of the island – the same place all your experts mentioned. Even if it's not Chicomoztoc, I think I can convince Rivera to buy into it.'

'And then what?'

'I'll figure that out when I'm in front of him. Selma, I need you to get me to Sulawesi. And then I need you to get me a seaplane.'

Chapter 46

Southern Sulawesi

Sam eased the Ikarus into a gentle bank and started bleeding off altitude in preparation for landing. Below and to the right, the airstrip emerged out of the haze. Sam lined the nose up with it, then dropped through a layer of clouds, made a few final adjustments, and touched down. He taxied toward the trio of Quonset huts at the edge of the tarmac and followed the hand signals of a ground-crew member to the fuel pumping station. Sam powered down the Ikarus and climbed out. As Selma had already done the legwork, Sam had but to sign a form. He did this, then walked around the edge of the hut. He dialed star six-nine.

'You're cutting it close,' said Rivera.

'I've only got sixty seconds or so left on this phone. Are you at the spot yet?'

'We're ten minutes away.'

'Let me talk to my wife.'

'Tell me the location of Chicomoztoc, and I'll do that.'

'Not until I'm standing in front of her.'

'You're pushing your luck,' Rivera said.

'And you've already tipped your hand. You said it yourself: You're not going to let us live. You want Chicomoztoc, then these are my terms. Put her on.'

Remi's voice came on the line. 'Sam?'

'Are you okay?'

'I'm fine. Where are you?'

'Close. Hang in there.'

Rivera came back on. 'We'll be waiting.'

The line went dead.

Ten minutes later he was back in the air and heading southeast toward Selayar Island. Another twenty minutes, and he was again dropping through the clouds. Below, the sea was a flat blue. He leveled off at two thousand feet and followed the coastline until the southern tip of the island came into view. He put the Ikarus down a few hundred yards offshore and taxied toward the beach. Sitting on the side of a dirt road was a pair of Isuzu SUVs. As the Ikarus's skids scraped the sand, the doors to the SUVs opened and out stepped Rivera, Remi, and the three men from Pulau Legundi.

Sam shut down the engine, climbed out onto the pontoon, and plodded ashore.

'Check him,' Rivera ordered. One of the men frisked Sam, then stepped back and shook his head. 'Search the plane, too.'

Sam said, 'I'd like to hug my wife.'

'Go ahead.'

Sam let Remi come forward, hoping Rivera would let her out of earshot. It wasn't to be. 'That's far enough,' he called.

Sam and Remi embraced. He whispered, 'Take the number three seat. Grab the sleeping bag and be ready.'

Despite the cryptic nature of the message, Remi simply replied, 'Okay.'

They separated. Sam gave her a reassuring smile, then she stepped back to Rivera's side. The man Rivera had sent to search the plane waded ashore. 'There's nothing aboard. No weapons. Just some sleeping bags, blankets, and camping gear.'

Sam said, 'In case we have to stay overnight.'

'That's a relic of a plane,' said Rivera. 'Are you sure it will get us where we're going?'

'Not even remotely,' Sam replied, 'but it's what you get for a twenty-four-hour deadline. We can cancel the trip if you'd like.'

'No, we're going.'

'I can only carry three of you.'

'Fine. What's our destination?'

'A bay on the eastern coast. As far as I can tell, it doesn't even have a name. It'll take us two and a half hours.'

'If anyone is waiting for us, I'll shoot you both.'

'And die in the resulting crash,' Sam replied. 'I have to admit that has a certain appeal.'

'I can fly a plane as well as you can fly a helicopter. Let's get moving.'

Sam should have compensated for the Ikarus's edge. It was closer to three hours before the coastline appeared through the windshield. Sam put the plane through an abbreviated checklist and began his descent. He banked gently to the north and pointed the nose at the mouth of the crescent-shaped bay. In the rear seat beside Remi — who, as instructed, had taken the seat behind Sam's — Rivera leaned forward for a better view.

'It's a small bay,' he remarked.

'A quarter-mile wide at the mouth and three-quarters of a mile at its widest. Six islands.'

'And you're sure Chicomoztoc is one of them?'

'I never said I was sure. It's my best guess based on everything we know. You seem to be forgetting that we managed to do in a few weeks what you couldn't accomplish in almost a decade.'

'Belated congratulations,' said Rivera. 'How did you find it?'

'Long story, but in a minute you'll see what put the frosting on the cake. The question is, will you recognize it?'

As Sam dropped the Ikarüs through a thousand feet, they passed between the headlands and into the bay.

'Where is it?' Rivera asked.

'Patience.'

A minute later Sam turned the nose slightly off center to let the thickly forested island pass beneath the starboard wing. 'Out the side window,' he said.

Rivera leaned sideways and looked down. 'This is it?' he asked incredulously. 'It's tiny.'

'Three hundred yards across and two hundred feet off the water.'

'It's not big enough to be an island.'

'An islet, then. Either way, it's what you've been looking for.'

'Why is the center concave?'

'It's called a caldera. You're looking at an extinct volcano,' replied Sam. 'You still don't see it, do you?'

'See what?'

'Remi?'

With a nod of approval from Rivera, Remi leaned over his shoulder and looked out the window.

Sam said, 'Squint. Think "big hollowed-out flower."'

A beaming smile spread across Remi's face. 'Sam, you found it.'

'We'll soon find out. Do you see it yet, Rivera?'

'No.'

'You're familiar with the traditional illustration depicting Chicomoztoc? Imagine that illustration viewed from above. Now imagine the points of the island rounded and more pronounced.'

After a few moments Rivera murmured, 'I see it. Amazing. Amazing! Take us down!'

'Are you sure?'

'Yes, damn it, take us down!'

'Whatever you say.'

Passing through two hundred feet, Sam banked the Ikarus one last time, following the bay's western shoreline until the plane's nose was again pointed north. Thirty seconds later, the pontoons kissed the surface; the Ikarus's fuselage shivered and the windows rattled. Sam kept a slightly nose-up attitude, bumping over the surface as his speed bled off.

He watched the needle drop to sixty knots, then fifty. When it slid past forty knots, he said, 'Remi, how many sleeping bags do we have?'

She leaned forward in her seat, picked up the pile of bags, and placed them in her lap. 'I've got three.'

'And I've got one,' Sam replied, pointing to the bag stuffed between his seat and the passenger seat. 'Rivera, how many do you have?'

'What the hell are you talking about?'

Sam's eyes flicked to the dashboard. The needle hit thirty-five knots. He turned toward the man in the passenger seat. 'How about you?'

The man opened his mouth to reply but the words never came out. In one fluid motion, Sam dropped his right hand diagonally down, punched the man's seat-belt release, then grabbed the sleeping bag, brought it to his chest, and shoved the stick forward.

The Ikarus nosed over and slammed into the water.

Chapter 47

Having never intentionally crash-landed before, Sam had a plan that was a combination of gut instinct and a fair grasp of physics. Traveling at thirty knots – roughly thirty-four miles per hour – the Ikarus had enough kinetic energy to throw everyone inside violently forward against their seat belts but not enough to throw the seaplane into a nose-over-tail tumble.

The impact was also enough to rip the passenger seat and the seat behind it free of the mounts that Sam had preloosened before leaving the airstrip.

Rivera's man in the passenger seat, already unbelted, was driven headfirst into the windshield, snapping his neck and killing him. Rivera, still belted in, flew forward and slammed into the back of the passenger seat, while Sam, clutching the sleeping bag in front of his face and chest, smashed into the dashboard. In the backseat Remi's impact was cushioned by two sleeping bags. She was the first to regain consciousness after the impact.

She released her belt and heaved herself forward between the seats. She grabbed Sam by the shoulders and eased him backward. Water was gushing into the cabin through the hole left in the windshield by Rivera's man. Already nose down in the water, the Ikarus began tipping forward under the weight of its engine, lifting the tail from the water.

'Sam!' Remi shouted. 'Sam!'

His eyes snapped open. He blinked a few times, looked around.

'Did it work?' he asked.

'We're both alive. I'd call that a success.'

'What about Rivera?'

Remi looked at Rivera, who lay slumped forward, bent at the waist.

'Unconscious or dead. I don't know and I don't care. We need to think about leaving, Sam.'

'How about right now?'

'Great!'

Sam braced his feet against the dashboard, fighting gravity, then punched the button to release his seat belt. He tried his door. It didn't budge. He tried again. 'My door's jammed. Try Rivera's door.'

'He's blocking it.'

Sam pressed with his legs and arched his back, sliding his upper body into the backseat. 'Get his belt.' Remi hit the release. Rivera slid forward into Sam's outstretched hands. He let gravity do the rest, and Rivera tumbled headfirst onto the remains of the passenger seat and his dead friend.

Remi crawled across the seat and grabbed the door handle. 'Are you ready?'

'Whenever you are.'

'Deep breath!'

She muscled the door open. A column of water surged into the cabin. They let the cabin fill up, then Remi shoved off and swam out. Sam was halfway out the door when he stopped and turned back. He kicked into the front seat and started probing the floorboard with his hands. Under the dead man's left boot Sam found what he was looking for: the semiautomatic pistol the man had been holding. He tucked it into his belt.

He made his way back out and kicked for the surface. He broke into the air beside Remi. Ten feet to their right the plane's tail was jutting straight out of the water.

'It's not going down,' Remi said.

'Probably a pocket of air in the tail. I'm going back down to see what I can salvage. My plan didn't include that part. I'll meet you on the beach.'

Sam took in a lungful of air, flipped over, and dove. His outstretched hand found the leading edge of the wing, and he pulled himself across the fuselage, then down into the doorway.

He stopped.

Rivera was gone. Sam looked into the tail section, saw nothing, and checked the front seat again. He saw movement out of the corner of his right eye and turned his head. A shadow rushed toward his face. He felt something hard strike his forehead. Pain flashed behind his eyes, and everything went dark.

'Sam!' he heard distantly. The voice faded, then returned. 'Sam!'

He felt hands on his face. He knew that touch: Remi. He forced his eyes open. She was leaning over him, her auburn hair dripping onto his face. She smiled. 'How many fingers am I holding up?'

'Very funny. None. I'm okay. Help me sit up.'

'Just stay there. You've got a nasty gash on your forehead.'

'Rivera . . . Where is – '

'I'm here, Mr. Fargo.'

Sam tilted his head backward. An upside-down Rivera was sitting ten feet up the black-sand beach. 'Damn,' Sam muttered. 'I'll give you this much, Rivera, you're one tough bastard.'

Sam forced himself up onto his elbows, then sat upright with Remi's help. He turned around. Rivera was in tough shape; his nose was broken, one of his eyes swollen shut, and his lower lip was split. The gun in his right hand was held in a rock-steady grip, however.

Rivera said, 'And you're too clever for your own good. As soon as you're feeling better I'm going to kill you and your wife.'

'I may have tried to kill you, but I didn't lie about this place. I could still be wrong, but I don't think so.'

'Fine. I'll kill you both, then find the entrance myself. The island isn't that big.'

'It doesn't look big now, but once you get into that jungle it'll suddenly get a lot bigger. It would take you months to find it.'

'And how long for you?'

Sam checked his watch. 'Eight hours from the time we get into the caldera.'

'Why that number?'

'Just a guess.'

'Are you stalling for time?'

'That's part of it. Also, we want to find Chicomoztoc as

much as you do. Maybe more. We've just got a different motive than you do.'

'I'll give you four hours.'

Rivera stood up.

Remi helped Sam to his feet. He leaned on her as though dizzy. 'Headache,' he said loudly, then whispered in Remi's ear: 'I had a gun.'

She smiled. 'You did. I have it now.'

'Waistband?'

'Yes.'

'If you get a chance, shoot him.'

'Gladly.'

'I'll try to distract him.'

Having toughened themselves over the past few weeks, first on Madagascar, then on Pulau Legundi, Sam and Remi found the hike up the island's forested slope relatively easy. Rivera, however, was struggling. His broken nose forced him to breathe through his mouth, and he was now limping. Still, his years as a soldier were shining through. He kept pace with them, keeping ten feet between them and his gun.

At last they reached the top. Below them, the caldera's slopes dropped a hundred feet to the valley floor. The bowl shape, having acted as a rain funnel for centuries, had caused the trees and vegetation to grow faster than their cousins on the exterior.

'What now?' asked Rivera.

Sam turned around in a circle, orienting himself. 'My compass was in the plane, so I have to estimate this . . .'

Sam walked to the right, picking his way through the trees for another fifty feet, then stopped. 'It should be right about here.'

'Here?'

'Below us.'

'Explain.'

'Right after which you shoot us. No thank you.'

Rivera's mouth tightened in a thin line. His eyes never leaving Sam's, Rivera shifted his gun slightly right and pulled the trigger. The bullet punched through Remi's left leg. She screamed and collapsed. Rivera shifted the gun back onto Sam, stopping him in midstep.

'Let me help her,' Sam said.

Rivera glanced at Remi. His eyes narrowed. He limped over to where she was lying, crouched down, and picked up the pistol that had fallen from Remi's waistband. Rivera stepped back. 'You can help her now.'

Sam rushed to her side. She gripped his hand hard, her eyes squeezed shut against the pain. Sam patted his pockets, came up with a bandanna, and pressed it against the wound.

Rivera said, 'Do I have your full attention now?'

'Yes, damn it.'

'The bullet hit her in the quadriceps muscle. She won't bleed to death, and, providing she doesn't stay out here more than a couple days, there's not much chance of infection. Between these two guns I've got thirty more rounds. Start cooperating or I'll keep shooting.'

Chapter 48

They made their way down to the valley floor, Sam in the lead with Remi cradled in his arms and Rivera trailing behind. They found a small clearing in the approximate center of the bowl, and Sam laid Remi down. Rivera sat down on a fallen log at the edge of the clearing. His gun never wavering from Sam's chest, Rivera lifted his shirt up; on the left side of his abdomen was a black softball-sized bruise.

'That looks painful,' Sam said.

'It's just a bruise.'

Sam knelt beside Remi. He lifted the bandanna on her thigh. The bleeding had slowing to a trickle. He whispered, 'Rivera's bleeding internally.'

Through clenched teeth Remi asked, 'How bad?'

'I'm not sure.'

'Stall until he keels over dead.'

'I'll try.'

'Stop your whispering!' Rivera barked. 'Move away from her.' Sam complied. 'Tell me your theory about the entrance.'

Sam hesitated.

Rivera pointed the gun at Remi.

'It's based on the illustrations,' Sam said. 'Chicomoztoc is always a cavern with seven smaller caves around it . . . like a flower. The cavern is beneath a mountain. The drawings vary, but the big details are the same – including the location of the entrance.'

'At the bottom,' Rivera said.

'Right. But if I'm right and this is the place, it means the exterior shape of the island was as important to them as the interior.'

'How could they have gotten an overhead view of it?'

'They didn't. They sailed around it and mapped it. As small as this island is, it would have been easy to do it accurately.'

'Go on.'

'If you're looking at the illustration face on as a two-dimensional image, the entrance to Chicomoztoc is down. If you look at it from overhead – and they oriented them-selves on the four cardinal directions like most cultures do – then the entrance lies to the south.'

Rivera considered this, then nodded slowly. 'Good. Now go find it. You've got four hours. If you don't find it by then, I'll kill you both.'

Rivera made the ground rules clear: Sam would search for the entrance while he, Rivera, guarded Remi. Rivera would call Sam's name at random intervals. If Sam didn't answer within ten seconds, Rivera would shoot Remi again.

As he and Remi had done on Pulau Legundi, Sam made do with what was at hand: a sturdy six-foot-long stick and patience. Facing what he thought was due south, he started up the caldera's slope, prodding ahead of him with the stick.

The first pass to the top took him twenty minutes. On

the rim he sidestepped to the right and started back down the slope. He felt ridiculous. Though his method was sound and still used in certain cases, the gravity of where he was, what he searching for, and the clock that was ticking on Remi's life blended together, giving him a nagging sense of helplessness.

The afternoon wore on. In twenty-minute intervals he hiked up the slope, then down the slope. Up, down, repeating until he'd made six passes, then eight, then ten.

Shortly before five o'clock, with the sun dropping toward the western horizon, he was picking his way through a particularly dense cluster of trees when he stopped to catch his breath.

Initially, the sound was just a faint hiss. Sam held his breath and strained to pin down the location. It seemed to be all around him.

'Fargo!' Rivera hollered.

'Here!' Sam called back.

'You have thirty more minutes.'

Sam picked his way ten feet farther down the slope. He paused. The hissing had faded slightly. He stepped ten feet to the left, listened again. Louder now. He repeated his test, box-stepping up and down the hillside, until he found himself standing before a bulge in the slope. He poked the bulge with his stick; the tip disappeared.

His heart thumped in his chest.

He dropped to his knees and shoved his head into the opening.

The hissing doubled in volume.

'Waves,' he whispered.

He pulled back, dug into his pocket, found his penlight.

He clicked it but nothing happened. 'Come on . . .' He unscrewed the bottom and dumped the batteries on the ground and used his shirt to dry each one in turn. He reassembled the flashlight and clicked the button. He was rewarded with a bright beam.

He stuck his head back into the opening and shined the light around. A three-foot-wide, smooth-walled shaft descended diagonally into the slope. At the edge of Sam's flashlight beam the tunnel curved right into darkness.

'Fargo!'

Sam pulled his head out. 'Here!'

'Twenty-five minutes left.'

He had a decision to make. With no idea where this tunnel led and without proper gear, he could easily find himself beyond earshot of Rivera or, worse still, he would hear Rivera's check-in call but be unable to answer it within the allotted ten seconds. He had no doubt that either of these circumstances would lead to Remi being shot again.

'He's going to kill us anyway,' Sam said to himself. 'Roll the dice.'

Feet first, Sam wriggled into the opening and started downward.

He hadn't gotten ten feet when Rivera shouted: 'Fargo!'

Sam scrambled back up the chute and stuck his head into the light. 'Here!' He checked his watch: nineteen minutes.

He backed into the chute and let himself slide, braking with his toes and palms until he reached the bend, where he had to curl his body to navigate the angle. The chute steepened, continued for ten feet, then suddenly widened out. Sam felt his legs dangling free. He clawed at the walls, trying to arrest his slide, but gravity took over. He slipped from the chute and started falling.

Chapter 49

His plunge lasted less than a second.

He landed feetfirst in a pile of something soft, rolled backward in a reverse somersault, and came to rest on his knees. His flashlight lay a few feet away. He crawled over, grabbed it, and cast the beam about.

The pile into which he'd fallen was almost pure white. His first thought was sand, but then he smelled it: the distinctive tang of salt. The rush of the waves echoed around him, bouncing off the walls, fading and multiplying as though he were caught inside a fun-house auditorium.

Sam checked his watch: sixteen minutes.

He looked up. The chute from which he'd fallen was ten feet above his head. He turned around, panned his flashlight. The wall nearest to him sparkled as though encrusted in tiny mirrors. He stepped up to it.

'Salt,' he murmured.

Beneath the faceted white veneer he could make out a darker streak. It was green – translucent green. The stripe rose up the wall, widened into a foot-thick band, then turned again, forking into dozens more veins. The branching continued until it was a giant latticework beneath the white salt veneer.

The cavern itself was roughly oval and no wider than forty feet in diameter. Eyes fixed on the ceiling, he started across the cavern. He felt a jet of air blow up his leg. He stopped and crouched down.

The four-foot-wide hole in the floor was perfectly disguised by a crust of salt, punctuated by pencil holes through which the air was being forced. Sam stood up, looked around. Now knowing what to look for, he could see dozens of holes within the beam of his flashlight.

He reached the center of the cavern. Spaced at regular intervals around him were what looked like salt-encrusted stalagmites, each one approximately five feet high. There were seven of them. These were ceremonial cairns, he realized. Each cairn a metaphor, perhaps.

'The Place of the Seven Caves,' Sam murmured. 'Chicomoztoc.'

Careful of his footing, he strode over to the nearest cairn, knelt down, and pressed the head of his flashlight against the surface. Beneath the crystallized salt he saw a dull green glow. He used the butt of the flashlight to lightly hammer the surface. On the third blow, a scab of salt fell away, followed by a Ping-Pong-ball-sized rock. He picked it up. It was a translucent green, the same as the maleo statuette. The stone absorbed the beam of his flashlight, swirling the light until the interior seemed to glow and sparkle of its own accord. Sam pocketed the stone.

'. . . argo!' Rivera's faint voice called.

'Damn!' Sam muttered. He whirled around, casting his light wildly about. He needed a plan. He needed something . . . His beam fell on the salt pile. The kernel of an idea formed. It was sketchy at best, but it was all he had.

Dodging holes, he sprinted back to the salt pile. He

grabbed a handful of it and stuffed it into his pocket. He scanned the flashlight along the wall beside him. It curved to the right. He followed it. The floor sloped down, then up, then left. The hiss of waves faded behind him. To the right he glimpsed a faint light source. He ran toward it. The walls closed in, and the ceiling descended until he was running hunched over.

He stumbled through a wall of foliage and fell forward. '. . . argo!'

Sam rolled onto his back, caught his breath. 'Here!'

'Eleven minutes.'

Sam lay still for thirty seconds, picking at his plan until satisfied it could work. But, then again, *could* was a far cry from *would*. He had no choice, no other options, and virtually no more time.

He picked his way to the bottom of the bowl, then made his way back to the clearing. 'I found something.'

'Are you lying to me?' Rivera replied.

'No.'

Rivera stood up. 'Let's go.'

'Give me a minute.'

Sam walked over to Remi and sat down beside her. She opened her eyes and smiled at him. 'Hi.'

'Hi. Does it hurt?'

'No. It's dull throbbing. I've been counting my heart-beats to pass the time.'

Sam chuckled. 'Never bored, are you?'

'Never.'

'I found something. I'm taking Rivera there now.'

'Is it – '

'I think so. I think we found it.' He leaned over and

kissed her on the cheek. 'I'm going to take him in there,' he whispered. 'With any luck, I'll be coming out alone.'

'Then I'll see you when you get back.'

Sam stood up and turned to Rivera. 'Ready.'

'Lead the way.'

Sam took Rivera to the exit, then handed him the flashlight and stood to one side as Rivera ducked his head into the entrance. Rivera tossed the flashlight back to Sam.

'What's in there?'

'I didn't go far.'

Rivera paused. Sam knew he was debating whether the Fargos had suddenly become extra baggage.

'But as far as I went, I got lost three times. In one of the side tunnels there's a drop-off; beyond that, I saw something on the wall. A symbol of some kind.'

This did the trick. Rivera gestured for Sam to enter the tunnel. He stepped inside and hunch-walked until the walls and ceiling widened out. Rivera was a few steps behind.

'Which way?'

Sam feigned confusion for a few seconds, then headed right and followed the sloped floor's dips and rises and turns until finally they emerged into the salt cavern.

'Are those waves?' Rivera asked, looking around.

'I think so. There's probably a maze of sea caves down there.'

'And the walls? Crystallized salt?'

'Sea salt, blown up from the caves. Do you see the dark streaks?' Sam pointed the flashlight at the nearest wall. 'Take a look.'

His gun fixed on Sam's chest, Rivera sidestepped to the wall.

Sam said, 'It's some kind of mineral deposit. Emerald or jade.'

Nodding absently, Rivera followed the veins with his eyes as they spiraled up the wall and across the ceiling. 'Where's this side tunnel?'

Careful to keep the beam off the floor, Sam shined the flashlight across the cavern. He held his breath, half expecting Rivera to notice the cairns and their arrangement, but he didn't.

'Go on.'

Sam started across the floor. Heart thudding in his chest, he tried to keep his pace steady, watching the placement of his feet as he stepped over holes or along their edges. As he crossed the cavern's center point, there came a crackling sound, like pond ice giving way. Rivera cursed.

Sam turned around.

'Don't shine that in my eyes, damn it!'

Rivera had stepped into one of the smaller holes and fallen through up to his crotch. He struggled to extricate himself, straining to get his free leg under his body. He tried twice more, then stopped.

'You're going to come over here and help me up. If you – '

'I know,' Sam replied. 'You'll shoot me.'

Flashlight in his left hand, Sam strode forward. He flicked the beam into Rivera's eyes, then down again. At the same time he stuffed his right hand into his pocket, grabbed a fistful of salt, and pulled it out again.

'Damn it!' Rivera growled. 'Keep the light – '

'Sorry.'

'That's close enough. Just give me your wrist. Don't grab ahold of me.'

Sam extended his wrist. Rivera grabbed it and used Sam's counterweight to pull himself free. Sam felt Rivera's weight shift forward. He twirled the flashlight in his fingers, shining the beam directly into Rivera's eyes.

'Sorry,' Sam said again.

Even as he said the words he was moving, sidestepping left, using Rivera's momentary blindness to get the gun barrel off him. Sam swung his right hand forward as though throwing a baseball. The salt hit Rivera squarely in the eyes. Knowing what was coming, Sam dropped to his belly.

Rivera screamed and started pulling the trigger. Bullets thudded into the walls and ceiling. Salt crystals rained down, sparkling in the glow of Sam's flashlight. Rivera spun wildly, trying to regain his balance as he staggered across the floor, the gun bucking in his hand.

Sam pushed himself to his knees, coiled his legs like a runner in the starting blocks, then pushed off and charged. Rivera heard the crunch of Sam's footfalls and spun toward the sound, firing. Still running, Sam dropped back to his belly and skidded across the floor, the salt crystals ripping at his chest and chin. He went still. Held his breath.

Rivera whirled again, trying to pinpoint the sound. He lost his balance again, lurched sideways, and stepped squarely into another hole. With a zipperlike crackling sound, Rivera's legs plunged through. He spread his arms to arrest his fall. The gun dropped from his hand and skittered across the salted floor, coming to a stop beside Sam's face.

He grabbed the gun and climbed to his feet.

'Fargo!' Rivera screamed.

Sam walked over to the hole. Rivera's arms were fully extended. Only the palms of his hands were touching solid ground. Already his arms were trembling; the tendons in his neck strained beneath the skin. Still blinded by the salt, Rivera rotated his head wildly from side to side.

Sam crouched down beside him.

'Fargo!'

'I'm right here. You're in a bit of a pickle.'

'Get me out of this thing!'

'No.'

Sam shined his flashlight into the hole. Salt-encrusted rock outcroppings jutted from the walls like barbs, leaving only a two-foot-wide gap in the center. Far below, Sam could hear the roar of waves crashing against rock. He grabbed a nearby softball-sized stone, dropped it into the opening, and listened to it ricochet off the rocks until the sound faded.

'What was that?' Rivera asked.

'That's karma calling,' Sam replied. 'About a hundred feet of it, based on Newton's Second Law.'

'What the hell does that mean? Get me out!'

'You shouldn't have shot my wife.'

Rivera growled in frustration. He tried to press himself upward but managed only a few inches. He slumped back down. His head dipped below the level of the floor. Beneath Rivera's shirt, his muscles quivered with the strain.

'I just realized something,' Sam said. 'The more your palms sweat, the more the salt dissolves beneath them. I think that's what financial experts call diminishing returns. It's not a perfect metaphor, but I think you get my point.'

'I should have killed you.'

'Hang on to that thought. Soon it's all you're going to have left.'

Rivera's left hand slipped off the edge. For a split second he clawed at the ground with his right hand, his nails shredding, before he tipped sideways and started to fall. He landed back first on one of the outcroppings, shattering his spine. He screamed in pain, then slid off and kept tumbling, his head slamming on rock after rock before disappearing from view.

Epilogue

Two weeks later,
Goldfish Point, La Jolla, California

Remi limped into the solarium and eased herself down on the chaise lounge next to Sam's. Without looking up from his iPad, Sam said, 'You're supposed to be using your cane for at least another week.'

'I don't like my cane.'

Sam looked over at her. 'And you call me stubborn. How's the leg feel?'

'Better. The doctor says I'll be fit for full duty in a few weeks. Given the nasty alternative, I couldn't be happier.'

'By "nastier," I assume you mean starving to death inside the crater of a dead volcano?'

'That's exactly what I mean.'

Though Remi hadn't been in danger of bleeding to death on what they'd since dubbed Chicomoztoc Island, the risk of infection and sepsis were all too real, Sam had known. He had only two choices: Stay put and wait for Selma to send help, which she was sure to do, but how quickly would her request for assistance take to make its way through the right channels in the Indonesian government? His second choice was to leave Remi alone and strike out on his own in search of help. In the end, Remi, knowing her husband as

446

she did, encouraged him to leave her the gun and go. That left Sam the question of which direction.

The next morning he said good-bye to Remi and climbed to the lip of the caldera, where he stood for a time scanning the horizon. He'd all but decided to head south when he saw a faint trickle of smoke rising from the forest a few miles to the north.

At a jog, he zigzagged his way down the slope, waded into the water, and swam the half mile to the shore, where he headed north until he reached a river. This he followed inland, his eyes never leaving the smoke column until he reached a small clearing, in the center of which stood a man in a safari vest and a blue baseball cap bearing the BBC logo.

Upon seeing the disheveled Sam stumbling into view, the director of the documentary yelled, 'Cut!,' and began demanding to know who'd just ruined his shot.

Two hours later Sam was back in the caldera with Remi, and an hour after that the BBC helicopter touched down on the beach. The next day they were back in Jakarta, Remi tucked safely in bed.

'We have to start making some decisions,' Sam now said.

'I know.'

They were keeping some gargantuan secrets. Given the momentous nature of what they'd discovered in the weeks following their improvised excavation of the *Shenandoah*'s bell, it had come as a shock to realize that other than themselves, Selma, Pete, Wendy, Professors Milhaupt and Dydell, and the Kid, no one was aware of what they'd found. The outrigger in Madagascar was still perched atop its altar in the Lion's Head cave; the *Shenandoah* was still sitting in the ravine on Pulau Legundi, buried under fifteen feet of Krakatoan ash; the maleo statuette they'd recovered from the *Shenandoah* was tucked away in their workroom safe; and the ceremonial cavern beneath the caldera remained hidden and unspoiled.

While they fully intended to hand over these discoveries to the world's archeological and anthropological communities, they also recognized the wisdom of taking a few weeks to consider the implications of what they'd discovered and prepare themselves for the media storm that was sure to follow the press releases.

Sam and Remi now also understood why Garza had never let the Mexica Tenochca's symbol, the jade statuette of Quetzalcoatl, be physically examined. If Garza's Quetzalcoatl ever faced testing, Sam and Remi were confident of a match between those results and the ones they obtained on their maleo. The jeweled bird was in fact not made of emerald or jade but rather a rare type of garnet known as magmatic demantoid. Except for the meticulous sculpting the maleo underwent, its characteristics were identical to those of the stone Sam had taken from the cavern.

Wherever and however Blaylock had found the maleo, its surprisingly pristine condition, and the *Shenandoah*'s unique fate had combined to leave behind even more compelling evidence: microscopic traces of Indonesian-specific pigments that suggested the statuette had once been painted – perhaps to better represent the maleo bird itself.

*

In the days following their return home, a number of minor secrets that had been nagging Sam, Remi, and the others slowly sorted themselves out: Blaylock's journal, whose eccentricities continued to reveal themselves in dribs and drabs, had solved the bell mystery when Pete found two pages stuck together. In Blaylock's own words he dramatically described being attacked by pirates while the *Shenandoah* was at anchor off Chumbe Island, two days before she departed for the Sunda Strait. Lest the bell, 'Ophelia's heart,' fall into the wrong hands, Blaylock jettisoned it overboard after removing a memento, the clapper, intending to reunite the two upon his return to Bagamoyo. In the same attack Blaylock lost his artillery sword, a short Gladius-style weapon, the same one Sylvie Radford found while snorkeling a hundred twenty-seven years later.

Blaylock's beloved journal and walking staff, both of which were rarely beyond his arm's reach, he'd left behind with one of his concubines the day before the *Shenandoah* departed for Indonesia; they eventually found their way to Morton and the Blaylock Museum and Curiosity Shop. Sam and Remi couldn't help but wonder whether the enigmatic Winston Blaylock had somehow known he wouldn't be coming home.

In the end, President Quauhtli Garza's paranoia sealed his fate. Good soldier that he was, Rivera had left no trail that could incriminate his boss, so Sam and Remi devised a disinformation plot that capitalized on the fact that Rivera's body remained missing. They were surprised when their scheme bore such spectacular fruit.

Armed with their suspicions about the tourists Rivera murdered in Zanzibar and the evidence supporting their theory about the true origin of the Aztecs, they used Rube Haywood's connections to start a leak that quickly became a torrent: Itzli Rivera was alive and rather than face extradition to Tanzania, he was talking to the authorities, who had details about not only the murders but also Garza's attempt to hide the truth about his Quetzalcoatl statuette and the Mexica Tenochca's power-grabbing ruse. Within hours of the story hitting American cable news channels, Mexican networks were running it nonstop. Within days, Mexican opposition parties and legislators were demanding an investigation, and hundreds of thousands of protesters had taken to the streets in Mexico City, surrounding government buildings and grinding the city to a near halt.

Having spent nearly a decade safeguarding a secret that had the power to both glorify and destroy him, Quauhtli Garza now realized all was lost. In the space of weeks, all of it was gone, torn asunder by a pair of treasure hunters, no less. Americans – imperialists, just like Cortés and his hordes. It was unjust. History repeating itself. How had the Fargos managed it? And so quickly?

Curse them, and curse Rivera for that matter, the traitorous bastard, Garza thought.

He would not suffer the same fate as his forefathers. He was alone, but his destiny was still in his hands.

On the fifth day after the story broke, Garza, now trapped in his office by mobs chanting 'Show yourself!' and 'Garza must go!,' dismissed his security detail and staff and stared out the window at what had been, just hours before, his adoring public – now treacherous Conquistadors returned to tear down what he'd built.

At sunset, a sunken-eyed Garza left his office, marched to the roof of his building overlooking Templo Mayor, took a final look at his city and what could have been, and unceremoniously leapt into the air.

Surrounded by thousands of stunned onlookers, his shattered corpse lay atop the jagged steps of the pyramid, the last remnant of the lost Aztec Empire.

Selma's strident voice came over the loudspeaker above Remi's chaise: 'I'm ready whenever you are.'

Remi replied, 'On our way.'

They found Selma in the workroom, standing at the end of the table.

'I just finished plugging in the last of the data: a similar scenario run by the U.S. Geological Survey a few years ago,' Selma announced. She'd collected information from dozens of other geological organizations and universities from around the world in addition to the USGS.

'Have you seen it?' Sam asked.

'And ruin your fun? Not a chance.'

One of the more troublesome questions that remained unanswered – or at least not answered to their satisfaction – was why, after traveling twelve thousand miles across the globe, had the Proto-Aztecs chosen Lake Texcoco as their ultimate home? Legend claimed they had been guided there by an eagle perched atop a cactus with a snake in its mouth, but Professor Dydell's MDI – Migrational Displacement Iconography – theory suggested that image had begun as a maleo perched atop a durian tree.

'Go ahead, Selma.'

Selma pointed the remote at the LCD, and a moment later a Google Earth-like overhead image of Chicomoztoc Island appeared. The camera zoomed out to encompass the nearby isles and the bay itself.

Selma pressed another button.

Slowly at first, then gaining more speed, the image began to morph as a time line at the margin counted backward in ten-year increments. Sea levels rose and fell; coastlines retreated and expanded; jungles thinned and thickened. A column of smoke drifted across the bay, followed by a second.

'Hold,' Sam called, and Selma paused the animation. 'Volcanoes?'

Remi nodded. 'Looks like it.'

Selma hit Play again. Water levels rapidly rose and retreated. And then land began moving.

'There it goes,' Remi murmured.

'Can you slow it down, Selma?' asked Sam

Selma touched a button on the remote.

The screen's time line read 782 A.D. The animation slowed to one-year-per-second increments. Sam and Remi watched, transfixed, as the horns of the bay gradually began rising from the sea and crawling toward each other as all the islands in the bay except Chicomoztoc disappeared beneath the surface. By the time the time line reached the year 419 A.D., the bay had become landlocked. All that remained was a lone island, shaped like the flower-shaped cave in the Chicomoztoc illustration, in the middle of what had morphed into a lake.

'No wonder that otherwise marshy piece of land in the middle of Lake Texcoco looked so appealing to them,' Remi said. 'They were coming home.'

Sam and Remi thanked Selma and returned to the solarium.

'Which one do you want to do first?' Sam asked.

'Which what?'

'Which excavation: the outrigger on Madagascar, Chicomoztoc Island, or the *Shenandoah*? Once we make the announcement, I suspect it won't take long for expeditions to begin forming. I'd like to think we'll have our first pick.'

Remi thought about it a moment, then shrugged. 'You?'

Sam smiled. 'Each one has its appeal.' He dug into his pocket and came up with a quarter. He made a fist and placed the coin on top of his thumbnail. 'Two tosses. We go with the winner?'

Remi nodded.

Sam Fargo flipped the coin and it twirled skyward.

He just wanted a decent book to read ...

Not too much to ask, is it? It was in 1935 when Allen Lane, Managing Director of Bodley Head Publishers, stood on a platform at Exeter railway station looking for something good to read on his journey back to London. His choice was limited to popular magazines and poor-quality paperbacks – the same choice faced every day by the vast majority of readers, few of whom could afford hardbacks. Lane's disappointment and subsequent anger at the range of books generally available led him to found a company – and change the world.

'We believed in the existence in this country of a vast reading public for intelligent books at a low price, and staked everything on it'
Sir Allen Lane, 1902–1970, founder of Penguin Books

The quality paperback had arrived – and not just in bookshops. Lane was adamant that his Penguins should appear in chain stores and tobacconists, and should cost no more than a packet of cigarettes.

Reading habits (and cigarette prices) have changed since 1935, but Penguin still believes in publishing the best books for everybody to enjoy. We still believe that good design costs no more than bad design, and we still believe that quality books published passionately and responsibly make the world a better place.

So wherever you see the little bird – whether it's on a piece of prize-winning literary fiction or a celebrity autobiography, political tour de force or historical masterpiece, a serial-killer thriller, reference book, world classic or a piece of pure escapism – you can bet that it represents the very best that the genre has to offer.

Whatever you like to read – trust Penguin.